# TURN THE OTHER CHEEK

Vaun faced straight ahead when he limped through the doorway, but the corner of his eye disliked something vague in the darkness to his left.

"Stop right there!" a girl's voice cried behind him. "Put your hands up. All the way."

He stopped, stretched his arms overhead, and turned, squinting into the rising sun. He couldn't see her clearly, except for a glint of light from the weapon. She could certainly see him.

"I'm Admiral Vaun." The words sounded stupid, somehow. "I am unarmed," he added, as that was probably what she was looking for.

"Turn around."

"I'd rather be shot on this side, please."

*"Turn around!"*

He obeyed reluctantly.

"Now drop your pants."

By Dave Duncan
*Published by Ballantine Books:*

A ROSE-RED CITY

*The Seventh Sword*
THE RELUCTANT SWORDSMAN
THE COMING OF WISDOM
THE DESTINY OF THE SWORD

WEST OF JANUARY

SHADOW

STRINGS

HERO!

*A Man of His Word*
MAGIC CASEMENT
FAERY LANDS FORLORN
PERILOUS SEAS*
EMPEROR AND CLOWN*


*Forthcoming

# HERO!

## Dave Duncan

A Del Rey Book

BALLANTINE BOOKS • NEW YORK

Dedicated to
Robert Runté
for labors
amid the alien corn.

# Acknowledgments

I am very grateful to Dan Cragg for reading the manuscript and helping me with terminology and procedures for the Space Patrol. The book was greatly improved by his efforts. Where I chose to ignore his advice, it was to emphasize how far Ultian Command has degenerated from a military force toward a hereditary aristocracy. (Warrior castes have evolved often enough in the last five thousand years that I am certain they will recur in future—Vaun would call them a design fault in human nature.) Thus any military absurdities remaining in the text are my own doing, and deliberate.

"**A**FTER THIRTY THOUSAND years, the Empire is dying," the lieutenant proclaimed. "And you're all too decadent to care." A haze of smoke from the firepool drifted slowly away through the foliage overhead, but the angry words hung unanswered in the night.

That boy had his mix set too high, Maeve decided. Possibly he was just drunk, although she had not noticed him drinking at all, nor even sniffing croil. Possibly he was just a natural loudmouth and his best friends wouldn't tell him. Whatever the cause, he was spoiling this corner of the party, standing by himself in the center and trying to raise trouble.

An uncertain light flickered over the dozen or so faces around the little grotto. Leaves rustled in the breeze, and sounds of laughter and music floated in from distant parts of the grounds to die in the sullen silence. The girls looked annoyed. The boys were embarrassed—they had come to party, not to fight, and especially not fight with a spacer. The lieutenant was big, and his was the only uniform in sight, although Maeve was fairly sure that a couple of the other boys were spacers also. One could usually tell, no matter what they wore. Or didn't.

"Security, identify last speaker," she murmured.

The expected voice came softly in her ear, "Lieutenant Hajin, navigator on Ultian Spaceship *Defender*."

Just what she'd been afraid of—that pup had teeth! His parents were both admirals, and even her own position in the Cabinet was not secure enough to risk annoying *him*. His family had been Patrol for generations, and virtually owned three states. When a spacer wanted the sidewalk, civilians walked in the gutter.

Some of the other faces were more familiar to her—a famous ballerina, a celebrated oenologist, the pretender to the throne of Lyshia. She suspected that the chubby boy nearest her was the heir to the fabulous Locab fortune. Mostly she wanted to speak with the girl in blue, who was an ecologist and reputedly had some novel

1

theories about the decline in the smallfish catch in the Narrow Sea. But the girl in blue was being squeezed tightly in a corner by a boy in green, and was presently not interested in anything else at all. Maeve could do no good there, and there was nothing she could do about the blowhard lieutenant. She decided she might as well leave and see how the rest of the company was doing.

There was also the Vaun problem to attend to.

Before she had taken a step, Security whispered in her ear, "Subject of special surveillance is heading in this direction."

Maeve nodded in acknowledgment, hoping that the signal would register—her household equipment was becoming distressingly erratic. During parties, it tended to panic at any sign of rowdiness and then overrun the place with innumerable sims of armed guards. She had almost given up trying to find anyone competent to repair it, and the newer systems were all junk.

Nothing more happened; Security did not ask for further instructions, so she must assume that it was functioning correctly.

She would wait for Vaun. Vaun had been skulking about the grounds all night, haunting the edges of the company as if hoping not to be recognized. If he knew who owned Arkady, he must have had a very special reason for coming here—Vaun had been known to walk out of a diplomatic function when Maeve arrived. He would stand up a king or president to avoid meeting her. But perhaps he didn't know.

"Decadent!" the lieutenant bellowed, growing madder as his victims sullenly refused to talk back.

Maeve wanted to know what Vaun was up to and why he was here. She wanted this bigmouth lieutenant to stop spoiling everyone else's evening. She wanted too many things, obviously. She wished Blowhard would get hungry, or that one of the girls would take him off somewhere and lay him. She was not desperate enough to undertake the job herself—she did not care for beefy loudmouths, and there were lots more interesting people around tonight to talk with or play with; more than she had seen here in weeks. Sometimes it happened that way. Other nights she turned on the beacon and almost nobody came.

She stood back in the shadows under a crimple tree, relishing the musky smell of it, watching the flames dance in the firepool. The night was sticky hot, heavy with the scents of crimple and the night-blooming creepers on the crumbling walls. A night harp trilled plaintively on a twig somewhere. Those walls, the mossy paving, the weathered stone benches—only recently had she realized that they were part of some centuries-old ruin, probably a church. Now they made very effective garden scenery.

Romantic, too! A faint swish of shrubbery announced that the girl in blue and the boy in green had vanished off into the dark. So very shortly they would just be girl and boy . . .

"You!" the lieutenant snarled, picking out the second-largest boy present. "Haven't you got anything to say on the subject?"

Before he could answer, Feirn spoke from the shadows at the far side of the court. "You've scared us all speechless. How many thousands of years have we got left?"

Maeve had not noticed her sitting there, half-hidden by a gupith bush, but she should have recognized the glimmer of her pale skin, the smolder of the red hair. Firelight suited Feirn. Her companion was almost invisible by comparison.

The lieutenant squinted over the flames of the firepool to see who had stooped for the gauntlet. "So all you care about is your personal existence? You are not concerned at all for future generations. That's decadence!"

The boy beside Feirn started to rise. She restrained him with a pale hand on his arm, and this time her voice was stronger as she gathered confidence. "And why worry about the distant future? Shouldn't we be more concerned about the famine down in Thisly, or the civil war in Agoan, or the grain plague in—"

"Bah! Details! There have always been local wars and famines. I'm talking about the galaxy!"

"Then tell me exactly what I should be doing for future generations. How can anything I do improve the Empire's chances?"

That was a fair question, but it happened to coincide with a burst of laughter from the buffet table on the next terrace up. A cascade of merriment rained down through the canopy of branches and gave the remark more sting than it deserved.

The lieutenant's beefy face flushed. "Support the Patrol, of course! The Commonwealth's record is abysmal, and the rest of the planet does little better. Press for far greater funding. More ships, more com equipment so we can find out what's going wrong, more men—"

"Better men would be a better start," a new voice said, and Vaun strolled in from the darkness.

*Well!* Maeve eased farther back under the leaves. She wondered momentarily if Vaun also might have his mix set too high tonight, or whether the lieutenant could somehow be his reason for coming, but she quickly decided that no mere lieutenant could ever be worthy of Vaun's notice. Not a male one, anyway.

He hadn't changed by one eyebrow hair since the last time she'd seen him, and she couldn't remember when that was. He was wearing only a plain white shirt and shorts—Vaun detested uniform—a slight, dark boy, with an arrogance as wide as the galaxy. Contemptuous of everyone—he hadn't changed.

The lieutenant was looking him up and down, smirking in satisfaction. Obviously he hadn't recognized this ambitious newcomer. Obviously no one had. Blowhard was naturally assuming that he'd found the opponent he wanted—which would not be what Vaun intended.

"I think I could take that as an insult," the lieutenant said, flexing his arms.

"If it fits, wear it." Vaun had been running. He was flushed and still panting slightly, and that suggestion of arousal added emphasis to the confrontation. It reminded Maeve of other things, wringing a pang from old wounds: *Vaun!*

A sleepy smile crawled over the bigger boy's face. "Insulting the Patrol can be dangerous."

"Disgracing it is worse," Vaun said mildly.

And that, Maeve suspected, was the only warning the lieutenant was going to get.

"Besides," Vaun continued innocently, "I don't see why you should be concerned about the remote future. Surviving the next four months ought to worry you more."

In a stage whisper, one of the onlookers said, "The next four minutes for you, bud!" A couple of his companions chuckled, but the lieutenant was now wary of Vaun's inexplicable self-confidence—civilians did not talk back this way.

"Why is that . . . *sir*?"

"Because of the Q ship, of course."

"What Q ship?"

"The one from Scyth. It should have started braking weeks ago. Even in our time frame, if it doesn't start in two days, it ain't going to, and in eleven weeks we're all spareribs. It'll smash the planet!"

This time the snigger was general. Drunk, obviously, or orbiting on croil . . . The tension faded. Some of the girls pulled faces.

Not Maeve! Her heart lurched. She knew Vaun, and lying was beneath his dignity. Whatever he was up to, Vaun meant what he said. If he said, "smash the planet," then he meant *smash the planet*. God Almighty!

"But the greenest ensign in the Patrol," the lieutenant smirked, "knows that it is impossible to get an accurate fix on an approaching Q ship. There's no definition to a fireball, and the singularity fouls up the Dopplering.''

"I allowed for that," Vaun said calmly. "It's close enough now for triangulation from the Oort stations. Estimation at the ninety-five percentile. But I don't suppose such dangerous information is allowed to seep down to your level.''

"Go get him, Haj," said the kibitzer in the background.

It was astounding that no one had yet recognized Vaun. No one would be more astounded than he. He certainly could not talk his way out of this now. The spacer would tell him to put his fists up, and then he would have to produce his ID. Or he might not bother—Maeve had never seen him fight, but if he was as good at brawling as he was at everything else, then the lieutenant was in much more danger than he realized.

Vaun was the most relaxed person present, supremely confident of his invariant ability to outdo anyone at anything. He thrust his hands in his pockets in calculated contempt, although his opponent was barely two strides away—and smiling.

"So now you're accusing the Patrol of incompetence?"

"Am I? I'm saying that it should be attending its immediate duty to guard the planet before it worries about the rest of the galaxy. Sure the Bubble's dying. It's been dying for most of those thirty thousand years you mentioned and I expect it'll continue to die for the next thirty.''

The lieutenant sniggered—only civilians referred to human space as the Bubble. Spacers called it the Empire. Vaun himself, in typically pedantic fashion, usually called it the Doughnut, but he had just set a trap, and the other boy had taken the bait.

Maeve began to move and then stopped. Vaun had expected to be recognized, but apparently she was the only one present who knew him. That did not mean that she had a duty to intervene. He did not even know she was there, or he would never have come to Arkady. He was old enough to take care of himself. And he was serious about the Q ship.

Then, without taking his hands from his pockets, he abruptly dropped his mockery and detonated a parade-ground bark. "Go home, Lieutenant! You're disgracing your uniform, and behaving like a snot-faced aristocratic boor!''

Without a word, the lieutenant stepped forward, swinging punches with both fists. They never came close. Vaun's hands stayed in his pockets, but his foot blurred up to take the lieutenant in the crotch, lifting him bodily. He crashed to the paving. A couple of girls screamed. In a chorus of oaths, the other spacers leapt to their feet, intent on vengeance. Maeve opened her mouth . . .

Vaun wheeled around to face toward the shadowy corner where Feirn sat, and bellowed, "Ensign!"

With an inarticulate yelp of horror, the boy sitting beside Feirn seemed to cross the little court in one bound. Suddenly he was standing beside Vaun with his cap already straight on his head and his hand snapping up in a flawless salute, while the rest of him stayed rigid and as motionless as a statue. Everyone else in the courtyard froze. Inexplicably, they all seemed rumpled and unkempt by comparison.

Oh, that one? Still? Maeve kept hoping Feirn would tire of that one.

Nicely done, though. With one word, Vaun had vaporized any possibility of a general brawl. Feet thumped in the background as the other spacers came to attention also. One of the other girls wailed, and then slapped a hand over her mouth.

Feirn followed her companion out of the shadows, sylphlike in a sapphire sheath. Firelight gleamed on pale arms and ran rejoicing over her copper hair.

Vaun ignored her, and that was ominous. "You know who I am?"

"*Sir!*" The ensign's voice cracked like a whip, but his lips did not seem to move. He would have looked more flexible had he been made of cast iron. "Do now, sir. You had your back to me—"

"Have you transportation?"

"Yessir!"

"Take this *thwag* back to his kennel and plug him into a medic. I don't trust him to obey an order."

"He is under arrest, *sir*?"

"Not unless he causes more trouble." Vaun scowled down contemptuously at his writhing, retching victim. "As soon as he can understand, you may inform him that his behavior here tonight was unacceptable. I shall require a letter of apology of not less than ten pages—in his *own* handwriting, *personally* delivered, every page initialed by his commanding officer. Within two days."

It was time to intervene. This was all typical Vaun. He could twist a situation to his own advantage faster than anyone and he reveled in tearing up rule books. Obviously he was after Feirn.

Maeve walked out into the light. "Welcome to Arkady, Admiral."

Had she goosed him with a handbeam, Vaun could not have

jumped higher. Then he said, "Oh, shit!" loudly, and spun around to face her.

I T HAD BEEN a corpse of a day.

The Q ship from Scyth was not due in for half a year yet, but he had checked on its progress a couple of weeks back, out of curiosity. Unable to believe his calculations, he had called for sightings from the out stations, but of course they were light-days away. It was only after breakfast that morning that he had returned to the problem and downloaded the new data.

While he was still trying to comprehend the measure of the ghastly answers he was getting, Phalo had called to say that Tham had gone into withdrawal. Trivial though it might be in comparison, that shock had been personal, and more immediate.

So Vaun had set the Q ship problem aside and spent the next few hours trying everything he knew to get a call through to Tham, and been balked all the way. Sometime during those hours, Lann had departed—left a recording and walked out on him. Not a word of thanks, either.

So he'd jumped in his torch and headed for Tham's place, only to discover that Tham had his armaments primed, with no entry for anyone. Not even Vaun. Especially Vaun, maybe. Crazy guy!

Eventually Vaun had given up in disgust and headed home. On the way he'd remembered Lann. Then he'd picked up a party beacon and decided to stop in and look over the exhibits, hoping to conscript a replacement bed warmer. He hadn't thought to query the beacon to find out whose place this was, or who was already there.

Maeve! It was enough to drive a boy to religion.

First the Q ship, then Tham, then Lann, and now Maeve! Rotting, fornicating, corpse of a day!

For a moment he teetered on the brink of leaving—just spinning on his heel and running off to the parking lot. But he wouldn't give her any more satisfaction. He stayed. He let her run through the introductions, mouthing the usual cool politenesses so that all the

nice boys and girls could go home and tell their friends that they'd
met the great Admiral Vaun. And all the time he was cursing the
fate that had brought him to Maeve's place of all places. On this
day, of all days.

The bitch was loving it, of course. But eventually she eased him
away from the admirers, off to an isolated stone bench under more
of the smelly crimple trees. Girls seemed to like the crimple odor,
but it always made him think of armpits. Maeve had filled Valhal
with crimples, and he'd turfed them all out right after he'd turfed
her out.

The night was warm for late fall, and was about to become
warmer, for Angel was just rising. Already its spooky blue light
was softening the darkness. Must be about midnight.

Maeve hadn't changed. The auburn gleams in her dark hair caught
the starlight, and her body could still stun a boy at fifty elwies. She
was wearing a slinky thing that seemed to consist only of silver
ribbons—it looked simple and had probably cost an honest politi-
cian's annual income. Very few girls could have worn such a thing
and gotten away with it. Never mind! If there was one human female in the galaxy he could resist, it was this one. Never again!
How long had it been? He didn't want to think how long.

It was hard not to think of it. She had the fair skin and sensuous
lips of Scythan ancestry, one of the three planetary stocks that had
populated Ult. Moreover, she had the innate arrogance of royal
blood, from the Island Kingdoms somewhere, back a century or
two. Self-satisfied whore! Always had been. Throwing her out had
been the smartest thing he'd ever done.

Behind a screen of bushes, down a level, a half-decent orchestra
was playing a fiery jig tune. Couples were dancing. Laughing.
This was quite a place she'd landed in here. Not Valhal, but quite
a place. He wondered whom she was hostessing for. Some government type, likely. He'd heard that she was dabbling in Commonwealth politics.

"Just coincidence?" she murmured. "Pure fate that you dropped
in like this, so unexpectedly?"

Bitch.

"It certainly wasn't deliberate."

"What's really surprising is that we've never run into each other
at someone else's party. You do query the beacons, usually? Obviously. And come late," she added.

"After your usual bedtime, I expect."

"Don't tell me you're jealous? Or that you're sleeping alone.
Who's hostess at Valhal these days? Anyone I know?"

"No." Bleeding, *stinking* bitch!

Maeve chuckled throatily. The sound brought back memories. "Not like you to travel alone, Vaun. Another girl walked out on you? How many does that make?"

"Hundreds," he said between his teeth. "Some walk out. Others get thrown out." The spies. The traitors.

"Don't be childish. It's too long to bear a grudge, far too long. Odd how no one recognized you tonight, wasn't it?"

He'd never let any other girl needle him as she did. "I was trying not to be recognized!"

And that was true—he'd hung around in the shadows, avoiding the groups, wanting to make his choice before he got mobbed. Besides, he'd noticed a couple of high-ranking spacers he disliked intensely, and he'd been avoiding them, too. The dislike was mutual, of course.

Maeve straightened and turned to study his face, laying an arm along the back of the bench. She had chosen her spot carefully. Behind her, Angel was growing brighter, striking in under the trees, turning the night sky a metallic, mysterious blue, running silvery highlights on her shoulders and the swell of her breasts under—and between—the ribbons. She was wasting her time. He was immune now.

"Yes, I marked your bashful approach." She shook her head, and the long hair flickered sultry auburn signals. "Is the celebrity thing finally getting boring? My, how times change! But I meant later. You did expect to be recognized when you took down that smart-ass navigator—and you weren't! You trapped him, Vaun!"

"Pompous spacer prig! He deserved it."

She sighed. "It was all part of the hunt, of course. The redhead, wasn't it?"

Oh yes, the little redhead! He thought of the slim arms and the pale skin and the cool touch of the girl's hand when they'd been introduced. He thought of the wide eyes, the tremor in her voice. He knew hero worship when he saw it. She'd been wetting her pants just looking at him. His desire surged, chokingly. "What redhead?"

"Feirn, of course. All that grandstanding was just to dispose of the boy, wasn't it? Unscrupulous as ever."

"What boy?"

"Oh, Vaun! The ensign."

"Oh, that one? He looked too good to be true."

"He is too good to be true. His name's *Blade*."

"You're joking!"

"No. Ensign Blade. Exercises five times a day, cleans his boots every fifteen minutes, reads textbooks in bed . . . and no, I don't know that from experience. I'm extrapolating."

Vaun was intrigued. Could Maeve have descended to making passes at lanky, pipsqueak ensigns? Been refused, maybe?

"Why your interest in him?" he demanded.

She shrugged, suddenly defensive. "Nothing. I just don't like the type. He must have other names. If he turns up again, why don't you pull some more rank on him and order him to use another one?"

"Such as?"

"I don't know. He must have several. I preferred Ephiana when I was young."

"Before we met."

"Indeed!" she snapped. "And just why do you think nobody recognized you, back there at the fire?"

He ignored that, and moved as if to rise.

She sighed. "Never mind. Let's talk business. What's all this about a Q ship?"

"Just grandstanding."

"Oh, no! You meant it." Her manner hardened. "The Cabinet hasn't heard anything about a runaway Q ship."

"The Patrol isn't about to start a panic by telling every tinpot government on the planet. But it's common knowledge. Anyone with a çom can work out that stuff I was spouting."

"But only a spacer would think to do so? Is there really danger?"

"At three hundred millies? If it hits anything at all coming through the system, it'll fry us with a burst of hard gamma and high-energy bosons. Even a civilian ought to know that."

"You mean the out stations, or the planet, too?"

"If it's close enough, the atmosphere may not shield us enough."

"What if it hits the planet itself?"

"Space is very big, Maeve."

"You're being evasive, Vaun. Could it?"

He shrugged. "It might. It's coming in coplanar with the ecliptic, tangential to Ult's orbit, so in theory it could."

"That sounds like a missile trajectory!" Maeve was no spacer, but she had brains and was not afraid to use them.

"It could be." It was. The velocity was three hundred and forty millicees, near enough—almost exactly one-third light speed. Nothing else was needed but timing, and timing was easy with a Q drive. The timing looked very nasty at the moment.

"Vaun! How much damage would a starship do if it hit Ult?"

"Would depend how big it was. Ships come in all sizes, and I don't know how big this one is."

But he did know it had left Scyth twenty-one years ago. Nobody made long hops like that in bathtubs. It would be big.

"Vaun, darling, you're starting to play the Patrol's game."

The *darling* made him want to puke. "Am I? All right. It's holding a standard cruising speed, roughly nine thousand times Ult's escape velocity. Say four thousand times as fast as an average meteorite."

Maeve said, "Shitty shoes!"

He'd forgotten that stupid, juvenile expression. He felt an odd pang at hearing it again after so long. "And kinetic energy goes up as the square of the velocity."

"But four thousand squared is . . . *sixteen million*!"

"Usually. So one ton of Q ship counts as twenty million tons of meteor strike, near enough. Any more questions?"

"You're saying that if it's any size at all, it will wipe us out totally."

"I'm saying it will wipe us out if it's the size of a racing bicycle. If it's the size I think it is, it'll sterilize the planet."

She drew a hard breath. "Why would anyone do such a thing?"

"Because the crew's dead and the mechanicals have failed, maybe."

Revenge was another possibility, but he didn't feel like mentioning it and Maeve wouldn't think of it. Her head did not contain such horrors. She pondered for a moment, absently playing with one of the ribbons on her thigh.

The torrid dance tune on the lower level died away into a sound of applause. Vaun thought about taking that redhead in his arms for a dance, or better. Feirn.

Maeve's throaty voice broke his dream. "So what's the Patrol doing about it, the ship?"

"The Patrol's chasing its ass like a puppy, of course."

She regarded him thoughtfully. "You know that, or just guessing?"

"I know it." Too late he remembered that he'd never had much luck lying to Maeve.

"You mean Roker trusts you now?"

"At the moment he hasn't got much choice, has he?"

Maeve hesitated, then chuckled and seemed to dismiss the matter with a flutter of silver starlight. "I expect not. But that's what Roker gets paid for, isn't it? That's why we have the Patrol?"

"How did you know about the Cabinet not knowing?"

She sighed. "I'm the Commonwealth's Minister of Resources. Oh, Vaun! You really didn't know?" She sounded more upset by that realization than she was by the Q ship problem. Why should she care what he knew or did not know? What sort of a girl would put her personal vanity ahead of the fate of a planet?

"I hadn't even realized I was over Commonwealth territory. I don't come this way much." This was close to Hiport—normally he would stop in there whenever he happened to be going by.

Again she sighed. "No."

Silence . . . Angrily, he found his gaze was sliding easily over starlit silver pathways, following familiar lines and curves, dipping into interesting places that he had once known better than anyone. Probably common knowledge now. Published maps . . .

Suddenly a voice broke into song down where the band had been playing. In a moment a chorus of male voices broke in.

Vaun was on his feet before he knew it.

Maeve made a vexed sound. "Wait! Don't leave yet. I'll have them stop it."

"Time to go," he said. "The longer I stay, the more we'll claw. Nice place. I like it. You've done well—Minister."

Traitors always did well in politics; it was their natural element.

"Thank you, Vaun."

Nice place, but if the Q ship was a missile, then she had only eleven weeks left to enjoy it.

She rose also, and for a moment he thought she was going to try and kiss him. Fortunately, discretion prevailed, but her laugh sounded brittle.

"I don't suppose I'd recognize Valhal now, would I? Lots of changes?"

She wasn't going to get the chance. *Think spying. Think betrayal.* "No, you wouldn't. Good-bye, Maeve."

The damnable singing was getting louder, twisting his nerves like hot wires. He'd turned and taken two steps when she spoke.

"Vaun?"

He stopped, and waited.

"What are you looking for?"

He swung around. "What the hell does that mean—what am I looking for?"

She recoiled slightly at his anger, then took a step forward. "Just . . . curious. You always seem to be hunting something. I just wondered what."

"Girls! Girls, girls, and more girls. Blondes, brunettes—"

"Oh, don't talk crap! There's more to life than screwing, and you know that. *You* know that better than anyone. No, you're ruthless. Hunting, always hunting! I knew it even back when . . . when you owned me body and soul . . ."

"Ha! Body, maybe, but it was Roker who—"

"Even then! You've got everything, Vaun, everything any boy could ever ask for, yet you're still hunting for something, and I never did know what, and now, tonight . . . I meet you again and I see you're *still* hunting, and I want to know *what for*?"

The singing was making him sweat. He needed to scream.

"So now we're into mind probing?" he shouted. "Well, I assure you that I have everything I want from life. And that includes changing the girl when I change the sheets. I just like it that way."

Maeve's expression was shadowed. "You want me to locate the redhead for you?" she asked softly.

Why did she have to bring that up? He wanted out fast; and he wasn't going to take any favors from Maeve. "Taken up pimping as a sideline?" he snapped.

He saw her wince as he spun on his heel and strode away into the darkness.

A S SOON AS he was out of earshot, Vaun began to run. The path was bright in the Angellight, and there were small glow lamps wherever the tree cover was heavy. It wasn't just the singing. He desperately wanted to be away from Maeve, although he wasn't sure why. He didn't want to know why.

A sim imaged in at his side, a girl in simple livery running with him. "You wish transportation, sir?" It wasn't panting like him. Sims didn't sweat, either.

He told it to bugger off, and it vanished. He went on alone, climbing steadily, listening to his feet pad on the pathway and the steady, strong beat of his heart. The sounds of merrymaking dwindled mercifully away.

The grade was gentle. He moved easily, enjoying the exertion in the hot fall night, thinking about the Q ship. Maeve assumed that the Patrol would deal with the problem. That was what the Patrol was for, wasn't it?

Everyone thought that way about the Patrol.

He could remember when he'd thought that way, too.

M EMORY . . . BACK IN Doggoth, a skinny recruit stands in a stuffy classroom with forty other skinny recruits, packed tight together, all shifting minutely from foot to foot and trying not to fidget in their unfamiliar uniforms. Collars cut at necks, boots pinch toes—and that particular recruit has never worn boots before. Somewhere machinery hums, rubbing on auditory nerves like sand. Everyone smells of soap, all scrubbed to the quick, and the boys' faces have been depilated raw. On a platform up front, a flat-voiced officer pontificates with well-rehearsed sincerity as he delivers the official welcoming lecture.

He tells the Legend, and calls it History, and Recruit Vaun listens and believes with the others. Humanity evolves and grows to knowledge, trapped on a single world! Humanity discovers that not all quasars are distant galaxies, that some of them have proper motion among the stars and must be artifacts! Humanity reinvents the Q drive! Humanity strikes outward from ancestral Earth to inquire what beasties already voyage among the stars . . .

Not *aliens*. Not *sentients*. We of the Space Patrol call them *beasties*. And don't you forget it.

There are no beasties near Ult.

Except politicians, of course.

You laugh when an officer makes a joke.

Louder!

That's better.

Behind the explorers come the settlers, and the Empire of Mankind spreads outward through the galaxy.

But Q ships are potentially deadly, and they fly blind. Someone will have to control the traffic, for ancestral Earth has just as many

petty, potty governments as Ult, or Bethyt, or any other of the
million worlds. And so . . . And so the Space Patrol is formed, an
organization dedicated to running the Q ships and keeping open
the spaceways, an organization above planetary politics, servant of
all humanity, owing allegiance only to High Command, back at the
Center.

This is the Legend, but the officer calls it History, and the forty-
one believe him. Recruit Vaun is part of thirty centuries of tradition! Recruit Vaun feels his bony chest swell with pride. His pulse
beats in march time. Recruit Vaun swears sacred oaths to himself
that he will be worthy . . .

S URE. HOW EASY it had seemed then!
        Civilians still believed all that crap. Many spacers believed
it still. That gawky Ensign Blade with his squeaky-pressed uniform
and iced-over eyes would certainly believe it. Even that underwit-
ted, overmuscled, overboosted lieutenant likely believed it, with
his glib talk of the Empire.

Panting hard, Vaun came to a crossing. The path went on, but a
narrower, steeper track transected it. That was obviously meant for
service vehicles, and it must lead up to the parking lot. Even without glow lamps, it would be a faster road. He accepted the challenge
and took off up the service track.

As soon as he reached his torch, he would be long gone away
from Maeve and her crimple-stinking Arkady. He wondered who
hosted for her. She certainly would not lack for volunteers to share
an estate so grand and a bed so generous.

There had never been an Empire.

Only the Patrol itself.

Thirty thousand years of tyranny disguised as service. Rape in
the name of love.

Now the simple people of Ult would expect the Patrol to defend
them from the runaway Q ship. Even Maeve, a minister in one of

the larger governments, had not questioned the Patrol's intent, nor its ability.

Except that there wasn't any way to stop a Q ship. Not in these circumstances. Coming in on the ecliptic was blatant aiming. Even to lay a simple trajectory for a target planet was a breach of space law. The accepted procedure was a flight path that needed end-course correction, just so that there couldn't be unfortunate accidents if things went wrong on the long voyage. There was no question that this brute was hostile.

And there was damned little the Patrol or anyone else could do about it now. If they threw up a missile or diverted an asteroid, it would just impact with the fireball. An asteroid vanishing to nothing in a singularity would emit enough hard radiation to cook the whole system, and the ship would be left unscathed. The intruder was only a third of an elwy away, and the time for throwing asteroids had passed. If death was their purpose, the bastards had won already . . .

Dark as a sewer . . . He raised his arms before him and slowed his pace to a trot.

They could have been stopped a year ago, maybe, but a year ago there had been insufficient evidence. Q ships still came to Ult from worlds farther in—rarely, of course, far fewer than in ancient times, when Ult itself had been part of the frontier—but there were still adventurers, exiles, and jittery refugees fleeing the Silence. After a journey of years, most voyagers had had enough, and even if they hadn't, the local Patrol might evict them and replace them with its own people. There was no way to avoid planetfall, because the ships themselves needed attention. Heated by their own radiation almost to melting point, stressed between their singularities, Q ships tended to stretch with time.

So some or all of the passengers would become settlers, buying entry rights with whatever scraps of unfamiliar technology they might have brought, and with their ship itself. The Patrol would refurbish it, rotate it to a new axis, and send it on again, outward to the frontier worlds. The new crew would be Ultian spacers, of course—keep it in the family. This steady Outward drift was what mankind had been doing since it fell out of a tree in some tropical corner of a minor world called Earth. It was the human way. Probably this one vessel had seemed no different from any of the others, except that it had come from Scyth.

That was significant! The Patrol should have been more vigilant. What had gone wrong? Tham was not only the most likely boy to know the answer to that question, Tham was almost the only high-ranking officer in the Patrol who might be willing to share the information with Vaun. Even if Roker had specifically ordered him not to, Tham would probably confide in Vaun if Vaun asked him to. Normally Vaun would not have forced him. Now Tham had withdrawn. Vaun had been viewing Tham's retreat and the Q ship as two unrelated problems. Perhaps the running was clearing his head, for suddenly he decided that that was altogether too much of a . . .

A sim imaged in his path, a girl in a security uniform, with a gun on its hip. It glowed faintly, so that he would see it under the trees, and it held up a hand to stop him.

"Sir . . ."

Some trick of Maeve's, trying to make him stay? Not likely.

Without a word, he ran right through the illusion and kept on going. Mirages couldn't hurt him. Mirage guns couldn't hurt him. Pants and shirt stuck coldly to his skin now, and his heart was racing, but the ground had leveled off at last and he must be close to the parking lot.

Then he heard a sudden rattle ahead of him, like dry sticks. With a stab of panic, he realized what the sim had been about to tell him.

*Idiot!*

Croaking aloud in his fear, Vaun sprawled to his knees on the path and ripped off his shirt.


K RANTZ! WHAT AN idiot!

Most of the crops and all of the vertebrates on Ult had been imported by mankind. The native life-forms were all primitive, and yet there was one species that came dangerously near to sentience. That rustling close ahead of Vaun was the sound of a pepod.

If he had blundered into its privacy radius, then he was dead, and he would take a lot of other people with him. The rattle came again, sickeningly close. He curled over until his forehead was almost touching the ground, holding his forearms alongside his thighs to cover the cloth. The position was not dignified, and it made panting damnably hard, but it was the only way to face pepods. Either they regarded clothes as a threat, or else they enjoyed watching humans grovel.

The chill on Vaun's back was fear and cooling sweat mixed. Mostly fear. Sweat trickled down from his armpits. *Idiot!*

Rattle . . . To the eye, a pepod was an armchair-sized bush of hard twigs, but those twigs were pseudolimbs and mandibles and poison spines and eyestalks—and also antennae, for pepods had a germanium-silicon metabolism, and communicated by high-frequency radio. How close? The size of the defended area depended on the size of the unit itself. When a pepod felt threatened, it assembled all the others within range into a group organism and they all went berserk together.

Pebbles clinked, but Vaun was still alive.

Gravel dug into his knees and he smelled the cold earth.

Suddenly a voice whispered in his ear. Possibly a sim was bending over him—he did not look up. "The quasisentient commiserates on your elevated body temperature, sir." Security was translating the radio jabber.

Vaun was shivering, but the pepod would be viewing him in far-infrared. Pepods favored the southern hemisphere, which was colder, and they disliked Angel, the supermassive star that warmed northern winters. In a few thousand years it would have drifted away, and the pepods would again inherit the planet.

"Inform the beastie that I also express my sympathies on the unpleasant weather."

"I have done so. It wishes you good grazing."

Vaun risked raising his head a little, to ease his neck. "Give it a suitable acknowledgment. Can I get up yet?"

"In a moment, sir. I congratulated it on its melodious song. It is moving away from the path, sir."

As Vaun sat up and fumbled to find his sodden shirt, he felt fury replacing his fear. Pepods were an unpredictable hazard and also a real nuisance. Of necessity, the law everywhere protected them from molestation, but simple radio screamers would keep them away from human settlements. Why would Maeve tolerate a pepod on her grounds?

The only reason he could think of, as he stalked angrily on up the track, was that there were always pepods around Valhal.

V AUN'S FAVORITE TORCH was a standard Patrol K47—a
seat on a star, as the old song said—but his had been considerably souped up before he had acquired it, and he had added a few
improvements since. The bench, for example, would fold down
into a couch just barely large enough for two. Even a regulation
K47 would fly a ballistic trajectory at the limits of the atmosphere,
and a surprising number of girls were interested in trying things
weightless.

He took off on manual, blasting straight up at max climb. The
sonic boom would rattle Arkady a little. Admirals were expected
to do things like that, and Maeve would learn that he had departed
before Security told her so. She must already know of his encounter
with the pepod, of course. Bitch! If she hadn't made him so mad,
he wouldn't have been so cretinly stupid.

He set course for Valhal, seeing the Commonwealth spread out
below him, ghostly blue in the Angellight, under a spooky sky of
slate-colored velvet. The lights of Hiport gleamed to the north.
Usually when he came this way, he would stop in there; that was
why he had not known of Arkady, and Maeve.

Less than a dozen other stars were visible, the few that could
compete with Angel. One day Angel would go supernova and take
half the Bubble with it. Somewhere high off to the left was mythical
Earth, three thousand elwies away. Sol was a nondescript star, visible at such a distance only through major telescopes. No one had
heard from Earth in a long, long time, or from any of the first
worlds. Inside the Bubble was the Silence.

Scyth had gone silent thirty-odd years ago. But it had sent out
the Q ship afterward, and that was very unusual. Tham said . . .

Krantz!

Like an echo of thunder came memory of the insight that the
pepod had interrupted. Why should Tham suddenly withdraw, just
when he was most needed? Yes, the galaxy was full of coincidences . . . It was full of trickery, too.

19

And anyway, what was Vaun doing, heading home to an empty bed when he hadn't completed the task he'd set out on? What sort of famous hero ran from a few alarm signals? He reached for the controls again.

The party beacons would all be turned off now. There would be no girl tonight he could dazzle with thoughts of hostessing the famous Valhal and comforting the famous hero. No naked little redhead in his arms tonight. Nights without sex brought bad dreams.

He had more important things to do than sleep.

He banked as tightly as the safeties would let him and laid in a return course for Forhil, Tham's place.

Famous hero . . . Vaun had killed Abbot and defeated the Brotherhood. This invading Q ship might be the Brotherhood's revenge.

Scyth had gone silent thirty years ago—which meant about forty if you allowed for the time lag—and Tham believed that the Brotherhood had been responsible. Vaun had heard him say so more than once. True, Prior had come from Avalon. Abbot and *Unity* had come from Avalon, but Avalon had not succumbed to the Brotherhood yet—probably. A couple of years ago, when the Avalonian Patrol had finally answered Ultian Command's urgent queries, Tham had passed the news to Vaun. The war had been won, the message said, the brethren on Avalon defeated and wiped out—and Avalonian Command had congratulated its Ultian comrades on their own victory against the infestation.

That message could have been a fake.

Scyth was part of the Brotherhood problem, too. Scyth's sudden silence had come later, long after *Unity* had arrived at Ult, and this new, deadly Q ship had certainly originated from Scyth after that. So what was the Patrol up to? What was Roker up to? The high admiral was a prick of the first water, but he did not usually allow personalities to interfere with business. Why was Planetary Command not consulting its great hero, Admiral Vaun?

He was the expert on the Brotherhood, wasn't he?

Despite Vaun's brave lies to Maeve, he had no idea of the Patrol's thinking on the threatening Q ship. He had tried to get through to Roker, but his calls had been refused.

And was Tham's withdrawal at this critical moment mere coincidence, or was it Roker's handiwork . . . or even the Brotherhood's? The brethren had subverted the Patrol once before. They might try again.

Now the torch was so high that the sky had turned black. Angel was a blinding pinpoint that polarized a jagged purple blot in the canopy field, but now and again it flashed brilliantly off rambling watercourses on the dark world below.

Down there was the Putra Delta.

That was another reason Vaun never came this way.

In all the years since he first left his birthplace, he had only gone back once. He had left in silence, an outcast. He had returned in triumph, a hero. He could still taste that sour memory . . .

A S THE TORCH canopy dephases, the heat hits him like a fist. Hot air steams in his lungs, a white brilliance of sunlight stabs knives in his eyes. He smells mud. His hands tremble as he grasps the edge of the hull to dismount.

He jumps down the last step, and grass squelches slimily below his boots. A tiny, sly voice in his right ear is prompting him, "Head higher. Look left . . . now right. Smile. Take a deep breath. You're happy, dammit! That's better. Now start to walk . . ."

*The hero returns.* Smiling. Dazzled. Walking—a little faster, now—walking over to where the welcoming committee huddles in terror and bewilderment. The hidden cameras watch, so the world can watch.

Admiral's epaulets weigh heavy on his shoulders. Already his chest glitters with medals and jeweled stars, and there are dozens more scheduled to come yet as the governments and rulers of the planet outdo one another in honoring the hero.

This is important for the Patrol, remember. Vaun's a hero. Good old Vaun. He saved the world. Everyone wants to watch him coming home to tiny Puthain. Good for the Patrol.

Taxes—a chance to raise taxes . . .

"Looking happy," the prompt says in his ear. "Looking happy. Hold out your arms now. Higher! Walking faster."

The grass is muddy, spurting under his shoes. The smell of the river . . . How could he have forgotten the ever-present stink on the river, the oozy, black mud of the delta? Or forgotten the unending drone of brownflies, the sigh of the empty wind in the long

green pozee grass; not a tree or a hill in sight, nor any building fit
for human habitation. The watchers burst into cheering, all together.

Puthain? It's been cleaned up specially for today's show. Rustic
simplicity is okay, but voters and taxpayers wouldn't like squalor . . .
Still only an ugly heap of driftwood, that's all it is. They never
called it *Puthain* when he was a child. Just the village. Probably
the name has been invented to put it on the map: Puthain, birthplace
of Admiral Vaun.

The hero.

But it's only a litter of hovels half-drowned in the mud of the
Putra Delta. He can smell eels under the mud smell. The scent
makes his mouth water, although he has learned that eating eels is
shameful. Now the crowd has been released and comes running
forward, arms out. So few? But it's a very small village . . . the
boys and girls of the village, and the children of his age grown up
now, and a new crop of stick-limbed, shock-haired youngsters replacing them, staring at his uniform. He recognizes Olmin . . . and
Astos . . . Wanabis. Underfed, bony, been cleaned up for the occasion. At least half the girls are heavy with child. The boys' beards
have all been removed and the lower halves of their faces painted
dark to match the sunburned bits. Beards are for savages. Bony,
brown faces . . . more puzzled than resentful, more resentful than
happy. What do they care? They forgot him years ago. Six years—
is that all? He doesn't belong here now.

He never did belong.

He wants to turn and run back to the torch; he wants that so badly
his knees shake. This is worse than hunting Abbots through the
bowels of a Q ship.

Faces . . . Faces missing. There's only one face he really wants
to see, and he won't ever see that one again. He knows that, and
yet he hasn't been able to remember the village without remembering Nivel. Nivel isn't here. Nivel would be smiling too, but
Nivel's smile would be real and shine in his eyes. It must be ten
years ago now . . . One day just like any other day, and then somebody, somewhere, alarmed another pepod, and this one came flailing into a work gang with poison spines lashing and put eight boys
and three girls into death agonies. A little place like this can't afford
screamers to keep the pepods away.

There were no cameras here that day.

Now the villagers are milling around, thinning out, backing away;
puzzled, cowed, being prompted by hidden voices, moving so the

cameras can see him, the hero being welcomed by his childhood friends. The freak is back.

Olmin is visibly shaking. Looks like he has to speak first. Place hasn't got a mayor, hasn't got a priest. Seems Olmin has been designated as Best Friend. That's a bitter joke! Olmin the taunter? Olmin the tormentor? Olmin who sat on his chest and beat fists on his face. Olmin who peed on him while the others held him down. Very reasonable—they just wanted to see if pee would turn his hair the right color. It never did. Best Friend? Well, why not? The rest were no better. Did you ever scare me as much as you are scared right now, big-kid Olmin?

Missing faces . . . Glora isn't there. They'd assured him that there would be no Glora. The Patrol doesn't want the world to hear Admiral Vaun's crazy mother screaming about meeting God and virgin birth and how she's always known her son would save the world. Glora's been taken away for treatment.

Olmin makes a croaking noise and lays an awkward, shaking hand on Vaun's shoulder, frightened of dirtying the epaulet.

"Vaun!" He is licking his lips and listening to his prompter with his eyes so wide that the whites show all around the mud-brown irises. "It's good . . . to see you . . . again. Vaun." Pause. His scalp shines through his sandy hair.

Vaun waits for his cue, tries to hold a smile, watches the goiter lump jiggling in Olmin's throat. Feels sudden anger—why isn't the local booster adjusted for iodine deficiency?

Still Olmin's turn. "And good . . . to be back . . . too, Vaun . . . I expect?"

" 'It's always good to come home, Olmin,' " prompts the voice in Vaun's ear.

He tries to say the words, and they stick in his throat like shit.

*Good to come home? No, it's horrible to come home. I hate this place! I hate the lot of you. You made my life a hell, all of you. If I saved the world, then it wasn't for you. God knows, it wasn't for any of you.*

"It's always good to come home, Olmin."

WAS OLMIN STILL alive, down there in the dark, living out his belly-crawling existence in the mud of the delta? It wasn't likely, because the peasants' booster was crude, all-purpose stuff, not tailor-made like a spacer's. But Vaun could almost hope he was, because a life like that was its own punishment. Long life to Olmin!

Now the torch was grazing the edges of space, where Angel could not hold back the flood of stars, and the night wore its finery. By habit, Vaun's eyes sought out the constellation of the Swimmer, and the eye of the Swimmer—Alpha and Gamma, two reddish stars, the suns of Avalon. The suns that shone on Monad, where it all began . . .

Angel was almost at the zenith. Dawn must be near.

He laid back his seat in the torch; he reclined at ease in the little bubble and thought about ciphers and electronics and passwords and missiles. In theory the problem was simple—Commodore Tham was entitled to barricade himself inside Forhil to his heart's content. If he wished, he could turn it into a modern version of one of those preindustrial castles whose ruins dotted the high borderlands. Vaun had flown over them a million times. Probably Commodore Tham would be technically breaking Commonwealth law if he actually fired any of his beams and missiles and brought down a torch and killed someone, but Commonwealth law wasn't going to do much about an officer in the Space Patrol.

The Patrol itself, though . . . that was another matter. To shoot down an admiral must certainly be a breach of some regulation or other. It would show a lack of proper respect, at the very least. Furthermore, Commodore Tham did not own Forhil, although he was free to treat the place in every way as if he did. When he died, it would revert to the Patrol and be deeded to some other senior officer, and he in turn would hold it for a century or so. An admiral outranked a commodore handsomely, and Vaun could *order* Tham to admit him to Patrol territory. He might be reprimanded later for

24

violating a subordinate officer's privacy and privilege, but that was a trivial matter.

Unfortunately Tham was not accepting messages, so he could not receive the order. He had apparently put his defenses on automatic, to shoot on sight, regardless of rank.

High Admiral Roker himself, now, or any of the senior brass . . . they would know codes that could override anything Tham might use. That was the practical problem—Vaun was the famous hero, the holder of renowned Valhal, the finest estate on the planet, and so far as the world was concerned he had all the status of his exalted rank, but in fact Admiral Vaun was never provided with high-class passwords and ciphers. Not likely!

The more he thought about it, the less Vaun could accept the coincidence of timing between Tham's withdrawal and the arrival of the approaching Q ship. There was dirty work afoot; waters were being muddied. If Roker was not behind it, then the Brotherhood was—at least two brethren had never been apprehended, and if they were still alive, out there somewhere, then they would certainly be still conspiring somehow. They would never give up. In either case, burning Vaun down out of the sky could be part of the plan, or at least an acceptable variation on it. Even Phalo's call yesterday might have been contrived, although Phalo himself was as trustworthy as Tham.

None of which would matter if Vaun could somehow manipulate the electronics of his torch to make them manipulate the electronics of Tham's defenses. And so he thought back to his days as a trainee, and racked his brains for everything he could remember from innumerable lectures. He came up with an enormous blank, a total void.

The Space Patrol was the biggest con job the galaxy had ever seen, on this and probably every other planet of the Bubble. States and churches, democracies, monarchies, empires, religions, faiths, philosophies . . . those were the visible rulers of the human body and soul, but behind and above them all, feeding on them, crouched the eternal aristocracy of the Patrol.

But Doggoth was one part of the Patrol legend that was factual. Indeed, Doggoth's grim reputation was but a shadow of its reality.

Doggoth was a carefully crafted hell, a bleak, rocky torture house in the remote north. There was absolutely nothing at Doggoth except screaming weather and the Space Patrol Academy. To Doggoth came the adolescent scions of the great Patrol families, sons and daughters of commodores and admirals, and there all the easy decadence of their pampered upbringing was callously ripped out of them. Day after terrible day, in Doggoth they were systematically driven out of their wits—ill-treated, humiliated, destroyed, ground to paste. And when they had been reduced to suitably gibbering zombies, they were skillfully refashioned, rebuilt in the proper mold, as spacers.

Graduate or die. There was no other exit. By ancient tradition, trainees and instructors alike bore loaded weapons at all times. Even minor infractions were punished by firing squad, and dueling was encouraged. The suicide rate was unbelievable. But the process achieved its objective. The survivors returned to the world as junior officers, a triumphant elite, all staunchly convinced that the galaxy now owed them a living.

Vaun had been even more of an alien at Doggoth than he had been in the squalid delta hamlet of his childhood. At Puthain—if that had really been its name even then—he had been the wrong build, the wrong color, black-haired, black-eyed. He had been the bastard son of the local madwoman. He had suffered abominably.

At Doggoth he had been the mudslug, a contemptible, ignorant, incomprehensible peasant thrown in among the sons and daughters of the galactic aristocracy. They had considered that he spoke wrong, ate wrong, walked wrong, thought wrong. His mere existence among them had been inexplicable and inexcusable. They had despised him utterly, and done everything they could think of to drive him to despair and self-destruction.

But the mudslug had proved to be smarter and stronger and tougher than any of them. He had surmounted every obstacle, triumphed in every contest, come first in every class. The officers had promoted nonentities over him, refused him recognition, treated him like garbage, done their worst on him—one of the many incidental skills he had gained was an ability to go without sleep for days at a time. His classmates had spurned him, cheated on him, mocked him, ignored him, insulted him. After his first dozen duels, he had begun attracting the suicides, and learned to maim instead of kill; after that he had been challenged less often. He had stubbornly refused to turn his gun on himself no matter how often that solution had been recommended, because the most important lesson he had learned at Doggoth was that he was better than anyone else at anything.

That he had never forgotten.

Recruits entered as frightened youngsters. The survivors emerged after six months or so as aristocrats in ensigns' uniforms, ready to rule the world.

Vaun had remained at Doggoth for five years, and never risen above the glorious rank of crewboy, second class. Had the Q ship *Unity* not arrived in the Ult system, he might be there still.

He had certainly learned everything there was to know about automatic defenses and missile systems and electronic recognition signals.

But he could think of nothing that would help him weasel his way into Forhil against Tham's wishes.

The Patrol had been perfecting its security systems for thirty thousand years.

A S THE YELLOW of dawn began to contest with Angel's cold blues for possession of the east, as the torch began its long descent from the ionosphere, Vaun's thoughts drifted to Tham himself. Tham was a solid, dependable boy—reticent and secretive, but emphatically not the sort of nervy quitter who would jump into withdrawal without as much as a farewell com to his friends. His family was Patrol stock from time beyond measure—Vaun had heard him mention in passing that his ancestors had come from Elgith in the *Golden Chariot* with the holy Joshual Krantz. Of course, if everyone who made that claim was to be credited, then *Golden Chariot* had carried a crew of several billion, but when Tham said it, a boy believed.

Tham had breeding, and more brains than most, and by definition toughness, for he had survived Doggoth. If he had a fault, it was that he was a nice guy—and nice guys never make the top. Early in his career, Tham had settled in as ComCom, chief of the Ultian Patrol's Network Section, and he'd run it ever since, seeking nothing more.

The Network Section handled interstellar communication. It should have been an important bureau in the Patrol's organization, and the fact that it never had been showed just how much of a myth the Galactic Empire really was. Each planetary command ruled its own world in its own way, and for its own benefit, oblivious of what the others did.

But if anyone knew what was really going on, it would be Tham.

Tham had many friends, and Vaun felt entitled to include himself in that list. Tham was one of the very few high-ranking spacers who would treat Vaun as an equal—even now, after so long.

They'd hunted together, drunk together, played together, even worked together, if you could rank Vaun's public relations nonsense as work. Tham had visited Valhal innumerable times. It was less than six weeks since the last time he and Zozo had dropped in, unexpected but always welcome. They'd gone gill fishing and sky buzzing that time—nobody ever just sat around when Tham was present. Just after that, Vaun and Lann had made a protracted tour of the Stravakian Republic, and they'd managed a side trip to Forhil. Vaun closed his eyes and counted, and made it nine days since he'd seen Tham. Or maybe only eight. There had been nothing wrong with the lad then.

Even if Tham's behavior was understandable in a boy so reserved, then Zozo's silence was not. Vaun could perhaps understand why she would ignore him, but he would have expected her to call for help from Phalo. She would certainly not have abandoned Tham.

Tham had shared his pillow with the same girl for as long as Vaun had known him. She was his *lady*—they'd gone through some sort of binding ceremony in one of the minor churches, and they were devoted to each other. Faithful, even! Once in a while any party with spacers present would degenerate into an orgy—spiking the drinks with stiffener was a perennial prank—but Tham would never join in those if he was still capable of any choice at all. He would grab Zozo and run.

Tham might have refused to call on his friends for support, but why hadn't Zozo?

It was all very suspicious. The more Vaun considered it, the more he thought he detected the sinister hand of High Admiral Roker.

And the less he understood. Why should Tham have to die like that?

Withdrawal was hell. Vaun knew that better than most. He could remember how once he'd nearly died of it.

**I**S THIS WHAT dying feels like? Vaun's head aches and dark things float in front of his eyes. Glora keeps telling him to sing up, but his mouth's so dry he can't make a word. And the pain in his bloated little belly is getting worse and worse.

Glora has turned to shout at him, but she's so far ahead that he can't hear anything she says over the wind sighing in the pozee grass. Probably she's telling him to keep up. He thinks Glora isn't very well herself, because she wanders from side to side as she goes along the track, and sometimes she slips in the mud. When he comes along later, he sees the marks where she's fallen.

There's no one else on this road. It's just a trail through the pozee, winding along toward the sky, with no ups or downs, and nothing to see. The river may be close, because the smell of it is making the air thick and heavy, but there's nothing, nothing, nothing to see, except Glora's gaunt shape, sometimes, weaving along the track ahead . . . arms waving like black sticks against the sky, hair and rags dancing out of time. Other times she disappears around a bend, and then he does hurry as hard as he can.

They're going home, Glora says, home to the village. The priests in the big towns are all blinded by the Father of Evil and won't hear the true word, or see the corporeal mani—manifest . . . something. Vaun doesn't know. He really doesn't care. He thinks he may die before he reaches the village.

For a moment the wind fades, and he can hear Glora's voice raised in praise. He ought to be singing praise, too, and maybe then God will make him better or let him die. Whichever God wants will be fine. God is his daddy. But if God wants him to live, then he hopes God doesn't want him to do it back in the village. Following Glora around and singing outside churches is nicer, and begging for supper much easier than eel skinning. The town kids jeer at him, of course, but mostly they jeer at Glora, and they don't pick on him the way Olmin and the others do. Fortunately, he doesn't think Glora really knows the way back to the village. They seem

29

to have been walking for an awful lot of days since she first told him they were going home to the village. They've spent the nights in the grass.

Oh, the cramps in his tummy . . .

Smelly mud in his face. He must have fallen, like Glora.

"Hey there, fella? Sleeping at this time of day?"

Vaun forces his eyes open. He forces his head to turn. He recognizes Nivel's withered foot.

He smiles a little.

Now Nivel is carrying him, which is very funny, because Nivel rocks when he walks, dragging his bad leg, and now Vaun had the same sway as Nivel does. *Hup—swoosh! Hup—swoosh!* He hears Glora singing praise somewhere behind.

"You hungry, Little Black Eyes?" Nivel is panting hard. "Got some eel soup for hungry lads."

"Not hungry, Nivel."

"What'sat? Young lad not hungry? Never grow up to be a big boy if you don't eat, Vaun."

"Not hungry," Vaun insists, forcing the words from his dry mouth. Sore tummy . . .

Nivel gasps, and lowers Vaun to the ground, and kneels down beside him. Glora is a long way back, her arms waving, doing a dance.

"Need a rest," Nivel pants, peering very hard at Vaun. He lays a raspy thumb on one of Vaun's eyelids and pushes it up, as though wanting to see what is underneath. "You been getting your booster every day, lad?"

Vaun nods uncertainly.

Nivel mutters something he doesn't catch. "You listen to me, Little Black Eyes! Listen good! And never mind what that muddy-wit . . . what Mommy tells you contrariwise, all right? You make sure you get your booster *every day*, understand? Every single day! And if you haven't got any in the house, you come and see me. Or ask anyone. Even in a big town. If you haven't got booster, you can ask any boy or girl at all, and they have to share with you if they have some. That's the law. Booster's free for everyone. Understand?"

Vaun has never seen Nivel look so fierce, so he nods.

"Eating isn't enough," Nivel says, seeming a little less sure of himself. "Food hasn't got some things in it that it should have, and it has things it shouldn't, and people who don't take their booster *every day* get sick awful fast and don't grow up to be big strong boys and beat the shit out of Olmin."

Vaun sniggers at that. It's a secret, private joke between him and
Nivel. Nivel isn't very big, and he can't work very hard with his
bad leg, and he lives by himself, when all the other boys live with
girls and little kids. Sometimes Nivel comes and lives at his house
for a while, and those are good times, even if Vaun does have to
sleep on the floor, because then Glora doesn't talk to God so much
and wake Vaun up in the night to sing praise, but those times never
seem to last very long.

Vaun likes Nivel better'n anyone. Even Glora. Specially Glora,
because the things she says about him make the other kids laugh at
him. Sometimes Glora is nice.

Nivel stands up again, and pulls Vaun up, too, and hoists him on
his shoulder again, muttering and heaving. "So you remember,
Black Eyes! People who don't get their booster can't live on Ult,
remember?"

After a few steps . . . *Hup—swoosh! Hup—swoosh!* . . .

Vaun says hoarsely, "Where do they live, Nivel? People who
don't get their booster?"

"They don't," Nivel says, between pants. "They sort of shrivel
up and die."

THE DREAMER IS Pink and Scarlet is It. There are dozens
of units—no, hundreds—no, thousands, all dodging and
laughing as Scarlet pursues them. They scamper and eddy all over
the grass, ebbing and flowing in millions of colors, always defining
a clearing around Scarlet, shrieking and yelling, mocking and gleeful. High overhead the twin suns are shining—two crimson pillows
in an indigo sky. But Scarlet is tiring. Scarlet is weary and laughing
no more. The Dreamer takes pity and fakes a brief stumble, so
Scarlet can tag him; now Pink is It and must tag another. *Come to
me, brothers, so I can touch you* . . .

The dream changes. The Dreamer is Blue . . .

Brown arms wheel in a chaos of shrieks and flying water as the
Dreamer's crop all reach the bank together. With shouts of *Cheat!*

and *He tripped me*! they scramble out, jostling, shivering, laughing, in a tangle of wet brown youngsters. The Dreamer is Blue today, but as he grabs his shorts from the pile, another hand snags them also. He grins and is grinned at, and both units let go together and reach for another. So the other becomes Orange and the Dreamer is Tan . . . and Black is poised right on the edge of the bank, so the Dreamer jabs a fast elbow and Black goes over in a howl, and then everyone is into that game and the Dreamer himself is pushed and falling into a splashing surf of brethren . . . *Brothers, I am coming . . .*

The dream changes . . .

There is no moon, and the dorm is dark. Youngsters are meant to be sleeping. But tonight is not a usual night; this night is full of weeping. News has come from Xanacor that the hive is gone. The randoms have attacked it, and the hive is no more. There are pictures, and terrible stories, and the big boys sent the young crops to bed early, saying that there was business to talk tonight, but the Dreamer knows that is just so they can do their own weeping downstairs and not seem sissy and set poor examples.

Small fry need to weep, too! The Dreamer was allowed to sit on a big boy's lap for a while and be hugged while he cried, but that is not enough. He has too many more tears to shed. He cannot sleep for thinking of his brethren. Others are sobbing in the warm dark, and just when one gets control of himself, then another unit starts, and the sound brings the lump back to the Dreamer's throat, and the pictures burn up into the memory again, of units being bayoneted, being strangled, bleeding and burning. His brothers, some no older than himself. Bleeding and screaming. So his sobs start again, gasping, retching, hard-to-breathe sobs.

He hears movements, and raises his head. Units are moving around, but even as he realizes what is happening, there is a unit already beside him in the dark. Gratefully the Dreamer makes room, and the other unit snuggles in beside him. They hold each other tight and weep together, dribbling tears on each other's pajamas, weeping for their dead kin in Xanacor.

" **A**DMIRAL?"

Vaun must have been dozing. The harsh voice of the cabin alarm startled him. "Eh? What?"

"You asked to be advised when you were at closest approach to Forhil."

"Oh . . . right." He was on his way to Tham's place.

He stretched and rubbed his eyes and pulled his wits up like wrinkled socks to straighten them. Dawn burned blood and gold in the east. He had laid in a course for Caslorn International, which would make him seem like an innocent flyby to Tham's defenses.

He had not thought up a way to sneak into Forhil; he would have to break in by brute force, and there was no way to do that in a torch.

Right! Go for it . . . Although this was his closest approach, he was still far too high, but he snapped over to manual and banked into a dive.

Two seconds later, red alarms lit up all over the board and the siren screamed in a replay of yesterday. Wishing he had a warm coat with him, he buttoned up his shirt and waited, tensing.

"Attention 80-775! Attention 80-775! You are entering restricted airspace. Retaliatory action will commence in three minutes. Attention . . ."

He let the voice shout, counting seconds, watching airspeed and altitude slide around the vids. Too fast . . . He eased back, but the scoops could not grip the thin air, merely making the craft shudder and a few more warnings flash on . . . About two minutes now until the defenses took command and diverted him. That was what had happened every time the previous day. He had tried three times, and three times the defenses had flown him an hour's flight away before releasing him. Today he wasn't going to argue.

One minute . . . He opened a com channel, voice and video. The warnings dropped to a whisper. The screen stayed blank.

33

"Calling Forhil. Tham, this is Vaun. I need to talk to you. I'm alone and unarmed. I'm coming in, Tham!"

As he disconnected, the shouting resumed. *Extreme Hazard* lit up on the board. The opposition wasn't going to blink. Any second now he would feel the controls go limp as command was taken away from him.

With his right hand, he slid the handgun from its holster beside his seat, and leaned over to press his left thumb on the *Eject*.

"*Refused*," screamed the speaker, drowning out even the siren. Every light flashed, including *Suicide*!

"Go ahead then, you bastards," Vaun muttered. He pointed his gun at the control board, and waited.

And waited . . .

**W**AITING? WAITING IS slow death and worse than death. Waiting is more exquisite torture than any horror in the blood-soaked history of religion or the annals of the Race Wars.

The cabin is midnight dark, full of mysterious, bulky shapes. Here and there a faint rainbow glow of instruments plays on an ear, a forehead, or a moving hand. Within this crypt, in a huddled circle of hunched ghouls, the crew attend their boards—two girls and four boys all as intent as musicians performing ancient masterpieces. Voices murmur, human and mechanical, small sounds overlain on a deeper hum. Vids flicker.

Ultian Command's shuttle *Liberty*, presently in high orbit . . .

Vaun is tormented by overload: crisp-new uniform rustling with every move and pinching his crotch, awesome omens of rank glittering on his shoulders, the smell of metal and recycled air, the vertiginous false gravity, and especially the view he has called up in his tank, a billion stars coruscating in glory.

This is not a Doggoth simulator. *This is real.* He rode this bottle through the Hiport launcher, out into the universe.

Maeve didn't say good-bye. Wasn't there to say good-bye. When the rest of the crew were kissing their lovers, he was alone. He'd been told she'd left Hiport. Better not to think about it.

Somewhere out there is a Q ship—name unknown, crew unknown, inbound from Avalon. The Brotherhood, maybe. He can't see it, but the vids tell him he should be able to. The boat's electrocrystalline mind makes no allowance for its commander being a rank beginner.

He could switch to infrared, of course. Q ships are hot, and he'd pick it up on long-infrared. Somehow that feels like cheating . . . He continues his search on visual.

Strangest of all and worst torment of all is the alien sense of authority. He is in charge. Excitement is a throb of pain in his temples, acid coursing his veins, but it is also ice in his gut. Five of those six spacers are genuine. They have spacefarers' blazes on their lapels and must know ten times as much about all this as he does. They all left Doggoth at least five years ago, before his time, and Ultian Command is large enough that a brand new ensign can posture as a commodore and get away with it as long as he isn't actually recognized.

They look to him for orders. They have no inkling that this seemingly routine mission threatens death for all of them, like a wisp of approaching storm cloud bringing winter. They must wonder why an exalted commodore has been assigned command of a lowly pilot boat, and why he is in such a fearsome, bat-fired hurry to make contact, but not one of them has shown any hint of further suspicion. Apparently he is still concealing his ignorance and inexperience, and that is all that is needed. The five trust their lives to his fake insignia; they will obey him without question.

He mutters a word to his board, demanding more magnification, and is absurdly worried that one of the spacers will hear him. They are all occupied with their own duties and wouldn't put any significance on the commodore wanting more magnification anyway. They don't know he can't find a Q ship in a view tank.

Still can't!

Vaun glances around the darkness and the hints of faces. At the far side of the circle, brightness of two eyes . . . Yather is watching him. Every pilot boat carries a political officer, of course, but not likely one hailing from the same branch as this one, and normally PolOff has no duties to perform until contact. This poloff is working already. Yather's job is to keep Vaun in line. The boat's seating is nonstandard, altered so that he sits directly across from the commander. He may have a gun pointed at Vaun already, a spacer's low-velocity slug thrower with soft bullets that won't damage equipment much, or knock holes in a metal hull, but will spread human flesh like a tablecloth.

He probably has orders to use it before the flight is over, regardless of what happens with the Q ship.

Waiting. Vaun is ashamed of the tightness in his chest, the dryness of his throat.

He sneaks another glance across to the far side of the cabin, and again Yather's eyes shine at him. Still watching. The last five years have been kind to Security Officer Yather, who is now Commodore Yather, but today he wears the humble plumage of PolOff Yather. His career has prospered since he met Vaun. He's shed a lot of his beef, none of which was ever fat. Either his job no longer includes bullying people or now his rank is high enough that he doesn't need muscle to show that he's a big man. He's still tall, and somehow the size of his bones is more impressive without all the meat cluttering them. He is still swarthy and suspicious. He still glowers darkly.

Vaun looks away.

And there is the Q ship in his tank. How could he have missed it earlier? True, it isn't very impressive, just a smoke-gray, irregular bulk. Rounded, not jagged. It isn't very big, either—the vids are estimating four kilos max axis, but nothing is going to be very accurate as long as the fireballs are on. It looks like a potato, not an ancient asteroid fragment blasted by the hellfire of space travel. This is a *ship*—a true star voyager, a *rock*—and compared to it, this shuttle is a mere toy. The insignificant smudge has raised Vaun's pulse by thirty points.

"NavOff!" Vaun barks, making everyone jump, even himself. "How long now?"

The navigator clears her throat, peering at her board. "About fifty seconds, sir. Assuming they're going for standard orbit."

Sloppy answer . . . "Why wouldn't they go for standard orbit?"

She flinches. "No reason, sir. Forty-four seconds."

Vaun drops his eyes back to the tank and the interstellar visitor, edging now into a parking orbit that will be a very fair approximation of what Patrol standing orders call for. Considering that a Q ship travels almost blind, with all its observations screwed up by the singularities, this one is doing very well—certainly better than the legendary *Gryphon* that tried to orbit City Hall in Kilianville a few centuries ago.

In less than forty-five seconds the singularities will be turned off and the visitor will then be nothing but a hollow rock, an artificial satellite. Then he'll find out who or what is aboard, and they will discover him already in place, on the job.

He toggles for close-up and notices a few tangles of spidery human artifacts, hinting at the complexities of the interior. He can see the singularity if he snaps his tank over to X-ray; then the Q ship blazes at both ends, where the rarefied ions of Ult's uppermost atmosphere plunge into bottomless nothings and themselves become nothing. The singularities show little on visual, only a faint blurring that he suspects is mostly imagination.

Infrared shows seven hundred kelvins max . . . Hot lady! An icy spot around the entry nipple says refrigeration has survived the journey. Turned on already? Makes a boy wonder if *Unity* maybe expected this extrafast welcome.

The gravity meters are going nuts.

NavOff has set up a timer on Vaun's board. *30 . . . 29 . . .* Trajectory is getting very close to critical. This feels much less real than a Doggoth simulator. Any minute now Safety will start bleating warnings that he's put his craft too close to the Q ship's predicted orbital station—not too close for business eventually, but too close while the fireballs are on. Safety won't let the pilot boat fall into a singularity, if only because its death scream would be a gamma flux to fry the planet below. The Q ship itself is falling into the pseudo–black hole also, and has been doing so for untold years, but the Q ship has another singularity at the rear to control acceleration. Dangerous things, Q ships. Patrol legends tell of ships falling and wiping out fair-sized nations.

An amber warning flickers. *15 . . . 14 . . . 13 . . .* Vaun is not going to back off unless he has to. Are the others sweating like him? He glances around, but the only spacer looking his way is Yather. Snake eyes. Still. The light has turned red. Verbal warnings will be next. *10 . . . 9 . . .* But the Q ship is very close to orbital velocity now. Relax, kid, you'll make it.

Inhabitants unknown.

Presumably human.

That is one answer: beasties. The Patrol has a million legends of aliens, although none around Ult. Something unhuman invented the Q drive first; other species roam the spaceways. Elsewhere in the vast Bubble of the Galactic Empire, there must have been contact, but the tales that whisper in over the radio static are distorted and fragmentary. And the worlds of the Silence . . . Something took them out and cut them off from human ken. Any incoming Q ship is suspect, always.

The Brotherhood? That is another answer, and the most likely.

That is why Vaun is here, to look out for the Brotherhood. And Yather is here to look out for Vaun. And Roker, down below, is watching both of them on his board.

7 . . . 6 . . . 5 . . . The pilot boat is accelerating, being sucked into the invisible maw of the singularity.

The Brotherhood? Or just another nameless load of human wanderers, heading Outward, driven by ancestral urges to try the next valley?

The lumpy mass is growing larger, nearer, more menacing. As the counter reaches 3, the Q ship turns off its drive. Gravity flux drops to zero. Emergency over. Vaun doesn't need NavOff's gleeful exclamation—the vids show a perfect interception ahead. All luck, of course, but a nice feeling. With the fireballs off, all the instruments can register. Radio contact can be established. The visitors ought to be surprised to find the pilot boat already in position. They won't have time to sneak off any shuttles of their own, which is what Roker wants. Vaun doesn't think they'll be surprised.

Roker is waiting, down there at Hiport, with his finger on the toggle. Q ships are solid nickel-iron, and so close to indestructible that even hardbeams won't penetrate them far. So Roker's little missiles are armed with neuron warheads that will short out every organic synapse within ten kilos. The Q ship may use hardbeams.

Boats like this one are a lot more maneuverable, but also very destructible. Roker promised enough warning.

Who trusts Roker?

Radio contact—everyone winces as the cabin is suddenly strident with static and garbled voices. Vaun glances at a nonstandard vid, one that the others' boards lack. Or so he has been told, but Yather probably has one also. It still glows green . . . Innocent until proven guilty . . .

The voices congeal into one, barely discernible, speaking Galactic with an accent that Doggoth would send to clean latrines. Every planetary command has its own way of pronouncing the ancient tongue.

The lanky, tow-haired com officer starts chewing a knuckle, worry written all over his peach-smooth face as he listens. He glances up guiltily. "I'm having trouble getting this, sir. Machine translation'll be along in a moment."

The accent is no problem to Vaun. He interprets for ComOff, and also for Roker and the other unseen eavesdroppers—not that any of them are likely to trust his translation.

"They're claiming," he explains, "that they suffered dust damage from cosmic cirrus on three separate occasions, which wiped out their supply of high-gain antennas. They're also spinning some fine yarns about their cryogenics failing, which explains the lack of sim. And so on. It's starshit. Suggest some alternative mock-ups and linkages, and tell them that if we don't get proper responses, we'll report them as hostile.''

ComOff gulps and says, "Sir!"

Then a new voice crackles out loudly, making them all jump. A male voice. "Q ship *Unity*," he says. "From Avalon. Do you read us now?''

''Yes! We read you now, *Unity*.'' The boy on the com runs hands through his sandy hair and glances across at Vaun with a huge grin of relief. He has been sweating.

Again the Q ship speaks, "Then don't jack us around, mate! We've been twelve years on this jaunt, and we didn't expect to make it for the last eight. Half the rotting junk on this hulk's falling apart on us.''

*That voice!* Vaun knows that voice, and the hairs on his neck stir. Have any of the others noticed? If even he can recognize it, then the computers must have made a match . . . Yes, the secret vid has turned to yellow. That's a tight-beam code from Roker. Yellow means *Suspicious: further data required*.

Suspicious, hell! Maybe Roker needs more evidence to justify destroying both a Q ship and a boatload of his own spacers, but Vaun has all the evidence he wants. The Brotherhood is on that ship.

Visual! Ult must see that speaker's face. That will do it. Then the vid will turn purple, meaning *Get the hell out of the way! Fast.*

"Get a visual, ComOff!" Vaun snaps, but he knows that there isn't going to be a visual. The Brotherhood is not so stupid. The sandy-haired boy speaks into a mike, and jiggles the toggles with his fingers at the same time.

The Q ship voice becomes garbled again.

Vaun looks at Yather's sour stare and sees no help there. There'll certainly be no help from Roker, who daren't send up more than that tight-beam code. Avalonian technology is superior.

The comoff boy is at his wits' end, and Vaun can sense the others' growing unease. They're all waiting for instructions. He's going to have to make a command decision quickly, because without a course correction they will drift past contact.

If he makes the wrong decision, Yather will shoot to kill.

If he alerts the brethren, then Roker will.

If the brethren suspect what's happening, then they will.

Oh well, he's made no plans for the afternoon.

And suddenly there is a visual, a girl's face peering out of the snowstorm in the tanks. A *girl*?

"Hello *Liberty*!" she says. "Do you read me?"

She is speaking Andilian, one of the principal languages of Avalon. Almost no one on Ult can speak or understand Andilian.

Prior knew it, though. And Vaun does. The hairs on the back of his neck prickle again, and his scrotum clenches. Yather is showing his teeth, waiting for Vaun to utter just one single word of warning.

"Calling pilot boat," the girl says, her voice crackling with static. "Do you read me?"

"She's a sweetie, isn't she?" MedOff mutters.

Is she, though? The image . . . the voice? With reception so poor they could easily be fakes, sims made by computer. Again Vaun looks to Roker's signal, and it is still yellow—so Hiport isn't convinced by that female image either.

The Brotherhood . . . If the Brotherhood is running that ship . . . The Brotherhood wants to know if Prior is aboard.

Vaun glances at Yather and gets a grudging nod.

"I'll take it, ComOff," he says in his unfamiliar commander's tone. He thumbs a toggle. The girl shows no reaction, but the readings say that his image is going out. He turns his head momentarily, as if checking something on a side display; in reality he is letting them see his profile. The static and jabbering fall off sharply.

He looks squarely back at the com and speaks Galactic. Conscious of Yather's jumpy trigger finger, he pronounces it Doggoth-style and a lot slower than he needs to. "Hailing *Unity*. This is Ult Command shuttle *Liberty*, Commodore Prior, commanding. Identify yourself, speaker."

Silence . . .

Contact is coming up. Downstairs, Roker is also waiting, with a finger on a trigger. Silence . . . Are the brethren waiting for Vaun to give a password? Or have they already guessed that he is not Prior, as he claims? Are their fingers reaching for triggers also?

Waiting . . .

E VEN IN AN age when half the equipment on the planet seemed to be failing from lack of competent maintenance or lack of the correct resources or sheer antiquity . . . even then, the Patrol's K47 torch buggies were so universally reliable that they carried only the simplest of emergency gear. Whichever previous owner had hot-rodded Vaun's unit had stripped out most of that and left nothing but a simple buzz cushion and a primitive cartridge to blow it clear. Why bother? Nothing ever went wrong with a Starseat.

Unless some maniac gave the control board a bad case of meltdown, of course . . .

Vaun spat into the howling ice of the wind, and coughed again. He thought he had been unconscious, briefly, but he was flying the cushion, so he must be still alive. Fortunate that sky buzzing was one of his favorite pastimes at Valhal—his reflexes were in good shape. There was a salty taste of blood in his mouth, and a red filter blurring his right eye. He felt as if he'd fallen about ten stories onto a concrete sidewalk, facedown. Ejection at that altitude and velocity was classified by the manual as "last resort."

The world spun crazily far below him, and he fought back with muscles already numbed by cold. He dimly recalled seeing his torch dissolve in a flower of red fire that dropped smoky roots earthward. That might have been one of Tham's missiles, or merely the self-destruct.

His left eye wasn't much more use than the right, but through the tears he identified the familiar hills around Tham's compound, and the lake, far below him still. He twisted the cushion and angled his dive that way.

They hadn't shot him down, at least, and they could have beamed him easily already, so probably they weren't going to. *Krantz!* but it was cold. He was a human icicle. He hoped nothing would freeze and break off before he landed.

41

Dawn flamed glorious along the peaks to the east. Good to be alive.

COZILY NESTLED IN a wooded valley, Forhil's steeply pitched roofs and sheer timber walls suggested one of the Early Gilbian reconstructions favored by asteroid brokers and armament tycoons; but Forhil was genuinely old, parts of it dating from before the Stravakian Revolution. It sprawled haphazardly, confessing to centuries of indecision, yet that very vagueness—plus a mangy coat of velvety moss on all the buildings—gave it real character. It seemed almost part of the hills themselves, something that mankind could borrow and use, but had never created. In fact, in its youth there had been a substantial city here. The surrounding forest was pocked and knobbed with masonry and old cellars.

Forhil had belonged to the Patrol for several centuries, and was a traditional perquisite of the ComCom; which was likely why Tham had hung onto the post. Vaun ranked it third or fourth behind Valhal as a fitting home for a hero.

He was aware that he must be a sight as he limped across the lawn, heading for the front door. His eye had cleared, but there must be blood and bruises all over his face, and he was still coughing blood. He had ripped his shirt and some skin in a fornicating crimple bush as he landed, and twisted a knee. But at least he'd landed in one piece, and nothing seemed to have fallen off yet.

He reeked of crimple like an unwashed locker room. Why did women go for the scent? He would drive Maeve insane if she came near him now.

Stillness oppressed him as he hobbled up the wide steps to the terrace. The pool shone unrippled silver in the morning light, and the ornamental shrubs had a disconsolate droop to them, although that was likely only his imagination. Maintenance robots must still be tending the gardens, even if he could not see any. He had seen no signs of Security, either, which was hopeful. No sims, even. A dog barked monotonously from the paddocks around the back.

The absence of people was eerie. Always he had known Forhil teeming with people, boys and girls laughing and sporting on the wide lawns, in the pool, among the trees—the lucky ones of the world: politicians, aristocrats, industrailists, royalty, famous entertainers . . . and spacers, of course. Now the only guests were a couple of unwanted gate-crashers: Death and Admiral Vaun. Was Death inspecting the wine cellar? Trying a few idle strokes on the putting green? He wasn't visible at the moment, but Vaun sensed the implacable presence more strongly than he ever had in his life.

Tham had had everything to live for, and all the resources of human science to help him do so. But Death was the most persistent of old friends—one who had refused to stay behind on Earth, or let mankind travel the spaceways alone. He could be delayed, but never denied.

Forhil's main house faced squarely to the rising sun, and Vaun followed his shadow over archaic flagstones toward it, puzzled by the lack of challenge—no robots, no trained carnivores, no energy beams smoking through the shrubbery. Tham had been bluffing, maybe? And if the defense was so weak that it must use guile against a lone man, then the perfect ambush was right here, at the front door.

The entrance itself was set well back in a lofty breezeway, which had been built large enough to shelter a coach and four. Now the flat, yellow light of dawn poured in through the eastern arch, but the arch was narrower than the cobbled interior, and its sides were shadowed.

Vaun decided he didn't like being an ambushee, even when he had volunteered for the job. He faced straight ahead when he limped through, but the corner of his eye disliked something vague in the darkness to his left. He was allowed another four paces.

"Stop right there!" a girl's voice cried behind him.

He stopped. It was nice to be right as usual, even if he were *dead* right this time.

"Put your hands up. All the way."

He stretched his arms overhead, and turned slowly, squinting into the rising sun.

She really was holding a gun on him. She was wearing a long, dark gown, and he still couldn't see her clearly, except for a glint of light from the weapon. She could certainly see him.

"I'm Admiral Vaun. I'm a friend of Commodore Tham." The words sounded very stupid, somehow. "I am unarmed," he added, as that was probably what she was looking for.

"Turn around."

"I'd rather be shot on this side, please."

*"Turn around!"*

He obeyed reluctantly.

"Now drop your pants."

"What!"

"You heard! Do it or I *shoot*."

He did not like that sudden squeak of hysteria. Slowly he lowered his hands and unclipped his belt, wondering if this was some obscure execution ritual or merely a horrible joke. His shorts fell to his ankles.

"Lift your shirt."

This was bizarre!

"All right," the girl said, and her tone had changed. "You're really Vaun. I had to be sure."

"Zozo?" Vaun crouched to retrieve his pants, wondering why he had not recognized her voice. He also wondered how many people knew of the toothmarks on his buttocks. They were a hunting accident, tolerated and retained because they amused girls, and sometimes inspired them to be innovative. If the brethren were to send one of themselves to impersonate him, they would surely be efficient enough to research his scars first.

Respectable again, he turned to meet the shadow coming to meet his shadow, wondering if she'd let him kiss her. She never normally did, unless Tham was present.

His greeting died in a croak of horror. It was Zozo. It was not Zozo. Unsteady, sagged, and *too small*! She stooped as if gripped by an awful sickness. Something unthinkable had shriveled her face. Fried it. He mouthed her name and barely resisted the urge to step back.

A bitter smile twisted loose skin around her mouth as she registered his reaction. This cruel caricature of a beautiful girl . . . Someone had taken a wax doll and started to destroy it, and then stopped halfway. There were dozens of tiny, shallow grooves scored around her eyes. Her neck was crooked on her shoulders and the skin of her hands was blotchy. He had heard of this, but never seen it, not even in pictures. It was appalling. His gut knotted in revulsion.

"You don't need to kiss me today, Vaun."

That was a challenge, and Admiral Vaun never refused a challenge. He'd known many dares he'd approached with more enthusiasm, but he overcame his horror and tried to embrace her. She backed away. "Forget it!" she snapped. "The good times are over."

He found his voice. "Oh, Zozo! You, too?"

She nodded, and her neck *puckered* horribly. He wondered about arms in the long sleeves, about breasts and belly and thighs, what horrors might be hidden under the voluminous gown. That wondrous fair body . . . Yes, there had been some good times.

Very good times. He had spiked the punch himself more than once to get Zozo. The last time, at least, she had guessed who'd been responsible. She disliked him because of it, and put up with him for Tham's sake.

If Vaun had a gun as she did, and was dying as she was, he would certainly want to settle all his old scores before he went.

"Yes," she said bitterly. "Now you've seen, Vaun. It's true. Go away, Vaun."

There was a shine of white at the roots of her hair that he did not understand. It repelled him as much as the crêpe skin and spidery veins . . . But Admiral Vaun's poker face had lured many boys to bankruptcy, and he had never been more glad of it than he was now. "I have to speak with Tham."

She shook her head fiercely. "My God, boy! You don't have any human feelings at all, do you? No compassion. No understanding. You never did. If Tham had wanted to see you . . . if he'd wanted you to see him . . . Just be merciful—go away." Her eyes glistened. Zozo had always been very controlled, an intensely private person—except when nobbled with unexpected chemicals, of course—and it was a shock to see the fear in her, the wavering, and the doubts. The hopelessness. Tham's obscure religion wasn't much good when the big bills came in, obviously.

"Listen, Zozo. I'm not doing this out of some misguided sense of pity or sympathy. I'm here on business, serious bus—"

The gun jerked up again, and she backed away. "Swine!" she said. The muzzle quivered.

"You don't understand!" he shouted. His voice echoed coldly inside the great porch.

"Roker sent you!" Her knuckles on her gun hand whitened. He could see real hatred in her eyes. He would not have expected so much of it.

"No! No! Roker did this to you, Zozo!"

At least she did not fire. "What?" she said.

"Both of you?" he yelled, and continued to yell over the echoes. "Don't you see that it's too much of a coincidence for both of you to go at the same time? And so suddenly? Damnation, Zozo, you were both all right last week . . ."

She lowered the gun again. She shook her head sadly. "Roker didn't send you?"

"I swear he didn't," Vaun said—more quietly, now that he was no longer a target, forcing a calm suitable for a famous hero. "It was all my own idea. I'm pretty sure the bastard is up to something. Or someone is." He decided not to complicate things with talk of the Brotherhood. "Obviously someone has been tampering with your booster, Zozo, but if we get proper medical . . ."

She was shaking her head again.

And almost smiling, which looked awful. "Tham's known for two years, Vaun."

Two years? He stared dumbly at her smug contempt.

"Medical advised him it was having to raise the dosage."

"But he's not that old!" Vaun protested. Then he realized that he had absolutely no idea how old Tham was. Older than him, yes—and he would have to work it out to know how old that was—but a boy's age didn't matter. Or a girl's. It wasn't something anyone ever worried about. A girl didn't ask a boy how old he was before she bedded him. Lots had spread their knees for their great-grandfathers, and not always by mistake, either.

But apparently his statement had been true, for Zozo was nodding. "Some people just go sooner, Admiral. The body starts resisting the drugs. You know that! The Lord grants some of us one century; others He honors with two. Blessed is the Lord!" Her voice sounded sincere, but her sagging face was bitter. "Sooner or later the Lord sends for all of us, and for Tham it was sooner."

"Two years?" Vaun knew the chill that death gave off when it was very close. He knew he could face it without wetting his pants, but he didn't know if he could control his bladder that way for two years. Yet Tham had never as much as dropped a hint.

Of course, if Vaun did have a weakness, it was picking up hints.

Zozo was driving away the silence with nervous words. "When the dosage becomes too high, there's a sudden rejection. A catastrophic rejection. It happened a week ago."

"But you? That can't be coincidence."

She looked down so he could not see her eyes. "We've been together a long time. We're going to go together."

He wondered if Tham knew of her decision, and what their precious church said about suicide. He also felt unusually lost. Absurdly, he was mostly aware that his knee was throbbing painfully, and he was enormously weary and hungry, as well as disappointed that his long journey probably wasn't going to do him any good.

It was morning now and he hadn't had his booster.

"I understand," he said. "I admire you for that, Zozo."

Two outright lies back to back, but she gave him a hard stare, and then said, "Thank you, Vaun." She looked comforted, as if anyone would believe words spoken in such circumstances. "I probably didn't have a great deal of time left myself, as I seem to be going fairly quickly. You miss it horribly at first. Every hour it shows more. I feel so tired . . ."

He could never remember hearing her complain before, ever. He would have expected more heroics from Zozo. When she ran out of convenient, empty words, he said, "What sort of shape is he in?"

"Tham? Hellish!" A trace of the old strength emerged briefly from the ruins as she became protective. "You don't want to see, and he doesn't want you to see. Withdrawal is everyone's right, Vaun. A boy wants his friends to remember him the way he was. A girl certainly does, and you had no damn business bursting in here like this."

Business . . . he forced his mind back to business, and why he had come. If Tham had been failing for two years, then Vaun's suspicions were unfounded. The ComCom's withdrawal at this time was just a horrible, ironic coincidence. But the rest of the world had a right to life.

"I need to talk to Tham, Zozo. There's a Q ship on impact trajectory. It's not just him and you that are going to die. It's everyone. The whole planet."

He saw the suspicion leap up again in her eyes. She remembered her gun, and raised it slightly.

"Why did you think that Roker had sent me?" he demanded sharply. And why the insane missile defenses, if they were real and not just a bluff?

The folds of skin tightened around her eyes. "It's Tham. He's having . . . not delusions . . . but he has a crazy notion that Roker may come here to get him."

Get him? Why would anyone go after a dying boy? Then Vaun understood, even as Zozo put it into words.

"He says Roker's threatening to do a mind bleed on him."

E VEN AT DOGGOTH, Vaun has rarely ever seen a human medic before, but this one is undoubtedly human—unusually dark skin, but quite human. Her snowy-white coat bulges over hip and breast. The whites of her eyes are tinged with yellow, her head and hands coal black. So is her thick, woolly hair. Recalling anthropology classes, he decides she must be an almost-pure example of one of the rarer Elgith stocks. He supposes the other boys would find her attractive. Not a machine, for sure.

He has no clothes on, but he stands at attention because of those metal tags on her shiny white shoulders. She is taller than he is.

She is studying a handcom she holds, and ignoring his nudity. That sort of thing never worries him anyway. All he can think about is that he is leaving Doggoth. The austere little room is damned chilly for bare ass, though.

"Interesting," she says. Then she turns her black-on-yellow gaze on him. "You are a very remarkable specimen, Crewboy. Medically remarkable, I mean."

With that complexion she couldn't blush, and he wasn't going to. If that was what she meant, she was wasting her time. It wasn't too likely she meant it that way, anyway.

"Ma'am."

She shrugs. "You are scheduled to participate in a mind bleed. Do you understand what is involved?"

"Yes, ma'am." He means he has a rough idea, and he suspects it's nasty, but he will do anything to leave Doggoth. Anything.

"I am required to certify that you are acting from free choice, that you understand that this procedure is not within standing orders, and that you may refuse to proceed without any prejudice to your record."

When an admiral wants it? Ha!

"I understand, ma'am."

She looks him over doubtfully, and her fleshy lips move into a

48

hint of a smile. "I think you're lying your head off, Crewboy, but you're on record now."

"Ma'am," he says automatically, and wishes they would get on with whatever it is.

"It won't hurt, but it will be unpleasant. We shave your head, you understand? And we drill holes in your skull."

Vaun says, "Ma'am!" a little less certainly.

Now she is certainly amused. "Very small holes. Hair size. They'll heal in a couple of days, and no harm done. Seven or eight of them. There will be another boy involved, and what happens to him is a great deal more unpleasant, but you will not be damaged."

She pauses, so he repeats his mantra again, "Ma'am!"

She glances down at her handcom again, and rolls her eyes. "You are a cool one! All right, you can put your pants on."

She doesn't move, so he doesn't. She regards him again, hesitantly. "Crewboy . . . The worst part of this is what happens to the donor. You have to be close, so you'll have to watch. It's not nice at all. Just remember that nothing like that is happening to you."

This time he merely nods.

She shrugs and turns as if about to go, then stops. She thumbs something on her handcom.

"Crewboy . . . You know about booster, of course?"

This big black girl is starting to irk him, leaving him dangling in a cold room like this. He is under an admiral's orders now, well out of reach of any pry-finger medico's powers, so for the first time in his whole life he can afford to be a little bit uppity. " 'Booster is the common name for the dietary supplement necessary for human metabolism on an alien planet, containing essential amino acids, vitamins, and trace elements, plus various therapeutic or preventative medications including antihistamine antidegrad—' "

"Quite!" she snaps, shutting him off. The jet eyes flash. "You may need a few more shots, Crewboy, and I can really lean on a needle."

"Ma'am!" he says apprehensively.

She chuckles. "You are about to receive your commission, I believe?"

"Ma'am." And leave Doggoth!

"One of the privileges of being a spacer officer is that you get to adjust your own mix, you know. Except when on duty."

"Ma'am."

She nods thoughtfully, studying the information he cannot see, and he is suddenly curious. She holds all of him there, in that coal-black hand of hers. Everything human science can know about him is right there on her palm, and he wonders what it says that she finds so interesting.

"You likely won't ever need mood adjusters. Off the record, Crewboy . . . this is a very personal question, and you needn't answer if you don't want to. Have you ever had a woman?"

"Yes, ma'am." Now he thinks he is blushing. Krantz!

"But not often? Not often for a healthy boy of twenty-two? An unusually powerful, intelligent, and reasonably good-looking boy?"

"Maybe not, ma'am." *Did it once, ma'am. On a bet, ma'am. The others said I couldn't, ma'am. Showed them I could, ma'am. Fuck your own minding business, ma'am.*

She looks down at her com and says, "Boys, ever? Voluntarily, I mean—I know what happens to recruits in Doggoth."

"No, ma'am." That would be even more disgusting.

She nods to the machine, and he is surprised to realize that she is embarrassed, and doesn't want this conversation any more than he does.

"That's what the numbers say. That you're physically capable if it, but your id . . . your drive is almost non . . . is low. You know about 'stiffener'?"

"Yes, ma'am." After lights-out, the talk is almost all about what the recruits will do with stiffener when they get back to the real world. The girls' version is called "loosener." He's heard of little else for five years.

"I'm going to give you some advice, Crewboy," she tells her hands, "as I don't suppose anyone else ever will, and a machine medic won't volunteer information. Most spacers add about three units a day to their booster. The machines know what you want if you ask for stiffener. Four or even five units for parties—maybe. Despite any stories you may have heard, almost no one takes more than that. Six or seven make a boy a human goat—he'll go after everyone and everything, including the canary. Someone usually shoots him in self-defense. Understand?"

"Yes, ma'am." Vaun is certain he is blushing all the way down to his groin. Blushing, after five years in Doggoth!

"For you I would prescribe an initial dose of ten."

*"Ma'am?"*

"You can experiment, but my guess is that seven will put you at about civilian standard and you'll need ten or so to be a normal, obnoxiously raunchy spacer. Twelve for parties."

He nods, wondering why he feels insulted and angry.

She gives him a real smile, and very white teeth flash in her very black face. "It adds to life, Crewboy. Believe me, you'll like it."

She slides the handcom into her pocket and turns away. "Prior did it," she says over her shoulder as she goes to the door. "It was the only way he could pass. Put your pants on and come out here."

THERE WAS NO stiffener available in Forhil. There was no booster of any kind. The medical stood silent and dark, and nothing Vaun tried would activate it.

Well, he wouldn't be staying long, and one day without booster wouldn't hurt. His metabolism was vastly superior to most, and he wouldn't lose much of his edge in one day. It would soon return. A day without stiffener might even be advisable, as he hadn't replaced Lann yet, but he knew that girls would soon start eyeing him oddly and the boys would catch on a day or two later. A spacer not on the make was not normal.

There would be dreams, too.

He had showered and shaved, and donned fresh clothes delivered by Zozo herself. Then he had gone to the medical, intending to have a full checkup, because of the battering he had endured in ejecting from the torch. Staring in baffled anger at the mass of useless, shiny junk, he resigned himself to bearing his bruises until he got back to Valhal.

But of course the bruises were not his real concern. In truth, he had been rattled by seeing Zozo's disintegration. He found that insight distasteful. How did a boy feel when at last he heard the warning—that inevitable warning—about increasing his daily dose of preservative?

How old was Tham?

How old was he?

Ruefully he recalled Maeve's shrewish comment the previous night about his not being recognized at the party. What she had been hinting was that Admiral Vaun, famous hero, was ancient history now. Probably none of the boys and girls present around that firepool had even been born when he'd boarded *Unity* and faced down the Brotherhood. That was a medicine more bitter than booster.

It was not the sort of medicine a boy wanted, though.

Well, if he could do nothing about black eyes, he should be able to cure hunger. Turning to go in search of the kitchens, he discovered Zozo standing in the doorway with the damned gun still dangling in one limp hand. Spying? He hid his anger in a bland look of inquiry and asked politely, "Can I see him now?"

She peered at him with a vagueness that only came from neverminds, the unmistakable appearance of being somewhere else. So, now she had chosen to meet her voluntary disintegration in a drugged daze, but that was her business. Tham had no choice, if his body was rejecting the booster, but she had gone into withdrawal voluntarily. Vaun didn't think he could ever do that, not for anyone.

Eventually she nodded. "He says so."

"Lead the way, then."

Zozo thought about that, then nodded. She turned and shuffled out the door. Vaun followed. He caught up with her in a couple of long strides and made a fast snatch for her wrist, twisting the gun away from her.

She made no attempt to resist. "Why didn't you just ask?" she asked bitterly, rubbing her fingers.

"Why didn't you just offer?" he snapped back. Surprisingly, the weapon was a spacer's bullet-throwing pistol. Unless Zozo had skills he was unaware of, she would not have been able to hit the planet from the ground floor with a thing like that, but he felt much happier with it safely tucked in his belt.

Long ago, he had shot Abbot with one of those . . .

Hunched and awkward, she led the way back along the corridor, and out into the lofty central hall. Again Vaun sensed the paltry neglect that he had felt in the gardens. Pale dust dulled tables and banisters, and the beams of sunlight from the high windows were alive with sparkling motes. Forhil was already in mourning for the boy who had owned it for . . . how many years?

He had hoped Zozo would lead him to the dining room, or at least the kitchens, but she headed for the library, and he realized that he was dreading the coming encounter.

He knew the comcom as an attractive, trim boy with oversize freckles decorating a snub nose, and curly brown hair above a notable widow's peak, a boy who smiled a lot and said very little. Either Tham preferred to run his mix very fast, or he was just naturally full of energy. He rarely sat down for two minutes at a time. He was a daunting companion in any sort of physical activity. At gill fishing he could swim even Vaun to a standstill, and then innocently suggest a half-hour run back up to the house just for the sheer enjoyment of it.

And now . . .

Now Tham was a shabby dressing gown full of bones, stretched out in a huge, heavily upholstered, brown chair. His eyes were closed; his breathing rattled. If that was what age looked like, then he must be as old as the galaxy. Most of his hair had fallen out, leaving only a taut stretch of skin to hide his skull, and yet his face hung in loose sags, frosty with stubble. His bare shanks were blotched and thin as sticks.

Vaun had never dreamed it would be this bad. No wonder people withdrew from the world when it started! He had known domestic animals grow old, of course. Favored pets were given their own booster, but when their bodies likewise rejected the preservatives, then pouncers and horses could be mercifully shot.

"He was awake a minute ago," Zozo said fretfully. "I told him you'd come."

The room was silent except for an ironic, cheerful crackling from the big stone fireplace. A dog howled somewhere in the distance.

Vaun stared miserably at the pathetic relic in the big chair. "Roker truly threatened him with a mind bleed?" he asked softly.

"So he says. They had a screaming row."

"About what?"

"About Roker forcing a com call through to a boy who'd gone into withdrawal."

So how would Vaun's behavior rank? "What has he been holding back, Zozo? What secrets has he kept from Planetary Command?"

She blinked vaguely. "None." They were both whispering. "Or so he says. He swears that every signal ever received has been fed to Archives as required. But Roker's a crafty devil. He trusts no one."

Roker was having delusions if he thought he could run a mind bleed on Tham now. Even the preliminary trephination would kill him. But the talk of mind bleeding might be Tham's own delusion, if his brain was rotting as fast as his body.

Oh Tham, Tham! Few indeed were the admirals or commodores who would accept invitations to Valhal, or invite the upstart Vaun to visit their own abodes. Many would turn off their party beacons if they detected the signature beam from his torch. Stuck-up aris-

tocratic prigs, all of them, while Tham, whose family was older
than any . . .

Suddenly the folds of skin twitched like blinds, and Tham's eyes
were open, staring up at Vaun. They were bleary and yellow, but
they were most horribly and certainly Tham's eyes, peering out of
that decaying monstrosity of a body in which he was imprisoned.

Nothing else moved and the strenuous breathing rattled on at the
same pace. The dog howled.

Vaun stepped close and knelt painfully to clutch the thin, cold
bones of the comcom's fingers. "Tham, I'm sorry!" The invalid
had a sour smell.

Sunken flesh around Tham's mouth began to move, and what
happened was apparently intended to be a smile—not a very happy
one, though. "Who did your face?"

"I bailed out a little early."

"You always did think that fences were for climbing, didn't you,
Vaun?" Even if Tham was as angry as Zozo, his gibes would be
more subtle than her shrewish reproaches. Tham was never dis-
courteous, even when his meaning was deadly.

"I should not have come if I . . . Damn!" Vaun wasn't about to
start telling lies to an old friend, and there was no use apologizing
now. "Listen, Tham, I came because of a misunderstanding. I just
need to ask you a couple of questions, then I'll go and leave you in
peace. This wasn't Roker's idea. Just me. A favor for an old friend?"

"How may I be of assistance, Admiral?" The voice was a scratch
of fingernail on old, dry bone.

"You know there's a Q ship coming . . ."

"Three, the last I heard."

"The one from Scyth, I mean. It was due in about this time next
year. Out of sheer curiosity, I checked on it—and I discovered that
it isn't braking. I thought we'd lots of time to . . . time before it
arrived. But it should have started braking by now." No need to
tell Tham that Scyth was seven elwies away, or that such a journey
needed a rock, which could not decelerate like a metal-skin boat.
"It's on impact course, and in about a hundred days we'll need an
*Eject* button on the planet. Suddenly it feels urgent . . . Tham."

What wasn't urgent to someone who looked like Tham looked?
Or what was? Did anything matter at all? Tham's *Eject* button had
already been pushed.

"And what can I do?" His mind seemed to be unaffected. The
boy Vaun had known so long was still in there, in that suddenly
ancient body. It was going to take him with it.

Vaun had never considered himself as being afraid of death, no more than any other living being, but he knew that some deaths were better than others. "I want to know if it's the Brotherhood, Tham. That's all that concerns me. If it's beasties or a runaway derelict or anything else at all, then Roker and his boys can do the worrying. But if it's the Brotherhood again, then . . ."

Vaun let the sentence fade out, wondering what the ending really was . . . *Then I feel responsible?*

Tham grimaced and squirmed, as if at a sudden cramp. "How the hell should I know? You think I can pick up signals from a Q ship?"

"Of course not. But when Scyth went silent, you told me you thought it was the Brotherhood's doing."

"Maybe I did. Thought so once. Still do, I suppose." Tham rubbed his eyes wearily. "Didn't you tell us that Abbot told you that the Brotherhood came from Scyth originally?"

What was going on here? Was Tham deliberately playing dumb, or was this just part of his illness?

"No," Vaun said. "Abbot claimed that the Brotherhood did not originate on Avalon. And you know damn well that Abbot could have been lying. Scyth went silent—what? Thirty years ago?"

"Thirty-three, our time."

"And twenty years *after* that—"

"Nineteen."

"Nineteen years after that, a Q ship leaves the planet, heading for Ult." Why hadn't everyone panicked then? But Vaun had had no need to storm the fortress of Forhil and consult Commodore Tham to find the answer to that question. Because the ship wouldn't arrive for years, so who cared? There had been lots of time, and everything else had been more urgent. Now the time was up.

Tham coughed painfully. "Vaun, you're as bad as Roker. In fact you're worse. You both think I have some enormous store of secrets about the Brotherhood, and The Meaning of Life, and How to Feed a Family of Four on One Gushima Egg. He seems to think I've been confiding in you, for Krantz's sake! Remember the Ootharsis of Isquat?"

"Vaguely," Vaun said, wondering if Tham was hallucinating. "Gibberish."

"Yes, gibb—" Tham coughed, and twisted in his chair, and coughed again. Zozo came over to him, and perched on the arm beside him. She laid a hand on his shoulder.

When he spoke again, his voice was an insectile rustle in the big, still room. "That is the secret, Vaun. The whole secret. That it's all like that. Scraps and fragments. Languages we don't understand. News that means nothing, and is hundreds of years old any-way. Static from the Q ships blanks most of it, and the rest is gibberish. Every world is an island, Vaun. We're on our own.''

Vaun remembered the loudmouth lieutenant at Maeve's party the previous night. The boy had been right, in a way—why did every-one not worry more about this? Scyth was one of the closest worlds, yet it had gone silent and no one had done anything. They had all gone on with their own little lives and trusted the Patrol to do any worrying required. And beyond Scyth, all the way back to the origin, thousands upon thousands of worlds had inexplicably gone silent in the last thirty millennia.

"But Avalonian Command say they've won, don't they? The war there is over, the Brotherhood defeated?''

Tham grunted, and rubbed his eyes.

"Don't they, Tham? Isn't that right? They finally answered, and said they'd won?''

"That's what the com said.'' Tham coughed. "It was garbled, though, and friggin' short. Maybe the Brotherhood won, and faked the message, mm?''

There was the problem—four elwies was too far to go to find witnesses. "Tham—tell me about the Silence? What took out the old worlds? Beasties? Destruction? Is it suicide, or murder?''

Tham shook his head as though unwilling to waste his fading time on trivia. "You know all the theories as well as I do.''

"Do I? I'm asking for the Patrol's real thinking here, Tham, not what the civilians hear, or the stuff that gets taught at Doggoth. What do Roker and his cronies believe?''

"Don't know that they ever worry about it.'' Tham closed his eyes wearily. "Same as everyone else, I suppose. Worlds just wear out, maybe. Like me. Or they invent something better than radio. And just talk to each other, not us. Or they stop caring. Like me. Why is everyone so anxious for my famous last words?''

"What happened to Scyth?'' Vaun demanded.

"Plague?'' the invalid mumbled. "They had a plague on Scyth.''

"That was a hundred years ago!''

"Close-run thing, though. Maybe it came back and next time took everybody?''

"No plague ever takes everybody!''

Tham wheezed for a moment. "Families?''

"Families? I never heard that one. What families?''

"Designer genotypes like the Brotherhood. It can't be the only one. There must be others, many others, in a million worlds. They wouldn't be any friendlier to each other than they are to . . . to us.

I don't know, Vaun. I never have. What is this strange superstition about wisdom on deathbeds?'' The familiar eyes glared resentfully in their unfamiliar, macabre surroundings.

"A chance to look back and review a life's work, I suppose."

"And Roker told me I had to file a report before I could go off duty." Tham bared his teeth, and again seemed to spasm with cramp. "Well, I told you, didn't I?"

"Er . . ." Vaun thought quickly over what had been said. He sat back on his heels to ease the pressure on his sore knee. "You did?"

Again the dying boy was racked by a spasm of coughing, and this time it was worse. "Yes, I did," he said at last, hoarsely. "So now it's my turn. Why don't you like singing?"

"Huh? I do like singing. I join in any—"

Tham was shaking his skull-like head. "I mean listening to singing."

"Opera? Folk songs? I—"

"Don't play dumb, Vaun. I haven't time for games. As long as there's a band, or any instrument . . . that's fine. But unaccompanied voices . . . They drive you nuts. You get almost hysterical. Why, Vaun? Tell me now."

Vaun shivered as some unwelcome memory tried to surface and he pushed it back down in its psychic swamp. "I've no idea. Is that true? Ask DataCen, it has all my synapses cataloged. No idea, Tham." He shivered again.

"I noticed that," Zozo remarked vaguely, not looking at either of them.

Tham sighed. "Then try this one. Vaun, *what did happen when you boarded the Q ship*?"

Vaun flinched. "Oh, Krantz, Tham! Not after all this time? Not you, too!"

The dying boy said nothing, just gazed painfully at his visitor. The dog howled, far away.

Even Tham? Had no one ever trusted Vaun?

"Go read the history books!"

Still Tham just waited, staring accusingly with his dying eyes. Zozo smiled mindlessly at a lithoprint on the far wall. Security would be monitoring the conversation. Roker himself could access those records—if not now, then very soon, when Tham's heart stopped. Oh, Tham!

"I pretended to be Prior!" Vaun snapped. "I fooled them. They gave me the run of the ship. I managed to trigger the self-destruct and I got the hell out, in the shuttle! That's the official story, it's my story, and it's the true story!" He looked for reaction, and saw none. "For Krantz's sake, Tham! *Unity* blew herself all over the sky. The whole of Shilam saw the flash. All over Ult, rocks were falling for weeks. You *know* that! What else *could* have happened?"

Tham sighed again, a long sad exhalation as if something vital were seeping away. He closed his eyes for an agonizing moment.

"You still owe me one, then," he whispered. *"Hercule!"*

The standard Security sim at Forhil was a testimony to Tham's former sense of humor. It imaged in now beside his chair, a hairy, beetle-browed boy, bulging with tattooed muscles and festooned with weapons. It glowered suspiciously at Vaun, then at Zozo on the arm of the chair, and finally down at its owner, all with the same belligerent expression. Vaun rose to his feet and backed away a couple of steps. He wasn't afraid of a mirage, although this one was admittedly oppressive and intended to be so. It was Tham he was wary of now.

"Transmit the Memorabilia file to Admiral Vaun at Valhal," Tham said hoarsely.

"Deciphered, Commodore?"

"No. Ciphered."

"Done, sir."

"Power down all circuits still active."

The sim's scowl grew even more menacing. "I need confirmation of that, Commodore. Code seven-four-three?"

"Eight-three-two."

The sim vanished instantly and the illusory flames dancing in the grate faded out into cold emptiness. Vaun had a strange sense of the building itself growing still, although he had not been aware of any other background noise. A house was a machine, and tended to have its own imperceptible hum of life. This one had just died.

The dog's howl sounded louder, and nearer.

"Good-bye, Admiral!" The dying boy glared up from his chair with a beady scowl only marginally less menacing than the sim's. "And thank you."

Vaun's mouth felt unusually dry. "Now wait a minute, Tham . . ."

As if it were a painful effort, Tham raised an arm to embrace Zozo, and she slid down in the chair beside him; there was plenty room for two such withered relics. But his eyes stayed fixed on Vaun. Obviously speaking was becoming an effort for him. "I was thinking of something Prior once said. Did you know that Roker threatened to have you tortured to death?"

"It doesn't surprise me," Vaun said sourly. "When was that?"

"Early in Prior's interrogation. You were still scrubbing floors in Doggoth. You know all the experimenting we did on Raj . . . Or perhaps you don't? We discovered that truth drugs didn't work at all. Truncheons and electric shocks weren't much better. We had three of the cuckoos by then, and Roker threatened to string you all up by your thumbs and skin you in front of Prior's eyes."

Vaun wondered if that had been entirely a bluff. "What did Prior say?"

"He said, 'The brethren cannot be distracted from their duty by foolish sentimentality, as you randoms can.' "

"The brethren are also very slow to anger," Vaun said, but he was thinking, *Truncheons and electric shock*?

"Then do it in cold blood. You owe me one. Maybe more than one?" Tham's eyes shone with bitterness, or challenge.

Startled, Vaun looked to Zozo—surely she would never have repeated her suspicions to Tham? But Zozo was spaced up on nev-erminds, cuddling Tham vaguely with her head on his shoulder, and not listening.

"Good-bye, Admiral," Tham repeated firmly.

Well, Vaun had come seeking trouble, and the request was reasonable under the circumstances. He eyed the distance to the window, and concluded that Security could block that before he could reach it; if Security was operational. He held Tham's steady glare for a moment, and could think of absolutely no reason why the commodore should have faked those instructions to the sim. Tham had never been petty.

"All right," he said. "Good-bye, Zozo. Good-bye, Tham."

Zozo grinned childishly, not comprehending.

Tham pursed his lips, and she turned her head to kiss him. Vaun blew out their brains while they were distracted, two shots so close that a single roar echoed through the empty house. No shutters crashed down over doors and windows, so Security truly had been powered down. It wouldn't really have mattered, he thought as he laid the gun on the nearest table. He would just have had to spend an unpleasant hour locked in with two smelly corpses. No court of law would ever convict the famous Admiral Vaun of wrongdoing when he had merely been helping out an old comrade; but he probably should report the matter right away.

The dog had fallen silent. Perhaps there was no dog.

At the door, Vaun turned to glance briefly back at the bodies, a single bloody tangle in the big chair. He would miss Tham. On the other hand, he had never understood Zozo, and her miserly reluctance to share that superb body with her friends.

But he would miss Tham.

Yet . . . *truncheons and electric shocks*?

"I did it for Raj!" Vaun proclaimed wryly, and went off in search of a com unit.

I N DISABLING SECURITY, Tham had also disabled every useful device in the house, down to and including the antique brass barometer in the vestibule. Eventually, in a tiny office he had never seen before, Vaun found an emergency com with its own power supply. As he put through a call to Valhal, he realized that he was sitting at a magnificent antique goldwood desk, almost certainly a genuine Fairinjian. For years he had wanted one of those to add to his collection, and here Tham had had one all the time, tucked away and probably forgotten in this neglected nook.

The sim that appeared in the tank represented an ugly runt of a boy with sandy hair and elongated, herbivore features. Its shirt was permanently misbuttoned and hanging half-in, half-out of its shorts; its arms and legs were thin as sticks, and it spoke with the sort of exaggerated Kilabran accent that sounded as if it came from under water. Vaun sometimes referred to it as Jeevs, and it was the standard projection used at Valhal; spacers meeting the horrible sight for the first time tended to look extremely puzzled for a moment, and then turn either very pale or very red.

His household equipment used a different image when it communicated with him alone, but on an outside call like this it could not inspect his environs for listeners. It could not even guarantee the channels, for while nosy persons or civilian authorities would never tap into the Patrol circuits that Vaun used, the Patrol itself certainly could. Thus the gawking, moronic lummox was a useful reminder that anything he said might be overheard.

"What messages?" he demanded. "Start with the Patrol."

"Two, Admiral. The first concerns protocol for your address to the Freedom Union. The second lists your schedule for the next twenty weeks." The sim leered toothily.

Vaun groaned. "Tell me."

"Eighteen functions in all. Four major speeches, two factory openings, three—"

"Cut. Nothing personal?"

The sim twisted its upper lip in an ugly mannerism and rolled its eyes. "From the Patrol? Noooo, sir."

So Roker was still not returning Vaun's calls.

"We have also received a ciphered communication, sir."

"Decipher it," Vaun said cautiously.

"Can't, sir." The sim scratched its tangled hair with enthusiasm. "It's in Idioplex, and can't be read without the key."

That confirmed what Vaun had expected. He hesitated, then decided to assume that he was under surveillance. Perhaps that was paranoia; probably he wasn't sufficiently important to merit observation, yet Tham had gone to some trouble to conceal the information in that file.

He frowned, as if at a loss. "From whom?"

"No source given, sir, but that is a Patrol cipher."

"Call on DataCen, then."

The sim shook its head, slobbering slightly. "Even Data Central cannot crack Idioplex without the key, sir. The seed key is expanded by cognitive association to a complex textual matrix of considerable size—do you wish an outline of the theory?"

"No. It's probably a practical joke, but keep trying." As soon as Tham's death was recorded, all his files and codes would revert to Ultian Command, so Roker would be able to read the file then, if he knew it existed and was important. "What else?"

The Jeevs image curled its long upper lip. "I withdrew your invitation to the President of the Kinarkian People's Paradise, as a sudden upsurge in the current unrest—"

"I did not authorize you to do that!" Charky was a bloodthirsty despot, but he was politically important and very good company in private.

"Sir, the late incumbent is presently dangling from a gargoyle of the palace. His most likely successor—"

"Ah, well, that's different. What else?"

With Vaun only just returned from his Stravakian tour, Valhal was empty of houseguests at the moment, but the sim rattled off a long list of visitors due to arrive within the next few days, and then began listing others who had called to request invitations—politicians, aristocrats, celebrities of one kind or another . . . A few captains, a couple of commodores, but no admirals. No spacers of any importance, in other words. As usual.

Lavish entertainment was part of Vaun's duty to the Patrol; he

liked to keep the company as large as possible, so his absence
would not be noticed if he decided to ignore them all and disappear.
But now he had a problem, and the sneer on the sim's face showed
that the computer was aware of it: Lann had left. Valhal had no
hostess at the moment, and the invasion would begin in a couple
of days. Valhal needed a mistress again, and so did he.

The personal need was more urgent, and more easily satisfied.
He ran through some possibilities in his mind.

"I want to call . . . Anything else?"

"The Air Traffic Control Board of the Western Common-
wea—"

"Oh! Right. I wiped my torch. No damage on the ground, I
hope?"

"No, sir."

"Good. Requisition the best replacement K47 you can find, and
refer the Board to DataCen." The Patrol system could be relied
upon to entangle the civilians in a bottomless morass of red tape.

"And some other callers, sir."

"Show me."

The reply was a lightning-fast flicker of images, as the computer
utilized the human brain's ability to identify faces more efficiently
than it could do anything else. In a couple of seconds, Vaun was
informed of about two dozen people who had called in his absence.
One face jumped right out at him—the diminutive redhead he had
been stalking the previous night. Red hair and pale arms in firelight . . . A ripple of excitement raised his heartbeat and took up
residence as a steady thrill in his groin. That little cutie had been
weak-kneed with hero worship before he'd even smiled at her.

"Citizen Feirn! Return her call. Top priority."

A call with Patrol priority on it would stop an earthquake. In a
few seconds the sim faded from the tank, and the girl appeared in
its place. She was using a civilian com, so that only her head and
shoulders showed, but there she was, looking as he had guessed
she would look in daylight, skin milky pale, her hair shiny curls of
pure copper. Her eyes were bluer than the sky, and she had faint
freckles like the stars of the galaxy.

Small but perfect.

Freckles could be natural or induced. Feirn's might be both, for
she had more than he had ever seen, a faint tan dusting all over her
face. They were just as numerous on her bare shoulders, and down
to the top of her halter. Now there was a challenge to the imagination! He adored freckles, and Feirn obviously did so also, or she
would have had them removed. She wore no trace of makeup, not

even to darken lashes so pale that they made her eyes seem curiously unfocused. Oh, scrumptious!

With an odd, very appealing nervousness she started to smile, and then gasped. "Admiral! You're hurt!"

He had forgotten his bruises, but he could guess that he had two beautifully swollen eyes by now. "Nothing serious, just another alien invasion. I do it to keep in practice. Seeing you makes it all better."

"Oh!" She hesitated, as if uncertain whether she was supposed to laugh, then settled on a childish snigger. "Defeated single-handed, of course?"

"Of course!" He thought her hero worship was less evident than it had been—but she had sought him out. "I'm very glad you called. If you hadn't, then I would have called you."

"I called on business." She smiled hopefully, just as he registered that her surroundings were quite obviously a commercial office.

His fever dropped a couple of degrees. "What sort of business?"

"You mentioned that Q ship . . ."

"Yes?"

"I'm . . . Well, I do interviews. 'Show-It-All,' on Commonwealth Central, and I was hoping . . . but your face . . ."

Interview? His duties for the Patrol sent him more than enough of that sort of public relations sewage—he had no desire to take on any more, even for this little flame goddess. He wanted her for fun, not business.

Yet, wait a minute! Maybe a pubcom interview was not such a bad idea. If the planet was going to be blown to gravel, then the people had a right to know, and Roker should not be allowed to bury his errors and incompetence under a heap of silence. Yes, Vaun must certainly arrange an interview—but he would offer it to one of the big name shows, any of whom would jump at it: "Truth-speak," or "Revelations." Not this pretty little unknown.

His hesitation had her staring at him in frank dismay. "I mean, I was so *awe-inspired* to meet you last night! I've always dreamed of meeting you, and I felt so honored and I just *wished* I'd got a chance to speak to you alone, and then I thought of the interview, and you can see what a wonderful opportunity this would be for you to make your views known—in such a very important, such a *catastrophically* important matter—and it would certainly be a boost to my career, because I admit I'm new to this, and if you'll only just say yes, then I'll be more than happy, I mean *overjoyed* to come to Valhal *any* time you want me to and it won't take very long.'' Last night she had been tongue-tied and shivery when he shook her hand. Apparently her tongue had broken free since then.

''. . . and of course those bruises on your face won't matter, because the gnomes downstairs can edit them out, and I won't be awkward, and I'll certainly ask any questions you want to be asked.'' She drew a quick breath, her blue eyes anxiously searching his face for signs of agreement. ''I'll be *so* grateful,'' she sighed.

Now that was more like it. Did he detect a trace of a blush?

''I'll have to think about the interview, Feirn. I'd be accusing the Patrol of gross incompetence, and that would be a pretty drastic step . . . Why don't you come and visit at Valhal for a day or two, so we can talk about it?''

''Can I? I mean, will you? Oh . . . Any time! I've heard so much about Valhal, and I've always dreamed of seeing it. Can I? Can I really come?''

Why did she doubt? ''And stay? Three days at the very least!''

''Oh, I'd love to!'' Yes, she was certainly blushing. Girls could be very complex and confusing creatures at times, but he had no doubts now that this one knew what was needed.

''I'll be home by noon, or a little after. You will come? As soon as possible?''

''Oh, yes, yes!''

''I shall count the minutes!'' He felt his bruises twinge as he smiled.

Citizen Feirn sighed soulfully. ''I feel terribly honored, Admiral.''

''No, I'm the honored one. Noon, then?''

She beamed and faded out, blue eyes full of stars.

He flexed his shoulders. He had the bed warmer he needed, obviously. The interview . . . Well, he would think about it. Maybe she could be granted a follow-up, after one of the big names had broken the story. It would still be a big score for a small-timer.

And yet, something felt wrong. He turned his attention to the sneering sim. ''Analysis of motives?''

''The girl's motives . . .'' The lummox scratched its head and twitched. ''Insufficient data for reliable analysis. Preliminary evaluation of facial expressions and other physical manifestations suggest—''

''Never mind the technicalities. Am I going to get laid?''

''Affirmative, at ninety-nine percentile.''

Vaun chuckled, wondering why he had ever doubted. ''For love or money?''

"Neither. Analysis at a relatively low confidence level indicates nonrational motivation."

He was startled. "You mean she's nuts?" If so, then he had a responsibility to turn the girl in for curing.

"Negative. Preliminary assessment . . ."

"No technicalities!"

"A tendency toward romantic delusions, is all, and a dominant self-image in the role of the Hero's Lady."

Ah! Vaun had been right in assessing her reactions as hero worship. Well, he would just have to perform like a hero!

"And your own motives," the sim continued, "were much as usual, in that you wished to be refused."

"*What!* Balls, I did! Why in hell would I want to be refused?"

"Sir," the sim said, with a complete absence of its usual sneer, "this conversation might best be completed in more confidential surroundings."

Vaun glared around the dusty little office and listened to the hush of the great house. It felt private enough, but of course the equipment was correct—the Patrol would almost certainly be monitoring the call. "Answer the question!" he barked.

"Sir, you followed your customary pattern, in that you also entertain habitual romantic ideals of a Hero's Lady. If a girl refuses your sexual advances, you classify her as a prude. If she submits, then you assume she is a whore."

Vaun bit back an angry retort that would have made no sense when addressed to a machine. Punching it on the nose wouldn't help, either. He reminded himself that the standard psychiatric programs were designed for the standard human mind; he was a long way from being a standard human, so the machine's confusion was understandable.

"You are computing from faulty premises," he snapped. "My duties require me to be assisted by a resident hostess with class and social know-how. My physical needs . . ." He fell silent. How could he possibly explain to a machine that some girls were more satisfying than others? "I was disconcerted to discover she was a wage earner . . ."

He didn't want to think that Citizen Feirn might be no more than a commoner lucky enough to have been picked up by that gawky spacer ensign and taken to a rich-folks party.

So she had dreams of being hostess at Valhal? She certainly looked the part. Perhaps she was not a bourgeois gold digger, but a bored little rich girl playing at holding down a job . . .

He wiped a strangely damp forehead.

A boy could hope, surely? A hostess and bed partner both, the ideal mate, able to flatter a duchess or tackle in mudball with the same finesse, pick out a fake in a set of Jing porcelain or spear a strealer with equally unerring eye, organize a fifty-plate banquet, or spend an evening before the fire reading poetry . . . inflame a boy right out of his skin all night long in bed and next day charm a bishop into blushes. And she would have to come equipped with red hair and freckles and generous breasts . . .

Maeve, of course.

Last night she had asked him, *What are you searching for?*

Old times, Maeve.

He wished he'd thought of that response at the time. Valhal parties had been more fun in the old days. When it had all been so new. When he had believed her lying protestations of love.

He discovered that he was scowling back at the contemptuous sneer of the Jeevs sim.

"Anything more, Admiral?"

"Cancel any visitors due within the next three days." There was something else, surely? Oh, yes. Tham.

"One other thing. Patch through a call now to whichever Patrol base is closest to Forhil and copy for my records. I have a report to file."

T HE PATROL WOULD certainly send in its own people before it informed the civil authorities. Oppressed by the dead, silent house, Vaun wandered out into the sunlight and stood on the terrace, drawing deep breaths of the dewy morning. Amazingly, the sun was still not very high above the hills. He had most of the day before him yet.

He was hungry, he remembered. He set off in the direction of the orchard, a little annoyed by his evident reluctance to return indoors, and amused by his reluctance to admit that first reluctance to himself. There was nothing in the galaxy more complex than a human brain, someone had told him once.

He was going to miss Tham, a twenty-four carat guy. He would not waste precious living time in mourning him, though. That would not bring him back. And certainly Vaun need feel no guilt over the manner of Tham's death, for what he had done was a kindness.

No guilt. The brethren regarded guilt as a sign of failure, and remorse as a weakness. They were ever practical, never maudlin. But their friendship knew no limits.

Forhil boasted a famous collection of fruit trees, and many were still laden. Apples he recognized, and ospers, but most of the others were a mystery to him—delicious products collected or invented on a dozen worlds as humankind progressed outward from ancestral Earth to Ult. Most of them would have long since traveled outward in symbiosis with their resourceful primate partners to the distant frontier worlds of the Bubble.

The Ootharsis of Isquat . . .

Years ago, when a thick-skinned, thin-witted girl at a party had been pestering Tham to tell her the latest news of other worlds, he had informed her that the Ootharsis of Isquat was dead. It was the most recent message to be intercepted, he had told her solemnly. No, he had no idea who or what the Ootharsis had been, or why his/her/its death should matter, especially as the message had been on its way at the speed of light for at least twenty-two hundred years, but he had it on excellent authority that the Ootharsis of Isquat had died.

For a long time after that, Tham had been asked at frequent intervals for the latest news of the Ootharsis of Isquat. The joke had also become his traditional response when pressed to talk business. And there was the problem—Tham had been naturally reticent, and had firmly believed that parties were for fun.

But he had obviously kept something out of Roker's reach in that secret file.

*Gibberish*, Tham had said. *News that means nothing.*

But not all news from other worlds was meaningless, and who better to wrest information from it than Admiral Vaun? He was the expert on the brethren. Moreover, he knew of nobody smarter than himself. He had spoken with boys who had crossed the voids between worlds—Prior, and Abbot. Willingly or unwillingly, they had given him knowledge of the Brotherhood.

He had gathered his first inklings from Dice and Raj, on a boat drifting along a sleepy river, when he had been sixteen, on a day that had felt like the first day of his life. Secondhand knowledge, certainly, but knowledge that had first opened his eyes to the Brotherhood, and the destiny for which he had been created . . .

The destiny he had rejected.
*Truncheons and electric shocks . . .*
Raj, who had rescued him from hell.
Oh, Raj!

R AJ . . .

"Multiply forty-three by seventeen and take away two hundred six," says the teacher.

"Five hundred twenty-five."

The teacher sighs. "You know all these problems by heart, Vaun. You know everything I have been given to teach."

"Then get more lessons!" Vaun begs. He feels desperate.

"I can't. I'm only a machine, you know." The sim depicts a tall, slim girl with dark brown hair. It stands with its hands behind it, and it glows faintly so that Vaun can see it in the dark. Otherwise, it looks very much like the government agents who come by sometimes—trim, clean, neat, well-fed people, nobly serving the despicable peasants.

The sim is worked by the big metal box in the corner. It breaks down often, and the village boys say that the wet air in the delta is bad for it. A real girl from the government came through yesterday and fixed it again, to Vaun's delight and everyone else's disgust. The pubcom never breaks down like that, and the pubcom doesn't just make sims of one teacher—it shows soldiers and spacers, acrobats and performing poisonfangs. Right now everyone else is gathered around the pubcom in the meeting place, watching the evening entertainment. Tonight's is a silly story about a female spacer who survives an endless series of very narrow escapes from monster aliens, usually losing parts of her clothing, but never any of her skin. Vaun's seen that one so often that he can tell where it's got to just from the sounds the audience is making. Every few minutes a monster rips her blouse, her breasts fall out, and the boys all cheer. Very dull and stupid.

No, the pubcom works much better than the teacher. Kids are

more use in the fields or the ponds than they are sitting idle in the schoolroom, no matter what the government says. The clay floor in that corner of the school shed is very battered, as if something heavy gets dropped there from time to time. This is the busiest time of the year, when the eels run, so the wet air will certainly get to the teacher again soon, probably right after the end of tonight's pubcom show. Vaun will be very surprised tomorrow if the sim is not so blurry and jumpy and squeaky again that no one can bear to watch it.

And if the parents come to meet the teacher tonight, Vaun doesn't want them to find him here, sneaking extra schooling. That would be more *strangeness*. More punch-ups, likely. So he keeps an ear open for the distant laughter. He very rarely bothers to watch pubcom shows, and when he does, he stays in the background, not mingling with the others on the driftwood benches. He would much rather be here, alone with the teacher in the dark. He knows he is strange to enjoy learning, but that is just one more tiny strangeness among many. He is a freak and a butt and a monster; he has black hair and black eyes, and he likes to learn. He is good at it, but maybe that is just because he wants to learn, and nobody else does, neither kids nor grown-ups.

He's not a kid anymore, so he never gets to come to the school shed during the day now. He has more beard than Olmin, or Astos, or others his age, and not a boy in the village would dream of giving him a fair fight, although he is not especially big. At sixteen he is still growing taller, wider, and hairier, but in a couple of years he'll stop changing and be one of the boys. Then he'll be expected to marry. He tries not to think about that.

"Teach me something else, then!" he begs the teacher.

The young girl purses its lips. "I've taught you everything I can, Vaun."

Summer has barely arrived and yet the evening is still chokingly muggy. Angel still hangs low in the western sky, so the night is not truly dark, but inside the schoolroom there is darkness, except for the faint glow of the sim. Bugs chirp and the wind brings the smell of the river and distant laughter from the pubcom in the middle of the village. Alone, Vaun sits cross-legged on the dirt floor of the school shack and tries to learn, because it is the only thing that makes him happy.

"There must be millions of things I still don't know!"

The sim flickers. "But not that you need to know," it says vaguely.

"Tell me about space."

"Again?" The sim sighs. "I have delivered that module . . . seventeen times in the last ten years, according to my records. Ten of those times you were alone, like this."

Vaun thumps a fist on the hard dirt floor. "Tell me again! Tell me!" Space, and spacers. The pubcom shows are often about spacers, but they're fake. He wants to *know*!

Sixteen—almost a grown-up. He dreams of leaving the village soon, but where can he go, what can he do? The teacher becomes very stern when Vaun asks about that, and says that the village is a good place to live, and the work the boys and girls do there is important, and he must stay and play his part in feeding the Commonwealth. If he runs away, he may be arrested and sent to a prison camp, which will not be a good place to live. Vaun doesn't believe everything the teacher tells him, but he believes that.

And there is Glora, his detestable, unbearable mother. Ever since the pepod killed Nivel, she has been getting worse. She says he must go away and save the world, but she had never been able to explain what she means by that, and he knows now what he didn't know when he was small—that she is mad. No one else believes her stories of meeting God, and Vaun being a virgin birth, not even the priests in the nearby towns. Especially the priests. If he does leave the village, who will feed her, dress her, bring her back when she wanders?

The teacher is explaining about the Bubble, spreading outward from the center, from ancestral Earth. Vaun could recite the words along with it, except that the teacher will stop then, and be angry. Five thousand elwies, twenty million stars, a million worlds.

Vaun raises his arm in the dark.

"You have a question, Vaun?"

"If people have gone out five thousand elwies in all directions, that means the Bubble is ten thousand elwies across, doesn't it?"

"Very good. Yes, it does, Vaun."

"But you told us that the galaxy is a sort of flat, round shape, and only two thousand elwies thick."

There is a pause. "That is a detail," the teacher says at last. "Please do not interrupt."

Which is what it always says. But the Bubble can't be a bubble shape; it must be a ring, like a wheel.

The teacher goes on with its lecture, word for word: the frontier worlds on the outside, the primitive worlds, and then the developed worlds, like Ult, inside. Vaun wonders what is inward of those, but that is another question that the teacher will not answer. *Over-*

developed worlds, perhaps? Or are worlds like people—first babies, then kids, then grown-up boys and girls, who don't change?

A board creaks.

There is someone outside the door, and Vaun is on his feet instantly, his belly spasming into a hard, sore knot of fear. He doesn't get set upon very often now by Olmin and the others of his own age, not since they all got interested in girls, but the younger kids have learned from them to gang up on the freak. There are so many of them!

The teacher stops and says, "Vaun? Is there something wrong?"

There is plenty wrong. The windows are set high, to stop kids staring out of them. Vaun knows he can scramble out because he has done it before, but if the little monsters are watching the rear again, then he'll come down in a snapper frenzy. The last time he almost lost an eye.

The door creaks and starts to open. Vaun runs silently over to the back of the room and reaches both hands up to the opening . . . and stops, seeing the rough driftwood wall visible in front of his nose. The faint light grows brighter, and yet he has no shadow. He turns—puzzled, excited. The glow seems to fill the room, more like a winter-morning fog than any lighting he has ever seen. There is an unfamiliar boy standing in the doorway, and the inexplicable brightness pours like smoke from something he holds in his hand; he lifts it higher, and light gushes out even brighter. It illuminates every knothole in the walls, starkly revealing the dirty, bare little shed.

He is not one of the village boys, especially with a tricky gadget like that. Instead of a grubby loincloth and sandals, he wears shorts and shoes and an open shirt. His face is beardless. So he must be a government boy, and Vaun's relief is enormous. Tense gut relaxes into shivery limp feelings.

The newcomer is returning Vaun's stare.

He has black hair.

He cracks a big smile.

"Hello," he says.

Black hair? Another freak?

He is very like Vaun. *Very* like, in fact—the same lean, hard build, the same height, more or less. The light isn't good enough to show his eyes, but . . .

"My name's Raj. What's yours?" His voice has an odd lilt to it.

"Vaun," Vaun says. His mouth is dry. His hands are shaking. He can see the newcomer very well now, and he can't believe what he is seeing. Before his mustache grew in, he saw that face every time he looked in the ponds.

Raj walks forward slowly, holding out a hand. "I thought I might find you in the school. Most likely place, in fact." He glances at the teacher, which is staring at him with a puzzled expression. "Authority override discontinue," Raj says sharply, and the sim vanishes.

Raj smirks at Vaun as if pleased with himself. He is not quite full grown—a little taller and heavier than Vaun, but not quite adult. His face and chest are hairless.

And he arrives in front of Vaun, still smiling, still offering a hand. As if to reassure Vaun, he raises his other arm straight up, and the light brightens even more. He is quite clearly visible now, and Vaun trembles at the sight of those twinkling black eyes. Does God have other sons? He is pressing his bare back against the knobby, prickly surface of the wall.

"Yes, Vaun, we are alike, aren't we? In fact, we're identical. Don't be alarmed. I'm your brother. I'm very happ—"

"I have no brother."

"Yes, you do. You were . . . sort of lost. But I've come to take you away from here. I've got a boat waiting."

"Away?" *Praise to the Bountiful Father!* Lost? As a tiny kid, Vaun always cherished dreams that perhaps he did not truly belong here in the delta; that he did not belong to Glora; that he had a real mother and father somewhere . . . Crazy, childish, wishful thinking! No, this can't be happening.

"Dice is looking after it. He's another brother. Come on—shake!"

Gingerly, Vaun clasps the proffered hand. It's real. Raj's palm is smooth, but he squeezes, and they both squeeze, hard.

And they both smile. "See? Evenly matched!" Raj says. He lowers the light gadget and hooks it on his belt, and the shack fades into dimness, but the shine of his eyes and teeth is enough to brighten it for Vaun like a summer noon.

"It's a shock, isn't it? I was lost, too. Tong found me a coupla' years ago—but at least I was raised in a half-decent little town. You don't want to *stay* in this mudhole, do you, Brother Vaun? Weaving eels, or whatever it is you do? Eating garbage? Doped stupid by the stuff they put in the booster? Frankly, Brother, you smell like the river. Come! The world is waiting! The galaxy is waiting!"

Vaun will not believe this. Others like him? He is as mad as his mother. He is seeing things. This can't be happening. If he takes one step, he'll be admitting that he thinks this is all real, and then the disappointment when it isn't will be even worse. His heart is pounding so hard he thinks he must be fevered, but it's the wrong time of year for fevers, and he doesn't catch fevers anyway. He pushes back against the wall, and Raj frowns, as if worried.

"Trust me, Brother!"

"Go where?"

"First to Cashalix. Big city! We're meeting Prior there in three weeks." Raj's voice throbs with excitement. "He sent us to look for you! Brother Tong'll be there too. They'll both be so glad to see you! Very glad! Like I am!" Raj laughs nervously. "Like Dice will be! We'll all be glad. You're one of us, Vaun!"

One thing at a time . . . "Brothers?" Lots of kids in the village have brothers but they don't look as much alike as Vaun and this Raj do. That's *himself* he's looking at. A little taller and wider and thicker, a little tougher around the face, in spite of the lack of beard.

"Brothers of a special sort. Vaun, oh, Vaun! It's all right!" Suddenly Raj hauls Vaun away from the wall, throws his arms around him, and hugs him; and that feels strangely right, except it reminds him of the time he tried hugging Wanabis to find out why the other boys hugged girls, and Wanabis burst into shrieks of laughter.

"What special sort?" Vaun demands, letting Raj squeeze him and very much afraid that he is about to start weeping. Scared of waking up, maybe.

"A very special sort. Brother Dice'll explain. Or Prior will. We're all brothers, Vaun, and you don't have to be alone ever again . . ." Raj's voice breaks off in a sniff.

He backs away, grinning and wiping tears from his cheeks. Vaun does the same, and they snigger ashamedly in unison.

"Vaun? Brother Vaun! Come on, Brother!"

"But the teacher says I must stay—"

"Fornicate the stupid machine!" Raj seems as overcome at meeting Vaun as Vaun feels at seeing him. "The government programs it to produce peons, that's all."

Whatever that means . . . "My . . . Glora? My mother?"

"She isn't your real mother! Just a foster mother. Never mind her, whoever she is. She's not important and *you are*!"

"I am?" Impossible. That's what Glora says.

"Yes! Very important! Just come! We've got food on the boat, and terrific beer, and Dice will explain everything. You'll love Dice. He's eighteen and Prior found him, coupla' years ago. You're sixteen?"

"Almost." Vaun wonders how this apparition knows that, and

is certain he is mad, meeting his own self like this—being hauled over to the door by his own self, a strong hand gripping his wrist.

Raj is both laughing and weeping with excitement. "You're the youngest. I'm seventeen. Gotta do something about that chin, Brother! We've got a shaver on the boat, and we'll get you done properly in Cashalix. Hairy faces are for savages. Vaun, Vaun! You belong with us! You're going to be with real friends, now. Real brothers."

"But I haven't got any brothers! Or sisters." Vaun stumbles as the light vanishes completely, and he is pulled out into the muggy night and the faint purplish glow of the setting Angel. Laughter rolls across from the pubcom beyond the first row of shacks.

"You have now! You can trust me! I'm closer'n any brother you can ever have!" Raj makes a happy, chortling noise in the darkness. He can hardly force out the words. "I know you inside and out, like you know yourself. And you know me. I'll help you, Vaun, any way I can. I'll share with you—anything I've got. I'll fight for you. If I have to, I'll die for you."

T HE BOAT IS long and narrow, with a high prow and a canopy amidships, just large enough for three boys to sleep sprawled out in comfort. In the heat of the following afternoon it smells faintly of varnish and old cooking. The design was invented centuries ago by water spider catchers over in the bayou country, Raj says airily, but this is a recreational replica for rich folk. With its diminutive motor humming softly, it lazes along, finding its own way through the mud flats without troubling its crew for guidance. The sun is a white glare in a muggy, white sky, and Angel a fierce blue smudge in the west.

Wide and mostly deserted, the distributary curves endlessly back and forth amid pozee grass. The three brothers wear broad-brimmed hats and scanty clothes of contrasting colors. As long as the boat shuns villages and gives a wide berth to other craft, no one is going to notice that its three occupants are virtually identical.

Raj sprawls on his belly in the shade under the canopy—mostly reading a book, idly joining in the talk when he wants to. Vaun sits aft, cross-legged on the deck in front of Dice, who is trimming his hair for him. Vaun's cheeks are shiny-shaven and feel odd.

Everything feels odd. Being clean. Reading books. *Friends!* Want to talk? Sure, what do you want to talk about? Why Q ships have fireballs at both ends? Why eels come upriver at this time of year? Why small Q ships accelerate faster than big Q ships but the big ones can go faster than little ones? And why do boys have nipples anyway? Anything at all.

All three of them are still hoarse from talking most of the night away, comparing their experiences, laughing, commiserating, joking; reaching almost to hysteria at times with the sheer joy of being united. Vaun has discovered within himself a great well of happiness that he has never known existed. He keeps wanting to weep, which is crazy.

Dice is a fraction larger than Raj, and Vaun is undeniably the baby of the three. He'll grow *this much* this year, and about *this much* next year, Dice says, and no, he'll not get much hairier at all. He mustn't judge what's normal by the mudslugs of the Putra Delta, who are unusually shaggy. Notoriously hairy people.

"We've got hair where everyone has hair," Dice explained at some point in the night. "And that's enough. Like other boys, we get our faces depilated once in a while. Our chests don't grow hair. What would you want chest hair for? That would just be—"

"—an unnecessary frill!" Raj completed the thought without a pause, and all three started howling with laughter yet again.

No hurry. They talk and doze and talk again under the hot sun. They will meet up with Prior in Cashalix in three weeks, and hopefully Tong also. Tong is another brother, presently hunting down yet another lost lamb over in the Stravakian Republic somewhere. Prior is the leader. Vaun notices that Prior is not referred to as "Brother" Prior. Just Prior.

Vaun's queries about Prior are politely and regretfully averted: Let Prior explain himself, Vaun.

It is all incredibly wonderful. They eat well and talk and right now they do nothing. Relax and be happy, Dice says dreamily; what else is life for? And Vaun thinks of the grinding toil in the village and says nothing.

Raj cooked the last meal, and Dice the one before, and Vaun is eager to be useful. "How about fish for supper? I can catch 'em. I know how to cook 'em."

"Mm," Dice says behind him. "I'm not too partial to fish."

"I like fish," Raj tells his book. " 'Slong as they're not eels."

"Hey!" Vaun protests. "I thought you said you were . . . we are . . . *Ouch!* . . . identical?"

"Sorry!" Dice says. "Well, you're certainly not identical now, Brother Vaun, missing half an ear like that."

"It's only a nick!" Vaun inspects the blood on his fingertips.

"Major artery," Dice mutters, angry with himself. "Terminal exsanguination. Hang on, I'll lick it."

"We're not perfectly identical, ever," Raj remarks sleepily. "You have a delta accent, and Tong's is Stravakian. Upbringing is important, too. I suppose Dice didn't get fed fish as a child. That must be why he now prefers to eat ears. Environment."

Dice finishes slobbering on Vaun's ear. "There, it's stopped bleeding. Almost. There's more, Raj. You want to tell him? See if you've got it right, now?"

Raj yawns and switches off his book. Then he scrambles upright to sit cross-legged in front of Vaun, like Vaun, right shin in front of left, forearms on knees, left thumb over right . . .

"You know about heredity? Genes? Cells? No? Mm. Thank you, Brother Dice! Well, every living thing is made of millions—billions—of cells. A baby starts from one single cell, and that becomes two, and then four . . . and then billions. And every single one of those cells has an instruction code inside it, like a how-to manual. Every organism is different, because it has its own unique how-to manual. It gets that from its parents, half from each, with the pages shuffled a bit. Then there's a brutal business called 'evolution' to remove the mistakes. Dice, do I have to go through all this?"

"Yup. Close your eyes, and I'll do your front."

Vaun closes his eyes and lets Dice twist his head around. Raj groans, but he probably likes to show off his knowledge. Vaun would, and already he knows that these uncanny replicas of himself enjoy the things he enjoys, like this teacher-talk. He can't imagine Olmin or Astos ever wanting to listen to talk like this; they only talk about girls. Dice and Raj haven't mentioned girls at all yet. Now Vaun has an odd feeling that he has been summed up, and is about to be trusted with something important. Dice suggested it and Raj agreed, all without words. They want to show him he is trusted, maybe?

They are more easily distinguished by their voices than by their looks. With his eyes closed, Vaun can tell Raj's husky youthfulness from Dice's deeper, more adult tones. But it doesn't really matter which one is speaking. They are interchangeable.

"The code is organized into forty-six strings called chromosomes," Raj says. "In people. Other animals may have more or less. In Earth species the codes are groups of four amino acids—"

"Bases," Dice growls.

"Sorry, bases, and I don't know what those are yet. I left that book back at the hive. Bases for Earth life, but other planets vary that a little . . . Life always uses much the same system, though. Two sexes for variety, plus trial-and-error sorting, to weed out the mistakes."

"You can open your eyes, now," Dice tells Vaun. "I think you should run through it simpler to start with, Raj."

"Who's doing this, you or me? Does it matter? Well, trial and error is wasteful. Forty-six aren't necessary. We have all our genes packed onto twelve chromosomes, and Prior told me that even that many aren't really needed. And we don't get ours by random shuffling. You see, some of the instructions . . . genes . . . are harmful. Humanity once thought it had left those behind on Earth, but they keep reappearing. Some are good. Some are good sometimes and harmful other times. Or harmful when there are two of them only. Or one of them only. They interact. It's complicated. It is very, very difficult to work out which are the best genes, the best mixture. But it's not impossible. Strength, and smarts, and courage . . . design the recipe for what you want to produce, see? Then you've got the Brotherhood. The best! The perfect human. No weak eyes or ungovernable tempers. And once you've got the design, then it's possible to make up the gene strings needed to produce that person—twelve are more than enough—and coat them with all the various sorts of goo that an egg . . . ovum . . . needs. Layer by layer. Then you put it in a machine that nurtures it, and it starts to grow."

He stops. Vaun stares down at his smooth, brown legs and unprecedentedly clean knees, at the fine, soft cloth of his unfamiliar shorts—all littered at the moment with black hair clippings—and no one speaks for a time, while ripples slap softly against the boat and a formation of torches drones across the sky, very high up. The air has a hot smell of river and boat varnish.

And finally Vaun says quietly, "You're saying that we came out of a machine?" His voice sounds strange to him.

Dice puts a hand on his shoulder from behind, and squeezes. "We know it's a shock, Brother. We've both been through this. Maybe it's worse for you. You see, in big cities .. rich folk often come out of a machine, too. The girls don't like the fuss of growing their babies inside themselves, so they have the ovum sucked out and let a machine do that bit. That's quite common, Vaun."

"What's not common is the making-the-egg in the first place,'' Raj explains, staring intently, almost fiercely, at Vaun from the same cross-legged position, like a wrong-way-round reflection. "In fact, anywhere on Ult that's illegal. It needs a big factory to make such a tiny product, lots of very special equipment, and the knowledge is suppressed."

"They do it with animals," Vaun says uncertainly.

"Animals is easy. There's nothing in the galaxy more complex than a human brain." Raj tries an encouraging smile, but it fades as Vaun stares back at him, not trusting himself not to say something wrong here.

Body, obviously. Mind, too? Look-alikes and think-alikes? His throat hurts.

"We weren't made on Ult," says Dice's voice.

Vaun continues to watch Raj. Wanting to trust, to believe, to be trusted, to accept . . . To be accepted.

"Avalon," Raj says, studying him carefully. "The ovums . . . ova . . . were put together on Avalon, and frozen. Prior brought them here on a Q ship, years ago. He had them machine-incubated, and then he put the babies out to good families to foster."

Virgin birth? Oh, Glora!

Oh, *Heavenly Father*!

"Something must have gone wrong in your case," Dice says. "From what you told us about your mother . . . foster mother . . . Vaun. I'm sure Prior would have picked a better foster mother than that. Something must have gone wrong. Kidnapping, or something."

"My family was all right," Raj says quickly. "Dumb and dull, but they took good care of me. I'm going to go back and visit them, often."

"Me, too," Dice says.

No use going back to the village and asking Glora where she found the baby. Get Glora on that topic and she makes no sense at all.

And Vaun doesn't think he can suggest anything like that just at the moment. There is one of him, and two of them, both bigger, and he's just been given some very dangerous information. He suspects that "illegal" means "major crime," if the whole planet has the same law.

It's a true story, though. Three boys as alike as three clams.

"Never quite identical," Raj says, perhaps guessing his thoughts—why not? Same brain. "First, there's lots of spare room on even twelve chromosomes, so they put a file number in there."

Of course machines have serial numbers. Even a dumb mudslug from the delta knows that. A baby-making machine that puts serial numbers on the product is very logical. Vaun wants to scream.

"And a little variation is a good thing," Dice says gently. "Sometimes you need a little extra strength at the cost of . . . well, a quick temper, maybe. Coordination rather than mathematical reasoning? I'm just guessing at the details, but that sort of thing."

"Not all environments are the same," Raj adds. "So you can modify the design for climate and stuff like that. And disease resistance—that's important. Add a small amount of trial and error to keep looking for improvements to the mix. But ninety-five percent is the same, always."

Dice squeezes Vaun's shoulder harder. "Remember that machines only do what they're told, Vaun. It's people who make people, even us. You follow?"

His lack of response is worrying them. "Roughly." He sounds hoarse. "It takes a bit of getting used to."

Back in the village he thought he was a freak because his hair and eyes and skin were too dark. Raj and Dice have told him that it's the mudslugs who are odd. His coloring is about the commonest there is. Far more people have black hair than any other color, so he isn't a freak at all.

Now they've told him how freakish a freak can be.

"The randoms are half-and-half. Half from father, half from mother. Two brothers share half their genes. But you and Dice and I, Vaun, are at least ninety-five percent the same. The other five percent is deliberately varied."

Vaun nods, still unable to accept that he is something that came out of a *machine*.

"Cheer up!" Dice says heartily. "Look on the bright side! You've got the finest brain in the world. Your muscles, gram for gram, are stronger than anyone's. Coordination, temperament, intelligence, adaptability . . . you are the best there is, Vaun! Not big, because size is no advantage in a technical culture. You can do anything better than any random can. The perfection of the human design. Prior . . ."

He stops, and must be looking to Raj for agreement, because Raj nods.

"Prior," Dice continues quietly in Vaun's ear, "arrived on a Q ship as a penniless immigrant twenty years ago, and now he's a commodore in the Space Patrol."

W HEN THE SPACER cops finally swooped down on Forhil, the first one out of the torch was a swarthy, husky boy,
who had the suicidal audacity to pull a gun on Admiral Vaun and
tell him to put his hands up. His sidekick went ashen-white and
made gurgling noises. Vaun dressed down the leader fluently until
he was the white one and his companion was smothering a smirk.
Then Vaun appropriated their torch, told them he would file a formal report in a day or two, and departed.

He gave the board Valhal's coordinates, telling it to use maximum speed and all of his priority. He settled back to endure the
cramped, smelly discomfort of a standard issue J9, but his mood
improved when he discovered the cops' packed lunches in the
locker. He munched greedily as the Forhil landscape dwindled
swiftly away below him.

He fantasized over his arrival at Valhal, with that freckled redhead waiting for him, all eager. That would be a worthy hero's
return, just the two of them to share the whole of Valhal. He would
show it to her in all its splendor. He would show her how heroes
lived. And loved. Which was a reminder that he had hardly slept
at all in the night, and had time to kill now. The seats were specifically designed to discourage somnolence, but he made himself as
comfortable as he could.

With the sky darkening to the black of near space, with Angel
waxing brilliant in the west, his mind returned sleepily to the problem of the Q ship. True, it was still a long way out, about a tenth
of an elwy. Also true, a Q ship's bearings were notoriously hard to
establish, but he had been using triangulation data from mining
bases and research probes, well spread around the system. If it
didn't start braking soon, it would not be able to do so without
being ripped apart by the tidal stress.

Unless it was a metal-skin, a boat. He wondered if even units of
the Brotherhood would face a twenty-year journey in a boat. He

decided that they might. The brethren were suicidally loyal to their kin, like hive insects.

But why come in on the ecliptic, aimed straight at Ult like that? It was a blatantly hostile move, guaranteed to rouse the Patrol's fury. If anyone on Ult should be able to think like the brethren, it was Admiral Vaun. Trouble was, he had been behaving like the wild stock for so long that he felt trapped now in their ways of thought.

But Roker ought to want him to try. The two of them detested each other, and normally they were careful never to meet, but now the fate of the planet was at stake. It was curious that Roker was still refusing Vaun's calls.

The com set *ping*ed. "Communication for Admiral Vaun," it announced in a satisfied tone.

Vaun had long ago accepted that the universe enjoyed playing with coincidences. "Who from?"

"Caller's identity is classified."

Vaun pondered that nonsense for a moment, but all it meant was that he must accept the call before Roker would admit it was from him. The big bastard probably had not even planned that, it was just a function of the security procedure, which would not switch to deep scramble until the channel was fully open. And it was very convenient at the moment, for Vaun had started to feel sleepy. He perversely decided that he was not in the mood to cross wits with the high admiral just now.

"Call refused," he said. "Accept no others. Disconnect."

Surprisingly, that worked. He squirmed himself around to try another position. No wonder the heavies were always so bad-tempered when they were given tubs like this thing to ride in! His left knee was in his armpit and his head kept sliding against the canopy field, which made his scalp tingle. His bruises hurt like hell and he hadn't had his booster.

There was a lot of unfamiliar geography visible out there now, and a fair amount of history also. The purple haze must be the Zarzar Mountains, whose warlike tribes had swept down over the Viridian Plain a dozen times throughout history, at first on riding beasts and later by kite and hang glider. Beyond the range would lie the Ashwor Desert—a symphony of reds and maroons the last time he'd seen it—where the Tolian Regicides had tried to build a nuclear capability a few centuries back and been blasted off the face of the planet by the Patrol, on the only occasion it had ventured a major interference in Ultian politics. Far away to the south, where blue moor and glinting lakes faded into the amber horizon smudge, would be Firstcome, site of the Holy Joshual Krantz's landing, ten thousand years ago.

Somewhere on the nearer green flatness, an invisible border divided the Western Commonwealth from Freeland. The former was a benevolent, ineffectual anarchy, and the latter a bloody military dictatorship. Some things never change. The Doggoth instructors had taught that every planet followed the same path: a simple rural settlement by a few dozens or hundreds, a period of rapid growth in wealth and population, leading to warfare and industrialization, and finally overcrowding and retrenchment, and a long decline. Then what? The Silence . . . but that was rarely mentioned.

Straight below Vaun now lay the mudlands of the delta, and the festering blotch of human pollution that was Cashalix.

Now there was a city he had never returned to.

Once was enough.

THE HOLIDAY IS over. The boat eases its way through a snarl of river traffic and floating garbage into the outskirts of fabled Cashalix, holy city of the Farjanis. Staying low, peeking out between the side and his hat brim, Vaun is conscious of a dry tingle in his throat and a madly pounding heart. He is amazed by the number of torches howling through the air, the way they seem to weave in and out of the towers in the distance. He is disgusted by the stench and alarmed at the way larger, faster-moving craft constantly threaten to swamp the boat with the sewage-laden soup of the river. He is so excited that he can hardly keep from giggling like a child. Monstrous trucks roar along the levees and pack the many bridges. Noise!

Three weeks ago he would have been ashamed of his excitement, but now he can sense that same thrill in Raj and even in Dice, who has visited big cities many times.

Not only are the three brethren virtually indistinguishable, but they are becoming more so. Vaun knows he is picking up Dice's way of speaking, although he is not conscious of trying to. It is fun to notice Raj doing the same. As the oldest, Dice tends to set the standard and sometimes he will quote Prior as an authority, but he will often conform to the others if he finds himself in a minority—he enjoys eating fish now. Better food and better booster are relieving Vaun of his extreme skinniness, and that means he must look even more like Raj than he did before. None of them has mentioned this convergence, but Vaun knows that if he has noticed, then the others must have done so also.

"There it is!" Raj is on the other side from Vaun, keeping down and peering out in the same uncomfortable crouch.

"Got it." Dice sits on the bench by the motor, at the stern, looking very calm and competent. He speaks a command to the controls.

Their destination is the marina where the boat was hired four weeks ago. Vaun glances at the sun, estimating time. At noon, Prior's torch will be sitting in the parking lot, waiting.

Soon Vaun will see himself or at least his double, in the uniform of a spacer commodore. That will be a memorable experience. Prior is much older, of course, but he looks exactly like Dice, Raj says. They both seem to worship Prior. He is the leader, the pioneer. Prior is not his real name, but a sort of title that he adopted as his name when he arrived on Ult.

"Even brethren have to have leaders," Dice has explained. "Sometimes a decision isn't obvious, and you can't have half jumping one way and half the other . . . So Prior says."

Only Prior really knows, of course. Only Prior knows how it feels to be not just one of a half dozen identical brethren, but one of hundreds. Vaun feels giddy when he tries to imagine it. Prior was born . . . conceived . . . on Avalon, and he embarked on the Q ship *Green Pastures* when he was about the age Vaun is now.

Soon, very soon, he will meet Prior. Then he will learn some more of his own future. Either Raj and Dice do not know what is planned, or they have been ordered not to say. Whatever it is, Vaun knows he will accept it. These are his people. He belongs, and after a lifetime of alienation, this is ecstasy. If Prior tells him to lie down on the street and be run over, he will probably do it.

Well, he might argue a little first.

And, of course, he can be certain that Prior will never betray him like that. He can trust his brothers, as he has never been able to trust anyone, except maybe Nivel, long ago.

The boat glides very slowly through a maze of floating jetties and small pleasure craft in a bewildering spangle of colors and shapes. And the people—clean, well-fed, well-dressed *rich* folk!

Peeking under his hat brim, Vaun sees that most of them do indeed have black hair. Their skin color and their shapes vary a lot, but light hair is not common at all. He sees a few boys of delta type, with sandy hair and shaggy chests. Already their oddly squashed faces look ugly to him, although he would never have thought so three weeks ago.

Randoms. Wild stock. He practices the brethren's terms and they sound good in his mind. He may be alien to the randoms, but they are alien to him. Perhaps the city of Cashalix is as alien to Vaun as Ult was to Prior, twenty years ago.

*Bump*.

Raj leaps ashore with a rope. Vaun eases in under the canopy so as not to be noticed, keeping his head down.

"Five minutes early," Dice says, stepping swiftly in beside him. "Not bad. Remember your orders?"

"Of course." For some reason Vaun feels a little nettled by the tone.

Dice raises his thin, dark eyebrows. "I'm Prior for this trip, Brother."

"Of course." Maybe Dice is not as cool as he looks.

Raj bounces back into the boat, and it rocks.

Vaun squares his shoulders, and Dice claps a hard hand on one of them.

"Good luck, Brother!"

Vaun stares into those wonderful black eyes and sees *concern*, and he wants to fall on his knees and sing hymns of gratitude—he won't, of course, because the other two look oddly at him if he mentions religion at all, and that is something else he must come to terms with. But Dice *cares*! So does Raj, of course. Two boys who care what happens to Vaun? That's a miracle. That's enough to make him weep. But he manages to flash his brother a cheerful smile of thanks and turn away casually, as if he knows Cashalix as well as he knows the village, as if his pulse isn't racing like he has a summer fever and his eyelids prickling.

He scrambles up on the jetty. He is going first, because first is safest. If any underoccupied busybody is going to notice three identical boys disembarking from that boat, then it will not be the first of the three that raises the alarm. There should not be an alarm, because wild stock breed twins and triplets sometimes. He does not know why any concealment is necessary, but this is how Prior wants it done.

He strolls. Rarely has he ever wanted to run quite so much as he does now, but he strolls. He tries to look as though he is interested in the myriad craft in the pool, but they are a meaningless blur to him. He reaches the shore and ambles up the stair.

The street is a madhouse of noise and crowds and confusion. Half the population seem to be giants. He shies back as a huge girl thrusts bare breasts in his face. "Watch me being raped tonight on 'Wonderworld'," she says urgently. Then he realizes that it is a sim. He turns away in disgust and is faced with a grotesque wall of rippling brown bulges. "The girls must all be laughing at you, lad!" the giant roars through the din. "Astal Booster will double your muscles in two weeks! No exercise required!" Vaun makes a fast dodge around the figure, walks right through a slimy reptilian biped waving a book at him, and finally reaches the curb.

And there is the parking lot across the street. *Watch out for the traffic,* Dice has told him. He attaches himself to a knot of jabbering, chattering girls, and crosses when they do. If anything goes wrong, he must make his way to the base of that silvery spire to the north and wait there. Under no circumstances must he run back to the boat. But nothing should go wrong.

So why is his heart leaping all around his chest like a sandfly?

For a long, terrifying moment, he looks blankly over the parking lot, appalled by the number of vehicles and torches, and by their diversity. He has never dreamed that there could be so many machines in the world. The whole of the village would not buy one of these shiny monsters. Female sims cluster around him, fighting for his attention, merging at times into gruesome many-limbed, multiheaded composites, all shouting, touting products and services he has never heard of. He has to peer around and between them. "I have no money!" he shouts, but they pay no attention. More come hurrying over. Then, with inexpressible relief, he sees the ominous black bulk of a Patrol torch, hogging two parking stalls.

He *strolls* across to it. He risks a glance around, and no one is watching. Frightened that he may have seemed furtive, he raises his chin and looks around again, defiantly. The torch is a monster, as big as Glora's cottage. The windows are all smoky-dark, so he can see nothing of what is inside.

He lays a thumb on the door plate. Astonishingly, the door slides open for him, as Dice had said it would. He thinks he will be very glad to see Raj and Dice again. Raj will be along in a minute; Dice must settle the bill for the boat.

Vaun steps into the torch and the door hisses quietly shut. He blinks in the cool gloom.

There are two men there in uniform, and neither of them looks in the least like him, or Raj, or Dice.

**N**OW COMES THE Dreamer, silent in the hot night. A shape, undetected . . . gone again . . . perhaps just a whisper, a breath of movement among the rushes? Hovering unseen, unheard, unfelt. The Dreamer crosses the black pools without rippling their stillness, and the rank grasses barely wave as he drifts above them. There is no moon. There is never a moon here, and the rank fog hides the stars. Hovering over the swampland, the hunter who does not kill, the predator that gives life . . .

Dark his pursuit, yet bright his purpose. Mean deed may craft great matter, as the teachers say.

This craft tonight is a mean and decadent means indeed. Such craft are not crafted anymore, for the means are depleted and the craft is lost. Very witty . . . No matter. No one here to appreciate his wit except the rightful owner, and he neglects his duties as host, for he lies a-snoring on the floor beyond the bed. Hyperdisneural hallucinosis, you say? Commonly known as stungun hangover? Well, fancy! A hefty shot of axilithene also? Poor fellow. But he may be capable of answering simple questions in seven or eight weeks, if he's lucky.

No, he cannot rightfully be called the rightful owner. Legal owner, maybe. He deserves no sympathy, that weak-faced Sybarite, that fleshy random, for he must surely have inherited this antique wonder, this luxurious drifter with its pseudobrain control and divided-quarkian suspension, and even if he has somehow earned it honestly, he has conceived no better purpose for it than to fit it out as a floating brothel. Not a rightful deed.

But a pleasant irony under the circumstances.

Wonderful old technology. Wonderful for getting around uncivilized country, perhaps of honorable purpose once. A model this size could house a band of six units in comfort—foresters or ecologists, say—and disturb nothing in the environment with its passing.

And now regard it! A cesspool of expensive bad taste. Thick

rugs, crystal chandeliers, silken bed sheets! Walls padded in lace and crimson velvet, pornographic sim equipment ready to depict every depravity imaginable. Pathetic, really. Thus do wild stock squander their lives and resources in the useless pursuit of transient carnal sensation. Sad. Decadent. Overdue for replacement.

Of course there are no tiresome control panels in sight to spoil the love-nest decor. Diminutive marshes, channels, bayous—all flow silently by within a sim imaged above the central gilt-and-crystal table. The craft itself rises and falls smoothly in a seductive, soothing motion.

There have been no signs of humankind for the last hour. Time is running out. Before morning the Dreamer must return to claim his torch from the copse by the Transdelta Highway, and this lust boat must be safely sunk in a convenient pond. It has served him poorly. He should have hijacked a more prosaic vehicle and hunted in the orchard country eastward. This delta excursion has been a regrettable folly.

But wait! Here comes something new—a jetty and a diminutive huddle of shacks. Alter course, change speed . . . A squalid little hamlet, drawing slowly closer as the drifter approaches. There may be quarry hereabouts—silent bog monster stalks its prey through the night.

This is the thirteenth mission, and the last. In two days the Dreamer must report to Doggoth, an appointment he will not miss—not after all the effort required to get it! Granted that randoms vary widely in their abilities, a rational boy would expect them to favor their best, and to define those best by merit. But no! Amazing! On Ult, access to the Patrol is restricted to the pampered get of spacers.

Even so, that same rational boy might assume that a space patrol containing almost no one with deep space experience would welcome a former member of a Q ship crew as an acceptable recruit. Well, barely. Only just. Only after two years' bribery and flattery and scheming and crawling around webs. Back in Monad, the teachers warned him: *Nepotism must always be an intrinsic weakness of random societies.*

The teachers would be proud of him now, he thinks; his brothers would be proud of him. He has done well so far. It will be interesting to see how the Doggoth teachers react to a recruit who can sport spacefarer blazes on his lapels. Badly, probably. But he can hold his own in any company of mere lust-maddened randoms.

Aha! A solitary figure is making its faltering way along a dirt track on the far side of the hamlet. In the false colors of the infrared, it shimmers as a violet ghost. Dare a boy hope that this lonely pedestrian will be the right age and sex? He demands more magnification.

Yes! He feels a hunter's visceral thrill. Luck is on the side of virtue. She is just what he needs.

It is easy. In a few minutes he has circled around and brought the drifter down astride the track, a dozen paces ahead of the plodding figure. He slips on his vision enhancers and douses the lights. The door opens with a barely audible hiss. He need not even stalk his prey on foot—moments later, she stumbles to a halt in front of him, recognizing the presence of something solid ahead of her in the mist. As she raises her hand uncertainly to feel for the obstacle, he shoots her down.

He holsters the stungun and stoops to lift her. She is not heavy, but she does stink.

Door closed . . . lights on. He glances around and concludes that to use that bed for his purpose would be altogether too ironic, even for him. He spreads her out on the little table, legs dangling over one end, head over the other. He tells the craft to retrace its course until it is above open water, and feels a gentle tremor as it rises from the ground.

His catch is scraggly, pale, and pocked by insect bites; not promising material at all. The medics back at Monad said that half the implants would take, but they hadn't counted on recipients like this. She may well be a total waste of time.

If her hair were clean, it would be blond. Her single garment is a disgustingly grubby rag, so rotten it rips apart when he pulls it up . . . pubic hair darker, breasts flat and hard. Given a better diet and lifestyle, she might have been attractive enough . . .

Horror!

Something has come alive inside his pants. His pulse beats harder. He feels a breathless tremor, a tightness in his chest.

Just two days from now he must report at Doggoth and begin his impersonation of a random. Career performance will be easy—he can outscore any recruit they have ever seen if he chooses to. Being accepted socially will be something else. Although the normal behavior of a wild stock male is utterly repellent to him, he will contemplate even that if he must. For the Brotherhood. So he has begun dosing himself with stiffener already, and now the sight of this squalid female peasant has set off the required reaction. No matter that he consciously rejects her flea-bitten carcass with revulsion and dismay—knowing that he has years of this abomination to look forward to—at the same time he craves it.

Business first : . . except that his pants are squeezing him so painfully that he has to open his fly, and that simple act, that meaningless gesture he has performed innumerable times without a thought, is suddenly erotic and sinful and exciting. His arousal grows. Striving to ignore it, he fetches his equipment and sets to work. Thirteenth time, and last time. Ethics? Is he still bothered by the ethics of it? Not really. He is an agent of destiny, of evolution in progress. The upward struggle of any life-form is a ruthless, savage contest, and he is merely a tool, like the predator that eliminates the unfit.

So why are his hands shaking? They never have before.

Insert the speculum . . . dilate vagina . . . laparoscope inspection—which finds no sign of a legitimate tenant to be evicted . . . catheter into the cervix . . . He fumbles. Damn! Damn! Damn! A slip here could puncture a major artery.

Then he rises and regards the scrawny patient, still oblivious. "That's it!" he says aloud. "Well, almost. I wish you safe labor, citizen, so that together we may launch one more unit of the Brotherhood on a promising career of subversion and conquest."

He strokes her thigh thoughtfully, and then goes for the syringes.

"You are the thirteenth, you know," he says as he inserts the needle in the first bottle, "and the last. There can be no more after you, for I have no more hormone." He squeezes the dosage into the muscle of her thigh. "I hope you appreciate this, mother-to-be? The months I spent deciphering pharmacopoeias, translated pharmacologies, plundering pharmacies, and concocting pharmaceuticals?" The second shot goes into a vein in her groin. "All just to stimulate you into producing a *corpus luteum*, you ungrateful wretch?"

Done. Except that there is more than half a dose left.

He ponders, regarding the emaciated limbs and shrunken belly. "Would you care for seconds? Why not! I really have no further use for it. You are most welcome."

Aware that the tremor in his hands is showing no signs of fading, he gives her the rest of the drugs and tosses the instruments into the bag under the table. Again he contemplates the disgusting female body before him.

"That completes our business, citizen. As you would see if you were paying attention, there is also a problem of pleasure to consider." It doesn't feel like pleasure. It feels like an irresistible compulsion.

Trembling, he unbuttons his shirt. "You understand that I do need the practice? I'm sure I can trust your discretion in the matter? More than I can trust anyone else's, and I will have to start sometime.'' He feels nauseated and invigorated at the same time. The worst part is the knowledge that stiffener acts primarily on the mind. It has made him *want* to couple his flesh with that of this filthy, naked animal.

There can be no harm in it, for forty-eight chromosomes can never meld with twelve, even if his testes produced viable sperm, which they don't.

"I do hope you feel honored," he says, as he removes his pants. He takes hold of the girl's knees to spread her legs wider, and feels a sudden reaction. Her head jerks up, chin on sternum, and she stares at him with wide-stretched mud-brown eyes.

That double dosage may have been an error.

He is absurdly aware that he is as naked as she is. Never in his life has nudity bothered him before, but it does now. The immediate result is to remove all trace of the burning lust he felt only a moment ago. What in the galaxy ever possessed him? Tongue-tied, he stands and stares back at her, wondering what to do now. The boy snoring beyond the bed never caught a clear view of his assailant, but the theft of the drifter will be discovered eventually, and now there is a witness to describe the thief's appearance.

He may not need to kill her, though. Her lolling tongue and uncoordinated eye movements are a sure indication of hallucinosis. Paradoxically, even her fast return to consciousness is a sign that he may have overestimated range and target weight. Complete recovery will follow much later than usual, if at all.

The girl rolls her head around, scanning the room. She comes from a world of driftwood shacks and utter squalor; she will never in her life have seen anything like this jeweled seraglio, and she must be viewing it through a jangling blur of psychotic distortion. What can she think of the place?

Then her wobbling gaze comes back to him, and he wonders what she makes of him. Has she ever seen any male other than the shaggy, fur-faced mudslugs of the delta? Well, likely. The Commonwealth must send agents through this wasteland often enough, for the eelskin crop is a valuable export. They will be figures of power to her.

Now what? To assume that she is too confused to remember him is a gamble, but to slay her out of hand does seem unfair, and he is reluctant to waste the whole evening's work.

She makes a gasping, choking noise, and her head lolls back. He thinks she has fainted, but then she grips the sides of the table with her hands and pulls up her knees.

He recoils in revulsion. "No!"

She lifts her head awkwardly again, peers at him between her scrawny thighs, and tries to speak around a limp and slobbering tongue. He thinks she says, "Lord?"

"I don't . . . ." He feels too nauseated to speak now. He points at the door. "Go!"

More wet noises, then, "Go?"

"Yes, go!"

She wails. "I have . . . have . . . offended my Lord!"

He rubs his forehead with a bare arm. "You have not offended. You do not understand . . . I . . . Oh, *God*!" He learned that meaningless expletive from the wild stock aboard *Green Pastures*.

There is a long pause, and then she says apprehensively, and with great effort, "Gladly will . . . I bear a . . . child to Your glory, Lord, if it be Thy will." She squints doubtfully at his flaccid condition.

This is absurd! But he remembers that political control of randoms is often achieved with the aid of state-backed superstitions. Evidently he has stumbled on some primitive incarnation religion, and it will solve the problem nicely.

"Gods do not lust as mortals do. You already bear the seed. Go and raise My son." He points at the doorway.

The girl gasps, whirls in an ungainly scramble of limbs, and falls off the table onto her knees. She presses her face into the pile of the rug. "Blessed be the—"

"Go! And take your clothes with you." The absurdity of her reaction is irresistible. He bursts into helpless laughter, and can say no more. She wails and cowers lower, and that makes him laugh harder yet. Throwing open the door, he pushes her out into the night. He has forgotten the instructions he gave the control board, and the resulting splash sprays muddy water over him and the fancy carpet bath. No harm done, though—she will benefit from a bath, and already she is rising to her feet, immersed only thigh-deep. The door closes, plunging her into darkness, and he gasps out a word of command that sends the drifter skimming swiftly and silently away.

The Dreamer reels across to a chair and collapses into it. He laughs until his ribs ache. The thought of what he almost did is sickening, but he wishes he could hear the tale she will have to tell when she returns to her village. He wishes even more that he had some of his brothers around to share the joke.

The worst part of his job is the loneliness.

# NO! NO! NO!

Vaun woke with a scream, thrashing in the cramped seat of the stuffy little torch. A jar of pain as his wrist struck the control board brought him fully back to reality. He wiped his sweating face and gawked around like a moron. His heart raced madly.

Dreams! Always he dreamed when he had not had a girl before he slept. That one was the worst of them all.

"Location?" he demanded with a sour-tasting mouth.

"Midway between Ajoolton and Besairb. Starting descent in approximately seventeen minutes."

He grunted. The ETA reading showed that he had almost another hour to spend in this airborne kennel. Feeling grubby and thick-witted from his nap, he eased to a more comfortable position and thought about Citizen Feirn and her freckles. He promised himself no more dreams for a long, long time.

Ajoolton was the site of the famous battle that brought down the Yiparian Empire. And Besairb was where Maeve had her fancy estate. He had forgotten its name.

He had forgotten *Maeve*! He had forgotten Maeve and her long years of treachery—serving him by night and Roker by day. Spy! Think of Feirn instead.

He would certainly be hearing from Roker soon. The big oaf must really be sweating over that Q ship. The idea of Roker trying to outthink the Brotherhood was ludicrous.

Roker had won the last time only because Prior had been cursed with a string of atrocious bad luck, culminating in an ignorant country yokel blundering into the clutches of Tham and Yather, two of the very few spacers in the whole force with more intelligence than a pondful of spawning eels.

**"I**T ISN'T HER *fault,"* Nivel says, wiping Vaun's tears. *"She was all right until that one night."* He hugs Vaun tight, and he has stopped the blood flowing, but he cannot stop the tears . . .

He clutches Vaun hard against his smelly shirt, but he cannot stem the tears.

*"We none of us believed her,"* he says another time, probably later, when Vaun is older. *"Because the girls examined her and there was no sign . . . But then she started bulging. A stranger. Some government boy. Must'a been some government boy."*

And yet another time—a time that must have been a very early time. *"Yes, God makes your mommy say such things . . . Don't mean they're true, though."*

Always it is to Nivel that Vaun goes when the other children set on him.

Raj said, *"He put the babies out to good homes to foster."*

But . . . *She started bulging.*

Someone has been lying.

Vaun has been thinking a lot, because he has nothing else to do. The cell is just long enough to lie down in it. The light never goes off. There is a hollow thing to sit on, and when you shut the lid it disposes of whatever you have put in it. There is food, passed through a hatch.

But there is no one to talk to.

He has no clothes. The room is all right for sitting, hunched up in a knot, but not quite warm enough for sleeping.

He does not know how long he has been there.

Now the spacer is back again, the one with the button nose and curly hair that grows down to a funny point on his forehead. Communications Officer Tham, he calls himself. He leans against the wall and studies Vaun quizzically.

"You still don't want to talk?" he asks.

Vaun hugs his knees and stares back and says nothing. His own bruises have mostly gone away, and the spacer's face looks better, too. Vaun is sorry that he hit this boy; he has a gentle, friendly voice, and he seems to mean well.

"You won't even tell me your name?"

Vaun just looks. He will not betray Raj and Dice, his kin, his brothers. He will not betray Prior. Raj had said he would die for Vaun if he had to.

"This isn't very sensible, you know. People go mad if they're left alone long enough."

How long already? By the fuzz on his face, it must be several days, but he doesn't know how fast stubble grows.

The spacer has an empty holster on his hip. He sees Vaun look at it, and chuckles. "Oh, I'm not dumb enough to come and talk to a prisoner with a loaded gun. You're not much to look at, lad, but that was some fight you put up. Yather must outweigh you two for one, but you broke his jaw, you know."

That's good.

The spacer sighs. "You're a tough one all around. Four days' solitary and still not a peep out of you? We can get much rougher, you know."

Vaun will not betray his brothers. He does not know if he walked into the wrong torch, or if Prior had been caught earlier and the two spacers were waiting to see who would turn up to meet him. He yearns to know if Raj and Dice have been caught, too, but he can't ask without speaking. He is not going to speak.

The spacer sighs and straightens off the wall. "All right. You win, Vaun. Yes, we know your name now. We know a lot. Come on."

He raps on the door. Someone must be watching through the little spyhole, because the door opens at once. A bundle is passed in. "Get dressed," the spacer says, tossing the clothes at Vaun irritably. "Then come out, and we'll show you a few things."

The shirt is all right, but the pants are so huge that Vaun has to hold them up. That keeps at least one hand occupied. He walks out, barefoot on the cold floor, and Tham is waiting in the corridor, alone. Without a word, he leads the way.

He throws open a door, stands aside. Warily, Vaun walks by him, into a big, dim room.

A dozen or so chairs arranged around a machine that looks like a complicated table, and that's all . . . except for the other spacer, the one called Yather, sitting on the far side. He is big and beefy, dark and surly, and the lower part of his face is hugely swollen. His eyes are definitely not friendly. "Dammit, Tham," he mumbles, "I'm crazy to go along with this."

"Sit, lad," Tham says, closing the door. "Anywhere you like. And you be patient, Yath. He's a tough one, and it would be a shame to damage him."

"It would be a pleasure to damage him."

Tham takes a seat also, and pulls a control board toward himself. "Give me half an hour. If he isn't singing lovely songs by then, you can have him. Remember, though . . . he may be as ignorant as moss, but he's probably smarter than either of us."

Yather grunts disbelievingly.

"Watch this, Vaun," Tham says. He does something with toggles, and the air above the machine in the middle seems to grow darker. Then a shadowy figure appears in it, smaller than life-size, and wavery, like a doll under water—muddy water. "Lousy quality," the com officer says.

Vaun knows this is a sim. He knows that the alien monsters he has seen on the pubcom are fakes, so this may be a fake, also. But he can't help watching.

The figure becomes clearer, gloom within murk. It is a very skinny boy, wearing only a rag, sitting cross-legged—a bearded savage. It raises one arm above its head. Vaun shivers with recognition even as the image speaks, in a squeaky, unnatural voice: "If people have gone out five thousand elwies in all directions, that means the Bubble is ten thousand elwies across, doesn't it?"

The sim dissolves, leaving the room brighter. Scared, Vaun looks to Tham for explanation. The spacer's gaze is bright and intense, dangerously wise.

"The teacher has a two-way      It can record, as well as project. Understand? That's supposed to be so that any exceptional students get detected. The Commonwealth . . . the government . . . most countries have that sort of equipment. They just never seem to get around to doing anything with the information, that's all. But you were recorded all through your schooling; such as it was."

He smiles, and Vaun feels a stab of anger that he does not understand.

"That was how Prior found you, Vaun," Tham says in his soft voice. "And how he found Tong, and Dice, and Prosy. It had been a long time—twenty years in some cases—and, of course, he had spread you well around, you understand . . . Not all of his efforts would have succeeded, and he needed to determine which ones had. We know he gained access to those educational records in several states."

Vaun has never heard of Prosy, who must be another brother. *But they don't know about Raj!*

Tham studies Vaun carefully, then says, "Now we know your name, and your village, and we know you disappeared from it twenty-five days ago, right after that scene we showed you. Who came, Vaun? Who turned off the teacher? Dice? Tong?"

Vaun says nothing.

Tham watches him for a moment, then says, "Well, leave that for now. Look at this one." He adjusts controls again, frowning.

"Dammit, Tham!" shouts the big boy on the far side. Then he yelps and claps a hand to his sore jaw. "We're wasting time!" he mumbles. "I've got stuff upstairs that'll get talk out of a nickel-iron asteroid."

"Patience, Yath, patience! Vaun, you know that com works by radio waves? There are millions of messages buzzing around the planet, and around all the settled worlds. Sometimes it's possible to look in on other people's coms, if you're lucky, or sneaky. Got that?"

Vaun nods before he realizes that nodding is a sort of talking and he has promised himself he will not talk, ever.

"In theory, we should be able to communicate with all of the other worlds of the Empire—the Bubble. But in practice, it never works out that way." Tham completes his adjustments, but holds one finger ready on a button, still talking to Vaun while the other boy glowers in silence.

"There's too much chatter, and all the Q ships among the million worlds put up interference. And radio takes time. It takes years for messages to cross between worlds. The Patrol is supposed to keep in touch. Ultian Command ought to report to—"

*"Tham!"* growls the Yather boy.

Tham ignores him, watching Vaun intently as if even his eyelashes may give off signals. "I'm going to show you a piece of a signal we picked up on a freak reception a couple of years back. It came from a world called Avalon . . . You've heard of that one? No? Sure? Well, never mind. Avalon is four elwies away, so whatever this shows, it happened six or seven years ago, when you were but a little tad."

He touches the button, and sound roars, making Vaun clap hands over his ears, and recoil in his seat. A fuzzy brilliance fills the room, completely obscuring the far wall and the other spacer and the chairs beside him, as though the building has just been chopped in half. The imaging is galaxies better than the pubcom back home—he is sitting in the middle of a sunlit street, filled with smoke. Motor noises, explosions, screams . . . and a girl's voice shouting over it all in words he does not understand. Trees explode in balls of fire, houses collapse, even the ground seems to rock and sway. Something like a giant beetle comes looming out of the smoke, knocking down walls and crushing smaller vehicles. Flashes and bright streaks come and go. None of it seems to make any sense, and the rocking is enough to give Vaun queasy feelings. He looks inquiringly at Officer Tham, who is still watching him, not the display.

Tham shouts over the din. "It's a war, apparently. We don't know who's fighting who. We know nothing at all, except that there was a battle. We suspect that some of that big equipment is being run by spacers, though. Now, watch this bit!"

The scene is shifting as though Vaun himself is running, coming closer to one of the ruined buildings, which is burning so fiercely that he thinks he should be able to feel the heat. He nears an empty window; a face appears in it—a bare-chested boy is trying to climb out before he is cooked; his hair is on fire; he is screaming; his face explodes in a scarlet flower. He topples back, out of sight.

Then smoke mercifully blurs everything, the sim vanishes, and the room is plunged into darkness and hard reality. Vaun feels horribly rattled, and his ears are ringing. Tham leans back in his seat, eyeing him thoughtfully. Time goes by in heavy heartbeats.

"We don't know what the commentary says. The grammar has the machines baffled, but they think they can pick out a few key words repeated here and there. *Hive* is one of them. *Brotherhood* is another."

Vaun hopes his face is showing what he wants it to . . . which is nothing at all. How much can he take? How long will he resist torture if they start on that? He wishes he could read what lurks behind Tham's odiously cheerful smile.

"And that boy in the window. Did you recognize his face? I think you did, Vaun. I know you should! When I first saw this, I thought he seemed oddly familiar. But how could I recognize a boy who died years ago and light-years away? I didn't know, and I daren't suggest such a crazy thing to anyone. But it bothered me so much I finally asked the Patrol computers to run an identity check on that image."

Vaun can guess what the answer was.

Tham's smile dissolves into darkness. "They said it was Commodore Prior of Ultian Command, attached to the high admiral's personal staff."

Still Vaun says nothing. He had just seen another of his brothers, obviously. Dying.

Tham crosses his legs and leans back without taking his eyes off his prisoner. "And I knew that, of all the spacers on Ult, only four had been born on other worlds—Q ship crews usually go onward with their ships or settle down in landlubber jobs, but there are four who have joined Ultian Command at one time or another, in the last century or so. One of those four was Commodore Prior, who came from Avalon in *Green Pastures*. But that could hardly be him. Even if the intercept was old history being rebroadcast, that could not be him, because he was only a kid when he left Avalon . . . not to mention that the boy in the clip obviously died. Yet DataCen said it was him!"

"So the ComOff came to me," the Yather boy growls, "and we started to do some checking on Commodore Prior. In secret."

Vaun clasps his hands on his lap and stares hard at them. Sweat trickles coldly down his ribs.

"We found him doing some very curious things for a Patrol officer," Tham says gently. "And when we went around to the places he'd been visiting, some very curious patterns began to emerge."

Silence falls. *He put the babies out to good homes to foster?*

Vaun looks up inquiringly, but this time Tham does not speak. Yather does not speak. The silence and the staring grow to screaming point.

After about four days of this, Vaun's own voice grates in his ears and his chin trembles. "Like what, sir?"

Tham nods approvingly, triumph starting to glitter in his eyes. "Like rape, Vaun. Do you know what rape is?"

Feeling sick, Vaun nods.

"The law doesn't care whether a boy uses his cock or a bit of pipe, Vaun. And morally it doesn't matter, either, I don't think. Do you think that matters?"

Vaun shakes his head. *She was all right until that one night?*

Tham pulls a face. "Even if you didn't know before, you can work it out now, Vaun. A human ovum is very small, barely visible. A couple of dozen in a special packet to keep them frozen would be easy to hide. He embarked on the Q ship as a Patrol cadet. The rest of the crew and passengers were legit. He was the only one of . . . of his kind . . . on the ship. Obviously we would have been curious about a gang of identical boys, so he came all alone. We don't think he had any accomplices among the normals, either. That clip I just showed you, of the battle; that suggests that Prior's kind is not universally popular on Avalon, doesn't it?"

Vaun nods. Raj had spoken of a hive once or twice, here on Ult.

But he hadn't said where, and it had sounded like nothing more than a hiding place. Remote.

"So Prior smuggled the package on board with him, and it's easy for a crewboy to keep something hidden on a Q ship. He brought the frozen ova from Avalon, and you were one of them. He smuggled them down to Ult on the shuttle. But he couldn't smuggle in money, because different planets—even different countries—have different sorts of money. He might have tried jewels or gold, but those would have led to questions. So he had very little money, probably just enough to rent a freezer to store you and your brothers."

Vaun shudders. Tham waits for him to speak, and then goes on when he doesn't.

"He made money, though, very quickly. He's an extremely clever boy. I know that from his career, although all of his medical files seem to have disappeared. And as soon as he could afford to travel around a bit, Vaun . . . Mechanical gestation is expensive; there would be questions, and records. He did it the cheap way, the secret way. Rape, Vaun! Women molested at night, Vaun. He implanted those ova in human incubators."

Yather says, *"Cuckoos!"* nastily.

"We have more evidence!" Tham stretches—he is a very restless person. "We have pictures of some of them, taken before they suddenly left home. Suddenly, like you did. I won't bother to show you—only the clothes differ, and the haircuts. I don't suppose all the implants thrived, but we know of several. You and—"

"That's enough, Tham!" Yather barks, and then winces.

Again Tham pays no attention to him. "And we noticed that about three years ago Commodore Prior took to traveling in much larger vehicles than the one-boy torch he had used till then. Four days ago, he took off for Cashalix. He had no official reason to come here, so Yath and I followed him. He parked, and went to have lunch, and we put a tail on him. Then we thought we'd check out his torch . . ."

"And I walked in on you," Vaun mutters, forgetting his vow.

Tham's eyes glint. "Yes, you did. I don't think you're really part of this plot at all, lad. I think you were sold a honeypotful of crap by some very smooth customers. Part of what those slickers said is true, I'm sure. But they didn't tell you the whole truth, now, did they?"

"No, sir."

"And you personally have done nothing wrong, have you?"

"I don't think so, sir."

Suddenly Tham's voice is no longer soft. "I know about your mother, Vaun. I can guess what happened that night seventeen years ago—she was assaulted, raped, and driven out of her wits. Prior did that, Vaun! It was an utterly disgusting, horrible act, and nothing can excuse it! Nothing! We know of others, but we'll never know how many there were altogether. So there it is, and now I want your decision, Citizen Vaun. Are you going to cooperate with me and justice, or do I let Officer Yather take you off to the lab? Answer this now: *Whose side are you on?*"

Vaun shuts his eyes so the tears won't show. Raj! Dice! It has been a wonderful dream. Now he will be sent back to the village, or to prison. Belonging . . . but belonging to what? If it started with rape, where was it supposed to end? What sort of person had his mother been before that night? And all the horrors of being a freak in the village all his life . . . Prior did that to him! What he suffered, and what happened to Glora . . . all Prior's fault! All Prior's doing.

He hears Tham sigh. "Okay, Yath. You can have him."

Vaun opens his eyes quickly. "I'll help all I can, sir." He is ashamed of the tremor in his voice.

Tham smiles a long smile, and says, "Good boy!"

Yather grunts as if disappointed. "Now what?"

"Now," Tham says, still smiling, "I think it's time to go to Valhal and tell Roker."

T HE PARKING LOT at Valhal was a tree-wrapped glade, set far from the house to muffle the traffic noise. Even the storage garages were well hidden, to preserve the dignity of the forest.

It was great to be home! After spending most of a day and a night in the air, Vaun jumped down onto the tarmac feeling as if he had just tunneled out of a dungeon. He blinked at the hot sunshine . . . stretched, scratched, and inhaled great lungfuls of the unique Valhal air, an unmistakable blend of sea and blossom, woodland and mountain. Nowhere else on Ult ever smelled so good. He shot a loving glance at the towering majesty of Bandor.

Security imaged in beside him, but not in the public Jeevs mode he had seen at Forhil. This sim was neither male nor puny, and there was nothing wrong with its clothes, because it wore none. Security was telling him he could speak in confidence. Instead of the unpleasant twang of a Kailbran accent, it spoke in throaty, seductive tones well suited to its voluptuous appearance. "Welcome home, Admiral. Transportation?"

Vaun felt fusty and rumpled after the long flight. More sitting was exactly what he did not want. He flexed his damaged knee, and decided the injury was not fatal. "No, I need a run. Send that junk heap back to its home base. Has Citizen Feirn arrived yet?" He began jogging without waiting for an answer, and the sim ran at his side, improbably barefoot and bouncing deliciously. Its hair streamed in the breeze realistically.

"At the parking lot thirty-three minutes ago, sir, reaching the front terrace seventeen minutes ago. There are pepods on the cliff path. Estimated time to disperse them is eleven minutes."

"I'll take the jungle trail, then." He left the parking lot, cutting into a narrow gap in the undergrowth, and the sim followed. The stiffness in his knee was fading. "Assign her the Pearlfish Suite."

"I assumed that would be your choice, sir. And her escort?"

"*What?*" Vaun stopped dead. In a feat no material body could have achieved, the sim was instantly standing in front of him again, smiling seductively.

"An Ensign Blade of the Space Patrol, sir."

"I don't recall inviting him!" Vaun felt a rush of anger. That whippersnapper who had been at the party? What game was being played here?

Of course, a guest could always assume that an invitation included a sleeping partner also, but he had thought that Feirn had other intentions . . . "Why do you ask?"

"He has requested separate quarters, sir."

"He has?" That was very strange, but Vaun would not argue. "Then put him in one of the Bay Cabins." He began running again, chuckling—how broad a hint would be needed to convince Ensign Blade he was not wanted? Hints did not come much broader than the Bay Cabins.

The sim was still ahead of him, voluptuous hips jiggling, twisting its head to look back. "There is an incoming call, sir. From Planetary Command. High Admiral Roker."

"Inform the caller that I shall return his com as soon as possible." *After I've told the world how he has failed to defend it!*

The sim vanished at last, the trail steepened abruptly, and Vaun windmilled his arms to keep his balance. The thick woods around him were a gala of bright-colored flowers, framing glimpses of the turquoise ocean far below, where sunlight glinted on snowy surf and multicolored blotches of seablossoms. As he went bounding recklessly down the slope, he realized with surprise that there were only three human beings on the island at the moment. It was rare for Valhal to be so sparsely inhabited. Except when Vaun himself was away on a speaking tour, a hundred houseguests was about average. Today only two—and tonight one, for Ensign Blade would certainly be leaving before dark, even if Vaun had to send him to Doggoth to borrow a corkscrew.

As for Roker . . . Whether he was home at Danquer, or tending to business at Hiport, he was half a world away, and should be allowed to enjoy the beauty sleep he so badly needed. "Service!"

The sim reappeared in front of him, running and looking over its smooth, round shoulder. "Admiral?"

"Any change in the Q ship forecasts?"

"No, sir."

Well, Vaun would return Roker's call after he had gone public with the story—and also after he had viewed Tham's mysterious Memorabilia file.

"How long is it?" he asked, puffing hard now, "since I approved that projection design you are using?"

"Seventeen years and thirty-nine days."

That long? Vaun was startled; he almost stumbled. "Modify it. The hair is too carroty. Make it match Citizen Feirn's."

"Like this, sir?"

"Much better. And more freckles. Now go away. I'm busy."

His insubstantial companion disappeared again, just as he rounded a sharp corner, where the path was banked the wrong way and coated with slippery pea gravel. A misjudgment could bring a painful wrench to an ankle, or even a fall into strategically placed daggerthorns. The jungle trail had been designed by some devious trickster centuries before Vaun's time, but successive owners had maintained it. It meandered up and down over half the island, missing few points of interest. To run the whole circuit in one day was a feat, and a challenge no boy worth his booster could resist; but few completed it unscathed on a first attempt.

Soon he was down to shore level, limping along the rocks. The tide was coming in, but the spray had not yet made the path slippery. The violet Iskanthia seablossoms were past their best now, but the yellow ones were glorious . . . Those were relative newcomers to Valhal; he must find out their name. Then came the long, killer slope they called Heartbreak Hill. Feirn was waiting—he pushed himself to his limit. Flocks of scarlet shrills panicked into the air as he emerged from forest at the start of a narrow suspension bridge. He trotted high above the Dragon Gorge without pausing to look for game. Valhal was stocked with the best hunting beasts on Ult, most of them imported, a few natural Ultian species, some artificial.

Artificial like him.

Memory: *You mean that wasn't just a sim, sir?*

The first time Vaun had ever come to Valhal, Tham had smuggled him along this same path on his way to meet Roker, and their cart had almost run into a behemoth.

‘‘**Y**OU MEAN THAT *wasn't just a sim, sir?*’’

Vaun stares back wide-eyed, listening to crashing sounds from the woods.

Tham chuckles. ‘‘No. And there are worse things around than that. Don't worry, they're kept pretty much under control.’’

‘‘By who, sir?’’ Vaun peers around at the soggy darkness of the jungle—more trees than he has ever imagined.

‘‘By Security.’’

‘‘But what can a sim do about a beast that size . . . sir?’’

‘‘The sims are just the visible part, lad. Security on an estate like this is a huge network, with all sorts of aggressive capabilities. It could put a ballistic lance into anything—or anyone—anywhere, in less than a second. And it would, too! Unless you were hunting, of course. Then the system allows a fair match and you're on your own! Roker loses a guest now and again. Makes it more interesting!’’

‘‘But . . . what was it?’’

‘‘I've no idea. Nothing native to Ult, but a lot of our plants and animals were brought by the settlers . . . evolved on other worlds or artificial, created in labs.''

*Like me.* Vaun is trying not to think about that. He almost grew accustomed to the idea while he was with Raj and Dice, because they had so obviously accepted their origin. Now he is back with real people, and he feels more freakish than ever.

The little cart rocks and bounces down the track, which is obviously not intended for vehicles at all. Vaun is hot, and weary, and hungry. He has never talked as much in his life as he has on the flight from Cashalix. Now Yather has gone on ahead to report to Roker, whoever Roker is, but Tham told the sim at the parking lot that Vaun must not be seen by anyone else, which is what brought on this backbreaking backwoods drive. A third boy, Lieutenant Hariz, piloted the torch while Tham and Yather interrogated Vaun. When they arrived, Hariz was ordered to Hiport, and has left already.

At last Tham has stopped asking questions. Vaun feels as if he has been squeezed like a lemon. Even his pips have popped now; he has held back nothing. So he may have revenged himself on Prior, and avenged his mother, but what did Raj and Dice ever do to him to deserve such treachery?

"Look!" Tham points up a grassy valley as the cart whirs across it, picking up speed on a flat stretch. "See those ruins? They're very old, preindustrial. Supposed to be the site of the first landing from Elgith. Some university types wanted to excavate it, and Roker threw them out on their ears.''

The cart crawls into more trees before Vaun can make out what he is supposed to be looking at. "Sir, who is Roker? And does he *own* all this?"

Again Tham makes his soft chuckling noise. He looks weary, but he is being friendly now. "Admiral Roker is my boss, one of the senior officers in the Patrol. When spacers win their pennants—that's commodore rank—then they're assigned estates. Those who go on to flag rank can choose another, grander one if they wish. It's the main source of motivation in the Patrol. Roker was either smart or lucky, because Valhal's acknowledged to be the best there is. High Admiral Frisde herself hasn't got any better.''

Vaun does not follow all that. While he considers whether to ask more questions, the orderly sim appears alongside the cart, jogging smoothly. Trailing branches pass right through it. No real boy could trot so effortlessly in such a uniform.

"Sir, the admiral requests that you come to the Crimple Arbor as soon as possible.''

"Stop this fiendish contraption, then." The cart wheezes to a halt, while Tham gives Vaun a mischievous smirk. "We can go faster on foot. I saw you give Yather a lesson in rioting. How are you at running?"

"All right," Vaun says cautiously. He should be good, considering how much of his life he has spent being chased.

"Show me!" Tham's teeth glint in a challenge.

"Can I take my shoes off?" Vaun was allowed a hasty wash before leaving Cashalix, and given better clothes, but shoes are a new experience, and an unpleasant one.

The spacer is amused at that. "Certainly. And make it an honest race, all right? No holding back just to please me."

Vaun shrugs, and nods. Win or lose, he is probably going to lose in the end. He scrambles out of his shoes and out of the cart.

"We'll proceed on foot, then," Tham tells the sim as he also dismounts. "See that neither of us gets lost. Ready, lad? Go!"

Vaun is off up the track. He wonders vaguely about monsters, but he can hear the spacer behind him, and he doesn't think that feeding him to some artificial alien horror is a likely prospect at the moment. Later, maybe. He won't think about later, and a humiliating return to the village. Or prison camp.

He slows down for a patch of boulders, then speeds up when the track becomes softer, winding through high bushes laden with fleshy purple and white flowers. The scent is enough to make him giddy . . . a view of the sea, shining blue-green, more beautiful than he has ever imagined . . . floating hillocks of vegetation smothered in red and mauve flowers . . . craggy spikes of rock rising from the jungle. He can't hear any pursuit now, and when he glances back, there is no one in sight. It's probably some kind of elaborate joke, with Tham following in comfort in the cart and laughing his well-educated head off. Well, Vaun would rather run and be by himself.

He comes to a branching of the path, and the sim is standing there, pointing to the right. It vanishes as he races by.

The exercise is welcome after four days in a cell. Booster is a poor substitute for the real thing. Then a steeper slope, his breath is coming hard, his shirt and shorts sticking to him . . . and he has arrived. He stumbles to a halt before a strange cagelike building in a clearing, a floor and roof and almost no walls, only pillars. It has a fine view of the bay and a silvery waterfall, but why should anyone need a building just to look at a view? Inside it, Security Officer Yather and another boy are lounging in chairs and eating off a stone table. A larger table behind them is loaded with enough food to feed the whole village. They stare at him—Yather with surly dislike, the other with openmouthed astonishment.

Winded, panting, Vaun points back the way he has come.

"He's just . . ."

"Yes, we know," says the one who must be Admiral Roker. "Security told us." Vaun realizes that Roker is even heftier than Yather, and therefore very beefy indeed. It shows because he is wearing only bright-colored trunks with a towel draped over his shoulders. He is as hairy as any boy in the village, and his hair is even fairer, but he is no delta mudslug. His face is the wrong shape, with a prominent nose and a very long upper lip, and village boys are never fed enough to grow muscles like those anyway. Yet he has a look of Olmin about him, somehow, mean enough to enjoy hurting. His eyes are a startling blue.

Not having been told to take one of the empty chairs, Vaun just stands and pants and dribbles sweat. He could use a drink.

Roker recovers from his surprise. Without taking his attention off Vaun, he shovels up something on a silver fork and pops it in his mouth.

"Astonishing!" *Chew.* "Alike as two pepods. This one's younger, of course." *Chew.* "Well, maybe there is something to this yarn of yours, SecOff." He curls his upper lip in a sort of sneer, showing his teeth like a horse. His voice has a strange nasal twang. Vaun doesn't like him.

Yather smiles grimly, but without concealing relief. Evidently Vaun's appearance has made the conversation friendlier.

"This war on Avalon? There was a ship in from Avalon not long ago."

"*Carina*, sir. Last year."

The blond boy tears a hunk from a roll and speaks with his mouth full. "Don't recall any war talk."

Yather looks uneasy again. "Fourteen and a half years, sir. Actually, I think *Carina* took nearer fifteen. The fighting may not have started when she left. People forget, too, in that time span, and they might not expect us to care about—"

Roker is glaring. "That's why we have interrogations, SecOff! Have you reviewed the *Carina* records?"

"Not in detail, sir. There was mention of unrest, of course. There always is. And there was mention of illicit biological experimentation, but no one knew any details, as usual. That should have been followed up, I agree, and we can track down the immigrants and work them over again . . ."

The admiral grunts disapprovingly.

"Only three of us, sir! Internal investigations are always sensitive—didn't want word to leak back to the suspect. No case number to assign extra machine time . . ."

"That will change," Roker mutters. It is a sign of forgiveness, and Yather's heavy frame seems to relax again. He fingers his swollen jaw as if it hurts.

The admiral works another load into his mouth and lays down his fork. He leans back and scratches his hairy belly, studying Vaun. Mumble: "Take off your shirt."

Vaun obeys uneasily. Busily chewing, Roker gestures for him to drop his pants also.

"Mm. Looks human enough. Prior has no hairs on his chest either. Wonder why not?"

*Because chest hair is an unnecessary frill,* Vaun thinks, but he suspects that it would be unwise to say so in front of Roker.

"But he does have tits!" Roker curls his lip at Vaun again. "Why have you got tits, lad?"

"I don't know sir. Why have you?"

The blue eyes narrow warningly. "Because I'm a product of evolution. Evolution progresses by trial and error, not by intent, right, Yather?"

"Right, sir. It does the best it can with what it's got to work with. No shortcuts."

"But if this . . . boy? It? Him? I suppose we call him human? If this lad was brewed up in a bottle, then whoever designed him could have omitted unnecessary things like tits. Right?"

"I would assume so, sir."

As the inspection seems to be over, Vaun begins to dress. He shivers at the clammy touch of wet cloth. There is an unpleasant odor around, but it doesn't seem to be him. He thinks it comes from the trees.

" 'Sthat hair or dirt on your chin?" Again Rather directs his questions at Vaun. The poor folk of the delta would offer a visitor a drink and a seat, but a peasant must stand before spacers.

"Hair, sir."

"Beards have no real function either, have they, Yather?"

"Only as a secondary sexual characteristic, sir, I think."

"What sex life has an artificial construct got? Do they screw test tubes? Why even balls?"

"Hard to say, sir, as their reproduction must be agamic."

Roker shoots a nasty glance at Yather, who flushes.

"Sorry. Asexual, that is. I've been reading up on this, picking up jargon. Testicles are needed to make hormones, I suspect."

Roker grunts. "Prior has a pretty impressive reputation."

"That could be stiffener, sir."

"Mm." Roker continues eating for a moment, scowling at Vaun. "We can check his intake. So it's camouflage? Nipples and beard . . . male chin and shoulders. Not purely functional—they're designed so they can pass as human?"

"We think so, sir."

The long, rubbery upper lip curls again in a sneer. "And what does this tell us about their intentions, mm?"

A scrabbling of boots on dirt, and Tham comes lumbering up the trail. He is scarlet-faced and gasping. He flashes Vaun a congratulatory smile, then comes to attention and salutes the half-naked admiral. The beefy boy shows his teeth in welcome.

"Come in, ComOff, sit down. Here, you look like you need a drink. Built for speed, is he?"

Tham swallows eagerly, then wipes his mouth. "Built for just about everything, I think, sir."

"Like Prior. Remember that night we all got into an arm wrestling match? You were there?"

"I think so, sir. The evening is blurry, but I remember my elbow the next morning."

"You were overall champion, sir," Yather says quickly. "You wiped the floor with us."

Muscleboy nods, scowling. "But Prior let me beat him—I could see it in his eyes." He looks Vaun over again thoughtfully, as if about to issue a challenge.

Then he seems to change his mind. "Well, this is a fine piece of work you've done, Tham. Well beyond the normal call of your duties."

"Thank you, sir. Security Officer Yather—"

"Of course." Roker waves his fork at the food table. "Help yourself to whatever you fancy. So we have cuckoos in our nest. What do you suppose Prior's planning, mm? Going to build a baby factory? What did you call it—a hive?" He stuffs a wad of meat in his mouth, and Vaun's stomach issues a loud rumble.

Tham rises and goes to the large table at the rear. "We tend to think not, sir. Yath?"

The normally surly Yather boy becomes almost exuberant. "The way we look at it, sir, the technology isn't available here. It's completely forbidden for humans, and even the animal work is rare nowadays. The Stravakians are doing a little of it, but as far as we know, that's all."

"There's a black market in baby improvement back in Kilbra. That I do know."

"Oh, you find gene stitching being done everywhere, sir, and a lot of it is just kitchen charlatanism. We haven't called on DataCen at all, yet, but so far as Hariz and I have been able to establish on our own, sir, the know-how to produce anything like this—" He waves a thumb toward Vaun. "—has never existed on Ult, or any of the founder worlds, even. Artificial animals, certainly—gnu-steeds, and yimyaks, and angorazebs—but no one ever managed to produce a workable human brain before. Moronic cripples was all."

Roker curls up his lip, chewing and speaking at the same time. "He may have brought the know-how with him."

Yather becomes diffident, as if contradicting the admiral is a touchy business. "Possible, sir, of course . . . but again doubtful. Even our best miniaturization could not reduce such a volume of data to invisibility, and those settlers were inspected closely. He did very well even to bring in the ova . . . and that is only one problem. He had four grown cuckoos that we know of, and maybe more still lost in the woods, but none of them are molecular biologists. Even if they were, they would have to acquire the equipment and the materials, and a safe location. It's certainly possible, of course, but if that's what he plans, then why become a spacer? Why spend seventeen years in the Patrol?"

Vaun doesn't understand, but Roker grunts thoughtfully, and nods.

Tham wanders idly by with a glass in his hand. "We can always ask ex-Commodore Prior, of course. Ask what he has in mind." Chuckling, he hands Vaun the glass without looking at him, and heads back to the food. Vaun drinks greedily.

Roker snorts. "He's long gone, surely?"

"Don't know that," Yather says, grabbing the conversation back before Tham can speak again. "He's due back at his desk tomorrow. Seemed inappropriate to com him, under the circumstances."

Roker's fork clatters on his plate. "Prior is no crumbrain! I say we'll never see him again!"

Yather flinches and looks nervously to Tham.

"Perhaps," Tham says calmly from the background.

The admiral twists in his chair. He clearly respects Tham's opinions more than Yather's. "Why do you doubt?"

"Look at it from his point of view, sir. He's had an incredible string of bad luck." Plate in hand, Tham has completed his inspection of the display of food, and made his selection. He spoons something white and lumpy onto his plate. "First there was the Avalon newscast, if that's what it is. Pure chance!"

"That's filed in Central, of course?"

"No, it isn't." Tham chuckles, and helps himself to some green stringy stuff. "Anyway, if he's monitoring the Avalon file, I can't find his prints. Secondly, I was credulous enough to believe my eyes and call for the ID check." He pours orange sauce over the white stuff. "Thirdly, he didn't know we were tailing him, or he'd never have left his torch unattended at the rendezvous, right?" Brown stuff next. "Fourthly, he got tangled up in a religious procession. None of our doing, but it delayed him getting back. Hariz almost lost him."

Roker's unfriendly blue gaze comes back to regard Vaun with surprise. "He doesn't know we've got this, you mean?"

Tham adds a couple of rolls to his heaped plate. "How can he? Hariz swears Prior didn't get back to the torch until three or four minutes after we—" He glances at Vaun with a smile. "—until after we hustled the evidence out of there. The next cuckoo arrived five minutes after that. Now, unless Yather and I left our wallets lying inside, Prior has no idea what happened to the—to Citizen Vaun."

"And we covered up," Yather adds. "I gotta contact in the Cashalix department, and he made up a roadkill for us with the kid's ID."

"He did look sort of run-over by the time Yath had done with him," Tham says, heading to the table.

Roker taps fingers on the arm of his chair. "And has the next of kin made inquiries?"

Tham and Yather exchange winks behind his back. "No, sir. But yesterday the file was illegally accessed by parties unknown."

Roker grunts again. "So he must assume the kid got lost and run over?"

"That's right." Tham sits down, looking cheerfully at his heaped plate. "It's the logical assumption. I'm gambling that he'll carry on as if nothing has happened. I suggest we do the same, just lay low and watch him. Nobody but us three and Hariz know anything at all."

Vaun wishes he had been included in that remark. His mouth begins running like the Putra as he watches Tham savoring his first mouthful.

"And hope he'll lead us to his nest?" Roker curls up his lip skeptically.

The other two say, "Yes, sir," in unison.

The admiral turns his blue eyes on Vaun in a cold, disagreeable stare. "And do what with the renegade?"

"The patriot, sir," Tham mutters, but all three now study Vaun for what feels like a long time. Evidently Tham and Yather are going to leave this decision entirely up to their boss. It is Prior the traitor they want, and the baby cuckoo from the delta is of very little interest now he has sung his song for them.

The cold liquid Vaun has been gulping seems be turning much colder inside him as he waits to hear his fate. He can think of all sorts of helpful suggestions he could offer. Why not just feed him to the monsters and dispose of the evidence? The medics and scientists will be interested in him, because he remembers Tham saying that Prior's files are missing. That's another useful idea he won't propose—ship him off to a lab to be dissected. He is a unique specimen, and by analyzing him they can learn about their enemies, the Brotherhood. He keeps his face impassive and braces his knees together in case they start knocking. He hopes they'll let him die on a full stomach.

Suddenly Roker smiles. "The patriot, of course." He heaves his bulk from the chair with ominous ease, and paces barefoot over to Vaun. He is slabbed with muscle, and a good head taller.

He wraps a meaty hand around Vaun's upper arm. In a friendly gesture. Like a tourniquet. He is beaming. Vaun's eyes are about level with all that golden chest hair, and the painful grip on his arm is saying that he is not much of a specimen, really, is he? The physical nearness is menacing. The smile is horribly reminiscent of Olmin's smiles.

"So you are loyal to Ult and the human race, are you, lad?"

Vaun looks up at the happy gleam in the blue eyes and distrusts it with all his soul. "Yes, sir."

"Not to your test-tube brothers?"

"I . . . I got along well with them, sir. They seemed like good guys to me."

The giant lowers shaggy, golden eyebrows.

"But I disapprove of what was done to my mother, and the other girls. And they lied to me, sir." He remembers Raj and Dice, their affectionate smiles and unfailing good humor. He wishes Admiral Roker were just a fraction more likable. He resents the contempt behind the big public smile. The admiral has been eating onions.

"Well, Citizen Vaun . . ." Roker turns on his cheerful voice again. "Well, I have a suggestion. Even if Commodore Prior is a traitor, I'll admit he's one of the best damned officers in the Patrol.

We've lost him, but I wouldn't mind having a replacement. How would you like to be a spacer?''

"Me, sir?'' Vaun says incredulously. Out of the corner of his eye, he notices Yather and Tham starting to grin at each other, and he doesn't like the thought that they can see something about this offer that he can't.

"Yes, you.'' Roker rotates Vaun easily to face the view, and waves a thick arm at the scenery. "Everything you can see here is mine, because the Patrol gave it to me. It's mine until the day I die. Not all of us live this well, but we mostly do all right. Don't we, lads?''

"Yes, sir,'' say the others on cue.

"Fine houses, lots of respect, travel, girls . . .'' Roker's blue-blue eyes lock onto Vaun's. His voice drops. "I forgot! Not interested in girls?''

Anger burns in Vaun's throat, and he forgets discretion. "Not in the least!''

Roker smiles pityingly. "We can fix that soon enough. Don't worry.''

Worry? True, Vaun worried about it back in the village, but Dice explained it willingly enough on the boat when he asked. "No, we don't want girls. We don't *need* girls. Wants and needs are weaknesses. Not needing or wanting girls is one of our strengths, an advantage we have over the randoms.''

Why should Vaun *want* a *want*? He has watched that *want* infect the boys in the village as they reach adolescence, a feverish yearning that burns up their thoughts and their lives and gives them no peace, and precious little time for anything else. Who *needs* that *need*? What use are the admiral's absurd muscles except to impress girls?

The big boy shrugs and releases Vaun's arm, but only so he can grip his shoulder instead, innocently digging a thumb into the pressure point over the bone. "Well, whatever you want, the Patrol's got it. Whatever's in you, the Patrol will bring it out, too. It's the best chance a lad of your age can ever have.''

It should be a wonderful offer. Vaun should be jumping at it. Why isn't he? "But I'm only a peasant.''

Roker frowns, blue eyes glinting out under golden brows. "That means 'No'?''

Vaun looks despairingly at Tham. Tham takes pity on him, and laughs. He walks over, and his presence reduces the tension.

"Doesn't that remind you of Prior, sir? He's cautious like that! Vaun, the admiral is making you a very good offer, and quite genuinely, I'm sure. There's one advantage that he hasn't mentioned, and that's security. Recruits go to Training School at Doggoth, and at Doggoth you'll be safe from your former comrades—which may be good for your health, until we can round them all up. You will be well hidden from view. There can't be anyone there who remembers Prior, and it won't matter if they do—you can quite truthfully say you're his brother. Everyone up there is someone's son, or niece, or something.''

Vaun has seen pubcom shows where the hero or heroine goes to Doggoth. It's reputed to be a tough place. He isn't afraid of that. He can handle whatever other recruits have to handle, but what special things might happen to him at Doggoth? The Patrol may have its own labs there. He will be utterly at Roker's mercy in Doggoth . . . Has Roker any mercy? . . . If he has, he hasn't shown it yet.

"So you'll be out of sight," Tham continues. "Besides, it's a fantastic opportunity for someone of your background, a very generous reward for the help you have given us. I think you'd be wise to accept."

And no alternative has been mentioned. Vaun studies Tham's friendly smile for a long moment, and finally looks up at Roker to say, "Thank you, sir. I accept." But he is really speaking to Tham.

There must be *someone* in the world he can trust.


RELUCTANTLY ADMITTING TO himself that he had been a refractory idiot in running on a twisted knee—and that the aforementioned knee was now a burning ball of utter agony—Vaun left the jungle trail by an inconspicuous branch path, which led to an obscure basement entrance.

He saw no need to visit his own quarters or the more frequented parts of the house, and he showered, dried, and dressed without once slowing below a run . . . except while inserting himself into his shorts, a process that science had not improved since prehistoric times. He paused briefly to scowl at his reflection and conclude that his face was even more battered-looking than it felt. In less than three minutes after entering the building, he was hobbling up the stairs to the terrace level. A new record.

He should, of course, go and get the booster he had missed that morning, but the medic would throw in some painkiller, and he perversely thought he deserved to suffer a bit longer for his stupidity. Another hour or so without booster would do no harm.

With his shirt hanging open, still toweling his hair, still panting hard from his exercise, he paused in the doorway to admire the view. The bay, Glory Falls, the West Face, and the icy spire of Bandor . . . he knew them of old. Today the major tourist attraction at Valhal was none of those.

Head haloed with red fire in the sunlight, Feirn was leaning over the balustrade, standing on tiptoe to peer down at something below. Vaun could not see what was proving so interesting—most likely a flock of spectrum orchidoforms, which were at their best just now, strutting their display on all the lawns—but he had a fine view of long, slim legs, and thin white shorts pulled tight over a trim little ass as fine as any he had ever admired. Beside it was a male posterior clad in spacer uniform pants, although the lanky ensign had no need to stand on tiptoe to see.

*That one* would have to go.

Amused to note that his pulse rate showed no signs of diminishing, Vaun threw away his towel. How would he be reacting to her if he'd had his usual dose of stiffener? There was an awe-inspiring speculation. *Ninety-nine percent probability!* Thrusting his fists in his pockets, leaving his shirt unbuttoned, he hobbled out onto the sunbaked flagstones.

Neither Blade nor Feirn heard his barefoot approach. He leaned on the lichen-dappled stone at her side. Oh, those freckles! All over everywhere visible—arms, legs, shoulders. Logical that they would be all over everywhere presently invisible also. He would count them all if it took him a year.

"I am very happy that you came," he said softly.

Like a bent spring released, Ensign Blade spasmed into a vertical posture, stamped, and saluted. Feirn jumped and turned.

"Admiral! You took me by surprise." She tried to smile, but at the same time a strange pallor suffused her translucent skin, turning her face chalky-white and showing up all her freckles like coarse sand on a porcelain plate.

Astonished, Vaun clasped her hands. They were slim, cool hands. He had rarely seen eyes so pale a blue, like sky above the sea. He knew his own eyes must betray his longing. ''You would rather be taken by storm?''

Feirn licked her lips and took a moment to find her voice. ''That's what heroes are for, isn't it?'' She glanced sideways, as if trying to appeal to her companion, but Ensign Blade was behind her, immobile as a marble statue, not even blinking.

Vaun was disconcerted. She was even smaller than he had remembered, and now she seemed so frightened and . . . *vulnerable*.

''Feirn? Is something wrong?''

She flinched, and glanced briefly at the house. ''No! No, of course not! I'm delighted to be here. I've always dreamed of coming to Valhal and what are those gorgeous things down on the grass there?''

''Orchidoforms. This is their mating display.''

''Plants or animals?''

Her hands were shaking. He lowered them without letting go, admiring the fine copper hairs of her eyebrows, the cryptic effect of the almost-invisible lashes. Why the tremor, though? And everyone knew about orchidoforms.

''Both. Neither. Mostly animal at this time of year. They take root over the winter.''

''Oh, they're lovely, it's all lovely.''

''You will stay a long time?'' He wanted to put his arms around her and hug her. That was understandable, except that somehow now he felt more protective than lustful, and that was certainly not his normal reaction to a redhead.

She licked her lips again. ''It's a heavenly place!''

''It's the finest place on the planet, and finer by far now that Feirn is here . . . That's a lovely name! I want you to stay on in Valhal and enjoy it. I want to show you all of it, day by day, one corner at a time, so that I can see it all anew through your eyes.'' But he noticed those sky-blue eyes flicker a sideways glance again and he was baffled. ''Tell me you will stay a long time!''

She nodded several times quickly. ''I hope . . . I would love to see all of Valhal, and I'd be proud if you'd give me the tour yourself, Admiral.''

*Freckle by freckle.* ''Vaun.''

''Vaun.''

He gazed appraisingly at the petrified figure of Ensign Blade and decided it could wait awhile yet. Raising Feirn's hands to his lips, he kissed a first freckle, but he glanced up just in time to notice her attention still wandering. There was nothing where she was looking except the house itself, and it was empty. She couldn't have brought anyone else with her, or Security would have told him.

Soon he would start to feel slighted.

He wanted to see her smile. Impulsively he decided to give her the interview she wanted. It wouldn't matter that an unknown could command only a small initial audience—Admiral Vaun announcing the end of the world would be a blockbuster story no matter who broke it, and every station in every country in the world would pick it up at once. In fact, it was astonishing that word of his remarks at Maeve's party hadn't hit the newscasts already, but Jeevs would have told him if the networks were calling.

"We'll get our business over as soon as poss—"

"Bandor!" she said quickly. "That mountain is Bandor, isn't it? It's beautiful. And the sea is so blue—and all those trees! Like the world used to be."

Puzzled, he said, "You really do work for . . . 'See-It-All,' was it?"

" 'Show-It-All'! It's the best news program—but let's not talk shop, Vaun! You invited me and I'm here, and I've come, and it's all I've ever dreamed of." She was babbling, smiling with ashen lips. What in the galaxy was wrong with her?

"Sorry. 'Show-It-All.' 'Fraid I don't watch pubcom much. But I promise you that you'll stun the lot of them with this one."

Still flustered, Feirn turned her head as if to speak to Ensign Blade, but of course he was still in a state of suspended animation, awaiting the admiral's pleasure. When she looked back to Vaun she seemed even more worried than before. Her fingers were icy.

Shadows of suspicion darkened the sunlight for him. He gazed around the terrace with its flowers and shrubs and carved benches. He saw nothing that should alarm her—or him. The big windows and glass doors were shaded against the sun, and the huge house was inhabited only by machinery. The nearest entrance led to his own quarters, the adjoining set to hers, the Pearlfish Suite. Everything seemed to be in order.

"I'm awfully new at it," she said. Her laugh was almost shrill. "And it doesn't matter. I only took the job because I was bored while Blade was away at Doggoth and Petly is a friend of Mum's and I thought it would be fun. I don't do it well at all, you know. I'm no good at getting the right answers, because I get flustered if the subject talks back . . ."

"Well, we can plan the questions together," he said, thinking that there were many other things he would rather do together. "Start with Q ships in general—"

"Oh, nothing so dull, Admiral! I'm sure you've done hundreds of interviews more than I have, and know all the best things for me to ask. The life of a world-famous figure . . . your favorite sport, and—"

Either this little miss was raving mad, or she was trying to divert him—but why? Because of Blade?

"You tell me your favorite sport, Feirn. Here we have everything—hunting, gill fishing, hang gliding, ashkinaling, surf walking, skiing, hiking, sky buzzing, archery, fooping, bungie jumping, falconry, chess, skating, golf, honeymoon bridge, leapfrog . . ."

That worked. The long catalog steadily widened her smile until she laughed and her laugh was all the joys of love and childhood, music and poetry and life itself. "Oh, I know hardly any of those! You'll have to teach me."

He paused a moment and then said, "I will gladly teach you."

She closed her eyes and said, "Oh yes!" with apparent relief.

He was completely baffled now. She was putting out very contradictory signals.

Needing time to think, Vaun turned his attention to the rigid Ensign Blade, who had not moved an eyelash since completing his salute. His eyes were a pale mauve that suggested Umbarian ancestors, but they stared out from the bony face as unvarying as glass. Looking him over, Vaun could find nothing to criticize in his appearance. Grudgingly, he concluded that this one would pass inspection by the meanest petty officer in Doggoth. On Admirals' Day Parade, even.

"At ease, Ensign," he said, trying to sound as if he had been guilty of an oversight.

Blade snapped into position, and he still made the stonework look flaccid—a typical Doggoth-made robot.

"Relax, boy! We don't stand on ceremony here!"

"Thank you, sir," Blade said politely, looking down to meet Vaun's eye for the first time, but not moving anything below the neck. Apparently his back was always poker-stiff, and it was hard to imagine even a trace of a smile on those intense features.

"I don't expect my guests to address me as 'sir'."

The mauve eyes flickered nervously.

"Is 'Admiral' permissible?"

"Why not 'Vaun'?" Vaun asked, but it was like torturing a mushroom. He wondered how long he would need to have Ensign Blade posted to some ice-mining station in the Oort Cloud. About four hours before the orders came through, likely, which felt too long under the circumstances.

"With all respect, si—" The mauve eyes seemed to brim over with sincerity. "With respect, I have admired you so greatly all my life that I feel unworthy to address you as an equal, Admiral."

If that was studied insolence, it was superbly done. And if it was sincere, it was somehow even more infuriating. Vaun recalled Maeve's catty dislike of Ensign Blade and it now seemed eminently understandable. *All his life?* How old . . . young . . . was this gangling upstart?

"How long since you left Doggoth, Blade?"

"Ten weeks, Admiral."

Vaun glanced at Feirn and was annoyed to see amusement in her jewel-blue eyes. "Most people show some signs of recovery by then," he remarked.

The twinkle vanished, and she shot yet another worried glance toward the windows. "I asked Blade to fly me over here, Vaun," she said. "He was going to leave, but—"

"Feirn!" said Blade.

"But?" Vaun demanded, and the prickles of suspicion were back again, stronger than ever. Blade's expression was impeccably blank and innocent, but the girl had understood whatever message he had conveyed, and her worries were back.

"Blade has a long-standing ambition to hunt strealers," she said hastily, "and of course Valhal is one of the few places—"

"Certainly! Nothing easier, but you'll have to do it before you eat, lad. Service!"

The gawky Jeevs sim imaged in instantly. "Admiral?"

"Ensign Blade wishes to go strealer spearing. They are still running?"

"Yes, Admiral." The sim writhed its long lip ruminatively. "There is a small school in the bay at the moment. And also *gaspons*." The nasal Kailbran accent made the word twang like a harp string.

A tentative snigger from Feirn's direction showed that she knew who was being caricatured. Blade did also, for his face was registering a slight frown, the first emotion it had shown.

Vaun ignored that reaction. "There you are, then, Ensign! Have you ridden a gaspon, before?"

"No, Admiral," Blade said calmly.

Vaun swung back to the sim. "Find him suitable attire, show him the way to the jetty, and be sure he understands the emergency procedures to follow when, I mean if, he gets carried out to sea."

"Yes, Admiral." Jeevs became two identical Jeevses. "Come with me, sir." one of them said.

Vaun liked a boy who knew when he was beaten. If Blade felt anger or resentment, he did not show it. If he truly did have a suicidal ambition to attempt one of the roughest, most taxing sports on Ult, then he did not show that either. "This is extremely kind of you, Admiral," he said serenely. With an almost imperceptible nod that somehow suggested a smart military salute, he spun around and went marching off after the sim, swinging his arms.

Vaun addressed the other sim. "Pick the liveliest gaspon you can find and let me know before you send out the floater."

The sim vanished with a hint of a sneer.

Feirn was staring after Blade. Then she felt Vaun's eyes on her, and turned to him with a quizzical grin that slid a stiletto of guilt between his ribs.

"He *can* swim, I hope?" he said.

"Like an eel."

"Then he is in no danger." Not too much, anyway.

She smiled understandingly. "He never is, except the danger of provoking homicide. He drives a lot of people to gnashing and clenching."

"But you . . ." Vaun demanded before he could stop himself.

Feirn glanced at the house briefly. "I trust him," she said softly.

But that was a lot less than what her eyes had said earlier, and again Vaun felt confused by this desirable minx. It was not unknown for female randoms to throw rival lovers together and watch the conflict, but to set an ensign against an admiral was absurd. Just what was she up to?

"And you, Feirn? What do you want? Really want?"

"I'd really like to see the paintings first, I think, and—"

"Stop!" He gripped her shoulders, thrilling at the cool smoothness of her skin. "Don't demean both of us with hypocrisy. I know what I want of you, and I haven't tried to conceal it. You owe it to yourself and to me to be equally honest." He watched the scarlet blush drowning the freckles again, and desire throbbed in him like a fever.

She gazed up at him for a long moment, big blue eyes wide. "I was told that Valhal is lacking a hostess," she whispered.

So Jeevs had been right! "Yes?"

"All my life I've dreamed of being hostess at Valhal for Admiral Vaun. It's my life's ambition! I know I'm very young, but—"

Now he understood those stupid twinges of protectiveness he had felt. "Feirn! How old are you?"

She dropped her eyes. "Almost seventeen," she whispered. Then she looked up again with an attempt at assertiveness. "But I've studied very hard! Mother's taught me everything! I know how to talk to a bishop, and how to judge a wine, how to divert a conversation when it gets onto dangerous ground and . . ."

Sixteen! But old enough! He tightened his grip on her shoulders, wondering if she could feel how sweaty his palms were. He knew that he was blushing now also. A chattering, inexperienced child, dreaming of being consort to a world hero . . . Only sixteen—why did that information excite him so?

"I just want a chance to try!" she said. "Don't you think I'd make a good hostess?"

*I think you'd make a really sweet fuck,* he thought. A sixteen year old running the estate of a world celebrity? It was a ridiculous notion.

"There's more to being a hostess than conversation," he said hoarsely.

She paused a fraction of a second, then nodded a solemn acceptance. "Of course!"

Ensign Blade was not going to be coming back for quite a while . . . "Now!" Vaun demanded, pulling her hard against him. *Ninety-nine percent going on a hundred . . .*

She slid her arms around his neck. She was warm and vital and thunderously exciting.

He tried to kiss her. She evaded the kiss and pressed her cheek against his. He felt, rather than heard, the whisper in his ear. "You have visitors."

The shock was paralyzing. That was what had been bothering her all along? She had started to tell him and Blade had shut her up . . . They had been ordered not to tell, of course.

No one could enter Valhal without Vaun being informed—except the top officers of the Patrol, who could override his Security.

There was only one who would dare.

Fury displaced desire.

Like the cold breath of an onrushing avalanche came certainty—plus an insight that told Vaun he had been subconsciously expecting this.

History was repeating itself. As he had done once before, Admiral Roker had come in person to enlist Vaun and send him into battle against the Brotherhood.

S UMMERTIME IS THE rainy season at Doggoth, because
the rest of the time it snows. At least once every summer, the
trainees are sent to trek up Bludraktor and plant flags on the summit. A permanent hurricane rips the flags away immediately, but
the spirit is what counts, say the instructors. The round trip is
supposed to take five days and never takes less than ten, which
means short rations or none at all on the way back. Usually that
does not matter much.

Vaun has made the trip eight times, and considers he has seen
the summit of Bludraktor more often than anyone else in the history
of the planet. This ninth trip is turning out no worse than any of
the others. In fact, the night raging outside is almost pleasant by
Doggothian standards—meaning that the tent may stand till morning and a boy can go outside for a few minutes without being
battered to pulp by hail. That does make the tent more pleasant
than some Vaun has known, because it is a very small tent for eight
adults, all with full equipment and seven with dysentery.

He lies on his back in the dark in soaking clothes and listens to
seven bellies gurgling and three boys groaning. The four girls, for
some reason, never even whimper. He thinks this will be his last
trip to Bludraktor. By next summer he will be gone from Doggoth,
dead or alive. The Q ship is coming.

Everyone but the green hands knows that the rations are spiked
on the Bludraktor jaunts, but regulations forbid throwing them away,
and very few human beings can resist food after two or three days
of strenuous exercise without it. The Bludraktor Trot, they call it,
a hallowed Doggoth tradition. When one in a tent gets it, they all
get it.

Except the mudslug. He never does, as his gut seems to be immune to the worst bugs the lab gnomes dare inflict. It's his delta
upbringing, of course; lucky stiff.

Vaun isn't sure that he wouldn't rather be ill than healthy in this
tent. His nearest neighbor is thrashing around in a near-delirium,

and someone else is struggling to climb over two or three more and reach the door before it is too late. Then, over the howl of the storm comes the sound of a torch, and the girl fighting with the flap says, "What the shit?"

Minutes later a brutal light pours in through the doorway, and a male voice bellows, "Oh, *Joshual K. Krantz*! You're a foul brood, you are! Crewboy Vaun?"

Vaun sits up, heart pounding with excitement. "Sir!"

"Get your ass out here, mister. You're wanted back at the base."

"Sir!" Vaun starts to gather his gear. The others all groan enviously. This is it! The ordeal is over and he will be leaving Doggoth. Dead or alive.

When he reaches the torch, they put him in a plastic bag and tie it around his neck so that only his head protrudes. He doesn't bother to explain that he is a safe cargo—he smells like the tent, and that is enough. He is dragged inside and left on the floor. The torch leaps up into the dark fury of the night.

Five years.

He is twenty-two now, and there is no record of anyone surviving Doggoth as long as he has. Within the first three days he understood what Tham and Yather had seen in Roker's offer. At Doggoth he has been captive in the most secure jail on Ult. At Doggoth the gnomes have had easy access to him to learn all they can about Brotherhood biology, and the instructors had obviously been told to find his limits. Thanks to Vaun, the Patrol brass now know exactly what they are up against. He hopes the information has made them all very happy.

He has learned, too, though. He is qualified in every branch of Patrol operations—communications, navigation, singularity control . . . everything. He is a one-boy Q ship crew. And he has gathered enough from the curriculum and the grapevine to see his own place in the overall scheme. He knows that there are three Q ships presently heading for Ult, and one of them is from Avalon.

That is what Roker knew from the first but did not mention. That has to be why Prior enlisted in the Patrol twenty-two years ago. And the ship is due in a few short weeks.

Vaun has no time to meditate further on his future. Four days of murderous slogging over scree and swamp, and the torch takes him back in a few minutes . . . A few more minutes and he comes pounding indoors on the double, soaking wet and half-blinded by the glare of the lights. Officers scream orders at him from all sides with the frantic impatience that only commodores or admirals provoke. His pack and gun are dragged from his shoulders while he is still running, and doors open before he reaches them, and the final doorway is flanked by two armed giants, but they do not question as he hurtles between them, into heat and brighter lights yet.

He stamps to attention and salutes as the door clicks shut at his back. He strains to breathe at regulation rate, staring straight ahead at paint peeling off the concrete wall and wondering who will have the honor of cleaning up what his boots are doing to the floor. He does not look down at Roker, who is sitting behind the table—Roker himself, in full dress uniform, flanked by two other boys of equally giddy rank. Those two suck loud breath in astonishment as they recognize the newcomer's face. Whoever closed the door at his back is remaining beside it. If Vaun were giving the orders, that one would be holding a gun.

Roker continues to study his papers for a few minutes. Then he looks up with a scowl and pushes his chair back.

"Phew! I understood you were immune to Bludraktor Trot, Crewboy?"

"Yes, sir."

"Your tentmates weren't, then." Roker's vulgarity provokes respectful chuckles from his two companions. Vaun studies the peeling paint. It is green, and the layer below it is a paler, older shade of the same green.

"You have changed since we met in my garden, Crewboy."

"Sir."

Roker hasn't. Without looking directly, Vaun can see the same gold eyebrows, the long nose, and droopy-lipped sneer. The nasal Kailbran accent is the same.

"Then you were a very bewildered young peasant. Now you are the most highly qualified boy in the Patrol—at least on paper."

"Thank you, sir." *Damn you to hell, sir.*

"Mm," Roker says thoughtfully. "You don't even sound like a Putran anymore. You know how you score on IQ tests?"

"No, sir."

"But I'm sure you know now why I sent you to Doggoth?"

"I think so, sir." The older paint is peeling in one small patch, showing a blue color below it.

"Then we must bring you up to date. What have you heard about Commodore Prior over the last few years, mm?"

Dangerous! "I understand that he is still a Patrol officer, sir."

"Not anymore. For two days now he has been shackled to a wall in Hiport."

Silence. Eventually Vaun says, "Sir."

"So are three of his cuckoos. We think they are Tong and Raj and Prosy, and Dice is the one we haven't yet located. We don't know for sure, they won't say, and I suppose it doesn't matter. They're as interchangeable as paper clips."

Vaun studies the blue paint. May he burn through eternity if he moves an eyelash for Roker.

"At ease, Crewboy."

Now Vaun can meet the pale and hateful stare.

"Vaun, you are impressive! None of us has ever read a report like this."

"Thank you, sir." *None of you will ever read anything on my face, either.*

The admiral's eyes narrow. "I remember the Doggoth grapevine, and you've had lots of time to put it all together. Remember that day we met? We speculated on the Brotherhood's strategy, mm? Well, what do you think about that now?"

The Doggoth grapevine is very effective. Vaun knows that Tham was promoted to commodore and also ComCom, four and a half years ago. Security Officer Yather is now Captain Yather. He also knows that High Admiral Frisde is well into her third century, that the upper echelons are counting days until she goes into withdrawal, and that one of the leading contenders to succeed her is Admiral Astin Link Roker Nev Spurth. Patrol politics are seething. But he is not going to mention any of *that*.

"I suspect that they had several alternative plans, sir."

"Go on. I want your thinking on this."

So the crewboy second class will lecture to three admirals, will he? Crewboy second class will do as he's told. Crewboy second class has just been warned that artificial constructs like him are put in cages now, and if he is going to be an exception, it will be only because he has shown he can behave himself.

"Sir. The primary objective will be to build a hive here on Ult and manufacture more brethren. I assume that back on Avalon— before Prior left, sir—they could not have been sure whether that would be possible, but it would be their easiest route. Second—"

"Easiest route to what?" asks the boy on the left.

Looking at him for the first time, Vaun sees another blond Kailbran, a miniature version of Roker himself, but still significantly larger than Vaun.

"To taking over the planet, sir."

His audience exchanges glances. Roker twists his lip in a sneer of distaste, but it is the third boy who speaks, the one on the right. He is dark-haired, he looks shrewd and bookish. Roker has the reputation of being adroit at picking good aides and exploiting their abilities.

"You didn't mention that objective when you were apprehended, Crewboy. Did either of the two cuckoos you met tell you that such was their ultimate purpose?"

Vaun directs his reply to Roker. "No, sir. I suspect they did not know that themselves, sir. Prior might not have told them. But I am certain now, sir."

"Why are you certain?" asks the admiral on the right.

"Did I report how they refer to . . . to normal human beings, sir?"

Roker shakes his head.

"They call you 'wild stock.' Sir."

Again the exchange of glances. The tension and anger rise.

"Go on," Roker growls. "You're correct so far, by the way. They've been trying. That's where we picked up the three cuckoos . . . an abandoned paint factory half-full of bio equipment. And of course the battle on Avalon must have been an attack on just such a secret hive. Secondly?"

"Secondly, they have sent reinforcements by Q ship." Vaun wonders how much he need spell out. In some portions of the electromagnetic spectrum, a Q ship is brighter than a star. Every incoming ship is tracked, and on arrival inspected right down to the bacterial content. The Patrol runs all the shuttles. There is no way a shipload of identical units could ever come to Ult without alerting the defenses. Interstellar invasion and warfare are dreams of pubcom fantasy, utterly impossible in practice. That is all obvious, surely? Even dumb Muscleboy must know that. "If Prior learned that he would not be able to establish a hive single-handed, his secondary mission was to infiltrate the Patrol."

"To what end?" Roker growls.

"I imagine he hoped to arrange things so that he would command the pilot boat when the ship achieves orbit, sir."

Obviously he has hit the gold. The left-hand admiral mutters oaths under his breath.

Roker appraises his companions' reaction and then nods.

"Very well done, mister. You've confirmed the official analysis perfectly. Now . . . Yes, Malgrov?"

The smaller Kailbran has been studying Vaun's face. "I think Crewboy Vaun has some more ideas to contribute, sir."

"Thirdly?" Vaun says. Are they really so dumb? Don't they know how to use computers?

"Thirdly?" Roker barks.

"They may have brought shuttles on the Q ship, sir."

"Mother of Stars!" says the one called Malgrov.

"Like an explorer ship?" Roker sneers. "Waggery?"

The bookish admiral clears his throat. "To carry even one atmospheric craft shielded against radiation would require a major change in standard design, of course. Tunneling on that scale significantly weakens a rock, and increases the cost enormously."

Yes, they are that dumb. Who cares about cost when they're playing for planets? These spacers can't think like brethren! Vaun can, maybe. His thoughts are his only coin to buy his way out of Doggoth, and when he has paid over every copper sou, then Roker may take it all and say it is not enough and give nothing in return. But to hold back anything will condemn Vaun as an enemy. This will be a war without quarter.

He offers another coin from his slender purse. "They would not require shielding, sir."

Roker's eyes send that remark to the bookish Waggery, who flushes. "After fifteen years exposed to a fireball, Crewboy, those craft would be deadly."

Vaun says nothing. Crewboys do not argue with admirals.

Roker half smiles, half sneers. "Well, what are we missing?"

"The brethren reproduce chemically, sir, not with their own body tissue. Radiation will be a much lesser danger to them."

"Krantz's turds!" says the blond Malgrov, and then sniggers. "He's right, you know! A lot of them might die of cancer in a few years, but that may not matter to them like it would to us. Almighty Mother, but he could be right!"

"They'll come down on us like a swarm of locusts!" bleats Waggery. Roker scowls under his shaggy gold brows.

Vaun has revised his opinions of the Space Patrol many times since he arrived in Doggoth five years ago as a wide-eyed adolescent, and always downward. These clam-brained admirals are doing nothing to raise it now.

Roker drums his fingers on the table for a moment. "Is there a 'Fourthly'?"

"Yes, sir."

"Tell us."

"If the pilot boat is not commanded by Commodore Prior, then they overpower the crew."

"We thought of that," Malgrov remarks. He seems to be amused at the way the conversation is going, while Waggery is angry. "That would let them bring down maybe six or a dozen boys at most, and we'd shoot it to bits anyway."

Vaun would not bet the planet on that.

Apparently Roker wouldn't either. "Six or seven qualified technicians would be enough." He does not take his pale blue gaze off Vaun. "Plus necessary equipment. What we're fighting here is an infection, an infestation. Let it once get established, and it will spread like foot rot. Go on."

"If the cuckoos have stockpiled shuttle fuel somewhere, sir?" Unmanned, a shuttle can return to orbit without the aid of the Hiport launcher. They are built that way in case they ever have to make an emergency landing . . . But admirals know such things.

Roker rolls his lip up off his fangs. "So that's what the fourth one's doing?"

That's what he would be doing if Vaun were in charge.

"Is there a 'Fifthly'?"

"No, sir."

Grunt. "Well done, Crewboy. Very well done! Thank you." Not only are the words surprising, the tone is almost gracious. Then the big man shows big teeth in a smile. "I made a wise decision when I enlisted you, Vaun. The Patrol needs boys like you. I'm going to make a place for you on my personal staff."

Vaun does not want Roker to have redeeming qualities. He wants to hate him wholeheartedly, single-mindedly. One day he is going to kill Roker for burying him alive for five years in this hell, but he doesn't want to think about that at the moment in case his emotions begin to muddy his wits. He needs all of those . . . and here comes the next thrust.

"Five years ago I asked Citizen Vaun where his loyalty lay. Now I ask that of you, Spacer!"

Vaun stiffens. "To the Empire and the Patrol, sir, according to my oath." Any other answer and he will be shackled in the cell next to Prior's.

This time Roker's stare seems to endure for an ice age. At last he says, "The traitor Prior is not being so cooperative. One thing we are seriously considering is a mind bleed. Have you heard the term?"

"Sir." Mind bleeding is some sort of last-resort technique for extracting information, but that is as much as Vaun knows. Whatever it involves, it must be his only chance of getting out of Doggoth and staying out of jail.

"It works best when donor and recipient are genetically compatible. In your case, it ought to be spectacularly successful."

And hopeless in any other, when Prior is the intended victim, for brother and random are about as incompatible as possible. For the first time Vaun begins to feel hopeful. They need him!

Roker continues. "It would be unpleasant, but not harmful—for you. Would you agree to do that for us?"

What choice does Vaun have? All he says is, "Sir!"

Again Roker pauses to think. "Well, gentlemen?"

The other two mutter hurried noises of agreement.

"Very well, Vaun. As of now, you have your commission. Ensign Vaun. And you're in the front line to help save humanity on this planet."

If he expects a gracious speech, he is going to be disappointed. "Sir!"

The admiral curls up his lip to show his big herbivore teeth again. "This is all still top secret. I've set up a situation center at Valhal, so we'll move you there, at least at first. But just because you're proof against Bludraktor Trot doesn't mean the rest of us are. Report to Doctor Thoandy in Medical."

Vaun stamps, salutes, and whirls around. He goes out on the double, and the boy who throws the door open for him is Tham, in a commodore's uniform. He flashes a brief smile of greeting as Vaun goes by.

He *is* holding a gun.

"WHAT'S WRONG?" FEIRN released Vaun and stepped back, looking worried. He was trembling with fury.

"It won't work!" he muttered, his tongue thick in his mouth. He turned around to lean on the balustrade and peer out at the bay unseeing. He felt raped. Roker had invaded his home and perverted his Security—and with unmitigated insolence had then ordered the legitimate guests not to mention his presence. Perhaps if Vaun had entered through a main door, he might have met the intruders . . . But Roker must have known he was here and had stayed in hiding. Swine!

"What won't work, Vaun?" She leaned beside him, her elbow touching his.

"Security heard what you said." Even a whisper could be detected, anywhere on the island, and be separated out from the animal noises, from the waves and leaves.

"Oh."

"But thank you. Nice try."

She was silent for a moment, then she said, "He hates you?"

"Mutual. You didn't know he was coming, did you?"

"Who? Roker? No, of course not! Blade had a major coronary." She sniggered, very softly. "He doesn't come here often, does he?"

"No he does not!"

"I think he was upset by your sims."

"I hope so!"

Swine! Now what? Then Vaun guessed the answer. He straightened up and turned around, and Roker was marching across the terrace toward him—in full dress uniform, complete with sword, his big face suffused with anger. Behind him, the door from Vaun's bedroom stood open and a half dozen security boys were emerging, as mean a crew as Vaun had ever seen. They were spreading out laterally and they were all armed.

This was not a social visit.

Roker came to a halt two paces away, working his lips as if chewing. Silence.

"Good afternoon, Admiral!" he said at last. Even at that distance, he was big enough to look down on Vaun, a behemoth of a solid muscle. Medals and braid twinkled bright in the sunlight. If he was waiting for a welcome, he would grow old waiting. After a moment he seemed to realize that, for his big jaw tightened. The Galactic Empire might be a convenient fiction, but the high admiral was de facto emperor of the planet.

"You have made some changes around here, I see."

"Improvements, sir."

The high admiral showed his teeth. His pale eyes moved to look at Feirn. Suspecting he was about to order her away, Vaun reached out and pulled her close. He was much too enraged now to enjoy the contact that had so excited him a few minutes before, but he did notice that her arm slid around him also.

"You have met Citizen Feirn, I understand?" His voice sounded satisfactorily steady, but it took effort.

"You were going to be interviewed for that scandal session on pubcom—is that correct?"

"Sir."

Now came the predictable sneer. "To reveal classified information! Secrets you blabbed at a party last night also."

"Not that I am aware of."

"Your topic was to be the Scythan Q ship?"

Vaun nodded. "It is no secret."

Roker's face seemed to grow even redder. "It certainly is, since High Command declared a state of emergency."

Vaun had not been informed, but there was no point in mentioning the obvious, and the records might not agree with his recollections anyway—the Patrol had always regarded history as more of an art than a science.

The big boy rarely came so close to losing control. How much of that anger was due to the parody of himself he had discovered in the Valhal household sim? In spite of his physical size, Roker was very small-minded, not one to tolerate mockery. He must be wondering how long it had been going on.

Let him wonder.

Roker snarled at Feirn. "Leave us!"

Thinking of the menace of those armed spectators, Vaun released her. In silence, she walked away along the edge of the terrace, not approaching the line of security goons. They were watching Vaun like crouched rapcats.

No bets that every one of them was a crack shot.

Vaun had mastered his fury now, reminding himself that the brethren were much less ruled by passion than randoms were. Anger was permissible, but to lose his temper would be a design fault. He could see that Bullyboy Roker was blustering, as he so often did—eight marksman against one unarmed boy? Absurd. And totally unnecessary. With his control of the Valhal Security, Roker could strike Vaun dead with a word.

The other shadowy figures huddled within the doorway must be the high admiral's usual gilt-embroidered entourage. If he had left them out of this discussion, then he was either up to no good or he was not sure of himself at all. And he would not have brought them to Valhal had anyone ever told him about the Jeevs sim.

Right. With studied insolence, Vaun stuffed both hands in his pockets and leaned back against the parapet. "To what do I owe the honor of this visit . . . sir?"

Roker's eyes flashed. "You resent my intrusion? But you established the precedent yourself, this morning."

"I had exhausted every other method of communication . . . sir." He had refused Roker's call as he arrived, but Roker had already been here, waiting. That had been a trick, and he had fallen for it. He reminded himself that his contempt for Roker always led him to underestimate the boy.

"And then you shot him dead!"

"At his own request . . . sir."

"There will be a Board of Inquiry, of course . . . Do you recall," Roker said, biting off each word, "a certain lecture you once delivered at Doggoth?"

"No . . . sir."

"Yes you do! You outlined the possible strategies the Brotherhood might use to infiltrate the planet. Four of them."

"Oh, yes. I do recall."

Roker came a pace closer. "You do recall! Excellent. Assume, for the purpose of this present discussion, that the ship now approaching from Scyth is crewed by the Brotherhood. Or a different brotherhood? Another family. After all, Scyth and Avalon are several elwies apart—"

"Eight, roughly . . . sir."

"Eight elwies apart. So they can't be the same brotherhood, can they?"

How much of his anger came from fear? Vaun had not thought to investigate the current state of Patrol politics. If Roker was being blamed for the pending disaster, then his crown might be working loose.

"They would be the same brotherhood if they used the same recipe . . . sir. They probably don't vary their formula very much, for just that reason."

"Explain!" Roker barked.

Vaun shrugged, wondering why he was required to repeat the obvious. "Sexually reproducing species favor their kin. A boy will normally defend his children against his nephews, his nephews against strangers, members of his own tribe or race against outsiders. His genes drive him to the aid of their own replicas, if you believe in molecular determinism. Genetic similarity generates loyalty. Two brothers have fifty percent of their genes in common. Cousins share a quarter—"

"But you, as a clone, share one hundred percent of the brethren's, don't you?"

Ninety-five percent, and the brethren were artifacts, not clones, but Vaun did not quibble. "A hive on Scyth and a hive on Avalon can work to the same recipe and produce the identical product. Thus they will be loyal to each other. If Prior were alive now, he would be just as eager to assist this new ship as he was to aid *Unity*.

Assuming that this ship . . .'' Then Vaun saw where the conversation had led. He heard the trap click.

Roker sneered in joy. "Prior is dead. Raj and Tong and Prosy . . . all dead. *But Vaun is alive!*"

Vaun took his hands out of his pockets. Suddenly the line of guards looked very much like a firing squad and he wondered if he was about to be offered a blindfold. But Roker merely pushed his advantage.

"So let us go back to that strategy lecture that I once heard from a crewboy at Doggoth. Plan One failed—now they know that a handful of cuckoos can't found a functioning hive. Plan Two failed— they no longer have a mole like Prior planted within the Patrol to help . . . or do they?''

"Sir?'' Vaun said, perplexed. Plastic surgery? No, the germ plasm was on file . . . No possible disguise would let one of the brethren slip into the Patrol now.

Roker ignored the query. "Which was plan number three? Of, yes. We're alert now, so they can't expect to launch a flight of their own shuttles and overwhelm unprepared defenses. And—fourthly— they certainly can't expect to hijack the pilot ship. So what is their fifth plan, Crewboy Vaun?''

"I have no idea. Except that the Q ship may be unmanned, a missile to take out the planet.''

"For why? For spite? For revenge? I thought the brethren were above such petty emotions?''

Vaun held the furious blue gaze steadily. "What about a preemptive strike? What if the brethren believe this is war to the death, and prefer it not be their death . . . sir?''

The irony of that theory was that it implied Roker and his Ultian Command had been lacking in sufficient ruthlessness. The idea of wiping out planets had just not occurred to them.

Roker did not like Vaun's suggestion. His mouth worked for a moment in silence before he decided to ignore it. "How about blackmail? Is there an ultimatum coming? *Let us in—or else?*''

Vaun had discarded that idea long ago. "Hold a planet to ransom? It'd never work. A few score at most against ten billion? We'd double-cross them somehow, sooner or later.''

That won a nod. "Yes, we would. So go back to Plan Three, the fleet of shuttle craft overwhelming the defenses. How about panic? Do you think they might be trying to rouse a planetful of people to such terror that social order breaks down, and the defenses can't function?''

"Seems farfetched,'' Vaun muttered, mind racing. But it

was a possibility, and maybe better than nothing. Chaos in the streets . . .

"Very farfetched. Seven-elwies-fetched. Seven light-years! But you do admit the logic?"

"I admit the possibility."

"And you were going to go on pubcom and spread the word, weren't you?"

*Oh, shit. Oh, unmitigated shit!*

"Start raising the dust, maybe?" Roker leered. "Once I asked Citizen Vaun. Later I asked Crewboy Vaun. And now I ask Admiral Vaun. *Where is your loyalty?*"

And that, Vaun thought, was a very good question in the circumstances.

"I didn't think of it," he muttered, and as an explanation it sounded weak as froth. Why wouldn't he have thought of it?

"Didn't you?" Roker's voice had suddenly gone very soft. "The smartest boy ever to pass through Doggoth—except maybe Prior, whose records were wiped. And you didn't think of it?"

"No, I didn't. I just thought that the people had a right—"

Roker lurched forward until he was almost leaning on Vaun, glaring down at him. "The people! May the Mother of Stars bless Her little folk! I'll tell you what it looks like to me, Brother Vaun! It looks like a backup plan. I don't think you ever were the great hero we made you out to be. We never had more than your own word for what happened on *Unity*. I think Abbot and his brethren saw that the game was up. Prior had been exposed and the game was up. Their mission had failed. So they blew up the ship deliberately! They killed themselves and left you alive. You were sent back to survive until the next time, to help the next attempt. *And now you're starting!*"

Roker had been a snake even before he became high admiral, and the ensuing forty-plus years had not made him any more lovable. Now he had Vaun on the dissection table. He might be going to send him after Tham in minutes. He needn't convince anyone else of the story, only himself. He could give the signal, walk away from the body, and explain later—if anyone bothered to ask.

So Vaun had better convince Roker.

"That's utter crap! That's raving psychosis! The brethren were fried and their Q ship turned into a billion tons of rubble and you're saying that they *won*? You had that same swill going round in your head when I first came back, you even accused me of not being the original Vaun, you . . ."

Roker opened his mouth and Vaun shouted him down.

"You tried to prove I was an imposter, one of the Brotherhood units, or Abbot himself—*and it didn't work*! And I was more use as a hero, anyway, wasn't I? You used me to pry more money out of ten billion hungry people so the spacers could fly a little faster and higher. And you used me to tighten your own grip on the Patrol. I was your step up to the throne, Roker. You built your career on me, and you're going to look pretty damn witless now if you come out and say it was all a mistake, the guy's a traitor after—"

"Mudslug! Upstart peon! I made you, I can break you!"

They were both yelling now.

"Crown a little loose now, Roker? Getting some heat, are you? All the minions wondering why you didn't stop the Q ship sooner? Looking for a scapegoat, Rok—"

"Mother of Stars, if I needed you as a scapegoat I'd have your ass mounted on my—"

"You big dumb prick! You've spied on me for years—"

"You haven't answered the—"

"—and you never caught me out in anything more than ringing your personal doorbell, Roker. Anytime I ogle a girl, you leap out of the shrubbery at her with a fat wallet and ask her if I talk in my sleep and with whom and how often and which way up . . ."

"Maeve, for instance?" Roker sneered.

*Maeve, Maeve!* Vaun choked into furious silence.

Roker continued, spraying a mist of spit as he shouted. "Loyal little spacer, are you? 'Loyal to the Empire and the Patrol, according to my oath!' That's what you told me at Doggoth. And I think it was true, then. I think you meant it then. But we ran the mind bleed on Prior after that, didn't we? Worked too well, I think. You picked up too many Brotherhood memories there, I think. You began to think like Prior. You got so you didn't know whether you were Vaun or Prior or both. That was when we lost you. You've been working for the Brotherhood ever since!"

"Gwathshit," Vaun snarled. "If that's the case, then it's your duty to have me shot and it's my duty to see if I'm fast enough to toss you over this railing first."

Triumph gloated in Roker's blue eyes. Vaun was blundering perilously close to threatening a superior officer, and of course Security now had his words on record. Roker's courts-martial had a tendency to be predictable and fatal. Fornicating scorpions!

The big boy waited to see if there was more to come. When there wasn't he continued, looking ominously pleased with himself. "So you want me to believe that you're loyal to the Patrol, do you? Then you won't mind proving it?"

Anything might surface now. "I am honored to serve . . . sir."

Roker curled his lip. "Where are the other two?"

"What other . . . The missing brethren?"

"The missing cuckoos, Dice and Cessine. We never did catch them, did we? Where have you been keeping them all these years? What have they been up to?"

Vaun felt much better. If Roker wanted to link him to those two, then he was welcome to try. "I don't know anything about them. I have no idea where they are, and never have had." Sincerity was wonderfully refreshing at times.

The high admiral bared his teeth right in front of Vaun's eyes. "Well, you are going to find them for me."

"I am?" Danger instincts flashed lights. He studied Roker's sneer and decided that it was unpleasantly confident. "How?"

"I'll tell you later. I have an expert coming to help you."

"That's a threat."

"Threat? No, no. Oh, not at all. You will merely demonstrate your loyalty to the Patrol by carrying out a . . . mildly risky? . . . Yes, a mildly risky mission. Of course, your courage is legendary. Quild will assist you. Together, you're going to find the missing brethren for us. Right here, in Valhal."

Roker knew something Vaun did not, obviously. There had to be something behind such insanity, something to explain the gleam of triumph in the blue Kailbran eyes.

" **A** ND LEAVE OUT the stiffener!" Vaun said.

The medic hummed and buzzed. It had already clicked disapprovingly over his bruises, but had issued no dire warnings about advancing age and extra medication and taking it easy. He still felt sour and shaky, but that was probably due to his suppressed fury at Roker, rather than to a few hours' delay in his daily booster.

He had greeted the odious collection of "guests" the high admiral had brought with him; then had watched as they quaffed his best liquor in the Rainbow Room while awaiting the banquet they had ordered. Not one of them had ever come visiting in the past. Socially Vaun did not exist, but pillaging expeditions were apparently permissible behavior for spacer aristocrats.

After enduring the fusillade of wit for a while, he had excused himself to attend to personal matters. Ironically, Tham's death had probably eased their mockery a little. Even that worthless crowd had liked Tham and now mourned him. Most of them seemed to approve of what Vaun had done.

A sinister purple position gurgled from the medic. Vaun tossed it off in one swallow. It tasted much the same as always.

It was years since he'd omitted his daily overdose of stiffener and he resented the need to do so now, but with Roker playing his deadly games in Valhal, a boy had better keep his head clear. Citizen Feirn would not be able to assume her new duties for a while yet.

So now he must dress up like a trained furpurr to entertain the parasite convention at dinner! Thinking murderous thoughts, Vaun went limping back to his own quarters, and his fury boiled up again like a pain in his throat even as the outer door dephased for him. The evidence was everywhere—people had been sitting on his bed, rummaging through his library, setting drinks down on the antique tables, sniffing croil. Every room stank of the filthy stuff. He threw open the big doors to the terrace to let in the air. This had been where Roker and his herd of flunkies had waited, eavesdropping on his conversation with Feirn and Blade and no doubt laughing their foul guts out. And if Service had not cleaned it up already, it was because Roker had given orders, so that Vaun himself could find the mess. How could anyone so petty have risen so high?

He ripped off his shirt and wadded it up. And paused. No! He was not going to dress up so he could go back and play gracious host for that gang. He could eat here . . . except that Roker's control of Security automatically let him run all of Household, so even that might refuse to obey Vaun now. Krantz! Raped and emasculated both!

He would go for a swim instead. Yes, he would head down to the bay and see how Ensign Blade was making out with the strealers or if he had already vanished over the horizon on a runaway gaspon. At the moment even Ensign Blade might seem like decent company.

Vaun also needed to view Tham's secret file, but if Roker had discovered it in the Valhal records, then that also might have vanished over the horizon. Vaun dearly wanted a peek at it, even if only to confirm that it was as useless as Tham had claimed, but it would have to wait until the marauders departed.

And this evening there would be the mysterious surprise that Roker refused to explain. *Mildly risky* sounded like a politic euphemism for *lethal*. Of course, it was impossible for the long-lost Dice and Cessine to be anywhere on the island . . . unless Roker had brought them with him. If the missing cuckoos had at last been captured and Roker could link them to Vaun in any way, then Vaun was a dead hero.

A shadow moved within brightness and he turned to the terrace doors. Crimson fires of backlighting outlined Feirn's head like a stellar corona. How could he have forgotten Feirn?

She did not wait for an invitation, and as she glided toward him, the bundled shirt tumbled from his fingers to the rug.

"Vaun?"

"I am sorry," he said, distracted from his anger by the graceful swing of those trim legs. "I did not plan it like this."

She smiled a wistful smile that knotted his heart. "I know. I am sorry, too. What you promised me . . . just the two of us, and you showing me all of Valhal, corner by corner . . . that would have been wonderful, Vaun. But maybe when the high admiral leaves?"

His blood raced insanely; she had come close enough for him to start counting freckles. Yesterday's stiffener had not worn off yet, obviously. His head would not clear for a day or two.

Red hair . . . Was his fascination with red hair common knowledge? Maeve had guessed, he recalled. If Maeve knew, then DataCen did also.

So perhaps his head was not supposed to be clear, and this cute little wench was another of Roker's spies.

"Maybe," he said, struggling with desire. "But that may not be for days. So as soon as your friend Blade finishes slaughtering strealers, he can fly you right back to wherever you came from."

He had been too harsh. She recoiled, then turned away quickly.

"You don't want me?"

"Not right now, thank you."

"But you said—"

"That was before I knew about Roker."

"Vaun?" She whispered, staring at the window. When he did not answer she continued, in a fast, nervous chatter. "Vaun, darling, I know this sounds crazy, but . . . Actually, I've never done it before. I mean most of the girls I know have been, well, you know, they started years ago, because their parents encouraged them, some of them, just kids even, and had lots of lovers ever since, but I waited, and I waited so long that now I'm scared to start, isn't that crazy? Just that first time, like jumping in a cold pool, and then I'm sure I'll be all right, but I've made such a big thing out of the first time now that, well, it is crazy, I know.''

Yes, it was crazy. He didn't know what to say next, but for some reason his excitement level was shooting straight up again like a Q ship. Never done it before? Why should that kinky idea arouse him so much?

Because it was supposed to.

''Pardon my asking, but what's wrong with Ensign Blade? You seem to be good friends.''

She continued to stare at the window, hiding her face from him. ''Oh, you won't repeat this to anyone . . . and I'm only guessing, of course . . . but I don't think he's ever done it either, and certainly not very often, and that would be silly, wouldn't it, two people both trying it for the first time and neither knowing what to do? I mean, two clumsy beginners?'' She sniggered nervously. ''But Blade says he understands, and when I'm ready, just to tell him.''

*Holy Joshual!* ''He is . . . willing?''

''Oh, yes! Quite eager, I think, actually.''

Utterly insane! But typical of the way wild stock got their whole lives entangled in their messy reproductive affairs.

''Feirn, Blade is a spacer officer. He has access . . . I mean, there is a preparation for girls called 'loosener,' and a spacer officer—''

''He won't. He says it would not be honorable.''

''Honorable? Not honorable? If you ask him?''

She sniggered again, and wiped her cheek with a slim finger. ''Blade has very strong ideas about honor.''

''Persuade him.'' Now Vaun was catching the insanity. Whose case was he arguing here?

''I'm not certain I could. Blade is awesomely well-disciplined. And it wouldn't be fair. He would hate himself afterward.''

''I'm sure he would survive . . . And where do I come in? Why me?'' he asked, while every cell in his body now was screaming *Why not?* Why did he have to get mixed up in the problems of this giddy little random?

''Well, I was told . . . I think you . . . You seem . . .''

''Who said?'' he demanded, suspicion rising again.

''A friend told me you were the finest lover she had ever known, and if I explained that I was nervous, you would be gentle and helpful, and . . . Oh, shit. I wish you'd just . . . You could have done it by now, couldn't you?''

"Maeve?"

She turned and stared at him with dismay, and then nodded.

*Maeve!* Always Maeve! He had blundered into her web like a blind bug the previous night, and he was still entangled. "This is some sort of elaborate joke, I suppose? What exactly is there between you and Maeve?"

Now the child was close to tears. "Oh, I've made a mess of this . . ."

"Tell me! What am I missing?"

"She's my mother."

With no memory of moving, Vaun had gone right by her, had reached the window, and was staring out of it.

"And she sent you to *me*?" Pimping her own daughter?

He heard a sniff. "No. It was all my idea."

"Why?" Another spy, of course. Was there no end to their foul suspicions, their prying . . .

"I told you."

"I don't believe a word of it!"

"Well, it's true!" Feirn snapped, and he turned to stare at her. He could see the resemblance now. Maeve's hair was darker, but it was certainly reddish. She had freckles, too, although not such a glorious abundance.

"And you want to be hostess at Valhal. That's the payoff?"

"Yes. I mean no!"

"There's a word for that, Citizen Feirn. It's called *whoring*!"

White-faced, she sat down on the couch and stared at him. He stared back.

"I know you're not really like this, you know," she said sharply.

"Like what?"

"Rude and arrogant, and all those things. I know that what happened between you and Mother made you twisted and bitter, and that before that you didn't hide your real self under that hard shell. I know you've had hundreds of girls here at Valhal, always hunting desperately to find a replacement for the one you really loved, but that's not the true Vaun at all, and basically you're a very loving, considerate—"

"Oh, for Krantz's sake! I suppose your dizzy mother put that crap into your pretty little head?"

Feirn was on her feet now, and yelling shrilly. "I thought you wanted to! I wouldn't force my body on anyone. I'm sorry if you find my request insulting, or demeaning, or think I'm too skinny. Maeve said she thought you were looking for a hostess, and I knew I could do that job all right because I've watched her running

Arkady, and as for the sex part, well, she's always said you were the finest lover she's ever known, so I didn't think you'd mind teaching me . . . I didn't think it was such a great favor I was asking—you looked like you wanted to *eat* me! Spacer officers are always chasing after girls. Or boys. I mean the girl officers chase boys. I thought a spacer—''

"Don't call me that!" he shouted. "I'm not one of them!"

"What? But . . ."

Krantz in a jug! What was he saying?

"Well, I am, of course." He had graduated from Doggoth. He was the Patrol's great hero. Of course he was a spacer. "It's just that . . . well, you made me think of that band of horrors that Roker has with him . . ."

Wild stock. Lust-crazed. But he'd never met anything quite like this mixed-up child before. And as for that ensign . . . "Does Blade know why you came here, or did he believe the interview story?"

Her anger faded into sad resignation. "Oh, he guessed right away. He said it would be good for me, and he didn't mind waiting if you wanted me to be hostess here for a year or two. He's very reliable, Blade, even if he is a little bit humorless. And I do wish I hadn't messed all this up."

She stooped to pick up Vaun's shirt and walked over to the door and pushed it at him in silence. For a moment he just stared at her, the shirt still clutched between them, fingers touching. He could see no guile in her jewel-bright eyes, blue and glistening. He discovered that he was inclined to believe her.

No spy, just crazy, and he felt that strange protective urge again.

"You didn't mess it up, Feirn," he said softly. "It was Roker did that."

She smiled with relief like a child forgiven. "Tonight, then? Not hostessing . . . but tonight, Vaun, please will you make love to me?"

God in Heaven! "Yes, if you want."

"Oh, thank you."

She had an innocence that was totally alien to him. Mixed-up, yes. Not especially smart, no. Sweet, but yet determined in her way. Ruthless, even, for she had no idea how cruelly she was torturing Blade. Maeve should have told . . . but Maeve did not like Blade.

Tonight, . . . he had better go back to the medic.

The sound of boots interrupted Vaun's thoughts—as if summoned by those thoughts, Ensign Blade was marching across the terrace toward him.

He was back in uniform. Or still in uniform—still flawless, looking ready to go on parade, valedictorian for Admirals' Day. He stamped to a halt, and his saluting hand rose, wavered, and hesitantly removed his cap instead. He tucked it smartly under his arm . . . his hair was unruffled, of course. His eyes avoided Vaun's bare chest and the rumpled shirt. He nodded politely to Feirn and spoke earnestly to Vaun.

"Admiral, I want to thank you for the strealer fishing. It was a very memorable and exciting experience."

The boy looked and sounded about as excited as a patch of lichen. He had no visible sprains or bruises. He was bluffing, obviously. He hadn't been out of those knife-edged pants.

"Catch anything?" Vaun asked innocently.

"Three, sir . . . I mean Admiral."

"Oh, that's very good," Vaun said with a straight face. "And you weren't gone long at all." In all his years at Valhal, only once had Vaun ever caught three strealers in one day, and *no one* rode a gaspon successfully on a first attempt. Some boys had tried for years and never succeeded even in bridling the slippery things.

The pale mauve eyes twitched just enough to show that Ensign Blade knew he was being called a liar, but he sounded completely sincere as he said, "Thank you, sir. It was mostly luck, of course."

Give him the benefit of the doubt—possibly he'd speared some bluetooths, or throilers, and didn't know any better.

"Big ones, were they?" Vaun asked.

"The sim tells me the largest is a house record for male strealers, Admiral."

*God the Mother!*

Feirn stepped forward and kissed his cheek. He blushed then.

How unexpectedly human of him.

"Congratulations!" Vaun felt shaken. "That's incredible. We'll have it mounted for you, of course."

"Oh, that would be very kind of you, sir . . . Admiral."

Vaun sighed. "As a special reward, I will even allow you to call me 'sir'."

The mauve eyes flickered again. "Thank you, sir. It does feel more appropriate."

Finally, though, a hint of satisfaction was showing on Blade's fresh-minted face. Yes, ice mining in the Oort Cloud, an extended posting . . .

Then he glanced past Vaun, somehow stiffened even more than

usual, and shot his cap back on his head. He saluted. Vaun twirled around.

"There you are, Admiral," Roker said heartily. "All finished what you were doing, mm?"

Vaun's fists clenched the wad he had made of his shirt. "I am at your service . . . sir."

The high admiral was enjoying himself immensely. "That's true. Professor Quild has arrived, so we can start as soon as the sun sets." He leered, gesturing expansively with an irreplaceable seven-hundred-year-old Palofi crystal goblet. "We are about to dine. Your other guests are starting to arrive, too, and I thought you might like to assign them appropriate rooms."

"Other guests?"

Roker nodded, curling his lips away from his teeth. "All those people at that party last night. Special powers under the state of emergency, you understand? You released an imperial secret, and we're trying to contain the damage. We have to put them some-where, so why not here?"

"You mean you're rounding up everyone who heard what I—"

"Everyone who was at Arkady." Roker gloated as he watched Vaun gauge the thrust. Then he clapped him on the shoulder. "Say, lad, why not give Maeve her old quarters in the Pearlfish Suite . . . just for old times' sake?"

Maeve? Coming back to Valhal? And nothing Vaun could do about it.

# LIFE IS IRONIC.

A torch outfitted in astonishing comfort lifts the brand-new Ensign Vaun from the harsh, mean life of the barracks at Doggoth and whirls him away into the night sky, one lonely passenger in civilian clothes, forbidden to talk with the crew. As dawn breaks the ensign arrives at the giddy opulence of Valhal and is conducted to a suite of rooms that would have shamed the most profligate empress of the Jolian Dynasty. This is not the main house, he is informed, merely outlying guest quarters, rarely used, but here he may enjoy himself. Respectful sims will answer all his questions, deliver any service, procure any dish or delicacy he requires. Robots will rush to do his bidding. He has only to ask . . . but the ensign is so weary that he just pulls off his clothes and falls into the silken sheets, asleep before his eyes close.

He awakens a few hours later with a raging fever and a headache so murderous that he cannot even see straight. He struggles out of bed to visit the john, and falls fainting to the floor.

The new Ensign Vaun likes to think he is tough. He likes to think that the genetic wizards of the Brotherhood on Avalon have crafted him a body superior to any male random on Ult. As a child he was never touched by the summer sicknesses that plagued the delta villages. He has been immune to the Bludraktor Trot and every other infection that has passed through Doggoth in the last five years. He has always done better than anyone else at enduring the physical stress so callously inflicted on recruits—mainly exhaustion and sleep deprivation, but also hunger, heatstroke, hypothermia, motion sickness, and an imaginative selection of others. He has come out of Doggoth alive and sane after five years, and that in itself is a stunning tribute to his toughness.

For the first time in his life he can experience luxury and comfort. And he only wants to die.

FIERCELY CLUTCHING THE carved ivory banister, Ensign Vaun picks his way gingerly down a staircase wide enough to march a platoon abreast. He sinks to the ankles in rug, and everywhere he looks he sees glitter—crystal and marble, gilded carvings and gold-framed art. He feels unworthy and unclean in such opulence. After all, he is only a peasant, and nothing he has learned at Doggoth will help him here.

He has endured three days of harrowing fever and two days of jelly-limbed weakness after it, and today he is going to go out and explore Valhal if it kills him.

The house seems to be deserted, apart from him. However, as his quavering legs bring him at last down to the safety of the hall, he sees a boy reclining on a padded sofa and watching his progress with a sardonic grin. He wears only skimpy red swim trunks and is wriggling bare toes in the rug. His curly hair grows to a point on his forehead. It is the comcom, seeming unusually relaxed for someone who is normally so fidgety, and who is so obviously out of place amid such finery.

Vaun himself is dressed in shorts and a singlet, as those were all he could find in his rooms, but he straightens up and . . .

"For God's sake come and sit down," Tham says, laughing. "You try to stand at attention, you'll fall over! We don't go for that bullshit here, anyway." He watches as Vaun totters toward him across the wide carpet. "Kowtow to Roker, maybe, but none of us lesser mortals."

To a lowly ensign, even a commodore barely ranks as mortal.

Sweating and panting with exertion, Vaun collapses on the seat beside him. His weakness is degrading; he feels as if he has run all the way from Doggoth.

Tham looks him over appraisingly. "Medical said you might be able to stand up tomorrow, and take a few steps the day after."

"I'll manage . . . sir."

Again Tham laughs, although not unkindly. "Ever been really sick before?"

"No, sir."

"Thought not."

Vaun gives him a studied stare. "Embarrassing for me, sir. Right after getting my commission, I mean. And being needed, now, to help against the Brotherhood."

"Yes." Tham nods faintly, but his eyes confirm what Vaun suspects. Tham is a decent boy. He obeys orders, but he has a conscience and he doesn't approve of what's happening. "You'll be all right from now on, I'm sure."

Vaun decides to trust that reassurance, and is relieved. He has been wondering what they might try next.

"Your indisposition hasn't caused any problems, though," Tham says. "We're going to do the mind bleed here, at Valhal—too many sharp eyes and loose tongues at Hiport. But it's taking time to get the equipment set up, and there've been some complications."

"What sort of complications, sir?"

"Oh . . . political stuff. Also, Roker's been clearing the place of outsiders. There's always dozens of guests around Valhal—admirals do a lot of political work at home, you know, wining and dining.

But it takes time to get rid of them. I mean, you can't just turn a president or a prime minster out on his ass! So we'd have had to keep you under wraps, anyway. They're all gone now.'' He smiles reassuringly. ''Nothing will happen for a few days yet. You'll have time to recuperate. So enjoy yourself—but do take it easy, okay? You're as weak as soap bubbles, and you won't help matters if you fall down and break an arm.''

''No, sir.'' Vaun measures the continent-wide plain between him and the front door and wonders if he can cross it without a rest in the middle.

''I'll leave you, then. Going to go hunt stingbats. When you've got your strength back, maybe I can give you a lesson. Terrific sport!'' Tham gives Vaun's shoulder a friendly squeeze, and jumps to his feet. ''Remember—take it easy!''

He goes striding along the Great Hall and disappears out the door. Vaun sets his teeth, heaves himself upright, and staggers after him.

He has achieved about eight steps when a girl comes out of a side door. She has obviously been listening.

Vaun stops and watches her approach. She is as tall as he, and very well built, and her brief garment is made of silver net and flower petals. None of the girls at Doggoth ever looked quite so striking. Of course, they were all scrawny from overwork and abuse and worry, with weather-beaten faces and hair cropped short. This one's hair is thick and shiny and a dark reddish shade. Her skin is deeply tanned all over, yet she has traces of freckles across her nose.

There is wonder in her smile.

''I'm Maeve, and I know who you are. Here, let me help you.''

He opens his mouth to protest, but she puts an arm around him and he leans on her. It ought to be humiliating, but he discovers the physical contact is strangely enjoyable. He has never felt anything quite like the texture of her skin.

''I'd heard you looked just like Prior,'' she says, ''but I wouldn't have believed . . . No, this way.''

''I want—'' He wants to go outside. She is leading him to yet another door, and he is too weak to struggle.

''I know,'' she says softly. ''But come in here a moment.''

He finds himself in a tiny cloakroom, with a toilet and vanity.

''Sit,'' Maeve says, closing the door. Bewildered, he sinks down gratefully on the toilet seat. He is sweating again, as if he has been running.

She leans against the towel rail, folds her arms, and grins at him.

"There are very few places in Valhal that aren't monitored, and this just happens to be one of them."

Vaun says, "Oh!" suspiciously. Tham has just been hinting that there were people around earlier who should not meet the Prior replica, but that they have now departed. But Tham did not give Vaun specific permission to talk freely with anyone he meets.

The girl seems to read his thoughts, for her smile grows broader. "I'm not trying to worm information out of you, Ensign. I just want to tell you a few things."

"Yes, ma'am."

"Maeve. Call me anything else and I'll kick you in the crotch."

"Maeve, then. Certainly, Maeve. Anything you want."

She laughs and pulls an arch expression. "Anything? You're in no state to promise that!"

"Probably not." Vaun remembers what the med officer told him back at Doggoth about adding stiffener to his daily booster. Suddenly he thinks he might like to try that. The girls at Doggoth never interested him, even when they were running around doe-naked in the showers and the other boys were harassing them and visibly lusting after them. A body is a body . . . but this heavy-breasted girl in her flower petals is exceptional. He'd quite enjoyed touching her skin.

She smiles cryptically. "I'm official hostess at Valhal. You know what that means?"

He has a rough idea, but he says, "No, ma'—Maeve, I mean."

"It means I am charming to guests, and see that they get whatever they want from Household, and I sleep with Roker."

Vaun puts on his poker face. "I see."

"And sometimes with the guests—if he tells me to, or I take the fancy."

He's heard stories at Doggoth, of course. Aristocrats do not have the same standards of behavior as peasants. "Why are you telling me this?"

She shows her teeth. Very pretty teeth. "Because I don't approve of what's going on." The red highlights in her hair are fascinating.

"No?" He doesn't approve, either, of course, but he senses a trap. He knows he is on dangerous ground, having intimate chats with the admiral's own girl. A washroom is not romantic, but it is a suspiciously private site for a meeting.

"Your sickness, for example. You know what caused that?"

"Overstrain, I expect. I was on an arduous cross-country—"

"Shitty shoes, boy! Prior is a lot smarter than that."

"They gave me some shots before I left Doggoth," Vaun says cautiously. "I expect I had a reaction to one of them."

"You were pumped full of attenuated virus vaccine. They've been trying to develop something that will infect the brethren and not the rest of us. Did you ever meet the one called Tong?"

Vaun shakes his head.

"They found a bug that would kill him. It wasn't easy."

Vaun shudders, then reminds himself that this is war.

"Obviously the vaccine needs a little more work, shall we say? But you lived, and they think you're now immune. Trouble is, it's about a hundred percent fatal to normals, too. I think they'll forget about germ warfare from now on—you designer boys are tough."

"How do you know this?"

"I snoop." Maeve turns to the mirror above the vanity, and examines her face. She can watch him from there, too, though. "Prior came here quite often."

"Yes?"

"He's very good."

"In bed?"

"Usually in the bushes, but that's what I meant. They've been spiking your booster. And really vicious doses, too, I think."

That explains things, then.

His face must have given him away, because Maeve laughs, and moves her body suggestively. "When you've got your strength back, we'll see. Listen, Ensign. I don't like all this. Mind bleeding is barbaric, and I enjoyed Prior. Yes, I know there's a war on, but I don't like it. I just want you to know that you've got a lot of stroke in this affair."

"I do?" Vaun feels like the humblest pawn in the galaxy.

Maeve swings around to face him. He cannot stop his eyes prowling around over her delectable body. He cannot help wondering what happens when the petals fall. And she knows that.

"Yes, you do. They're going to try to put you in Prior's place, right? He planned to go up with the pilot boat to meet the Q ship, so you're going to go instead, right?"

"I don't know." But he assumes that is the plan.

"And Prior must know some sort of password, right? That's what the mind bleed is for, because they can't trust him to tell them the real password. I'm told the usual drugs don't seem to be working, and if they torture him, he could lie. You, though, they can trust." The bountiful lips shape a crafty smile.

"I'm loyal to the—"

"Oh, don't be a fool, boy! Roker isn't, however much he likes to play the part. Why would they trust you? Give me just one good reason!''

"Prior raped my mother."

"And Roker buried you alive in Doggoth. You know how it feels, now."

Roker has sent her to find out Vaun's loyalties. Perhaps when she discovers them, she will tell him, too, because he doesn't know them himself. All he does know is that, after five years in Doggoth, if he had both Prior and Roker in his sights and only one charge left in the magazine, Prior would live.

The big girl leans forward a little as if to impart a secret, and her breasts move within the netting. "They'll have to bribe you as well."

Of course they will! Why hasn't he seen that?

Maeve steps across to him and puts a hand under his chin and lifts his face up. She is so close he can feel the warmth of her, and smell her musky scent. Her eyes are dark and intense, and embers glow in her hair.

"They'll ask you what you want as a reward, Ensign."

"They will?"

Maeve smiles grimly. "Don't sell yourself too cheaply. I learned that a long time ago."

"What do you recommend as a reasonable price?"

"Demand the frigging world. They'll promise you anything at all—make sure you ask for it."

With a sudden shiver of excitement, Vaun knows there is one thing he wants that he has never wanted before. "Will they keep their promises?"

"It may be possible to arrange things so they have to." She studies him darkly for a moment. "There are many ways to trap ordinary people, but you are a lot different. That's why they've been spiking your booster. Understand?"

"Yes, I think so."

"Soon they'll start flaunting girls around you. Girls they trust. They want all the holds on you they can get. Follow?"

He nods. "Why are you telling me this?"

"Because I want you to have a fighting chance in the bargaining. Because Prior made me feel important. Because I despise Roker."

That seems improbable. She sees his disbelief, and her tone grows more urgent. "When I sleep with him that's all I do. Oh, he can fake it when he has to, but his taste runs to juvenile males."

Even after five years in Doggoth, this is beyond Vaun's understanding, but then the whole copulation idea has always disgusted him. "Why doesn't he use stiffener, then?"

"Oh, he does. Then he runs to *more* juvenile males."

Vaun thinks about that with all the old distaste. "Was that why Commodore Tham was parading around in next to nothing?"

Maeve shrugs cryptically. "It's not his way, but he may have been told to see how you were leaning."

"No. Not me." But the other thing seems a lot more understandable now.

"Good. Now listen, ensign boy, if what I told you about Roker ever leaks out, then he'll never get to be high admiral, and that's what he's after. If he learns I told you, he'll probably feed us both to the raptors. Can I trust you not to betray me?"

Vaun nods. He levers himself upright, and he is much steadier on his feet than he expected. She melts into his embrace, and their mouths meet.

AFTER AN ABSENCE of years, Roker had returned to Valhal in triumph, accompanied by a verminous crew. The high admiral himself was a perfect turd, but some of his companions were worse. The shrewd advisers he had favored in the past, like Waggery and Malgrov, were long gone. Now he consorted with trash—Gargel, Legarf, Tawlet, Lepo—a collection of the most insufferable, incompetent sycophants in the Patrol, carefully selected for their ability to annoy Vaun, no doubt. And now they feasted and wassailed in the Great Hall like a victorious gang of Viscan raiders.

Vaun picked listlessly at his food as each masterpiece was laid before him. Obviously whoever had selected the menu had spared him no expense: strealer caviar, iced firebird from Gangador, jellied dilforms' tongues, arctic truffles . . . And he noted glumly that the most jealously guarded corner of his wine cellar had been looted also.

Roker was enjoying himself hugely, booming out ribald stories that his cronies applauded with cannonades of fabricated mirth. In between times, the others splashed acidulous wit in Vaun's direction and made poisonous asides that he was expected to hear.

He had been carefully placed between two women he detested, Admirals Gargel and Boorior. Gargel was a deadly bore, also a notorious flirt, and reputedly as dull in bed as she was at conversation. Making passes at Vaun would not be politic at the moment, so she chattered of nothing at great length, when she was not giggling and sniggering with her neighbor on the other side.

The awful Admiral Boorior was worse, needling Vaun like a embroidery pattern for everyone else's amusement. Boorior had a bony, angular figure and a hatchet face. He disapproved of her appearance, her politics, and her recreations. Only once had he ever accepted an invitation from her, and then she had clawed him half to death, forcing him to use his strength in ways he preferred not to.

"All these crumbling antiques!" she proclaimed. "So dull and musty! I do think Valhal was much nicer in the old days."

Roker picked up on that. "When Maeve was running it, you mean?"

"Well, it does take a girl's touch to make a place a home."

"One girl?" Roker said, and smirked around so that the audience would know to laugh.

"One girl at a time," Boorior agreed. "Or at least for longer than a week."

The dessert came at last.

"This is an excellent wine," Boorior said poisonously. "A celebrated year. I had no idea that there was any of this left in existence."

"I agree, my dear," Roker said heartily. "Let's have a few more bottles brought up, shall we?"

Vaun smiled thinly. "Why not? After all, we have only a few more weeks left to enjoy such trivia, haven't we?"

Roker scowled darkly. "Perhaps less than that, for some of us."

The audience laughed uneasily.

"But let us not be morbid!" The high admiral's face was flushed with drink and triumph. "This should be a joyful occasion." He did not explain why, but then a high admiral never needed to explain. "Tawlet? Give us a song."

Vaun flinched. Tawlet was a small, darkish man. He had no special reputation as a singer, but he was a notorious bootlicker. He hiccuped, smiled out of focus, and finally launched into a vulgar ballad.

Roker joined in, as a signal that everyone should.

Vaun could take no more. He was halfway to the door by the time his chair fell over with a crash. He heard Roker bellow his name over the tumult, but he did not stop. Slamming the door behind him, he broke into a run. He needed to find a burrow and lick wounds.

THE CLIFF HOUSE was the only place on the island where he could be certain of being unobserved, the one place where Security had no detectors. Even Roker could not be aware of it, because Vaun had discovered it himself while rock climbing, later tracing the access tunnel back to a bricked-up doorway in the cellars. With Maeve's help, he had refurbished it from a pestilential ruin to a cozy bower for two, a hideaway overlooking the bay, fashioned ages ago from a natural cave, high on a steep face.

After he had thrown out the traitor, Vaun had shunned it for years. Eventually he had taken to using it when he wanted solitude. He rarely even brought girls there, although that must have been its original purpose. It was a convenient refuge from the randoms' endless twittering over power and sex; it was a handy studio for pursuits he preferred not to advertise, like painting and sculpture. The unknown geniuses who had designed his psyche had not neglected his artistic talents, for which he had always been grateful.

The household robots never came to the Cliff House. That afternoon it clearly demonstrated their value. Just comfortable informality, he told himself as he looked around; the detritus of books and sketches and garments that covered floor and furniture was a distinctive personal statement, an antidote to the perfection of the rest of Valhal. Pig's nest, retorted his conscience; slovenly and disgusting. Dirty glasses, dried-out pots of clay . . . he rarely let it get this bad. The bed was still rumpled from a half-forgotten visit by the Archpontiff of Caslorn's sprightly lady.

Pouring himself a tumbler of the fine Gisthan brandy he had collected on his way through the cellars, Vaun slouched down in a soft chair, and wished that whoever had designed his liver had made it less efficient at metabolizing ethanol. Getting really drunk was almost impossible for him. There were other drugs, of course, but he would need his wits clear by sunset, when Roker unveiled his mysterious surprise.

For some time, Vaun sat and tried to deduce what that surprise might be, but halfway down the tumbler he gave up the task as fruitless. When he reached for a refill, he realized that he had been brooding about Maeve instead, and that was even more unproductive . . . more than forty years since he had discovered her treachery and thrown her out . . . almost fifty since he had overcome the Brotherhood and returned to glory and a hero's rewards . . . almost *seventy* since that addle-witted girl in Puthain had borne the freakish black-haired son she thought had been conceived by God to save the world.

Pouring a second glass rather shakily, Vaun decided that saving worlds should be a onetime thing. Worlds ought to stay saved. Once was definitely enough.

Small wonder he had not been recognized at Maeve's party. In natural biological terms, he was getting old. He couldn't recall what the natural human span was—and his might be different—but probably less than a hundred years, and a lot less if you discounted the final decrepitude. With good booster he would escape that altogether, and enjoy another virile century or more before that sudden disintegration he had seen so terribly in Tham.

He thought he had earned that century. He was entitled to it! Girls. Parties. Strealers. Even painting . . .

Then he realized for the first time that he had been unwittingly staring at the board on his easel, and for so long that if he closed his eyes now he saw it on the inside of his eyelids. It was an imaginative representation of a nude reclining on grass, decked in sunshine and flower petals. He'd dashed it off one blue afternoon weeks ago, and forgotten all about completing it. She had auburn hair, he noticed, hauling himself out of his chair. Too voluptuous, he decided, picking his way through the litter toward it. Not as pretty as Feirn, he mused, carrying it over to the balcony. Worthless waste of time, he concluded, hurling it far out into space. He watched it swoop and flutter off into the void like a wounded bird, following it with his eyes until it plunged into the surf.

He wondered what the brethren painted, on Avalon, or Scyth. Themselves? Lying on grass surrounded by flower petals? There were no female units in the Brotherhood. Dice had explained that to him on the boat—the male form was more effective. The female body was physically weaker, subject to unwanted attentions from male randoms, and too much taken up by reproductive organs that technological species no longer required.

Did they know what they were missing? he pondered, as he hurled his glass after the painting.

There was a small com unit in the Cliff House, although Security had it registered as being located in one of the Bay Cabins. Vaun switched it on manually, and slumped back into his chair. He might reveal himself to Roker . . . worse, he might reveal the secret file to Roker . . . but in his present plight, risks were necessary.

"Service!"

The female sim imaged in at once, and lounged seductively against the easel, which would have toppled over at once had that been a real girl leaning on it.

"What progress in deciphering the message we received this morning?"

"None, Admiral!" It sighed. "We need the key. Sir, forty-two guests have arrived, and I understand that another two hundred are expected shortly. I need directions about accomm—"

"Put them anywhere you want! Try decoding that file with 'Ootharsis of Isquat'."

The sim vanished. So did that end of the room, with everything it contained, including the easel.

"Machines are good at analyzing data," Tham said from the far side of a goldwood desk, "but they are less adept at analyzing the absence of data." He fidgeted with a book for a moment, and then smirked rather shamefacedly out of the simulation. "At any rate, that's my excuse for recording a few hunches."

"Dammit, Tham! Why didn't you warn me? Two years, boy, you kept it bottled up."

"Look at this," the image said, and dissolved into a street scene, noises of voices and motors, people in strange clothes hurrying along a shadowy alley.

"Save me the party tricks, Tham," Vaun said grumpily. "It's you I want to see. Your smile. Your—damnation—laugh!"

"Did you notice?" Tham had returned, still smiling. "That was from Scyth, recording in 29,416, our time. Nothing unusual, except that it seems very peaceable for an obvious slum. No one very nervous."

"You always did like secrets and mysteries, you bastard. Why didn't you confide in me? I could have helped, couldn't I? Cheered you up?"

"Did you notice the cops?"

The scene returned momentarily, a still shot of two uniformed boys extracted from the rest of the crowd. They might have been Raj and Dice. Or Abbot and Prior. Or Vaun and Vaun. Brethren.

The brandy fumes began to condense. Vaun sat up.

"That's just one example," Tham said. "Now look at this. This was the one that tipped me off. It's a newscast. The boy on the balcony is some big shot, making a speech. See there, behind him? An adviser, or a minister? A secretary, perhaps. Now this one—observe the spacer driving . . ."

Five or six clips flashed in sequence, obscuring the easel and paint-spattered table and the shelves behind. Sunlight from the window was climbing the walls, now, but Vaun was intent on the picture show, no longer worrying about Roker.

"So." Tham was back again, looking a little smug in his self-deprecating way. "There's the pattern. Never making the speeches or cutting the ribbons, but always in the background. That's not what we saw on Avalon! They couldn't have been secret, not so many of them, and did you notice the absence of visible repression? Back a century or so, right after the Great Plague, the surviving Scythan cultures—"

A hinge creaked. *"Discontinue!"* Vaun barked as he lunged for the bed—for the gun below the pillow. He whirled as Tham vanished, and Ensign Blade stood in the doorway, staring into the deadly lens. Then he looked at Vaun and raised his eyebrows. Behind him was Feirn, hand over mouth.

"Ill-begotten idiot!" Vaun yelled. "You almost died!"

"I apologize for the intrusion, sir," Blade came smartly to attention, staring over Vaun's head. "I thought there would be more doors."

"And I thought you were Roker!" Vaun tucked the gun in his belt.

Blade frowned slightly at the implications, and then went blank again. He seemed quite unperturbed by his narrow escape, but Vaun saw his mauve eyes surreptitiously scan the room.

"If I knew you were coming, I'd have waxed the floor."

"Sir, the high admiral sent me to tell you that he is ready for you."

"Tell him to come himself!" Vaun's anger had returned and encountered enough residual brandy to brew a potent mixture. Worst of all, perhaps, was the bitter knowledge that he so often underestimated Roker. Which girl had run from that bed to report the secret love nest? Of course, the big boy had more sense than to come himself, here beyond Security's vision.

Blade turned and spoke to Feirn. "Tell Admiral Roker that we're coming, please." He closed the door on her. Then he swung back to Vaun.

"We are, are we?" Vaun said.

Blade took a step forward.

Vaun pulled the gun from his belt. "Over your dead body."

Blade stopped and made his irritating little frown again. "Sir, the high admiral—"

"Screw the high admiral!" Of course, that had been another of Maeve's lies, and Vaun should have realized it years earlier than he had. Roker had no interest in juvenile males. And the little cloakroom in the guest house . . . It had been when Vaun discovered how well it was supplied with sensors that he had recognized the extent of Maeve's treachery.

Blade sighed. "Sir, I have orders to bring you."

"And a good spacer obeys to the death?"

"Yes, sir," Blade said sadly.

He probably meant it, too. This was the boy who had speared three strealers and come back without a bruise.

Vaun was beginning to feel extremely foolish. "Even if I didn't have a gun, you couldn't force me, you know. Big Pig himself might, but you can't."

"No, sir. But I have to try."

"Are you human?"

"Sir?" Blade eased another step closer. The room was very cluttered for fighting. There were two chairs and a pile of paintings and a stool between them.

Vaun clicked off the safety. "Are you a random, or another construct, like me? Another, better formula, perhaps?"

The mauve eyes were dark in the fading light, very sincere. "I am quite human, sir. I am not better than you, not in anything. I know that from your record at Doggoth." He was taller, but not much heavier. His youth would be a serious handicap against an experienced brawler like Vaun. "We all studied it, sir."

Vaun grunted, then spoke to the com. "Service, access DataCen. Verbal report: Doggoth record of Ensign Blade."

"Blade Strong Virtu, born 29,385, only son of—"

"I must tell Maeve you have no choice," Vaun said.

"Sir?" Blade advanced another step.

"Your name."

The com was still talking. ". . . with extreme distinction, First in class of ninety-three, First in physical proficiency training, First in electronics, First in Galactic, First in gravitics, Expert in marksmanship, First in navigation, First in ordnance, First in physics, First in track . . .''

For a random, it was an awesome litany of accomplishment. Blade was on record as the best all-around student since Admiral Vaun, forty-eight years earlier. The catalog of his honors rolled on and on, but he seemed to take Vaun's interest in it as some sort of mockery, for his face grew grimmer and his lips whitened. He continued to edge forward.

Eventually Vaun snapped at the com to cease. "Were there any possible Firsts you missed?" he inquired.

Blade had arrived within reach, and too close to watch both the gun and Vaun's eyes. His attention flickered up and down uncertainly. His next move must be open violence, and while he might have met the situation often enough in a gym, this was reality, against a real weapon. He would not be reassured by the total lack of concern Vaun was projecting.

"Political history, sir. Martial arts.''

"Why not martial arts?''

"Broke my arm, sir.''

He was fortunate that his classmates had done no worse than break his arm. Vaun tossed the gun over his shoulder, to land on the bed. "If I'm not up against a First, then I don't need that. Know something? You're too precious to shoot, anyway! The Brotherhood would likely pay real well for a sample of your genes; they're always keen to improve their mix.''

The lad's eyes flickered as they did when he was suppressing anger—or what would be anger in ordinary wild stock. There could be no doubt that he was human, though. Doggoth's gnomes would have checked his cell nuclei very carefully.

Vaun smiled. "So go ahead and take me in by force. I rarely back down for ensigns.''

At last the ridicule drew blood. "It was easy for you," Blade said bitterly. "You're naturally superior.''

"And it wasn't easy for you? You were obviously far superior to anyone else in the school.''

"No, it wasn't easy," Blade said, but still very quietly. "I worked like hell for it, every minute. Ever since I was seven years old, I wanted to come as close to being like Admiral Vaun as I possibly could.''

His mother was quartermaster at Hiport; he would not have been a mudslug misfit as Vaun had. But nobody as effective as Blade could ever have been popular, even had he been gifted with a sense of humor and a few human weaknesses. And now he was obviously planning a jump.

"You're too perfect for your own good," Vaun said reflectively. "Wits all fouled up by juvenile dreams of honor and heroism. And you have never suffered enough humiliation; I can tell. Very character-forming, humiliation. Leave now, because once I get started, I'll surely do you a favor and beat all that shit out of you."

Blade smiled thinly. "I would prefer that you strike first, sir."

"Think you've got a chance?"

"None at all, sir. But I'll still try."

Vaun ought to be feeling much madder by now. Where was his adrenaline? Blade's lips were white, but he wasn't flinching, and that should have been enough to rouse Vaun's blood lust. "I'll make a terrible mess of you."

"I expect you will, sir."

Crazy, suicidal bonehead! "Why? What's Roker planning, do you know?"

Blade hesitated. "Feirn knows of Quild. She says he's an authority on pepods, sir."

Gods and stars! Pepods? Vaun's heart stopped and started running again, but not running on brandy anymore.

"Oh, that's it!" he said, and shivered. "I see. Of course." What a fornicating awful way to die!

"Sir?"

"I'll tell you what the high admiral is planning. He's going to feed me to the pepods."

"That seems unlikely, sir." Blade had sensed the fight draining out of Vaun; he relaxed enough to lick his lips.

"Even if you believed me," Vaun sighed, "you'd still try to take me to him, wouldn't you?"

"Yes, sir. It's my duty, sir. And yours."

He did mean it. And he was too good to shoot. Too good, Vaun reluctantly decided, even to suffer what Vaun had done to that overloud lieutenant the previous night. And to repeat that exercise now would give Roker all the excuse he wanted, anyway.

"All right," he said wearily. "Let's go! Take me in."

Wild stock pursued territory almost as obsessively as sex. Roker had found a really fun way to win back Valhal, which Vaun and Maeve had stolen from him, so very long ago.

IN HIS MINT-NEW uniform, Ensign Vaun stands so rigidly at attention that he almost vibrates. He stares stonily ahead at the high crystal windows, and the endless ocean beyond, running blue to meet the sky. All around him, the big salon shimmers with rich fittings and furniture, and also with the braid and medals of its occupants. Slumped back at ease in the down-packed chairs and sofas are the assembled nabobs and shoguns of the planet, the admirals of Ultian Command assembled. They are gazing in fury at this perfect replica of the Commodore Prior they have known for so long.

Power and wealth.

The undoubted center of the array of might is High Admiral Frisde herself. Her uniform outshines all others, glittering with jeweled honors and orders; one glance from her green eyes can silence even Roker. Close beside her on her divan sits an incongruously humble captain with a thick neck and long eyelashes. He has the excessively broad shoulders of a Galorian, and her slim hand rests on his thigh.

But Maeve has explained Frisde for Vaun. Two hundred and thirty years old, perhaps even two-forty, she has been high admiral for over a century, and a ruthless destroyer of potential successors. She changes lovers frequently, and flaunts them as proof of her continuing vitality; she revels in scandal.

From what Vaun can see while staring fixedly over her head, he would be more than willing to oblige her in scandal making. Gorgeous! The thought reminds him of Maeve, and her parting good-luck kiss when he was summoned to appear before this council.

The council now awaits the high admiral's comment.

"Yes, the resemblance is astonishing," she says at last. Her voice is low and husky. "Say something, Ensign. The Pledge of Allegiance might be appropriate."

As stiff as an automaton, Vaun recites the ancient words.

"The accent is wrong, of course. But we can correct that. At ease, Ensign."

That means *Look at me!* so Vaun obliges.

Frisde continues to study him for a moment, and then removes her hand from the husky captain's thigh. "In what ways do you differ from genuine human males, Ensign?"

*Krantz!* What is she hinting? "Only in biochemical detail ma'am, so far as I am aware. I understand I have fewer than the normal number of chromosomes . . . things like that."

"Nothing that can be detected by the naked eye, you mean?"

A few of the onlookers smile uncertainly, but Vaun feels a sudden flush heating his face. "That is correct, ma'am."

Frisde smiles mysteriously, and looks at Roker. "He is really as durable as the Doggoth reports say he is? An all-round super-achiever?"

"Apparently, ma'am. He seems to learn anything without even trying. He caught his first strealer on a second attempt."

*And I caught your mistress, Roker. I have even bedded your own girl in your own bed, Roker. Ask Security to play it back for you, Roker.*

Apart from Vaun himself, Roker is the only person standing. The boys sitting around him are people Vaun knows to be his especial cronies and advisers: Waggery, Malgrov, Shrin. Again, Maeve's briefings make sense of the roiling undercurrents of tension in the room. Frisde is well past the normal age of withdrawal—gossipmongers whisper that she needs booster every two or three hours now, and rejection can not be long delayed. The scavengers are fighting for first bite at the carcass, and Roker's coup in unmasking Prior has catapulted him into lead position. His opponents are ganging up in desperation, and Frisde has called this meeting to adjudicate.

If she backs Roker, then he will have won. Always in the past, though, she has ruled by division, slowing the pack by felling the leaders.

Obviously she still enjoys the game. She is being cryptic. "Ensign, I understand that you have agreed to participate in a mind bleed of the prisoner Prior."

"Ma'am."

"You have never met him?"

"No, ma'am."

"I suppose he must be much older than you, but biologically he is your twin brother. You must know what will happen to him. How do you feel about destroying your twin?"

"Ma'am, he raped my mother. He drove her insane."

Frisde purses her lips, and nods. Her gaze wanders thoughtfully around the august company. "Are there any precedents for mind bleeding a commodore?"

The silence stretches slowly, until a stringy, oddly red-faced boy says, "Evidently not, ma'am, or Admiral Roker would have recited them for us."

Frisde looks up at Roker. Her neck is no thicker than Vaun's forearm.

Roker's long lip curls only slightly. "If you recall the history of the *Thunderstrike* Mutiny, ma'am, you may agree that what was done to the leaders was considerably worse than a mind bleed."

She pulls a face. "I hope we are not going to slide back into the barbarism of ancient times, Admiral. Let me have a show of hands . . . a preliminary sense-of-the-meeting. How many feel that a mind bleed is justified under the circumstances?"

Vaun dare not peer around to watch the result, but he can see Roker, and Roker is displeased. No totals are announced, and perhaps the high admiral does not bother with an exact count.

"You do not seem to have convinced us yet, Admiral," Frisde says sweetly.

Evidently Prior's fate has been made the point of issue. The lines are drawn there.

The ruddy boy raises a hand, and Frisde's glance gives him the floor. "With respect, ma'am . . ." He must be one of the leaders of the anti-Roker coalition, for the room stills. "All I can see here is that some curious charges of rape have been brought against Commodore Prior, and he has reserved his defense. Quite understandably so. We may ask why the matter has been suppressed for so long—five years, isn't it? I agree that there is enough evidence to proceed to a court-martial on those charges. The rest is all cobwebs, ma'am."

Frisde waits, and he shrugs and continues.

"We have been given no proof of this alleged war on Avalon. We were merely shown a couple of ambiguous com interceptions, fragmentary and cryptic. They would not be admissable in any courtroom, civil or military. The testimony of the last emigrants is contradictory and hearsay. They think that some enclave of illicit technology was destroyed at some obscure settlement in a remote corner of the planet . . . when was it?"

"By our calendar, it would be 29,364," Roker says coldly.

The other smiles nastily. "And how long was that before *Green Pastures* left Avalon?"

"Seven years, Ultian years."

"Prior was a cadet then, was he not? Your witnesses do agree on one thing—that Prior was an adolescent when the journey began. He could not have been more than a child at the time of the trouble, whatever it was. Now another ship is arriving from Avalon. Absolutely no evidence has been put forward that it is anything other than a routine interstellar—"

Roker breaks in. "Prior appointed himself to command the pilot boat."

The tall boy seems to snuggle down more contentedly in his comfortable chair. "Unusual, but hardly seditious! And perfectly natural. He was born on Avalon. He would be interested in hearing news of his former world."

He flashes a rosy smile up at Roker, as if asking him to confirm the score. Then he returns to addressing Frisde. "Absolutely no evidence has been presented that standard security precautions would not suffice, ma'am. They could be augmented, perhaps. We might go that far. But to trash the constitutional rights of a senior member of the Patrol and subject him to the barbarity of a mind bleed . . . that should need evidence, ma'am! Real evidence!"

All eyes switch to Roker, whose head has drooped low on his bovine shoulders. He glares across at his opponent. "We are not contemplating an attack by pirates here, nor a canoe full of cannibals! Our standard security can detect ordinary subversive elements, yes, and I am not suggesting that any sort of conventional armed invasion across interstellar distances could ever be more than the stuff of pubcom fantasy. No, this is a disease we are fighting! Let the infection once gain a hold, and we may never stamp it out! One boatload of technicians and supplies would be enough."

He is not very convincing, Vaun thinks. An impalpable mist of disbelief seems to rise from the distinguished audience. Ingrown aristocracies are never cordial toward revolutionary ideas.

"You are risking the whole planet for one boy!" Roker barks.

Worse—he will have to do better than that.

Vaun wonders what his own fate will be if the mind bleed is refused. Then he will be merely one more piece of evidence to be thrown in jail and held until the Q ship has been inspected and the truth discovered. Before that happens, much of the evidence may vanish in the labyrinthine obscurity of Patrol politics, especially when the stakes are so high. And if Roker is wrong, if crew and passengers are normal human beings . . . then what?

He has enjoyed two wonderful weeks with Maeve in the paradise of Valhal, but a Putran mudslug does not belong in this lofty, shim-

mering world of power. He will certainly never be tolerated within
the Patrol on a permanent basis, and the best he can hope for—the
very best—is to be thrown back in his swamp. The meeting is
concerned with Prior. Nobody here or anywhere cares about Vaun's
welfare . . . except Maeve, and for all her noble birth, she is only
a spacers' recreation girl.

The ruddy-faced boy smells triumph. "After all," he says jo-
vially, "if the human race is indeed battling such a peril on Avalon,
then surely Avalon Command would have sent us a warning? Radio
waves do still travel faster than Q ships, surely?"

Roker smiles.

Before he can seize the opportunity presented, Frisde demon-
strates that she can still cut both ways. "Ensign?"

Vaun is so taut already that he can not stiffen further. "Ma'am?"

"Answer Admiral Hagar's objection."

*Ouch!* "Q ships travel along line of sight, ma'am. Their singularities generate interference which impedes radio transmission between the destination and the world of origin . . . ma'am."

Kindergarten stuff. The room squirms.

"Thank you," Frisde says agreeably. "I thought there was some
rule like that."

Hagar's face has turned an unbelievable scarlet.

The high admiral lays a hand on her escort's knee and another
on the arm of the divan, and flows easily to her feet. She saunters
forward to inspect Vaun more closely. Her delicious red lips still
wear traces of a smile, but what he sees in her eyes appalls him.
He wonders which is more dangerous to meddle with—the Brotherhood, or High Admiral Frisde. He realizes with shock that his
present peril is even greater than Prior's.

She stands in front of him, and yet speaks to the whole room.
Her voice is the purr of a starving predator. "We must not forget
that there is more at stake here than the fate of one commodore.
Ensign Vaun?"

"Ma'am?"

"This Q ship will be arriving very soon. It may represent a
considerable threat to our . . . to our culture. Admiral Roker reports that you are willing to attempt an investigation to confirm—
or disprove—its hostile intent. If it is hostile, then it will be because
it is crewed by more facsimiles of yourself."

The green eyes have noted the sweat he can feel running on his
face, and they glitter in contempt.

She has paused, though, so he says, "Ma'am."

"In that case, they will certainly regard you as a turncoat, and you will be in extreme danger."

Here come the big, big questions. Fortunately—oh, how fortunately!—he has been well coached by Maeve.

"You are willing to undertake this mission?"

"Ma'am."

*"Why?"*

"I am loyal to the Empire, ma'am."

She smiles sardonically. "And at the moment you really don't have any choice, do you? If you don't cooperate, it's lab cage for you . . . right?"

Vaun says, "Ma'am?" as if shocked.

"Understandably, you prefer to keep your body cells assembled in one place, so naturally you wish this mission to proceed. So far your motives are clear. But if it does not proceed. Ensign, there must come a time when you do have a choice. You will be in communication with the Brotherhood—assuming the ship is what Admiral Roker suggests it is. You will be impersonating Commodore Prior. You will be in command of a spacecraft. So tell me why you will then continue to take our side and not theirs?"

"Ma'am, my culture is your culture. I was not reared as a unit of the Brotherhood. With respect, ma'am, you know my background. I am an Ultian, and a spacer."

"A well-prepared one," Frisde mutters very softly. She turns and paces toward the window. All eyes follow. This is the famous stagecraft Maeve has mentioned.

She speaks without turning, but her voice, like her personality, fills the room. "If you then defect to the other side . . . what then? The Brotherhood would reward you, I expect. I cannot imagine what form their gratitude would take . . . can you?"

"No, ma'am."

"Whatever it is, they will tender something of value, so we must outbid them. We must make you an offer they cannot surpass."

She whirls suddenly. "So? What do you crave, Ensign? I know what most people seek from life: power and wealth and fame. But those are not entirely valued for their own sake. Partly they are the means to sexual gratification and—ultimately—the means to raise offspring in the hope of biological immortality. You are effectively sterile. There are no girls with twelve chromosomes. What promises can we give you to take with you on your mission? What will motivate you?"

The words are almost exactly what Maeve has predicted in the dark, hot nights, in the calm tutorials between the storms of passion. And he plays by her coaching.

"Power and wealth and fame, ma'am."

The room murmurs like a nest of gishsaths.

Frisde stares hard at him. "How much fame? How much wealth? How much power?"

"You are asking me to name an exact price, ma'am?"

"I certainly am."

Vaun takes a deep breath and wonders if it will be one of his last. *Oh, Maeve, be right!* "I wish to be publicly recognized as savior of the planet and promoted at once to the rank of admiral in the Patrol, with all the normal monetary compensation and perquisites, and an endowment of an estate of my choice."

The room erupts in clamor. A few shout oaths, most just laugh—angry laughter, patient laughter, tolerant laughter. But Roker is not laughing, and neither is the high admiral. Frisde stares at the upstart, and the tips of her teeth show.

"Extremely well prepared! Have you any particular estate in mind, Ensign, or must we all tremble, awaiting your decision?"

"With respect, ma'am, unless I do save the planet and manage to survive the effort, then I shall be making no decision."

Frisde nods slightly to acknowledge the point. But Maeve is right again.

"Nevertheless, I think exact terms should be specified, and in advance."

"Ma'am. I want this one. Valhal."

Louder yet—those who laughed now curse. Those who profaned now laugh. Roker's face drains of color.

Frisde glances at the big boy appraisingly. "Whoever's been prompting him, it wasn't Admiral Roker, I think."

"No, ma'am, it was not!" Roker's glare bodes no good for Vaun when the admiral can get him alone. "Of course I agree, ma'am, that the ensign's continuing loyalty should be ensured by a promise of a generous reward if he succeeds. But his ambitions seem somewhat excessive."

"Do they?" Frisde glances thoughtfully around the room. The power-infested chamber has gone very still. Vaun almost can hear his own turmoiled heart.

Then she strolls forward again, across the downy carpet, stalking him. Drawing close, she lets the fear and hatred and contempt burn up in her eyes, for him alone to see. And her words are soft enough that only he can hear. "So that is your price for saving the world, Ensign?"

He meets her glare steadily. "Yes, ma'am."

Quieter yet . . . "No pay, no play?"

"Highest bidder wins, ma'am." He speaks without moving his lips, and the insolence draws color to her face.

"I can have you destroyed, you know."

Cold rivulets run down his chest. "You need me."

"You think I don't have any real choice?"

Choice is power and power is choice. After more than a century, she has been cornered at last, and cornered by an artificial pseudo-person, a peon from the mud of the Putra. If she could scratch him to tatters with her nails, it would be a great joy to her.

"You're bidding for a planet . . . ma'am."

Then neither speaks for a long lifetime, as Frisde weighs duty against personal satisfaction . . . and finally it is Frisde who blinks, and turns away. "Dismissed."

Fighting to conceal his exultation, Vaun salutes. He is sure now that another of Maeve's prophecies is about to be fulfilled. Who can put a price on a planet? Frisde must support Roker. His friends certainly will, and his enemies need settle for whatever they can get, even if it is only a chance to spite him by throwing Valhal into the pot. So Ultian Command will argue and discuss and debate for hours, and then accept Vaun's terms.

After all, his chances of collecting are barely more than zero, and Roker himself will do his best now to see that they become even less.

THE SUN HUNG close above the sea, splashing red on the breakers that rushed suicidally to death on the sand. Gritty-eyed with fatigue and still mildly hung over, Vaun stood within the gaggle of assembled sycophants, and listened with all the calm he could muster to their oily insinuations as they taunted his impotence.

"I do find surprises exciting!" Boorior told Legarf, peering around her bony nose to make sure Vaun was listening. "I wonder who this mysterious Quild boy is?"

Vaun chose not to spoil her fun by explaining. Few of Roker's lackeys were effective enough to be killers; they would be genuinely shocked by the tragic accident Roker must be planning.

Long shadows scored the sand like wounds. Bandor wore pink and peach before a darkling sky.

A couple of senior officers were tossing a football. The flirtatious Admiral Gargel, head of the Medical Corps, was clowning with Lepo and Tawlet and screaming shrilly as they tried to force sand down her cleavage. That was clearly foreplay, and any minute now all three of them would vanish into the bushes.

There were several other people huddling in the wind—unnamed civilians whose presence had not been explained. Mostly they seemed awed by their distinguished companions and were staying very quiet. One or two looked unnervingly apprehensive.

Feirn stood a little back from the beach, half-hidden in the trees, and Vaun wished she weren't there. Whatever the nature of the child's peculiar fixation on him, the forthcoming disaster would upset her mightily. The inevitable Ensign Blade was with her. Blade's protection might well be fearless, but he would be less use than a giant sea slug if she needed comforting.

Valhal's largest thicket of pepods was rustling around on a shingle bank not far away, stirring into life as evening cooled the air. Security should be herding them off to a less-populated area and obviously wasn't, so there could be no doubt that Blade's information had been correct, and pepods were the business of the day.

At last a hovercart came whining down the trail and squirted out onto the beach in a blinding cloud of sand. Roker's massive form was squeezed aboard beside a boy even larger, undoubtedly the cryptic Professor Quild. Vaun distrusted all academics on principle, and any who consorted with Roker would be worse than most.

Quild, when he grasped Vaun's hand in what he obviously expected to be a crushing grip, was a most unlikely-looking scholar. Not only was he as tall as Roker, and even bulkier, but he had hair hanging to his shoulders and a primitive's beard trailing almost to his waist—an obscenity that belonged in a swampy jungle rather than an ivy-coated college. Moreover, his arms and legs were coated with black fur, and black curls sprouted from his neckband like weeds. Any normal boy cursed with such a pelt would get his booster adjusted.

Vaun turned a bland face to the smugly sneering Roker and waited to hear what *mildly risky* fate was in store for him. The gang of accomplices clustered in close to listen.

"Professor Quild," Roker announced loudly, "is Dean of Aboriginal Biology at the University of Stravakia.'' The beribboned sycophants all nodded delightedly, watching Vaun and waiting for his reaction when enlightenment finally arrived.

Vaun looked along the beach at the spreading thicket of pepods. Had the long-lost Cessine and Dice been creeping around disguised as pepods all these years?

*"Silisentiens horribilis,"* boomed the hirsute scholar. "What do you know about our pseudosentients, Admiral?''

"Less than I shall know in a minute, I expect.''

"Quite.'' White teeth showed in the jungle of beard. "Have you even been close to one?''

"Twice.'' Conscious of the forest of eyes and ears around him, Vaun schooled his poker face.

"What did you do?''

"Ripped off my clothes, and then groveled.''

*That was last night. But the first time I ran away screaming, and Nivel . . .*

Quild nodded grudgingly, as if a bright class was failing to live up to expectations. "The undressing tactic is sound. We have not established why garments incite them, although we suspect that they view any extrinsic augmentation as weapons, but our recent tests have amply confirmed the aversive reaction.''

"I hope you didn't kill too many students in the process?''

The bushy brows dropped in a shaggy frown. "This is a serious matter, Admiral. We used convicted felons, if you must know. Those who survived received reductions in their sentences.''

"So did those who didn't, I expect. Can we get to the point, Professor?''

"Groveled, you said. Why grovel?''

"As a child I was taught that the pepods were less likely to attack anyone who crouched down as small as possible.'' *But I forgot. I ran. Nivel screamed and screamed . . .*

"Ah! That is where the conventional wisdom is at fault. It is not the posture that matters.''

"It feels right to me,'' Vaun said, recalling his narrow escape the previous night.

Quild scowled. "What matters is the aspect you present to them. What do they see—although of course pepods' perception is keyed to frequencies we cannot appreciate, but 'see' is an adequate approximation . . . What does a pepod see when you grovel before it?''

Oh, of course! "Hair?''

"Exactly! Hair. Being fibroid themselves, they may associate sentience with filamentary texture. Hairy, in other words, although of course this is anthropomorphic speculation. When we shaved the convicts' heads, the effect of groveling was below the five percentile confidence level. In other words, not significant.''

Perhaps it was fatigue, perhaps it was fear, but Vaun felt a virulent dislike for this oversize anthropoid pomposity. ''I think I see why you have met with success in your researches, Professor.''

An angry flush showed above the monstrous beard, but Roker broke in impatiently. ''Professor Quild made the initial discovery quite serendipitously. He—'' Quild tried to interrupt and was quailed into silence by one of Roker's sneers. ''He was challenged to a duel. A pepod duel. Illegal, of course, but an old Pharishian custom. Perhaps you have heard of it?''

Vaun hadn't. *Nivel screamed all the way back to the village. There were eleven of them carried back screaming, and even Nivel's withered foot, which had never moved before, was twisting and writhing.*

He shivered in the cold sea wind. ''I can guess. Am I being challenged to a Pharishian pepod duel?''

''It would be murder,'' Quild snapped. ''They would react aggressively to you long before they did to me. I could go much closer.''

''And I would let you.'' Vaun shot an exasperated look at Roker. ''Sir, is this relevant?''

Clearly, Roker was enjoying the game, playing to his pet audience. Even Gargel and her playmates had come back to enjoy the show.

''Tell him about the standing wave, Professor.''

Quild grew suddenly coy. ''Well, this is a little premature for publication, but we do have evidence that the pepods' long-range, low-frequency radio communication is a much less discontinuous behavior pattern than has hitherto been appreciated. There seems to be an ongoing form of . . . well, our working terminology is *continuum* . . . of emission and response. A sort of background murmur, if you like. And at times it may even have a holographic quality to it. *Standing wave* is a relatively—''

''I don't see what any of this has to do with me, sir,'' Vaun snapped. But it did. Oh yes, it did.

Roker rolled up his lip as if about to wrap it around a juicy bunch of grass. ''Where are Dice and Cessine, Admiral? Where are the cuckoos?''

Vaun waved a hand. ''Out there somewhere, among ten billion other people. Working as salesfolk or bakers or painters—who knows? Staying in the slums, where spacers never go. Nor pepods, either! I expect plastic surg—''

"Plastic surgery would be quite ineffectual!" Quild boomed. The interruptions were annoying him. "At the wavelengths used by pepods, such detail would be quite undetectable."

Crazy! Vaun wheeled on him. "Are you saying you can talk to those vegetables, Professor? You think they have the sensitivity and the brains to tell the difference between one human and another? You—''

"Not brains, but the answer to both your questions is yes." The big boy smiled and stroked his beard with a furry paw. The sycophants were all smirking. "We have established quite clearly by simple reinforcement conditioning that they can distinguish between human beings. They 'see,' to use that approximate term, deep within the human physique, certainly to the cellular level, probably to the molecular. They may even be able to read DNA itself. They may not be quite as discerning as you are, Admiral, but they have surprised us several times."

"I hope they don't surprise us tonight." Vaun turned to the high admiral. "Sir, have you considered the dangers in this?"

Roker exchanged amused glances with his entourage. "Your personal courage is a legend in the Patrol, Admiral Vaun. Your annual address to the recruits inspires—''

"Not to me, dammit! This boy is claiming that there is some sort of worldwide pepod network, isn't that so, Professor? I don't believe him, because in ten thousand years we should—''

Quild could shout louder. "There are many early records of simultaneous pepod outbreaks on a continental scale."

"And that's exactly my point! A massacre's exactly what you're risking. We're within range of the mainland—you know that, Roker! There was a pepod eruption on the coast back in '98 or thereabouts, and the Valhal thickets rampaged also. If you start messing about with these, then you're endangering all the coastal settlements from Asimfirth to the cape and God knows how far inland—''

"Your concern has been noted, Admiral," Roker said, leering.

The sun had set; the salty wind from the sea was as sharp as a knife. Vaun shivered again. What a frigging horrible way to die! And if he refused to obey orders during a state of emergency, then Roker could have him shot. That might be preferable.

"Let's get this clear," he said, while his mind raced around the problem in search of escape. "First, you claim you can actually talk to these creatures? Secondly, you think they are sufficiently intelligent to provide useful answers? Thirdly, you think they will then oblige you by going off to look for replicas of myself, and fourthly, that they can somehow direct you to where those replicas may be found? What sort of gullible half-wit would believe all that? What sort of motive can you provide them with that they will give one damn about your problem? What—''

"I repeat, Admiral," Roker barked, "that your concerns have been noted. After all, the concept of a group mind may be alien to us . . . but I would have thought that you could comprehend it more easily than most."

Boorior cackled merrily at such wit, and some of the others followed her lead.

Several of the pepods were wandering in the general direction of the human spectators. Security would never have allowed them to come this close had Roker not already tampered with Vaun's standard orders.

The high admiral's sneer told Vaun he was beaten. The smirks on the faces of Roker's toadies confirmed it. They all thought they were safe, because Roker's armed band had arrived now, and because Security could call down a firestorm if there was trouble. Had they any idea how fast an angry pepod traveled? Well, he would not give them the satisfaction of hearing him plead. All mortals died in the end. Defeat was inevitable, but to go bravely was the closest a boy could come to victory.

He could not even just punch Roker on the jaw and earn a nice quick firing squad, because Roker would know what he wanted and would surely tie him up and throw him to the pepods anyway. There was no way out of this.

"Sir, I request specific orders."

"Very well. Admiral Vaun, you will accompany the civilian auxiliary Quild to the vicinity of that pepod thicket for the purpose of facilitating communication with them. You will aid Professor Quild's research in every way possible. Is that clear?"

"Sir!"

"And then we shall track down your missing brothers," Roker said, leering in satisfaction. "After so many years, a family reunion should be a very touching experience for you."

Vaun wondered briefly if he could break that thick neck before Security stopped him. Regretfully he decided that he could not. Randoms! Wild stock! Sex and power were all they cared about.

"Excellent!" Quild said, showing his teeth in his beard. He glanced at the pepods. "We can go a little closer before we remove our garments, Admiral. In the interests of propriety."

"Lead the way," Vaun snapped.

He trudged across the sand, following the big boy. Randoms! Lust and avarice would drive them to anything. The brethren could be ruthless—as Prior had been ruthless—but at least they committed their crimes in higher causes than mere personal greed.

Prior had paid dearly for his.

N OW THAT'S WHAT I call a sexy outfit!" says a teasing, throaty voice.

Vaun has been examining his image in the mirror above the basin. His head is as smooth as a fresh-washed Doggoth cookpot and decorated with eighty shiny silver buttons, marking the holes drilled in it. Sexy? He has no eyebrows, his eyes are red-rimmed, and his shapeless white gown ends at knees and elbows.

He turns to face the girl in the doorway. Can it be only four weeks since he met her at Doggoth? Tall and black, and wearing medoff insignia . . . She still outranks him, but his commission is official now. And besides, he has other things going for him.

"Ma'am!" he says. "The last time we met, I was even sexier."

"Ah!" her midnight eyes twinkle. "You have been taking my advice about spiking your booster."

"I had no choice. Blood tests?"

She shakes her head, laughing. "The way you look at me is enough. Besides, rumor has it that you ball the high admiral."

"Krantz, no!" Vaun starts to make a smile and lets it become a yawn, leaching any trace of sincerity from his denial. It is Maeve who comes to his bed in the little hours, the fleet, sweet hours of the night while Roker sleeps, but the Frisde slander won't do his career any harm.

Yet he feels himself color, knowing he has indeed been looking at the black girl, wondering if her nipples are the same shade as those rich, sultry lips now spread to show snowy teeth.

"And I don't need to be any medical genius to know that you haven't been getting enough sleep, Ensign."

"Absolutely correct, ma'am."

"Well, she's gone now. We can get to business." The medic's bright glance is still testing the rumors about him and Frisde. Let her pry! Yes, Frisde has gone now—gone without a word of farewell, or thanks, or anger; just gone. Call for her torch and her spade-shouldered Galorian captain to fly it, and gone. Whatever the gossips say, Vaun has never been her lover.

He was never asked.

"Nice place you have here," the medic says. "I'm going to enjoy this posting, brief though it may be. Ready for the mind bleed?"

He shrugs, remembers that she outranks him, and says, "Ma'am!" But he still doesn't use his Doggoth voice. She has noticed, and flashes him another amused glance of jet-on-amber as she turns and leads the way.

Barefoot, he follows, and two doors down the corridor she stops and gestures. "Take the empty chair. I'll be right back."

Suspicious, he goes in and blinks in the glare. The makeshift surgery is cluttered with metal, it smells of chemical and hums as if it were alive. The most obvious equipment is a pair of inclined chairs, set back to back. Through the web of wires and pipes and monitors around them, he sees that one is already occupied. He picks his way among the tangle, going to look at the other patient.

A slim, well-knit boy, almost slight . . . Dice, of course. His eyes are closed and the gaunt cheeks are pale. Shins and forearms project from another of the shapeless gowns; wrists and ankles are bound in place by shiny bands. A metal bowl encloses the top of his head, sprouting a tangle of tubes and wires.

Five years ago—three boys in a boat, drifting lazily on the sunbright waters of the delta. Dice. Happiest days of . . .

Of course, it isn't Dice. Dice is still at large. And of course Vaun has always known that Prior looks like Dice, but the reality is enough to tie knots in his innards, and his hands have started to shake. He feels cold trickles run down his ribs. Oh, Dice! Oh, Raj! Oh, me!

Dice, who learned to enjoy eating fish.

Then the familiar eyes open, slowly.

"Hello, Brother!" The smile is the same. The voice is not quite the same, and very weak.

How *dare* he try to be friendly?

"You raped my mother."

The smile weakens. "I prefer not to discuss it here, if you don't mind, Vaun."

Of course this is a setup. There will be cameras and listeners. But Vaun at least has nothing to hide.

"You drove her crazy!"

Prior's peaked face bears no expression at all now. "That was an accident."

"The raping wasn't." Vaun feels a strange rage; his blood pounds in his ears.

"You want revenge?" Prior whispers. "Take it! Take this abomination off my head and push a finger in."

"In what?"

"Pink jelly." He seems to find Vaun's shock amusing. "They took the top off. Then they gave me a mirror." He forces a thin smile. "Not many people get a chance to see themselves so clearly." A trail of spittle runs from the corner of his mouth.

"Tell us the password, then, and maybe they'll let me do that. It'll be a pleasure." Could he really push a finger into a living brain?

"Password? Is that what they told you—password? There's no password, Brother."

"We'll see." Vaun is annoyed to find that his anger is becoming contaminated by a sort of pity. He remembers *rape*, but it doesn't help as much as he would like.

"No password," Prior insists. "Language."

"Oh." Well, that makes sense. A whole new language? This is to be a bigger job than Vaun expected, and the thought is chilling.

Prior's eyes have closed, but he continues to whisper. "A world. A life. So you can pass as me. I know."

"You deserve this, and more!" At least Vaun can speak louder than he can.

"I don't mind. They're good memories, and you're welcome to them, Brother. Enjoy them."

Vaun is at a loss. He can't find his anger now, only fear. And pity, damn it. His brother, helpless. The machinery hums. Fluids sob in the tubes.

"I'll try," Vaun says. "I'll certainly try. And I'll use anything interesting I find in there. Your forgiving attitude is very touching. I'm just sorry I can't share it."

Prior opens his eyes again and smiles weakly. "You were reared as a random; you're a little confused still. But don't worry—in the end you'll never betray the Brotherhood."

"Oh, won't I? I would say 'Watch me!' but you won't have that pleasure."

"No, Brother Vaun. When the chips are down, you'll side with your kin." There is a chilling deathbed certainty in that quiet statement. Remembering the hidden listeners, Vaun almost panics.

"This is war!" he shouts. "And you started it."

Prior's eyelids lift partway. "Did I? Is it? Do cats and dogs wage war? Wait until you know more, Vaun. Xanacor Hive . . . they burned it. Burned down our brothers like vermin. Little kids . . . And Monad. I suppose they showed you that clip? I wept when they showed me. I was raised at Monad. You were conceived at Monad."

"I don't care!"

"You will. When you remember. The woods . . ."

"You started this."

"No. Cats and dogs. It's evolution."

Vaun makes a scornful noise, because he isn't sure what words may come if he tries to speak.

The dark eyes open wide, staring, intense. "You know about evolution? Go read up on it. Survival of the fittest. We're the next stage, Brother. The perfection of mankind, a whole new species, *Homo factus*. Whatever happens to me, or you, doesn't matter. Maybe it'll take centuries. Doesn't matter. The end is inevitable. The wild stock have had their day."

"And you'll wipe us out, I suppose? Bury us?"

Again Prior tries a smile. " 'Us'? Them!"

"You think I'm one of you? Well, I never asked—"

"No, you didn't. But you're still our brother."

Vaun wishes he could feel as confident and self-assured as the prisoner looks. How can he stay calm when he knows the awful things that are about to be done to him?

Prior sighs. "No hard feelings, Vaun. I'm only sorry you're on the losing side at the moment. But I understand."

"Oh, now that takes confidence! You sit there with no top to your head and tell me you're doing fine, you've got them on the run?"

Prior manages a faint echo of Raj's chuckle. "Not me. I'm only one unit. I'm no more important to the Brotherhood than a single cell in your epidermis is to you, and you shed those by the million all the time. Perhaps the Brotherhood won't win on Ult. I hope it does. But whether we win here or not, though, the wild stock will lose."

"We all die in the end, you mean."

"But a whole species doesn't have to kill itself, Brother. I wish I had time to explain. Maybe you'll pick up my memories on this. You know the random population on Ult?"

"About ten billion."

"And it used to be over twenty. You think they've reduced it by choice?"

"Certainly."

"Never. The wilds breed like bugs, all the time. And they exist by competition, so if one group does restrict its procreation, then another grows faster and takes its place. Didn't Dice tell you any of this? If their numbers are down, it just means that the die-off has started. Vaun, planets *wear out* if they're not looked after properly. The wild stock have just about finished this one."

"That's not true! Yes, there was a lot of waste in the early days, a lot of unnecessary pollution and bad development, but the international resource councils . . ." Vaun stops, sensing that he is running along a predictable pipe.

Prior sighs. "Too many people. Far too many. You know what the indefinitely sustainable population is for a planet this size?"

"No."

"Nor I. But the Brotherhood would be content with a couple of hundred thousand. Cooperation, not competition . . . We have no insane compulsion to multiply, you see."

"So you're going to rescue the globe from its inhabitants, are you? Who's going to thank you?"

"They'll all die soon anyway, and take their world with them. If you can't see your way to supporting us yet, then think of your duty to the biosphere." Prior closes his eyes wearily, and at that moment a couple of medics come in and the conversation is over. It will have been recorded, of course.

Vaun makes his way to the other chair and sits down. The fabric of it feels cold through his flimsy gown, and he shivers. A random would come up in goose pimples, but his skin has no vestigial hair follicles.

Two more orderlies arrive and start fussing with the equipment around him, muttering to each other and ignoring him, treating him like just another item on the manifest. They attach things to the buttons on his scalp. But he hears someone speaking to Prior.

"We're going to start in on the left lateral cortex. So if you have anything else to say, you'd better say it now."

Prior does not answer.

T HE DREAMER IS racked by monsters, pursued by terror.
He thrashes and fights, helpless in the coils of horror, and
there is no escape.

The hippocampus . . . now they're going for the hippocampus.
They brought him in on a cart today.

Brought me in on a cart today.

Two red suns and the trees are lime below a purple sky. I am
Blue. I am Yellow. I am Red. I am all colors and my brothers are
with me. We laugh and run and play. I am loved. I love. I am one
with my brothers.

They take me around on a cart. No need for shackles now; too
much damage to the motor cortex. Poor Vaun was shouting at them.
They hadn't warned him. Typical. He really can't have known what
to expect. He cares, though, whatever he says. The expression on
his face . . .

Who am I?

They're going to dig for the amygdala today, and process another
piece of the hippocampus, and the nucleus basalis in the forebrain.
That'll fix the bastard.

No pain; it's only jelly.

Brown is a full grown unit. He is talking about the female gender
persons that the wild stock have. I've seen them around Monad, of
course, but I didn't know about their special organs. This is very
important to the mission. Only one of us will get to go on the Ultian
mission—Tan or Rose or me. We spend so much time together that
I am learning to distinguish the other two, although of course I
would never be so unkind as to tell them so. Yesterday we were
Green, Violet, and White, and the teacher was a Black, but the
same unit, I am sure.

There isn't much left of him now. Not a brain in his head, one
of the lab gnomes said. And laughed. I wanted to kill her, choke
her slowly, but I laughed, too, because Roker is suspicious of me,
shooting questions. Even Maeve asks me who I am at times.

176

This unit has been very bad. I tried to poke a stick in my brother's eye. I have to go without pants all afternoon so everyone can see the number on my butt and know that this unit may have a design fault.

We're going to have to go faster. The Q ship will enter parking orbit in three weeks. Not much of Prior left now. Good riddance! I can speak Galactic with Avalonian-Command pronunciation now, and jabber in his native tongue, whatever it was called . . . Andilian?

Some of the memories are fading already . . .

North of Monad Hive, about an hour's flight from Zindir . . .

If I can win this bout . . . but I think this is the unit who threw me yesterday . . . just a hunch, of course, but if it is, then he favors his left hand a little . . . and he can't know that I was crop champion last year . . .

*Vaun! Vaun! It's a nightmare, Vaun. Wake up, Vaun! Maeve's here, love. Wake up, Vaun! It's all over, Vaun. Prior died, Vaun. It's all over, Vaun.*

Warm arms around him . . . his face buried between her breasts . . .

"No name!" he sobs. "I was happy, but I had no name. How could I be happy when I had no name?"

# HOW COULD YOU tell one pepod from another?

There was one good thing about the wind—it excused shivering. Quild did not seem to feel the cold at all, but then he was twice as thick as Vaun, and thatched all over. More important, he wasn't scared spitless.

"This is close enough for you," he said suddenly.

No argument there. Vaun had been forcing every reluctant step with brute willpower. The nearest pepod loomed directly ahead, seeming almost within touching distance, although that was his imagination making it seem closer than it really was. Even over the surf, he could hear its rustling complaint and the chittering noise it

made on the shingle. Something out to sea was shrieking plaintively.

His knee still ached, and the bruises on his face were throbbing.
Not, likely, for long.

Quild went on another dozen paces, and stopped, watching that
big mother of a pepod flickering and writhing like a dead bush
possessed.

Vaun hugged himself, hunched against the wind, and watched
also. The pepod was a big sucker, full gown, taller than he, and
that meant a large privacy radius. He could never work out how
they moved, whether they rolled or walked. Antennae, limbs, poison spines, all seemed to flail around simultaneously—they blurred,
when the brutes moved fast. Eyestalks and mandibles . . . nothing
seemed to be attached to anything else. Pepods had no centers.
Ordinary weapons were useless against them, and he was unarmed
except for fingernails. Unarmed, unlegged, untorsoed, undressed,
bareass. *Krantz!* it was cold.

The summit of Bandor glimmered in starlight; lights danced in
the woods by the parking lot. Once in a while a torch would purr
overhead, as Roker's goons brought in more unwanted guests, anyone who had been present at Arkady the previous night. There must
be hundreds of them here by now, but doubtless most would enjoy
a visit to the famed Valhal, provided it did not go on too long. Had
the traitor herself arrived yet?

Vaun's teeth wanted to chatter, but who knew what that sound
might convey to a pepod? A hundred meters or so back along the
beach, Roker was watching with his band of bootlickers, faces
indistinguishable in the faded light. Along the edge of the woods,
the armed guards stood in a row like fenceposts. Vaun wondered
what sort of armament they had been issued—eight of them, and at
least three times that many pepods in this thicket alone. He didn't
like their chances, but he wouldn't be around to laugh.

"Admiral Vaun?" a girl's voice said in his ear.

He jumped and looked around, but there was no one there.
"Yes?" he said cautiously.

"My name is Elan; I am one of Professor Quild's graduate students."

"Pleased to meet you." No point in saying he was pleased to
*see* her; she was invisible, elsewhere.

"I will keep you posted on what is happening this evening, Admiral."

He choked down a fatuous comment about coming to join her in
the control room . . . frivolity would just reveal how scared he was.

*Krantz!* but he wished they would get it over with. "I'll appreciate that."

"At the moment, we're still trying to distinguish the specimen closest to you. They toss frequencies back and forth so often . . ." She fell silent.

"Why does it matter which is which?" Vaun asked, mostly for the comfort of hearing his own voice, or hers.

"It lets us set up a reference point. They orientate on each other and the planetary magnetic field."

Quild said something that was lost in the sound of the waves, but he was probably speaking to the control room. He edged back a few steps, and Vaun was grateful of the excuse to do the same, keeping the distance between them the same. The pepod was coming slowly in their direction.

A few moments crawled by. "Still trying to calibrate here. They have a different pulse ratio from what we've met in Caruva." Elan's voice sounded apologetic.

Apologetic, hell! She sounded worried.

The news, whatever it meant in detail, merely strengthened his opinion that Quild was a conceited blowhard, rollicking recklessly far beyond his safe boundaries.

Again Quild backed up. Again Vaun copied him. He thought the pepod was gaining on them, though.

"Ah!" said the youthful voice in his ear. "We're starting."

Quild raised both arms, bowed, and began to dance.

"You don't have to do that, Admiral."

"I am delighted to hear it."

"We call it Attention Getting. There is no significance to any of the gestures, but the pseudosentients seem to react faster when there is a . . . When they can relate to someone, er . . ."

"Making a fool of himself," Vaun suggested. Quild continued to cavort and leap, but at least the exercise would warn him. The pepod had changed direction ominously, coming to investigate.

The girl sniggered slightly. "Well put! We are transmitting a standard prerecorded greeting. Some of the symbol groups have been identified—cool temperatures and melodious harmony are two well-established wave package symbols."

She could pontificate almost as well as Quild, but Maeve's Security had known as much the previous night. Of course, it might keep up to date by reading Quild's publications; that was entirely possible.

"It's answering!"

Good. Let us talk, by all means.

"Now we're starting the introduction. The professor has transcribed some greetings from other thickets he has visited."

Quild himself was still spinning and leaping and waving like a maniac. Vaun could hear his breath. Strenuous work, talking to pepods . . . but there did seem to be something to it. The oversize bundle of kindling itself had stopped moving around, although its individual twigs were all still rustling and writhing. All right—so it was listening. That was a small part of what the big ape had claimed he could do.

Give him his due, though; he had the courage of his beliefs. That monster was terrifyingly close to him. But suppose this meeting did get down to business? Just suppose, for example, that the thing asked a question? Then Quild's flunkies would have to translate it, and tell him, and he would have to think of an answer, and send it all the way back through the control room for transcription and transmission . . . How patient were pepods? Did a pepod interpret a long silence as a rudeness?

Quild slowed to an exhausted stop and doubled over, panting hard, and also trying to speak instructions to his assistants off in their control room. That might be half a world away, or up at the house. Somehow they would be patched into Valhal's Security.

Elan said, "They're responding now, in chorus."

If the pepod didn't get Vaun, then the cold would. This nonsense should have been put off until Angel rose, around midnight, this time of year. God of fools and innocents . . .

The monster began to wander away, seemingly more interested in gravel than people. Quild straightened, and renewed his dancing, although less exuberantly than before.

"This is the main question now," said Elan's whisper. "We're asking them to notice you standing behind him. He is saying that you are one of several . . . Seek others like you . . ."

*When Nivel died,* Vaun thought, *I fell in a ditch. There are no ditches here.*

Quild was slowing, out of breath.

"We have asked them to look for another like you." Elan's voice began to sound distracted. "We are getting a reply now . . . Negative, of course."

The pepod's writhings became more agitated, its rustle louder. Was it creeping closer? Quild began to dance faster.

"Now we are asking them to look farther—look far away, look for another like you. I do wish they had a better idea of *tense.* I think . . . Yes, the other thickets are melding in!"

A long, painful pause . . .

"Admiral? Elan, still. Sorry to neglect you like this. The quasi-sentients are definitely asking a question. We're having a little trouble relating the content to known semantic packages."

*You don't know what it wants, you mean.*

The girl's voice faded, as if she had turned away to speak to someone else. "No, Dik, that grouping definitely refers to aggression. . . ."

The pepod lurched into motion. It scurried right past Quild, heading for Vaun. His legs jellied. He wanted to run, to grovel, dance like Quild . . . mostly to pee. Anything!

A squeak from his invisible guide . . . "It's all right, Admiral! It's just coming to inspect you. At least, I think it is. Just stay still."

Easy for her! This was it, Vaun thought, as the rustling, clicking monster writhed over the beach toward him.

Then it veered, and stopped alongside him, so close he could have reached out and touched it. He could not stop his shaking, and his throat was as dry as the sand under his toes.

*Chitter,* said the pepod. *Click! Chitter! Chitter!* A twig reached out and stroked his head. Another reached toward his groin, and his flesh crawled.

"Yes, it's all right," the girl said weakly.

Vaun heard faint voices beyond hers, as if an argument was raging. "And definitely the emission is increasing . . . I think . . . yes . . ." She faded again. "Dik, see? We have a continuum!" Then she was back. "Beg pardon, Admiral. This is very exciting. We have some unique patterns developing here in the higher frequency bands."

Vaun hoped they knew what they were doing. He didn't think they did, though. The venomous mass beside him fidgeted and rustled; tendrils waved and peered, and occasionally touched him, very tentatively. He had a horrible certainty that it was shouting at him in frequencies he could not sense and of course wondering why he did not respond. How patient was a pepod? How long until it decided he needed a lesson in manners?

"And now we are picking up the mainland!" Elan was squeaky with excitement. "The fugue is expanding at an incredible rate . . . Dik, do you see *that*? Tell Quild!"

Vaun felt a shiver that had nothing to do with the cold. The rest of the pepods were certainly doing something, dancing maybe. He could hear them, even if he could barely see them.

Without warning, the pepod beside him scuttled away in a spray of sand, heading for the distant audience.

Elan shouted a warning. The rest of the thicket was moving,

vague in the dark, but definitely advancing, rolling forward in a shapeless rush, following their leader.

Quild cried out briefly, and spun around to flee, and shrieked as he was overrun.

Vaun took to his heels, angling toward the sea, hearing Elan wailing senselessly in his ear. The darkness ahead came alive with the green flashes of small arms fire. Screams of terror or pain from the distant audience told him the first pepod had arrived.

He wasn't going to make it. From the corner of his eye he saw the rest of the thicket almost on top of him. He whirled to face them, fell on his knees, and pressed his face to the ground.

## "WASH MY FEET,
Wash my hands.
Put me back in
The ditching bands . . ."

The air is hot enough to bake bread. The mud is thick and heavy and putrid. In the distance girls are singing.

Late summer is ditching time in the delta. No matter that the sun is a torturer and Angel its apprentice. Eclipse Day is a holiday, when the sun is closest to Angel—and it is said that long ago Angel would hide behind the sun on that day—but for weeks before and after Eclipse Day the two blaze side by side in the sky, and it is ditching time. The water is low then, and the ditches must be dug out, ready for autumn flood and next year's eels.

Vaun works alone, shoveling just as hard as any—harder, so no one will accuse him of shirking, off here by himself, and he stays in clear sight for that same reason. If he tries to join a band, sooner or later a shovelful of mud will come down on the top of his head, just by accident, oops, sorry, very funny. Mud is full of leebs, and it is bad enough to be bitten raw up to the knees, but get leebs in your hair or your ears and they drive you crazy. He knows.

This morning he started out with Nivel, and they kept each other

company for a while. But Nivel's withered foot slows him, and
Vaun has drawn so far ahead that it isn't worth shouting to and fro.
He's twelve now, and can throw mud as fast as any grown boy in
the village. Even last year he could dig a full boy's lot, and this
year he's bigger and stronger. Soon he'll go back to Nivel and
suggest they change ditches, and he'll dig enough so that by night
they'll have two lots dug, one for him and one for Nivel, even if
Vaun has dug most of both of them. He did it yesterday and the day
before and the day before. He'll show them! It feels good, except
for the blisters.

The mud squelches around his ankles, the pozee grass waves
overhead, but the only shade in the delta comes from the bugs;
everyone knows that. They're not quite thick enough today to cast
a shadow, but not far off.

He swings his shovel relentlessly, throwing muck up on the bank,
wash my *feet*, wash my *hands* . . . *slurp* . . . *slurp* . . . *slurp* . . .

Somebody screams.

And somebody else, even before he is up on the bank, dancing
on tiptoe to see over the pozee. People running, shouting.

Nivel's head and shoulders appear over the grass . . . not as far
back as Vaun had thought . . . and then the terror takes on a name—
*pepod*. There is nothing to see except the people, though. People
running, and yelling, and throwing their hands up and vanishing in
earsplitting screams as the thing in the grass gets them.

Nivel shoots a wild-eyed look at Vaun, and shouts, "Down,
lad!" And disappears. But Vaun sees Shil fall, and then Lonaham,
and two others are running toward him, and he turns and takes to
his heels.

He hears Nivel shouting his name.

He catches his foot in something and pitches headfirst into a
ditch . . .

A moment of sheer terror, and then he hears Nivel screaming
also.

**I**T HAD HAPPENED again. The day Nivel died, the pepod had gone right by Vaun. The trail of crushed pozee had been quite clear to see afterward—Nivel had jumped up and run also. He had drawn the monster away from Vaun, because it had gone right by where he had been lying, within a couple of feet of him. It had caught Nivel easily, of course.

And last night, even—how close had that brute of Maeve's come to Vaun?

As the explosions began brightening the night, Vaun rolled over and sat up, and reflected that it had happened again.

This time a whole thicket of pepods had gone by him, over him, and around him. His ears had been full of their clatter, and he had sniffed a dry, fruity odor. Sand had been thrown up, he had felt a few gentle, probing touches stroke his hair, nothing hostile.

They could see to the cellular level, Quild had said, perhaps to the molecular . . . Quild was still screaming . . .

Meaning, obviously, that they could see Vaun wasn't human. Did they know he was an artifact, and one of many? Did their group mind respect replicates more than randoms? More likely they just recognized that he was a freak and not one of the too-numerous, dangerous majority. To a pepod, he obviously did not look/smell/sound/feel human. He wasn't one of *them*. If there really was a group mind, then it had been battling the human race, on and off, for ten thousand years. Humans kept making threatening approaches that must be resisted. Over the centuries, a group mind might have developed very specific ideas about what constituted a human being. Forty-six chromosomes, for instance.

Nivel had died in vain. Oh, *God*!

Security had joined in the battle, gouts of fire erupting among the trees and even in the sea. The racket was astonishing, but it did not drown out the screaming. The human guards had not lasted long—at least Vaun could not recall hearing their weapons in use for long, but, of course, at the time he had been underneath a stampede of pepods, and not paying quite as much attention as he should. Red and orange fire detonated in deafening tattoo, and the sea bursts were yellow and steam-white.

Apparently pepods did not mind water. Vaun had never known them to go into the sea before, and had always assumed that it would be a refuge in case of attack. Others had made the same mistake that night, and not been as lucky. He could see bodies rolling among the waves, and fragments of pepods being washed up. The beach was bright with bonfires of burning pepods, shedding a cheerful glow and streaming pale smoke. But there had been no party, and those prone figures were not drunks.

More flashes up the hill located the other two thickets, which would certainly have attacked at the same instant, and Valhal was full of God knew how many people that Roker had been ferrying in.

And the mainland would have caught it, too.

What an unmitigated fuck-up!

He heaved himself to his feet, and went over to inspect Quild. His thrashing had almost stopped, and he was beyond screaming now, his whole body striped with poisoned welts and starting to swell. He was conscious, his eyes as big as fried eggs with the pain. He tried to speak, but the whisper was lost between the sound of the sea and the blood in his mouth.

Vaun could do nothing for him except perhaps choke him to death, and—he reflected wryly—he reserved such lethal mercies for his friends. Serve the murdering bastard right! He turned and trudged back to where they had left their clothes.

Even when he had dressed, he was still shivering. Reaction and shock. Brethren were tough, but not immune to adrenaline.

The battle was dying down, the bursts of green fire becoming less frequent. A fair part of the forest was burning. Security could work out what to do. Security was totally immune to adrenaline, and therefore should be left to cope.

How far had the carnage spread? Valhal was free of pepods now until they reseeded, but elsewhere the vermin were probably still on the rampage, and might stay that way for days. What had gone wrong? And why?

Here came the first of the torches now. There would be no medical help from the mainland for a while—in most areas, civilian resources would collapse completely if the casualties were high. One of the Patrol's few genuinely useful functions was the organization of disaster relief in cases of natural catastrophe like earthquakes. That it could handle, and handle well, but the Patrol must have its own problems this time.

Vaun started to run. The first torch was touching down on the beach among the bodies. Some of those bodies were still thrashing, and two survivors came running out of the trees, hand in hand, also heading for the torch.

A pepod emerged from the woods behind them and streaked in pursuit. Security let it scurry clear of the bushes, until it offered a clear shot, and blasted it in a bright violet flash. The pepod bounced, rolled a few steps, and then remained in place, burning with smoky orange flames. That must've been just about the last of them. The barrage rumbled among the hills for a moment longer, and died away.

Vaun went by at least a dozen victims, some moving and screaming, some not. A few were struggling to rise. So much for Roker's cronies. So much for Roker's armed bodyguards. How about Roker himself? Was he injured, or even dead?

The pilot of the torch was standing beside it, staring all around and muttering, "Oh, my God!" over and over. The two survivors from the woods were half carrying, half leading one of the wounded forward—Admiral Lepo, blood-soaked and barely conscious. All three were staggering whenever he was seized by muscle spasms. The rescuers were Blade and Feirn, which was not too surprising, because they had been back near the trees. Feirn lacked the weight and strength needed, though.

*"You!"* Vaun bellowed at the pilot. "Help that boy! Ignore the serious ones, Ensign. There's nothing to be done for them."

Blade shot him a shocked look, and said, "Sir!" His face was black with smoke, he had lost his cap, and his hair was ruffled. He looked more human, somehow.

Feirn released her side of the writhing patient to the pilot. "Oh, Vaun! You're safe?" She sounded vague, and was obviously in shock.

"Yes. Security!"

"Sir?" Roker had changed the Jeevs sim to a nondescript male in his own Danquer livery, but that was unimportant. The underlying software was the same, and there was none better on Ult. Besides, even Vaun would not mock Roker at a time like this . . . Roker? . . .

"Where is the high admiral?"

Vaun thought he detected a minuscule pause, as if the system had to think back and replay the disaster. "Over there, sir." The sim pointed.

"Dead?"

"Uncertain, sir . . . My processors are close to overload and there has been loss of sensitivity."

Blade and the pilot were already running. Blade knelt, and then rose and shook his head at Vaun. Feirn gasped. Roker dead!

The sim wavered and became transparent. "Admiral, I have a request for authorization. A Citizen Maeve, minister of—"

"What for?"

*"Vaun!"* Maeve's voice spilled urgently from the sim itself. *"I want to take over the sick bay here. It's chaos!"*

"Level One granted!" The night was heaped with irony—Maeve back and given authority! But no one would do a better job of organizing the human helpers, and tonight Valhal would have to depend on human helpers; the systems had never been designed for disaster on this scale.

"Any report from the mainland?"

"Nothing conclusive yet, sir. The networks are confused. Pepod attacks just about everywhere."

"Worldwide, you mean?"

"Yes, sir."

"DataCen?"

"Not operational."

*Krantz!* If the Patrol's own systems had crashed, then the anarchy was universal, and unbelievable. How fortunate that the Scythan Q ship was still ten weeks or more from . . .

*Merciful Mother!* Was it possible?

Create chaos, Roker had said . . .

What greater chaos than a pepod attack? How much of the mainland had it affected? If it had any range at all, then half a dozen nations were going to be accusing their neighbors of starting it. Roker was dead. There would have to be a conclave to elect a new high admiral . . . Total, utter, screwup!

Blade came staggering by with another screaming victim draped over his shoulders. He glanced curiously at Vaun as he went by— the great Admiral Vaun standing like a dummy with his mouth open. Blade was functioning, and functioning well, and that was both remarkable and fortunate, a tribute to Doggoth's ruthless training. Very few people would fly a level flight path so soon after surviving such a massacre.

"Ensign!"

Blade, having laid his burden in the torch, straightened and spun around. "Sir?"

Three more torches were settling down in swirls of sand. That was one good result of Roker's stupidity—there was plenty of transportation here tonight. "Blade, you take over the rescue here. You're in charge, regardless of rank, hear? Leave the worst till last, or shoot them. Get the rest up to the house. Don't forget the woods. Security, accept this man's orders to Level One. Feirn, get in. I'll take this lot.''

He pushed Feirn into the torch ahead of him and told her to control the moaning, writhing heap of people in the back—Blade and the pilot had loaded four. It was a bad overload. The torch was already airborne as the canopy phased in, but it skimmed a few wavetops before Vaun realized that the Valhal control systems were overloaded also, and not to be trusted. He snapped over to manual, and for a moment thought he'd cut it too fine. Then the craft steadied under his hands.

He banked, and banked again as he saw how little climb he had. A bloody arm came crashing over his shoulder, and someone fell on him, and he yelled at Feirn over the ravings. She hauled the delirious boy off him.

"Keep them back there!" he shouted.

"Vaun . . . How did you do that?"

"Do what?" The trees were still too close.

"Make the pepods attack like that?"

"What?" He turned in horror to look at her, and an updraft from the forest fires struck the torch, and for a moment he wrestled disaster. Motors screaming, the torch steadied. Now all four of the patients seemed to be shrieking at once. Pepod poison was fast, and he wouldn't give a peppercorn for their chances, any of them. He was ferrying corpses, but it had to be done.

"I didn't do that!" he bellowed. She probably couldn't hear him over the free-for-all going on back there . . .

"Security—where is the sick bay?"

"In the Great Hall, sir.''

Good! He wondered if that was Maeve's doing, and dropped the torch to an extremely rough landing on the front terrace, probably taking out half the windows in the west facade in the process. As he killed the motors, a gang of at least a dozen boys came running to unload. Someone was organizing.

Vaun stumbled out, and lifted Feirn bodily after him. He identified a commodore he knew slightly and told him to take over the torch or find another pilot, and then he headed for the house with a firm grip on the girl's slender wrist, almost dragging her. Before they reached the doors they were both coughing and weeping from the smoke of the burning forest. From indoors came a sound of bedlam.

"Now listen, Feirn! I had nothing to . . ." But her eyes were as wild as her red hair, and he saw that smoke was not the cause. She wasn't comprehending. "I had nothing to do with it."

She stumbled groggily, and he slowed. She was only a kid, and only a civilian, and the nightmares had been too much for her. Nevertheless, he daren't have her running around suggesting that he was responsible for the catastrophe. She hadn't heard Roker and Quild outline their crazy scheme, hadn't heard Vaun's protests. She'd watched Vaun and Quild go off to the pepods, and then the whole thicket had charged in and started slaying. Hers was not an unreasonable assumption, perhaps, but she must not be allowed to spread such ravings around tonight. Things were bad enough without that.

"You stay with me, all right?" he said as they reached the doors. He started to babble some nonsense about her being a professional eyewitness, and how important her testimony would be, and then saw it wasn't needed.

"Oh, yes, yes, yes! Yes, please!" She moved close, and clung to him.

Fair enough—her fixation on the great Admiral Vaun was still there, and now he was going to be her personal protector. Her thinking was just muddled, and she would not deliberately make trouble.

He blinked in the lights of the Great Hall. The tables had been pushed back, and bedding was being spread on the floors. He saw medical robots, and human attendants, and a lot of wounded. Amid all the noise and confusion, he sensed an undercurrent of method. Very few of the pepod victims would survive, but there would be burns and trauma and blast to deal with also. He could not see Maeve.

Security imaged in before him, a transparent face on a misty torso. Even its voice was faint. "Sir, a great many male persons are heading for the parking lot. My resources are inadequate for peaceful deterrence."

Half a dozen girls had surrounded Vaun and were shouting for attention. The boys had taken a more direct approach, but all those innocent bystanders Roker had rounded up, Maeve's guests of the night before . . . they would all want to head home now, to find out what had happened to their families and friends. Oh, gwathshit!

"Use force, then. As little force as necessary. Zombie gas, or something. But do not let any torches leave without my authorization. *Quiet!*''

The girls recoiled, and the hubbub around him stilled momentarily. ''As soon as we know it's safe, you can all leave!'' he shouted. ''But not until then! That is final, and you are under martial law. Tomorrow you can leave. Now go and help the wounded!''

Angry and frightened, they began to disperse. Were Roker here, he would agree with Vaun's decision. The Q ship was a dead issue now, until Ult recovered from this more immediate and tangible disaster.

Just in time, Vaun grabbed Feirn's arm as she moved to follow the others. ''You stay with me, remember?''

She nodded, and he hurried her out into a corridor.

''Vaun?'' she gasped breathlessly. ''What happened? Why did you and the other man go to the pepods?''

''It was Roker's idea, not mine.''

''But what was he trying to do?''

''Vaun!'' shouted another voice. ''Feirn!''

He turned as Maeve came running up. Her thick hair hung loose and disordered, and she wore an opulent white gown that seemed stupidly inappropriate for a major catastrophe. She looked from him to her daughter and back again. ''You're all right? Both of you?''

Feirn huddled close to Vaun and said, ''Yes!'' defiantly.

''We're both fine,'' Vaun said. ''Can you cope with the wounded?''

Maeve nodded, giving her daughter a worried frown. ''I can use more help, though.''

''No!'' Feirn yelped the word, and clung to Vaun with both arms. She was shaking violently. He put an arm around her also.

''She stays with me. I need her.''

Maeve hesitated, then shrugged in agreement, her eyes asking questions she obviously dared not put into words. Maeve as a mother was a strange concept for him, one he found oddly disturbing. He smiled and shook his head ever so slightly. She seemed to take that for reassurance, and relaxed a little. ''They're going to die, aren't they? Most of them?''

''Yes. Almost all. Just make them as comfortable as possible.''

She shuddered. ''Gods, it's awful. And not just here. What in Heaven's name happened, Vaun?''

Good question! What had Roker really wanted? What had Quild intended? Had Quild being playing for the Brotherhood? Quild had certainly not been one of the brethren, and surely he would not have chosen to die so horribly. Assume Quild had been a victim of his own folly—had Roker really expected the weird pepod seance to produce results, or had he merely been plotting murder? The dead must be given the benefit of the doubt.

"Roker was trying to find Cessine and Dice."

Maeve blinked. "Who?"

"My brothers," Vaun said. "My long-lost brothers."

L IKE THAM'S ESTATE of Forhil—like all the great Patrol houses—Valhal was equipped for defense. In a dark corner, Vaun triggered a hidden catch, and ushered Feirn through the door that slid open before them. It hissed closed as he followed, and the elevator fell swiftly.

She yelped, and turned scared blue eyes on him. "Where are we going?"

"To the bunker. Control center." There he could run a much tighter operation than he could through the sims.

Roker was dead. Until the conclave assembled, the Patrol would be commanded by the senior surviving officer, and Vaun had no idea who that was. It might even be the famous Admiral Vaun himself. Roker had cleaned out most of Frisde's cronies when he succeeded, and all of Hagar's clique. Many of the real old-timers had long since gone into withdrawal and been forgotten, others had lost interest and buried themselves on their estates, partying and leching and making merry. They would decline the honor. Vaun's first duty was to establish contact with Data Central.

The floor heaved upward underfoot; the door slid open on brilliance and a sense of busy activity. That was an illusion created by dozens of view tanks and overhead screens, all flickering information as if reporting to an army of invisible human operators. The big room was not quite as unoccupied as it should be, though—two boys and a girl sat at the long table in the center, slumped and silent. Vaun strode angrily forward and they lifted shock-dulled eyes to him.

"Elan?" he demanded, and the girl nodded.

So this had been Quild's control room, and Vaun gritted his teeth at Roker's impudence in making it available to a rabble of civilian academics. Nevertheless, he was delighted to have this lot fall into his hands.

"Right!" he barked in his best Doggoth voice. "Report! What went wrong?"

The girl shook her head blankly and looked to one of the boys. He just stared, licking his lips. It was the other who spoke.

"We don't know!" he said hoarsely. "They just went crazy."

"Well? Find out!" Vaun gestured at the tanks and consoles. "You've got all the brain power you can use right here. I want answers, and you don't leave until I have them. Do I have to drug you alert, or can you function?"

"You can't—"

"Oh, yes I can! We have a state of emergency in effect, and you three were responsible for the death of the high admiral himself, not to mention hundreds or thousands of people elsewhere, or haven't you got that through your pretty heads yet? You are in terrible, terrible . . . Shut *up*! I can take you out and shoot you if I want to, or I can turn you over to the crowd upstairs, who will assuredly rip you all to shreds—so which is to be? Cooperation? Good. Then get busy!"

The threats seemed to work, at least temporarily. The boys rose angrily and strode over to a board, and the girl followed.

Vaun doubted they would produce results, but he left them to it, going to the commander's seat in front of the primary tank.

Then he remembered Feirn. She was leaning straight-armed on a chair back, watching him with lips drawn back and eyes like two holes in a snowbank. The harsh lighting did nothing for her. He had seen recruits at Doggoth look like that on their third or fourth day, but with much more excuse—Feirn still had her gorgeous copper hair, even if it was hanging in tangles, and she had not been raped even once that he knew of. Recalling his overwhelming physical response to her earlier, he squirmed with disgust. He certainly had no time for such reactions now. Or perhaps his head was clearing, although it felt as though it had been buried under a pile of sand. But he had promised Maeve he would look after her daughter.

"Sit!" he said, gesturing at the next tank. "You can work one of these . . . You keep an eye on Blade for me. I've given him too much to do for his rank, and he's probably too pigheaded to shout for help if he needs it. Let me know if he gets in trouble, all right?"

Silently she nodded, like a frightened child, and sat down at the board.

Putting her out of his mind, he set to work.

First he ran a quick scan of the grounds. The wounded were being brought in, and Blade was coping so far, snapping orders, wielding the system like an expert. That boy had promise.

There was Maeve, in the Great Hall, shouting down a hysterical female admiral. Excellent. The parking lot was being held against an angry, but so far nonviolent, group of boys, and two captains were organizing food in the kitchens.

Satisfied that his immediate responsibility, Valhal, was running smoothly, Vaun turned to external affairs. He discovered that Data Control had been coming on line for a few nanoseconds at a time and then crashing again. He thought about that. . .

"Archives. Isn't there some regulation about field command when the C-in-C dies in action?"

The overworked system creaked for a moment, and then flashed up a text in the tank: *Para. 3-1a(1), Patrol Regulations 520.50.* Unchanged since the Faorian Civil War, centuries ago, but still in effect . . . Senior officer on location takes command. Which is what Vaun had thought. Good old Doggoth!—when it taught a boy, he stayed taught. He needed several minutes to prepare his move, but the next time Hiport came up it was rammed by a priority override invoking 520.50 and clearing everyone else off the system.

It worked.

He sat back and rubbed his eyes.

"Why are you grinning?" demanded a thin, scared voice.

He looked around at Feirn. "Am I?" He grinned more. "I suppose because I just got a promotion."

"You did what?"

"I just appointed myself emperor of the planet."

Nice.

"**C**OMMODORE! COMMODORE PRIOR?"

That means him. He is Prior, here in Hiport. He is a commodore. The mudslug from the delta is a commodore now! People salute him. Highborn lieutenants and captains salute the mudslug from the delta.

Rank and power and authority, and people groveling.

He turns to the girl's call, and something in his mind somersaults. Blue eyes, snub nose, big tits. Who is she? She knows him. So familiar! Memories . . . Prior's memories. Prior knew this blond girl smiling so hopefully at him, Vaun. Prior laid her, and more than once. Name? Name! *Name!* . . . She's not in uniform, so she's probably some sort of flack or historian or something weird. Pretty face, fair hair swinging loose, blue eyes . . . and terrific pillow fodder, as Prior recalls for him. Greedy little wildcat.

Lots of girls will do almost anything for a commodore.

Name? Name! *Damn it, Prior, give me her name!*

"Well! Hello, Gorgeous!"

"Commodore Prior, how wonderful to see you again!" She is smiling and laughing. Ooops . . . She obviously doesn't want to be kissed, at least not here in a busy corridor. She backs off, alarmed. "It's been weeks! Where in the galaxy have you *been*?" And adds quietly, "Oh, darling, how I've *missed* you!"

No wonder he collected this memory, then. It's a current affair, and would have been near the surface. Prior always had at least three affairs on the go, the gnomes told him, and showed him sims, but this girl wasn't one of them. Well, the next move is obvious.

"Oh, but I've missed you, too!"

Her blue eyes mist over. "Truly, darling? Oh, do you mean that?"

This looks very promising, provided he can discover her name. Of course Maeve will not like it if he stays *too* much in character, and he does talk in his sleep. The nightmares are waning, though, and he probably doesn't make enough sense for her to find out.

194

". . . next week?" asks the girl hopefully. "Hani's going to the Resources Conference." The blue eyes widen with appeal.

That's why she's not in uniform—she's Admiral Haniar's lady.

*Down, Prior!* "Next week, I'll be gone again, I'm afraid. The same mission . . . I'm only back for a couple of days . . . Oh, beloved, I'll count the minutes . . ."

He is really getting quite good at this, he thinks, as he continues along the corridor with What's-Her-Name's protestations of unlimited devotion still tingling his id, plus assurances that tonight would be all right if he can let her know early enough. At times he can almost believe he truly is Prior, spacer veteran, spy, double agent, lecher extraordinary. At times both Maeve and Roker have accused him of it. But he has Prior under control now. The bastard is *dead*!

I touched his brain, or what was left of it.

Dead!

The conference room is on the two-hundred level, circular and vertiginous. Walls swoop down to blend with floor, and all is transparent, even the seats. The impression is of floating high above Hiport, and on bad days the clouds float by. On those days it is easier to concentrate on the subject of the meetings.

Operation Modred—top secret. Today there are four commodores and a dozen mere mortals and they are all staring in horror at Roker as he outlines the mission.

*Destroy a Q ship?*

Vaun listens with less than half an ear. He has heard all this before, and besides, he doesn't want to hear it. If those missiles do get fired, he is going to be awfully, nastily, wet-armpity close to the target point. There's some question as to whether the damned things will work at all, of course, which is comforting. They are so old that no one knows how old they are. Nowadays no one wastes resources building weapons for wars that can never be fought, but these beauties have been the Patrol's treasure since time immemorial, and actually to fire them sounds like heresy. Attacking a Q ship is bad enough.

Q ships are sacred.

Vaun has been in Hiport for three days and Hiport is mindblistering. The coils of the launcher are the largest artifacts Ult has ever known. Gangs work on them continuously, repairing the corrosion. By the time they get to the top, the bottom needs rescuing again. Almost half the metal ever mined on the planet has gone into the Hiport launcher.

And maybe half the nonmetal materials into its buildings, Vaun suspects. Hiport is immensely old, and immensely impressive. It is too huge to comprehend. They don't make 'em like this any more. He hates it. In Hiport he can almost never be alone with Maeve, and when he isn't with Maeve his longing for her drives him lunatic. He dreams fantastic dreams of actually pulling off this crazy mission and returning as a hero, to inherit Valhal. Then he will throw Roker out and keep Maeve. Just the two of them together alone for always.

Not extremely likely.

An intercontinental is coming in. Traffic is heavy today. May be going to rain, later.

Roker drones on. He will not tell this group why the Q ship is suspect, for that is the heart of the most secret, but soon he will explain how Commodore Prior will be taking up the pilot boat.

Eventually someone will object that it is dangerous to run boats around Q ships when the fireballs are active, and Roker will say he knows that, thank you. He may or may not explain the need to stop the intruder dispersing a few quick shuttle craft on the sly. What he certainly won't say is that the pilot boat is going to be in a lot more danger from the crew of the Q ship than from its singularities.

At least there is no longer any doubt about motive, no doubt that Prior was an advance scout for an invasion. Vaun has Prior's memories, or some of them, enough of them. He remembers Prior remembering that the brethren plan to be on that ship, if they can. Of course if the Brotherhood lost the war on Avalon, then the ship will be harmless and Vaun will disappear very soon after he makes planetfall again. If the brethren are on board, then they will want to talk with Prior, but they will be very suspicious.

Vaun will have to play it by ear, both ears.

If he can give Roker enough evidence to justify attacking the Q ship, then he will probably die in the neuron blast.

If he finds the Q ship is harmless, then he'll be disposed of afterward, but quietly.

If he alerts the brethren on the Q ship, then they may get him before Roker does.

Issa. That's the name of Admiral Haniar's lady. Issa.

Tonight would be all right, she said. Yes, tonight would be all right for him, too. He'll have to make it awful quick, but it would be all right. Nice being a commodore.

# E MPEROR OF THE planet!

Roker was dead and Central had accepted that Vaun was in command—it was a heady feeling, but unfortunately he had no time to savor it.

When he finally had time to inquire, he learned that the senior surviving officer in the Patrol was Admiral Weald. He knew of her vaguely as a recluse interested in nothing outside her collection of antique porcelain. In all his forty-eight years as an admiral, he had not met her once. She turned out to be a slight, frail-seeming girl who looked as if she could never have survived toilet training untraumatized, let alone the rigors of Doggoth. Yet her eyes were steady as she stared out of the tank, and her pale smile seemed genuine. A spacefarers' blaze was nestled in the lace on her blouse.

"I was afraid you might call," she said.

"Ma'am, I have the honor—"

She shook her head, and her dark hair waved. Her home must be a long way east of Valhal, for sun streamed through the window behind her. "You're doing very well, lad. I've been watching you all morning, and no one could have done a better job. I think you should continue to act."

Strangely, despite all his years of frustration as a figurehead admiral, Vaun felt no ambition to retain command of the Patrol. He had enjoyed the challenge of the last few hours, but it was over now, and he wanted to wheel himself off to bed. On the other hand, this sprig of a girl hardly looked like a high admiral, even if the records said she was twice his age. Not even if she did call him "lad."

"It would not be appropriate," he said.

"Very appropriate! You've done a splendid job. The flacks must be ecstatic." She laughed as he pulled a face.

*Space Patrol to the Rescue—Famous Hero Takes Charge* . . .

"Seriously," he said. "I've got a couple of reports here. Look them over and you'll see what I mean."

Weald pouted, but did not object as he had expected. She faded out. He sent her his work on the Q ship trajectory, and Tham's Ootharsis of Isquat file.

He leaned back and stretched sensuously, enjoying his aches and a world-sized yawn. Then he looked around, and the three biologists were sprawled over the table, heads on arms, all apparently asleep. He must have been here for hours.

"Why inappropriate?"

He had completely forgotten Feirn. She was sitting cross-legged on the next chair to his, and regarding him with a steady, if understandably bleary, gaze. Obviously she had recovered her wits and poise. She had combed her lovely hair, too, sometime in the last however-long-it-had-been. Good for her!

"Why aren't you watching Blade, as I told you to?" he snapped.

She smirked. "Because he's in the shower."

*"Shower?"*

"He's finished. Wounded and bodies, all collected. He tried to report to you and I told him you were busy." Feirn tossed her head pertly.

Obviously she had resilience as well as impudence. "Then tell him to come down here as soon as he's ready," Vaun said, hiding amusement.

"I already did! He's done very well, hasn't he?"

"Yes. He's done extremely well. He's one of the night's heroes."

She frowned at that. "You're the biggest hero. Why are you trying to give up now?"

As Acting High Admiral, he was no longer free to babble Patrol secrets to Feirn, if he ever had been, so he laughed off the question. "I don't want to overdo the hero-saves-the-world act. People may get bored of it."

"But you just did. Did save the world." She seemed quite serious as she said it.

Vaun shrugged. "The pepods have erupted many times before, and Ult has always survived without any help from me."

"This was the worst outbreak of modern times. It was the worst since at least 19,090, if you're interested." She smiled cockily at his surprise, and indicated the tank beside her. "Blade didn't need me, and your conversation began to get boring."

He apologized solemnly.

She considered the matter, head on one side, eyes as bright as a bird's. "Well, I admit you were busy saving the world, but don't expect that excuse to work every time."

There was a sparkle there that he had not anticipated, but if she thought their date for this evening was still on, then she had chagrin coming. Admiral Vaun lusted for bed, and bed alone.

"The cities escaped, of course," she said seriously. "And the winter weather was a godsend, wasn't it?"

"I suppose so."

"Kept people indoors. So now we all stay indoors for a few days, until the vegetation calms down?"

"That's about it." Vaun covered a yawn. He had apparently impressed both Feirn and Weald, but in fact Hiport's computers had done most of it. He had been helped by the special powers he could invoke under Roker's state of emergency—that had been a fortunate irony—and all he had needed to do was keep his head, set priorities, and issue orders. He had dispatched air strikes against the worst infestations; he had untangled communications; he had organized rescues and medical help; he had restored public calm. Almost every operational torch and spacecraft on the planet was operating on his behest right now.

It had not been difficult. If the Brotherhood was planning to create worldwide chaos, as Roker had suggested, then it could hardly do better than what had just happened, but the effect had been very brief, in spite of Roker's death. And that had been a fluke, for high admirals did not normally spend much time near pepods. Moreover the timing had been wrong, because the Q ship panic had not started yet. So the pepod outbreak had nothing to do with the Brotherhood, right?

*Right,* said logic.

*Wrong,* said instinct. Paranoiacs live longer . . . But if there was a connection, he couldn't see it. He yawned.

"So why give up your command?" Feirn had turned serious, her blue eyes glazing over with hero worship.

"It's been an interesting exercise in priorities, is all. Now I want to hand over the paperwork to someone else."

"But I get first interview!" In one of her sudden changes of mood, she showed a gleeful collection of teeth. "And now it isn't just the old folk who'll recognize—Oh shit! Sorry, Admiral." She turned red, and then redder.

"Oh, I save the world every couple of generations, just to keep my face in the news."

"I said I'm sorry! Now you can see why I'm no good at—"

"I'm sure you're fine. You do very well for a kid."

"Swine! Rub it in."

"You're tired, is all. We both need to get to bed."

"Yes, please." She grinned nervously. Hero worship again.

Before Vaun had time to straighten out her confusion on that topic, Weald's fine-drawn features returned to the tank, brow creased with worry. He swung around to face her.

She was nodding solemnly. "I see what you mean, Admiral. Of course, no reasonable person would doubt your loyalty for a minute, but . . ."

"But they should," Vaun said, smothering yet another yawn. "It would be unreasonable not to. And I certainly must not be in charge of the Patrol when that Q ship arrives." Some hotheaded xenophobe would certainly assassinate him.

"Let me see if I've got my ancient mind round this. Standard arrival will be in twenty-eight weeks if it begins deceleration no later than today, at a normal half gee. That's about the limit for rocks, right? And if it doesn't . . ."

"Seventy-eight days till impact."

Weald frowned. "That doesn't seem to add up."

"One hundred and eighteen in their frame of reference, less light lag of thirty-nine."

"Of course. Stupid of me. No way to contact it, of course?"

"None."

Weald looked exasperated. "How long does it take to call a conclave?"

"Your decision, ma'am. I'd give them a couple of days to assemble, and a few more to talk about it. Then vote."

She nodded impatiently. "And then I can come home and be myself again . . . Very well. Is there a ceremony to this?"

"I think you just record your acceptance, ma'am."

"Right. I accept the position of, and will serve as, high admiral *pro tem*. Carry on, Admiral, you're doing great. Call a conclave, let me know where and when it is to be and if there is any development in the Q ship matter. You handle everything else."

The tank was empty.

Feirn sniggered. Vaun used a Doggoth expression she had not likely heard before.

"Two can play that game," he said grimly, and glanced at his Valhal situation board. The Great Hall was dim and quiet. Heavy equipment had brought the forest fires under control. The parking lot was deserted, with the last of the casualties removed. Blade was on his way to report. As soon as he'd done so, he could remove the irrepressible Feirn. Satisfactory!

The Hiport board was more cluttered, but nothing seemed critical. The duty officer's face appeared, gray with fatigue. "Sir?"

"Find a relief, and get some rest," Vaun snapped. "Advise all hands that Admiral Weald is Acting High Admiral with myself as ExOff . . . I am copying her acceptance to Archives . . . Process a promotion for Ensign Blade to lieutenant, effective at once . . . Hold all messages until I check in . . . Has Admiral Phalo arrived yet?''

"No, sir."

"When he does, he's in charge. Any questions?"

"About two hundred, sir."

"Tell your relief to deal with them."

The worry lines curled into a smile. "Sir!"

Vaun broke the connection and spun his chair around to look at the three biologists, the last problem to clear. One of the boys was still sleeping. The other two were sitting up, looking almost as scared as they should be. He wondered how long he'd been holding them here.

"Well? Have you an explanation?"

The girl nodded. "Yes, Admiral. It was an accident."

"Show me."

Elan rose stiffly and went to a board. In a moment she had called up a map of Shilam. She spoke without looking around. "This shows the pepod transmission on what we call the linking mode." A blue spot appeared at Valhal's location, and began to spread out over the continent like a stain, advancing irregularly but inexorably.

"What time lapse are you . . ." Then Vaun's eyes found the display on the screen overhead, and saw that he was viewing a real-time display.

"Real time." Elan's voice was hoarse and dull with fatigue. "The radio travels at light speed, but each thicket takes a few seconds to react."

"Right." It was impressive, and creepy. In a very few minutes, the blue had reached the sea almost everywhere. "That means that every pepod on Shilam was then linked into the group mind?"

"We believe so," she said.

The elevator door hissed open, but Vaun did not turn.

"You'd created a monster! And then what happened?"

"This." She touched a toggle, and the display turned red.

"Attack mode?"

"Yes, sir. But it didn't start here!" Her voice had risen to a squeak. "See it again in slow motion." The map went back to blue, and then to red again, but now there was time to see that the red had spread up from the south, from somewhere near Gefax.

"Something set them off at Gefax?" Vaun asked uneasily. Why did that feel wrong?

Elan turned around to look at him and he saw that she was terrified. "It must have done, sir! Not our doing at all! Some pepod was provoked while we had them linked . . . Professor Quild had never considered that possibility, so far as we know. It should have been just a local disturbance, but because we had them all linked . . . That was why they all went. We couldn't have known." She stared at him beseechingly.

Both boys were awake now, and both had the same dread look on their faces.

"Well, I suppose it's reasonable," Vaun said grudgingly. "And I'm not the judge. There will have to be an inquiry. You can go, but you will stay here in Valhal."

"We are under arrest?" one of the boys demanded shrilly.

"You are. You may communicate with your families, though. Or lawyers. Now scat!"

As the three stampeded for the elevator, Vaun turned wearily to Blade, who was standing stiffly at attention, of course. The last time Vaun had peeked at him, he had been a scarecrow running around the woods in bloody rags. Now he was his former impeccable self, in a clean uniform, with every hair in place . . . Insufferable perfectionist!

"Congratulations. You did a fine job, *Lieutenant*." .

The mauve eyes widened. "Thank you, sir! I just did my duty." Not a hint of a smile.

"And I just did mine." Again Vaun paused for a yawn. "Now escort Citizen Feirn to her quarters, and if you want my advice, Lieutenant . . . but I'm sure you don't."

"Vaun?" Feirn said softly.

He turned to her to shut her up, and then said, "Yes?" when he saw that he had guessed wrong.

She paused until the elevator door closed. "They missed something."

"Who did?"

"The three ivy-brains." She smirked, pleased with herself. Dropping her feet to the floor, she turned to the board beside her chair. Blade was frowning.

Her fingers jabbed at keys. "I was doing a little research, too. I saw what they were up to, and pried their data out of the banks . . . Here's the big picture." The map appeared again, but this time Shilam was smaller, and the three minor continents of the southern hemisphere appeared below it. Slowly the blue tide spread out from Valhal to fill Shilam—and cross the sea. "It never reached South Thisly, right? The pepods' range is too short to jump the straits."

Damn! Feirn had seen what Vaun and the students had over-looked—Thisly and Paralyst had been infested, but South Thisly had escaped the disaster. He should have remembered that, after spending so many hours dealing with the results. And she was obviously right about the range, because the blue stain spread down the Broach Peninsula to infect Paralyst, and leapfrogged through the Imbue Archipelago to Thisly. South Thisly stayed clear, isolated by the width of the Terebus Strait.

Lots of pepods in the cooler, southern continents.

"Well done!" he muttered crossly. "So the trigger wasn't at Gefax, it was somewhere down in Thisly?" So what?

"Er, yes. But . . . well, it's not important, I guess. But they still weren't quite right." She shifted the map to a close-up of Thisly. "Whatever provoked the attack didn't happen *after* the linkup. See . . . watch this. Did you see? The blue wave comes down to here— Kohab. That's its name, Kohab—and then bounces right back in red. No time break when you have the whole picture. So what happened was that the edge of the linkup ran into a thicket that was already on the warpath, and . . . Vaun!"

Vaun was on his feet, shoving her hands aside. Then he switched to vocal. "Show me that again. With more magnification! No, round Kohab. Bigger. Right . . . Again . . ."

Mother of Stars!

"Vaun?"

Vaun glanced at Blade, who had not said a word, but Blade was still frowning, and Blade was smarter than he acted. Vaun cut the display quickly. His throat was dry, his pulse racing. Was it possible?

Kohab had been blue *before* the linkup reached it—one tiny, isolated spot of blue, which had immediately turned red, and the red had then taken over everywhere, spreading back north. But even the front of the wave heading on south had been red after it passed Kohab.

"Summary of Kohab, in Thisly."

"Mining settlement dating from first millennium," said the dry, calm voice of the equipment. "Present population: zero. Aban-doned and reactivated fourteen times. Occupied by religious cults four times. Also used at various periods as penal station, artist colony, and germ warfare laboratory. Most recently reactivated, after three centuries of abandonment, as marine life research station in 29,399—"

"Cut!"

Possible! More than possible!

"Ens—Lieutenant. Are you familiar with the Moloch Sheerfire?"

Blade blinked. "No, sir."

"What d'you suppose its range would be?"

"I'd estimate a lot, sir. They don't make 'em like that any more."

"No," Vaun said, struggling to control his excitement. "No, they don't. Well, I have one more small task for you tonight. A job for a First in electronics."

The mauve eyes flickered. "Sir?"

"The high admiral's barge is a Sheerfire, and it's sitting up there in my private garage. Go up there and see that's it's fueled to the limit. And disconnect the auto."

The new lieutenant stiffened.

"And if you quote one word of regulations at me," Vaun said softly, "I'll bust you to crewboy!"

Just for a moment, he thought Lieutenant Blade was going to smile . . . but the fit passed. "Sir!"

Vaun headed for the elevator without another word. He heard Feirn call his name and he ignored her.

Maybe Roker hadn't died in vain. Maybe the bastard's crazy scheme had worked after all.


"**Y**OUR FATIGUE TOXINS level is elevated," the medic said, humming angrily. "Your last intake of booster was barely sixteen hours ago. I prescribe a sedative to counteract your current agitated condition, followed by extended bed rest. Personal history suggests that coitus would be advantageous, but your current level of testo—"

"Mind your own furtive business!" Vaun snapped. He hadn't slept for two nights, but he didn't feel tired now. He was running on adrenaline again. "Give me my booster with no extras . . . No, throw in something to keep me awake and assume that I won't get more booster for at least thirty hours . . . and leave out the stiffener." He was going to need a very clear head—an extremely clear head—if what he found at Kohab was what he suspected. And there would be no girls there to justify taking stiffener, only a couple of boys.

Dice and Cessine.

With a few clicks that sounded suspiciously like grumbling, the medic dispensed a tumblerful of booster. Sipping it as he walked, Vaun hurried off through the shadowy house. Here and there he saw lights under doors or detected low voices and moans, but all of Valhal had become one huge field hospital, and infinitely depressing in consequence.

Angel greeted him as he walked into his bedroom, flooding the sea with its spectral blue light. Normally that was a sight he could not ignore, but tonight it meant that he was running out of time. Dawn could not be far off, and he must leave before there were witnesses around.

It was going to be another long day.

He threw off his soiled clothes as he headed for the shower. Either the water or the pep in his booster began to take effect right after, and he was almost humming with excitement as he hurried into his den. Reluctantly he decided he had better wear full uniform, for he was going to be flying the high admiral's personal barge, and there would be questions when he stopped to refuel on the way back.

Tunic still unbuttoned, he padded barefoot across to the windows and coded open his gun cupboard. He found a regulation Dilber 16k handbeam and a Wassal Giantkiller that would bring down a behemoth or small aircraft. He'd better take some good, strong hiking boots and a warm . . .

"Good morning, Vaun," said a sleepy voice from one of the armchairs at the dark end of the room.

He swung around with the handgun, and then said, "Oh, damn!"

"You're improving." She yawned. "Not so coprolaliac as last time."

He was more visible in the Angellight than she was. In fact, it was only her voice he could recognize. He could barely be sure that there was no one else present.

"What're you doing here?"

"I was sleeping, actually. I feared you would think me presumptuous if I took the bed."

"Take it if you want. I'm not going to be using it."

"No, this is a very comfortable chair. I might as well go and make some rounds, anyway." She yawned again, and he saw her arms stretching overhead.

Maeve, right outside his bedroom door! Truly the night was filled with ironies. Oddly, though, he did not feel the burning anger he had felt the previous night . . . which was already the night before last now . . . Need to hurry. Blade would have the Sheerfire ready to go and dawn was pending.

Maeve! Well, she'd done a great job, too. He'd given Blade a promotion, but he could hardly promote Maeve to anything. He must go past her to reach the door, and now he was almost at her chair. He stopped.

"Thank you, Maeve—for all your work tonight. Great job!"

She was swaddled in a bulky, shapeless housecoat, color indeterminate in the shadow. When she looked up at him, he saw the whites of her eyes, mostly.

"I didn't do it as a favor to you, Vaun. But you're quite welcome if you want to take it as one."

"Sure, I will. Thank you."

"Ah, these rare little courtesies! Then I'd better apologize for gate-crashing, hadn't I? But it was the late Admiral Roker's fault, not mine."

"I understand that. Not your fault."

"And you're going to let us all go home tomorrow . . . today, is it now? So I'll be out of your hair."

"Well . . . Look, Maeve . . . I'm likely to be away for at least another night. You can stay on until I return, if you want." He couldn't promote her, but at least he could offer her something.

"And just why would I want to do that?" she asked, her voice a little sharper than before.

"Valhal?"

"What about Valhal? What's wrong with Arkady?"

He shrugged, surprised. "I just thought . . . Well, please yourself."

"Oh, I shall." She sat up straighter. "Thought what?"

"Nothing." He was too excited about the Kohab thing to want a knock-'em-down tussle with Maeve. And he hadn't had any stiffener lately—funny how that changed his feelings toward her. The adipose tissue that had fascinated him before would now seem merely an inefficient redundancy.

"No, do tell. I'm really curious now. Why did you think I'd want to stay in Valhal?"

There was no way to say it without being offensive, but he tried to keep his tone dispassionate and matter-of-fact. "Because you whored and lied and cheated and betrayed everyone and everything just to stay on as hostess in Valhal if by a miracle I did manage to get it away from Roker. So I assumed you would still be interested, that's all. A reasonable assumption. Doesn't matter. It was a long time ago. As you said, it doesn't matter now.''

She seemed to consider that for a moment, while he slung the Giantkiller on his shoulder and buttoned his tunic.

"Well, shitty shoes!'' she said softly. "Is that what you think? You've been looking at it that way all these years?''

"How else?'' He wondered again about spare boots.

"Well, I admit I wasn't always truthful. And I never claimed to be a bashful virgin, but I never realized . . . You still think that, do you?''

"With some justification,'' he retorted, beginning to feel testy. "And maybe one day you can drop me a note, explaining my error. Meanwhile, *if* you will excuse me, I must run.''

"Danger? When a boy packs guns and runs in the night, he must be in danger.'' She rose, a shapeless blur in the housecoat. "Trouble, Vaun? Can I help?''

"No. Well, one thing—keep that giddy little daughter of yours quiet, will you? I'd prefer she not go public until I get back. Appreciate that. Good-bye, Maeve. And thanks again for looking after the wounded.'' He turned.

"Wait! Vaun . . . be careful!''

He paused at the door. "What does that mean?''

"It means trouble. It means Q ships and pepods and the Patrol and the Brotherhood. I suppose it means I'd hate anything to happen to you.''

He snorted with a sudden surge of bitterness. "A tearful farewell? Do you remember when I went off to intercept *Unity*? When I was pretending to be Prior? When my chances of coming back were one in a billion?''

"Yes. Of course I remember. Why?''

"We were lovers, then. Or I was. And you didn't say good-bye then, Maeve. You left Hiport. You ran away back to Valhal. So why say good-bye now? Old age softening the hard edges a little?''

"And that has bothered you all these years?''

"Of course not! But it sure as hell bothered me then—that you'd leave without saying good-bye.'' When she tried to speak he spoke louder. "I was very stupid, wasn't I? I should have realized then that I wasn't anything to you except a future meal ticket, and that had stopped seeming very likely. That was all you'd been interested in. Oh, I should have seen right there! I should have known. But I didn't. When I came back alive and you rushed into my arms . . . I really believed.''

"Vaun . . . That wasn't what mattered!"

He laughed, and opened the door.

"Vaun! Please!"

He stopped.

"Vaun, please don't go off mad like that. I didn't say good-bye that time because I couldn't bear to. I was cowardly, yes, but it was because I *loved* you that I ran away."

He chuckled.

"Roker had told me that you wouldn't be coming back—no way! Yather was going to shoot you if the brethren didn't, he said. That was why Roker didn't mind risking Valhal, because there was no way you were going to come back alive. And I couldn't face you, knowing that! Can't you imagine how I felt, knowing what I'd done?"

"The expression is 'shitty shoes,' I believe."

"Its true. Damn you, it's true! If I was faking it in bed, I could have faked a fond good-bye, couldn't I? No, please listen. And I was never hostess in Valhal until you made me hostess in Valhal."

"What?" He spun around to look at her, but she was against the Angelbright windows and he couldn't see her face.

"I thought you knew! Yes, Roker threw me at you, but I wasn't his bedmate. Never."

"That day in the cloakroom . . ."

"Lies, of course!" Her voice cracked. "Yes, Roker planned all of that and told me what to say. He had three girls lined up, I drew short straw, and you took the first hook. All that crap about his liking boys . . . He planned it all, even to telling you to demand Valhal as your price. *All of it!* But I was never his mistress! Never. Before or after. Beefy loudmouths ain't my fun."

"Well, it doesn't matter now," he said angrily.

"It does, I think. I didn't do it for Roker, and I sure as Krantz didn't do it for Valhal. I did it because of the Brotherhood."

He said nothing. The torch was waiting, he ought to run.

"I did it because the human race was in danger, here on Ult! Isn't that a little more forgivable? Do you know how old I was?" She took a step toward him. "You still think I'm older than you, don't you? Something you said last night in Arkady . . . I was seventeen, Vaun. You were twenty-two."

He grunted. "It doesn't matter now."

"But it mattered then! You were so green! You thought you were a tough nut from Doggoth, and oh, you were tough. Tough physically. And emotionally, I suppose. I was younger, but not quite so green as you. I'd been one of Prior's statistics, I don't deny it. That was one of the criteria Roker used in selecting—"

"Come on, Maeve! Oh, come on! You're asking me to believe that you'd never had any boy except Prior? Because—"

"It's true, Vaun."

*Good God!* And Roker was dead now. Why should she lie now?

"Prior, twice. Once drunk, once sober. Then Vaun, Vaun, Vaun . . . All the Vaun I could get. I only agreed to whore for Roker, for the Patrol, because the world was in danger from the Brotherhood. He persuaded me that you were the secret weapon, but the Patrol needed to keep you under control and know what you were thinking. And you needed love."

"Sex!" he said sharply.

"No!" Her voice was softer now. "The stiffener made you need that. It still does. You were a motherless, friendless boy, and you needed love. I don't think you've changed very much."

"You forget I'm not human."

"You're human that way. All those girls who came after me in Valhal . . . And from what I know of the brethren, they need love even more than we do."

"You don't know much."

"More than you think. They have each other. They love one another, don't they?"

Raj? Dice? And Prior's memories of Monad Hive and . . .

And *Unity*, the Q ship, most of all.

"Maybe," he said gruffly. "Yes, they love one another."

Was that why he was rushing off now to Kohab? Just to see Dice again? Ask forgiveness?

"And you had no one," Maeve said. "I set out to be a whore and saw I had to be a mother and discovered I'd become a lover. Bed had really nothing to do with it, Vaun. Oh, you were great! Terrific. Never found a better. But it wasn't bed I wanted from you."

He felt sick. "It was Valhal!"

She shook her head, and took a deep breath, and he realized that she was probably weeping. He could never remember seeing Maeve weep, not even the day he threw her out. The idea of Maeve weeping was unthinkable.

"Why then?" he snapped. "When I came back? For five years you balled me by night and tattled to Roker by day. Security had records of your calls. If that isn't whoring, I don't know what is! And for what? It certainly wasn't for me. For Valhal, is what." He turned to go.

"Blackmail! Don't you see, even yet? When you returned, we all thought you must be one of the brethren. It was impossible that the Vaun we knew had survived! So Roker demanded that I come back. To watch over you and see if you were genuine, the real one—that was what I was supposed to do, and that was what I did, and I told him you were the real Vaun, and I loved you, but then I couldn't stop tattling to him because he blackmailed me. He said if I changed sides, he'd tell you the whole story and then you'd throw me out. DataCen did psychoplots."

"Crap! They're worthless."

"No. In the end they proved right enough. When you discovered, you did throw me out! And I always knew you would. I couldn't bear to see you hurt any more . . ."

"Gwathshit!" he muttered, still not looking at her.

Maeve sighed. "The tragedy was that there were no secrets to spill, except medical ones."

He bristled. "Medical?"

"The medics were curious about the effect stiffener has on you. You're either indifferent or a raging satyr. The same as Prior. Don't tell me you haven't noticed?"

"You preferred the latter, of course."

"Oh yes! I enjoyed the effects! But I loved you best when you were content just to be yourself: self-contained, competent, honest . . . not trying to act like a great celebrity, or a spacer stud, or a social snob. But even then, even when you became all those things, I still loved you."

Silence. Then she laughed ruefully. "I think I still do."

"Who's Feirn's father?"

"A minor poet with carroty hair and political aspirations. He died in the Cashalix food riots, before she was born. You didn't bed her?"

"No, I did not!"

"I wish you had."

*"Maeve!"*

She made a noise somewhere between a snigger and a sniffle. "I made a terrible mess of Feirn. All her life, she's heard me jabbering on about Vaun, Vaun, Vaun, and how I loved him. Still love him."

Roker was dead. She had Arkady. She had a career. Why would she say such a thing now?

It certainly couldn't be for pride.

He had a painful ache he couldn't place. "Maeve . . . when I get back, in a day or two . . . may I come and see you, in Arkady?"

"Of course. Anytime, Vaun."

"Thank you," he said gruffly. "I must go now."

"Do take care, won't you?"

"You, too."

He left the room before he was tempted to do something foolish.

T HE TIP OF Bandor was already turning pink when Vaun jumped down from the cart, shivering in the clammy dawn air. Half a dozen nondescript torches stood on the tarmac. The magnificent Sheerfire had been hauled out from under cover and waited in full sight, but there was no one around to see. That was no mere torch; that was a cruiser.

The passenger door stood open. He closed it behind him and wandered forward with his hand on his holster. Roker had done himself proud, from kidskin chairs to gold taps. The high admiral's barge was a miniature flying palace—bedchamber, office, lounge, galley . . .

Flight deck.

Lieutenant Blade was sitting in the copilot's seat, going through a hardcopy manual. He was almost at the end of it, too.

Vaun took the other seat, laid the Giantkiller out of the copilot's reach and regarded his companion quizzically.

"Thank you," he said. "Dismissed."

The mauve eyes held his scrutiny without flinching. "Estimated flight time to Kohab nine hours, sir."

Vaun could have said, *What makes you think I am going to Kohab?* He didn't.

"I disconnected the automatics as you instructed, sir." Blade could have added, *And that means they can't detect you coming.* He didn't.

Nor did he say, *It is a flagrant breach of regulations and civilian laws, also, because neither Hiport not any air traffic control center is going to know you are airborne.*

And he did not point out that Vaun had not slept all night and a tub like this was going to be a brute to fly on manual for nine hours.

The staring continued. Any boy who collected virtually every medal Doggoth offered must have brains in unusual quantities, however monolithic he pretended to be. He did not have all the data, because he did not know that Vaun was immune to pepods, but it was a fair guess that Lieutenant Blade knew what Vaun expected to find at the isolated outpost of Kohab.

Blade did not ask what Vaun planned to do about it. But he had certainly noticed the guns.

He did not say, *If you forbid me to accompany you, then my duty is absolutely clear and I must report you immediately to Acting High Admiral Weald.*

It was.

He would, too.

Vaun's trouble was that he did not know exactly what he planned to do at Kohab. Dice? Invite his two brothers to come and spend a comfortable retirement at Valhal?

He snapped open his holster.

Blade's thin face showed no reaction.

*Juvenile dreams of honor and heroism . . .*

Crazy mixed-up randoms!

"Are you prepared to obey my orders without question, no matter how they may seem?"

Flicker. "Of course, sir."

Vaun sighed and rubbed his eyes. He did not say, *Do you really think you can fly this bitch without autos, sonny?*

What he did say was, "Take her up, then."

It was the first time he had seen Blade smile.

T HE RENOWNED MOLOCH designers had been a brilliant and imaginative lot, but they had never conceived of anyone being crazy enough to try flying a Sheerfire on manual. Blade did clear the treetops, but he probably lost some paint. He certainly lost Vaun's stomach. After that nothing seemed too terrible; he took her up to cruising altitude and headed south over the sea. Under the circumstances, he was flying very well. Of course. Not a word was spoken.

Dice. Cessine.

If Roker's thugs had extracted the truth, then those were the two cuckoos who had never been apprehended. Dice had been second oldest. Cessine had been third. Vaun, the youngest, had never met Cessine, but he would be indistinguishable from Dice, if he still lived. One or other might be dead, of course, because it had been a long time. The others had all been murdered in Roker's horror chambers—Tong, and Raj, and Prosy, the eldest. Prior also, of course.

But someone was messing about with pepods, in secret, at an uninhabited nowhere-place in Thisly. It had to be either Dice or Cessine, or both.

What *was* Vaun planning? What did he want?

Information about the Q ship? If Prior had ever been told of the runaway Q ship gambit, then Vaun had failed to assimilate those memories. That was possible—the language complexes had transferred smoothly, but after that the brain had been so traumatized that later retrievals had been extremely spotty. Much had faded after the first few days, too. But Prior might have known, and he might have told Dice and Cessine.

Or was this a peace mission? There was Tham's Ootharsis evidence. Whatever bitter conflict had erupted on Avalon, the brethren had obviously lived in peace on Scyth once, and been valued citizens. Here on Ult, Vaun had been accepted and put to good use. Unless his brothers were up to some conspicuous mischief at present, he could certainly obtain a pardon for them now, so that they might live out their days in comfort.

Scyth, though, had gone silent.

Remembering what Maeve had said, he chuckled. Love? Was that all? Family reunion?

Small wonder that Lieutenant Blade did not trust Admiral Vaun. Admiral Vaun did not entirely trust himself.

After an hour he saw the beaded sweat on Blade's brow.

"I'll take a turn, now," he said. "Grab me a snack and then try that feather bed."

He took the con, and was appalled at the concentration needed to keep the brute stable. The Sheerfire tried to wander like a fistful of water; he gritted his teeth and swore by every god worshipped on Ult that he was not going to do worse than Smarty-Pants Lieutenant Blade.

Who had vanished to the rear in search of the galley.

And who was shortly to be heard shouting . . .

When the two of them burst into the cabin, Vaun risked a quick glance back. Blade's face was crimson with shame. Feirn was pale and bedraggled and had obviously been asleep. The barge lurched and Vaun hastily directed his attention to the controls again.

"Under the bed, I suppose," he said when he had leveled.

"In the closet," Feirn said grumpily. "Ouch! You're hurting my arm, Blade."

"Leave her be, Lieutenant. My fault, too. I must have gone right by her." But it had been Blade who had left the door open.

Realizing she had won, Feirn at once become cocky. "You told me to stay with you, Admiral! Besides, this will be a historic confrontation and I represent the media."

"You represent a gigantic pain in the ass."

"You say the sweetest things," she murmured, and leaned over his shoulder to kiss his cheek.

The Sheerfire wobbled violently and Vaun yelped in disgust. "Lieutenant! Take her away and throw her out!"

Feirn giggled and struggled as Blade tried to remove her. He did not make a sound, and Vaun wished he could see the expression on his face.

So now they had a press corps along! Vaun would not dare try to put this wallowing monster down anywhere except a standard strip, and to do that would incite the wrath of authority, uncovering and probably terminating his secret mission. He was stuck with the muddle-headed kid. His one-boy scouting trip was becoming a bandwagon.

Going to meet the brethren . . .

"Well, you might as well be useful," he said. "Can you cook?"

"No, I can not!" Feirn shouted, stamping her foot. Evidently cooking was not romantic enough for a hero's lady.

"I can," Blade said glumly. "You weren't serious about throwing her out, were you, sir?"

# GOING TO MEET the brethren . . .

Maybe. Maybe not. But what happens if we do?

Space Patrol shuttle *Liberty* in orbit, Commodore Prior commanding . . .

The fake Commodore Prior has a fearful urge to scratch the itching, healing scars on his stubbled head. He wonders for the hundredth time why Maeve did not stay to say good-bye. He can remember dozens of Prior's innumerable mistresses, and none of them compares with Maeve. He tries not to think about Yather and his gun.

The shuttle is almost within contact range, drifting ever closer to the Q ship, whose fire-scarred bulk now fills the tanks and blots the stars. Roker's clandestine vid stays stubbornly amber on Vaun's board, meaning he still does not have enough evidence to launch the missiles. If High Admiral Frisde herself is not holding the knife to his back, then she will certainly have appointed others to do so. Destroying a Q ship is sacrilege.

The voices from *Unity* have remained infuriatingly ambiguous, and the only image has been that of the girl, who does more smiling than talking, and even Vaun can make out little of what she says.

On Vaun's left, GravOff mutters an aside to his other neighbor, the medic. "Perhaps she's being held prisoner by beasties and would be grateful for being rescued."

MedOff counters on predictable lines. "But rescued by something human, like me."

So neither suspects that the girl is only a sim, or that there is nothing truly human on the Q ship at all. Or is Vaun's imagination seeing guilt where there is only reasonable doubt?

"What I want," MedOff continues, "is a hot shower."

"We'd all appreciate your getting that," says GravOff.

They have been sitting in this tin bucket for hours. A few formalities, and then showers and food and rest. Inspections start

215

tomorrow. That is the usual program. God knows what's planned
this time.

"*Liberty*, stand by for umbilical," says the boy's voice, quite
legibly. A cloud erupts from the ship's surface, and rapidly dissi-
pates into the vacuum. The umbilical floats out, a deceptively lazy
rope, for it bridges the gap in seconds, its free end swelling like a
monster snake with a circular mouth, shooting little puffs of steam
out of six nostrils as it lines up with the pilot boat's door. . . .

*Thump!*

"Contact, sir!"

Vaun acknowledges, and catches Yather's baleful gaze again. He
wants to apologize, somehow, as if there has been anything at all
he could have done to avoid this part, when *Unity* has taken control.
That physical linkage has increased the boat's danger. Now it is
tied to the target in Roker's sights. If the Avalonians go, she goes.
And MedOff will have to board that sucker, and Vaun may be
sending the boy to his death. Yather's glare says it's all his fault,
but there has been nothing he could do to avoid this. He's only an
ensign masquerading as a commodore—a mudslug masquerading
as a spacer . . . a unit of the Brotherhood playing on the human
team.

At least, he has played on the human team so far.

The prizes for this team are Valhal, and Maeve. The other team
doesn't get prizes.

"Pressurization complete, sir."

The first order of business must be to remove that gun of Yather's.
It is too distracting. How can Vaun think straight when his guts are
in danger of being blown out? Of course, neither side wants him to
think straight; they all prefer to do his thinking for him, but his
neck is closer to the ax than anyone's, and he feels stupidly responsible for the crew, for the five innocents among the crew, at least.
Not Yather—Yather knows the score and can look out for himself.
And if anything startles the big man, he may make a nasty mistake
in Vaun's direction.

ExOff snaps switches on her board, cutting the boat's pseudogravity, just as a sudden lurch tells of the umbilical starting to haul
it in. For a moment Vaun's head swims with vertigo, and then
steadies. Radiation monitors begin to flicker as *Liberty* approaches
the rock, but the cabin is well shielded.

MedOff unfastens his harness. "Permission to—"

"No. I mean permission denied." Vaun glances quickly around
the dim ring of faces, but he sees only surprise, no outrage or
mockery, so his disguise is holding. Nor is his decision unprece-

dented, for ships' captains are allowed to be wary. "PolOff will make first contact."

The big man opposite bares his teeth at this innovation by the supposed-commodore, but to talk back will alert the listeners, and the channels to *Unity* are still open. Glaring, he yields to the inevitable. "Sir!"

Yather unclips his belt and slips out of his chair. Probably only Vaun realizes that the gun in his hand has been there all along.

He floats to the doorway and ExOff breaks the seal for him. Air hisses; the hatch dilates. Then Yather has gone, into the circular dimness of the still-retracting umbilical. The MedOff is puzzled, barely concealing a sulk.

ExOff sniffs and wrinkles her nose. "Phew! Can you imagine twelve years in that stench?"

Vaun smells nothing except a faint mustiness.

"And I'm really looking forward to a nice bowl of algal soup," says ComOff. His hair is floating around his head like a tawny fog.

"That goop?"

"Tastes like poop!" says MedOff.

"Poop soup!"

"It's bench stench," ExOff announces solemnly.

"Wench stench! Makes you clench . . ."

ExOff and GravOff scream with sudden laughter.

"Stop that!" Vaun shouts. "ExOff, prepare—"

The lights go out. He stares in shock at his board, which has gone equally black. No vids, no lights. Nothing. How did they *do* that? Close the hatch manually . . . He fumbles for his belt, and watches in horror as MedOff levitates slowly upward, eyes closed. NavOff is snoring, hands rising limply in loathsome prayer. The only illumination is from the doorway, brightening steadily as the umbilical retracts.

Roker has the evidence he needs. Roker can press the button now.

There is another gun aboard, attached to ExOff's console. ExOff is mumbling, with her eyes rolling. Vaun must get that gun . . .

He snaps loose from his belt and lunges for it. In his agitation he misjudges, yanking the weapon from its holster as he goes by, then impacting the board with his shoulder. He bounces off, drifts backward, arms and legs flailing, helpless until he can find some purchase. *Up* and *down* interchange a few times, nauseatingly. Mostly the cabin seems to be upside down, with the dead or dying crew over his head.

Roker's missiles are surely on their way by now.

He tries to orientate on the light streaming in through the hatch, but it dims, blocked by a shadow. It goes *up* and *left* and *up* again and *right* and settles for being *down*, below him.

Then, in desperation, he manages to land a kick on the floating MedOff; the recoil sends Vaun spinning toward the hatch. He impacts, grabs at the jamb, reaches for the crank, and is blocked by a sinewy arm. Suddenly he is face-to-face with a mirror.

His reflection is wearing nothing but shorts and a soft cloth cap. He grins and says, "Well met, Brother!"

*That voice! His own voice, Prior's voice.*

The missiles are coming. Vaun jabs at the newcomer with the gun barrel and screams, "Out of the way!"

The boy's grin vanishes. "Hold it, Brother! Wait! I'm Abbot . . ." He grabs for the gun.

Vaun shoots him in the chest.

F AR BELOW, EMPTY ocean moved so slowly that it seemed motionless, and the Sheerfire hung in space as if time itself had died. On the borders of space, the sky was a rich cobalt-blue. The sun was overhead, Angel low in the northwest.

Vaun was flying, but his eyes ached, and every limb seemed as stiff as a board. He peered sourly across at Blade, who had taken no rest either. Sometime during the day, though, he had found time to sew a lieutenant's bars on his shoulders. Where in hell had he found those? Infuriating efficiency!

Well, if it was an endurance match, then Vaun had lost. He must grab some sleep, even if only a few minutes—but he would doze here, in his seat. If he went aft to the bedroom, he would be there for a week. He knew that he had started one night behind Blade, but he still hated to admit defeat by sleeping first.

"Lieutenant?"

"Sir?" The mauve eyes were rimmed with pink, but not much.

"Do you believe in love, Blade?"

"Yes, sir."

"Do you? Do you really? Do you love Citizen Feirn?"

"Yes, sir."

"Much?"

"Very much." The angular features displayed only respectful attention, no sentiment or emotion.

"So?" Vaun said sourly. "If I ordered you to go back there and bed her, whether she objected or not . . . would you obey?"

Not a blink. "I do not believe you would ever give such an order, sir."

It would certainly make for a sensational court-martial.

"Suppose I thought it would be the best thing for both of you? Suppose I did?"

Blade turned to stare straight ahead for a moment, and then looked squarely back at Vaun and said, "I would obey, sir."

"Why?"

"My duty to obey, sir."

"That's all?"

"No, sir."

"Well?"

"My father always told me I should never answer hypothetical questions, sir. But if I must, he once said, then I should always choose the most unreasonable answer. I . . . I'm not sure what his reasoning was, sir."

Vaun grunted, admitting that he had lost again. He did not believe in the hypothetical fatherly advice, either. "Do you ever play poker, Blade?"

"Yes, sir."

"Well?"

Solemnly Blade said, "Yes, sir."

Now that was believable!

"Take the con, Lieutenant. I'll go brew some coffee."

Vaun rose and dragged himself aft, reflecting that if many randoms were as good as Blade, there would be no need for the Brotherhood.

T HE KICK OF the gun rams Vaun back, and his head hits something hard in a shower of stars. For a moment he lashes around in panic; too many thoughts, too many obstacles . . . Roker's deadly missiles must be on their way by now; the rest of the crew are perhaps dead already, but perhaps only drugged, and he must try to save them, although two of them are drifting around loose and getting in his way.

He comes face to lurid face with MedOff, and sees a swollen tongue protruding from cyanic lips . . . heaves by him to reach the hatch. Now the hatch is *up*. He must close the hatch, fire the emergency disconnect, and start the drive. His crew may be all dead already, but they'll be certainly dead when those missiles arrive, and so will he.

A dark smoke hangs in the doorway lit by brightness behind, and when his hands touch it they turn red. He grabs a handhold and swings loose, scrabbling with his feet for purchase. The boy he shot has been blown back into the umbilical—by the impact of the shot, and by the jetting of his own lifeblood. His body would be evidence, real evidence. And Yather is out there, somewhere.

Can't abandon Yather without at least looking . . .

So Vaun peers through the hatch to see if Yather is within reach, and vertigo grabs him. Suddenly he is staring straight *down* and he hurtles headfirst into the umbilical.

But the umbilical is fully retracted now, and he flails through into the greater width of the caisson, spins around in the pseudogravity that has pulled him, and slams down hard on a painfully hot metallic floor.

For a moment he is jarred and winded. When he tries to scramble up, he discovers that he can't. The heat is terrific, here in the outer skin of a Q ship.

Yather is not there, but the boy he has shot is lying by a doorway at the far side. He is a huddled, bloody relic, absurdly small. Two other boys are kneeling over him, and they scowl across at Vaun.

220

One of them wears blue shorts, and the other black. They are Raj and Dice again. Or Vaun himself—slim, slight, and tanned by the sunlamps of a Q ship.

"I'll take it," says the one in blue. He jams Abbot's cap on his own head and stands up. It is not military headgear, just a nondescript cloth thing that a ballplayer might wear. He regards Vaun sadly.

"That was a great shame, Brother."

Again Vaun tries to rise, and cannot get past a kneel. His body is a heap of sand, and the gun as heavy as a tombstone. Dribbles of sweat rush over his skin in the high gee.

"Give me the gun, please." The boy with the cap moves forward slowly, hand extended.

"Stop!"

The boy stops, frowning, but more puzzled than angry.

*I am Blue. I am Yellow. I am Red. I am all colors . . .*

"You're Blue!" Vaun says, and does not recognize his own voice in that loathsome croak. The gun droops lower. They have caught him in a gravity trap, like a bug in a web.

"I am Abbot."

"He was Abbot!" Vaun has hardly breath enough to speak.

"And now I am Abbot. And you are not Prior." He begins to move again, slowly. "Give me the gun."

"Stay there or I shoot!" Vaun grips the gun with both hands and forces it up. They can't take it from him without getting into the gravity trap themselves. He is crushing his own legs and his neck is breaking. Soon he will not be able to breathe.

"You won't be hurt, Brother. We won't hurt you."

"One more step and I shoot!"

"We are your brothers." Abbot continues to come.

With a sob, Vaun shoots him in the thigh.

Abbot screams as his feet fly from under him and he falls, slowly in the erratic pseudogravity. Black jumps to catch him, and lowers him to the floor. The bullet must have gone right through the muscle; it would have taken off the limb had it struck bone.

Black finds the pressure point with his thumbs to stanch the blood, and then turns an angry, perplexed look on Vaun.

"Will you shoot us all, Brother?"

"Roker will! They've launched missiles! We're all going to be neuroned!"

Black shakes his head. "That's no excuse!"

Another brother hurries in through the doorway with a first aid kit. He is wearing green pants. Abbot moans and whimpers.

Vaun begins pushing himself backward, but he needs his hands to do it, and then he cannot aim the gun. Inch by inch he strains . . . his heart is bursting. He comes to a halt, and it is a moment before he realizes he has reached the wall. The lip of the entrance to the umbilical is waist-high behind him. Somehow he will have to rise.

Two boys are carrying Abbot out. Blood-spattered and wearing the cap, Black is coming toward Vaun, and his face is bleak.

"I am Abbot now, Brother. Give me that gun!"

"I'll shoot!"

Abbot continues to come. Abbot, Abbot, Abbot . . . There will be hundreds of Abbots, all the same, all Vaun himself, all Raj and Dice and Prior . . .

Crumpled into a heap, unable to lift the gun from the floor, Vaun manages to tip it up with both hands, pointing at Abbot. He blinks helplessly as sweat runs into his eyes. He fires. And misses. The bullet detonates deafeningly on the background wall.

"Give me the gun." Abbot is still coming—puzzled, angry, worried, but coming. He holds out a hand in a scarlet glove.

It is too late now to escape *Unity* before Roker destroys her. Too late. The gun slides from Vaun's limp, damp grasp.

The steely bands of gravity spring loose. Abbot takes the gun and tosses it away into the pilot boat. Then he kneels down beside Vaun and puts his arms around him and hugs him tight as he sobs, with fear and frustration and shame.

"I THINK YOU ought to kiss me," Feirn said brightly, although she was eating a large and untidy sandwich. Vaun had come aft to the galley to fetch yet more coffee. He'd found enough to fill the mugs halfway, and he could work out who had drunk the rest. Having spent most of the day in bed, she looked pert and bright and refreshed. Her pale green dress set off her copper hair admirably.

Vaun was limp with fatigue; his eyelids ached. Neither he nor

Blade had slept during the trip, or even left the flight deck for more than a few minutes. They had spelled each other off at the controls, which was certainly good flying practice in a craft so unwieldy, but in this case mutual stubbornness had played no small part. The barge was descending steadily now, and Kohab not far off.

"Why the hell should I kiss you?"

Trying to discourage Feirn was as useless as mopping up the ocean.

"One—you would certainly enjoy it. Two—I need the experience. Three—I discovered Kohab for you, and it would be a nice way of thanking me." She smiled triumphantly, revealing a fragment of green caught between her front teeth.

"I don't feel in the mood." Remembering the absurd hypothetical conversation he had held earlier with his copilot, Vaun added, "I'll send Blade back to do it. How many kisses, and how many minutes each?"

"Don't you dare! I can kiss Blade anytime. Now I want a real, *genuine* hero." Her frivolity was probably hiding a genuine appeal for affection. The child had troubles.

Right now, so did Vaun. "You won't get kisses from either of us if you steal all the coffee. Brew up some more." He bent to peer out the port.

For a couple of hours their course had paralleled the coast of Thisly, but without the autos he had been able to make out very little. Now, as the barge descended, he could see the barren, scabbed landscape, and even the minute remains of buildings and settlements. Lots of them. Once this had been prosperous, fertile farmland. Overproduction in ancient times had stripped away most of the soil and left the rest salinified and useless, a desert. Too many people once, so now no one . . . Why did that concept make him think of Prior?

Feirn was pouting. "What do you expect, Admiral? What are we going to find at Kohab?" She bit into her sandwich with enthusiasm.

"Nothing."

Mouth too full for speech, she raised fine copper eyebrows inquiringly.

"I think they must know what happened last night. The pepods would have told them . . . Hell, they must watch pubcom like everyone else. They'll be gone."

That was a pretty wild guess—as the girl's expression told him—but his only justification for this mad escapade was speed. Common

sense and fatigue together were telling him that he had blundered.
He should have dispatched a Patrol strike force.

By disconnecting the autos Vaun had arranged matters to let him
sneak into Kohab without announcing his arrival, but he had also
made the Sheerfire so maladroit that he dared not attempt a back-
door landing—on a beach, say. He would have to come in on the
strip, if it was usable. The gazeteer said that it wasn't, but it might
have been repaired. If it hadn't, then all he would achieve was a
quick overflight, and he could have called up more information than
that from a view satellite without ever leaving Valhal.

In other words, Admiral Vaun had apparently gone off half-
cocked. He didn't like that idea. He liked the alternative even less—
what *did* he hope to achieve?

As he turned to go, Feirn choked down a wad, and said, "Vaun?"

"Yes?"

"When are we going home?"

"Home?"

"To Valhal." She fluttered her lashless eyelids at him.

Krantz! The girl had a one-track mind—but of course her mother
had called it an obsession.

He wondered how she would perform in bed. Awful, likely. Her
mother at least was well padded, although that had never slowed
her at all. Feirn would be agile enough, but too skinny for comfort,
emotionally unpredictable, subject to crying fits and temper tan-
trums—exactly the sort of girl he could not tolerate for more than
a quick bang. He should have known that at once, but he had been
bewitched by her unusual pigmentation, flattered by her hero worship. He wondered if his fixation on red hair was a design fault or
something he had picked up somewhere, like a disease.

What a stupid, disgusting business it all was! If he had any sense,
he would give up stiffener altogether and save himself all the hassle
and heartache. Wild stock had no choice, but the Brotherhood was
immune, and he had no real need to play the silly game.

Well . . . he did. The one thing that had kept him at it all these
years was dreams. Prior dreams, Brotherhood memories. The
psychs had never been able to explain why screwing kept them
away, but then Ultian psychs had no experience of boys who did
not care for screwing . . . boys without parents, boys who lived
only for their brethren and hive.

Feirn had colored under his stare. "Mother says . . ."

"Yes. What does your dear mother say?"

"Nothing. Vaun, I really will try! I promise I'll try as hard as I
can!"

"Try what, Feirn?"

"Try to make up for the way she broke your heart. Try to give you the *real* happiness a hero deserves."

He sighed. When they got home, he would see what the Patrol shrinks could do for her. For her age, she was bearing up remarkably well. There was much there worth salvaging. With medical help and a few years' maturity, she might turn into someone worth befriending.

Meanwhile, he was too tired to be patient or tactful, and he no longer burned with lust whenever he set eyes on the child. He didn't like to think about that now. The trouble with stiffener was that it turned half the population into targets.

"Feirn, you are far too young for me. And you are just not my type."

She bristled. "What does age matter? And I *am so* your type! You *always* go for redheads and freckles, because of mother. Have you *any* idea what these freckles cost?"

He shook his head in sad disbelief. Half the troubles of the race came from its instincts for reproduction. Three-quarters? Or even more. No wonder the brethren were superior.

The floor tilted slightly. Blade was turning the barge landward . . . Time to go.

Feirn was smiling hopefully. "I was meant for you, always!"

"You are a stupid, misguided little tart!" he said wearily. "Some boy really ought to put you over his knee and spank you hard on your freckled little ass."

Feirn flushed again. "If that's how you want it. Mother never mentioned that."

"You," Vaun said, "are absolutely disgusting."

Even that, he reflected as he spun on his heel, might not jar Citizen Feirn out of her delusions. He was right.

"Vaun!"

Still clutching the coffee mugs, he glowered back at her through the doorway. "Yes?"

Blue eyes were glistening. "You still love *her*, don't you?"

"Who?"

"Maeve, of course!" *Sniff* . . . "That's why you don't want me."

*Krantz!* He would not even think about that problem now, let alone discuss it. "Feirn, will you promise to keep a secret?"

"Oh yes! Of course!"

Vaun glanced up and down the corridor, as if Blade could leave the controls or there might be more stowaways aboard. He lowered his voice. "Even your dear mother doesn't know this . . . But after she left, I discovered that I really prefer other boys. We of the Brotherhood are made that way. Didn't you know? All those girls who come and go at Valhal are just camouflage. That's why so many of them get mad and leave—they feel neglected. I've managed to keep it hidden and that's good, but now, if you'll excuse me, Blade and I were having an important discussion about ways in which he can advance his career."

He left her with her mouth hanging open and stalked back to the flight deck.

Too intent to notice his superior officer's smirk, Blade accepted a mug and contrived to drink coffee and fly the high admiral's disabled barge at the same time, which Vaun would not have attempted. They were coming in due east, and the barren coast of Thisly lay straight ahead.

"In the saddle between those two peaks, sir."

Vaun did not ask him if he was sure. He wouldn't say so otherwise.

"Head in for a landing, then. If it looks in the least bit dicey, pull up smartish, and we'll take a look around afterward."

It was riskier to do it that way, but it would use their surprise arrival to maximum advantage. It was riskier to let Blade do the work, too—for, in truth, Vaun was still a far better pilot—but the kid had earned the opportunity. He was almost smiling again.

The hills had to be smaller than they had seemed, for they rushed forward impetuously. The shore surged upward, a rocky moorland still spotted with a few patches of dirty snow. Vaun saw surf outlining a spit of rock that still held traces of a jetty—he thought that part of it had been repaired and might be usable for small craft—and then the beach. The ground seemed to rise to meet the cruiser. As Blade had said, the saddle held the only signs of life, a few tumbledown sheds and crumbling brick buildings. No trees and almost no cover. The strip lay straight ahead, and it was clear. Vaun glimpsed a thicket of pepods rummaging at the far end, but then the tarmac swept up and the Sheerfire came down to meet it.

*Bump. Bump.* Brake . . . and Blade was taxiing quietly over to a ramshackle hangar.

Vaun released his breath. "Beautifully done, Lieutenant."

"Thank you, sir." He sounded surprised that what he had done merited a compliment. Feirn, Vaun recalled, had mentioned Blade's tendency to provoke homicidal impulses in others.

The valley was wide and hummocky between the two hills, and seemed deserted. Summers were hotter and winters colder in the south, but with Angel gone from the sky, this barren moorland was cool enough for pepods to be active even in a late-spring afternoon. That might be the very thicket that had triggered a massacre across most of the planet. The pepods alone justified a visit to Kohab, even if the Brotherhood theory was all dustbunnies.

"What do we do now?" asked Feirn, who was peering out over Blade's head.

"Now I leave you." Vaun was lacing his hiking boots. "There's not much cover, but I'll try to disappear before anyone comes, and have a look around. *If* anyone comes, that is. Blade, you were ferrying the high admiral's barge from hither to yon and your autos gave out. Emergency landing. Okay?"

"Sir."

"Look out for pepods, of course. Play dumb for the natives, if any. I'll try to get back before midnight. That ought to hold . . . Uh-oh!"

The Sheerfire was just coming to a halt before the hangar. It was a very large hangar, and perhaps not as decrepit as it seemed at first. Lined up inside it, well back from sight, were half a dozen torches.

"Those look new," Feirn said.

Grabbing up the Giantkiller, Vaun hurried by her without a word. He threw open the door and jumped out into a cool and blustery wind, smelling of ocean. If there was anyone tending those torches, then to dive for cover would be idiotic. If there wasn't, then he would have plenty of time to burrow before anyone could arrive from the main buildings.

The problem solved itself instantly. A boy had been standing back in the shadows. Seeing Vaun, he emerged and strode quickly forward, wiping his hands on denims so grubby that they must have been used for that purpose many times. He wore a bright orange shirt, sleeveless in spite of the chill, and his dark hair blew free in the wind. Then he broke into a run. He was smiling widely.

Vaun knew that smile . . . hard to see it because the wind was making his eyes water. He stumbled forward a few steps. "Dice?" he croaked—there was something wrong with his throat, too.

"Vaun! Really you, Vaun?"

The Giantkiller clattered unnoticed to the tarmac as the two boys met, threw their arms around each other, and tried to crack ribs. Then they pummeled each other on the back a few times and went back to hugging.

"Vaun! At last! The admiral in the flesh!"

"Dice! You are Dice? Or are you Cessine?"

"No, Brother. This unit was never Dice . . ."

"Then—" Vaun stopped in midquestion, staring over his brother's shoulder. Another three boys were coming at a sprint, shouting in glee. By the color of their shirts, they were Green, Violet, and Tan. Tan could not keep up, because he wasn't fully grown yet, maybe sixteen. But he was close behind, and he cannoned into the melee and was absorbed also, while Vaun, in the middle of it, thought he would be battered to death, or crushed to death, and there were arms everywhere, and laughing. His eyes had misted over completely.

Back with his brethren. Home. A hive.

How many of them would there be?

Tan was unbelievably like Raj. He sounded like Raj, he grinned like Raj. And he said, "Wow! Really Brother Vaun!" in the sort of awed, excited tone that Raj might have used. "I know all about *you*, Brother!"

Raj had been dead for almost half a century. Vaun had betrayed him, all of them.

Orange or maybe Green said, "Oh, it's wonderful to meet you at last, Vaun."

"Know all about you," said another.

"You can't know it all!" Vaun protested—Raj and Prior and *Unity*?

The voices blended all around him. "Sure!" " 'Course!" "Watched what you've done for years!" "You're a hero!" "We've got plans for you!"

"What about the wilds, Brother?" asked Violet or Orange.

"Wilds?" Then Vaun remembered, and looked around. The sunshine seemed brighter than it had before, the sea wind sweeter, the hills in the background greener. Blade and Feirn were standing on the tarmac, she clinging very tightly to him, her cheek pressed against his chest; he with one arm around her. She looked horrified; his face was as unreadable as concrete.

Vaun thought, *What on Ult can I do with them?*

Then he realized that decisions were no longer his to make. What on Ult can *we* do with them?

He glanced at his brothers and saw a puzzled frown on Violet's face. Then Green caught it . . . and Orange . . .

They didn't know why he was in any doubt.

"We'll have to kill them, of course," he said.

Feirn screamed, *"Vaun!"*

"Could give them to the pepods?" young Tan suggested, as if he had just had a brilliant idea.

"That would still leave a couple of corpses," Green said, but he was clearly relieved that Vaun had admitted the obvious.

"Vaun!" Feirn shouted. "You don't mean that!" Her face was ashen-pale. She turned to look up at Blade, and hugged him tighter. "He's not serious, is he?"

Blade did not even look down. He continued to stare bleakly at Admiral Vaun, his lifelong hero. Blade knew the answer.

Vaun did mean it.

If he supported the Brotherhood, then he must guard the secret of the hive, meaning that those two must not leave Kohab alive. If he was still on the other side—and at the moment he was too shocked to know where his loyalty lay—then he must pretend not to be. Apparently the brethren would accept him as one of them, but he must play the part. The two randoms must pay the price. His own life was in danger, too.

Either way, he had no choice.

"They'll have to die," he said. "But when and how, I'm not sure. Let's lock 'em up somewhere and decide later, okay?"

"There's a storeroom in the air plant with a lock on it," Tan remarked, ever helpful.

"Fine. What did you all mean about having plans for me?"

The boys' voices jumbled all around him. "What you can do to help, of course." "What you can do for us." "To help the hive when Armageddon comes." "Your part in Die Day."

The infection Roker had spoken of so often was rooted now. Two untrained fugitives, Dice and Cessine, had somehow succeeded in establishing a hive, which everyone had said was impossible.

So the great hero Admiral Vaun had not succeeded at all. It had all been lies. For half a century he had lied to everybody—even, it would seem, to himself. He had not destroyed the Q ship *Unity*, and the Brotherhood.

Abbot had won in the end.

**T**HE STUNNING REALITY of *Unity* is bright and exciting, with every wall and doorway swirling in color and pattern, and no bare rock in sight. This is a far, far cry from the make-believe of the Doggoth simulator, which was only a web of drab tunnels like abandoned sewers. Despite his anger and danger, Vaun feels the thrill of being in a real Q ship at last. The artists who executed these intricate mosaics may be members of the present crew, or they may have been dead for centuries. Some Q ships are thousands of years old.

The air is fusty and unbearably hot. His flight suit is soon sodden, and even his shirtless companions shine with sweat, but for years the ship has been flexed by the gravity waves of two singularities, and soaked in radiation. Living quarters are refrigerated; the main mass of the rock will be considerably hotter.

A hidden PA is spouting a stirring march tune, which seems to be an assembly call, for everyone he sees is heading the same way. As he is led farther into the rock, the hum of machinery grows louder, the air mercifully cooler.

He feels choked with nostalgia. The colors and the bare-chested brethren and the voices—all are rousing Prior's memories of Monad Hive. Monad, the home where Vaun was conceived, the home he never knew until the mind bleed.

He is being hurried along in a group of a dozen or so, led by Abbot in his black shorts and his cap. Others are appearing and joining the procession. Invisible hills in the pseudo-gravity make his gut heave, and he is still oppressed by the beetling threat of Roker's missiles. Voices chatter all around him, all the same voice, so that he can not separate out the words.

They may seem friendly, but they are killers.

"The spacers," he demands. "You gassed them?"

" 'Fraid so," Abbot replies offhandedly. "Wouldn't have known what to do with them otherwise."

"What sort of gas?"

"No idea. Ask Bio. I do know we have a little modification to the hemoglobin alpha chain that comes in useful in technical environments. It's more selective for oxygen."

Four boys and two girls callously murdered! Vaun chokes with anger. He was in charge of that boat, responsible for them. So far he has managed to kill one brother and wound another—he hasn't leveled the score yet. He cannot believe this miraculous forgiveness and friendship. They are trying to trick him somehow . . . and yet, what does it matter? He is as good as dead.

Maeve and Valhal seem a long way off now.

He is ushered into a large, circular hall. A couple of dozen boys are there already, with others streaming in through other doors. The only furniture is a single bench, an unbroken ring big enough to seat sixty or more. Abbot steps over and sits down, facing the center. He gestures for Vaun to join him. Others are doing the same. In minutes the circle is completely filled, boys sitting side by side, squeezed shoulder to shoulder, all facing inward. Then they somehow wriggle enough room for another ten or so more to squash in also, and make a real crush out of it. There is much squirming and joking and friendly complaint.

The Brotherhood! A hive assembled. He sees again the high-raftered hall in Monad, open to the wind and the birds, its floor carpeted in brown cave grass. Often in summer, birds would soar through even when the brethren were meeting. He recalls the earthquake of mirth the day when droppings hit the brother speaking.

Vaun discovers he is gawking up witlessly at the dome overhead, whose mosaics depict strange winged monsters and mythical beings. The art may be ancient human, but the bright colors make him suspect the Brotherhood's handiwork. On a twenty-year voyage, there would be plenty of time for art.

He does not know what is about to happen, and he will not ask. This gathering feels suspiciously like a court called to try him for shooting Abbot—the first two Abbots.

A couple of heavy hands come to rest on his shoulders as latecomers line up around the outside of the circle. Small children wriggle through underneath, emerging from the forest of bare legs to climb into the nearest lap. Both of his immediate neighbors—Abbot on the right and Blue on the left—get landed with lads almost large enough to be called adolescents, a White and a Purple, who grin and bounce and wrestle and get tolerantly grumbled at, but the toddler who raises expectant arms in front of Vaun cannot be older than four. Vaun does not recall when a child last came to him.

Feeling strangely touched, he scoops the youngster up and makes him as comfortable as possible in the crush.

"Hi."

"Hi."

"What's your name?"

"Huh?" The kid twists his head around and gives Vaun a worried look. "I'm Pink, of course!" So he is—today. He frowns at Vaun's uniform, and fingers it curiously.

The center of the circle is apparently sacred, and stays empty, but from the space back from the bench to the wall is now packed solid with Vauns of all sizes and ages. Everywhere he sees his own face, always willing to smile if it catches his eye. Everywhere he sees his own legs, all much more tanned than the pair he walks on. The air is hot and stuffy, as rank as an unwashed locker room, and yet he finds the sweaty odor familiar and inoffensive.

Conspicuous in his uniform, Vaun peers over Pink and around White to see Abbot. "Why pants at all?" he asks. "Why not just run around bareass?"

"Pockets!" says White firmly, bouncing.

Abbot shrugs. "Hygiene, I suppose. Sit still, varmint!"

"And it saves a lot of *Hey you*," adds the Orange who is leaning on Vaun from behind.

The colors repeat around the circle, of course, but a group this large must be rare.

"Time to start," Abbot says. "You do it, lad. I'm nailed in here."

With a gleeful grin, young White snatches the cap from Abbot's head, slides off his lap, and starts to strut around the circle, waving the cap high for all to see. The babble of talk fades away.

A Brown says, "Eighty-four." There is a pause, and then a Green sighs and says, "Eighty-one."

Eighty-one, eighty-four . . . The numbers must be years, but they will be Avalonian calendar, and nothing like Ultian dates, so Vaun cannot tell what age they represent. How old is the Brotherhood itself?

No one else betters Green's eighty-one, so White throws the cap spinning across to him. He is feeding a very small baby, but a youngster on a neighboring lap snatches the cap from the air and arranges it on Green's head for him—back to front, of course.

White comes racing back and leaps bodily on Black, who says, "Ooof!" and then, to Vaun, "You are surprised by something?" His voice comes muffled from under a writhing tangle of younger brother. Purple similarly assaults Blue, and Vaun is suddenly busy trying to shield little Pink from the overall scrimmage.

"Yes," he admits. "The way you gave up power so easily. You're not Abbot anymore?"

Black masters his burden, turning young White upside down and pinning him between his thighs, holding his skinny legs up so that Orange can lean over and tickle the soles of his feet. Wild shrieks come from somewhere near the floor. Similar roughhousing is going on all around the circle. "Why should that surprise you?" Black seems surprised himself.

"Wild stock murder and conspire in the pursuit of power—I've watched them!" Vaun knows that even Frisde's nefarious court is not the worst on Ult. "They never yield power voluntarily."

"Power?" snorts his neighbor. "It's responsibility, is all. There's no power involved."

Vaun senses achievement of an age-old dream. In the Brotherhood, it is evident *that all boys are created equal*.

On a million worlds, where else is that true?

Cuddling his baby, the new Abbot strolls out into the empty center, and the noise fades away. He could be any one of them past puberty. He could be Dice, or Prior.

The brethren come to order. Young White is released, and allowed to resume his seat, red-faced and grinning.

"We welcome a new brother," Abbot tells the silence. Even the small fry are listening intently. He smiles Raj's smile at Vaun. "This is your hive, Brother. All we have is yours."

Vaun jumps as the whole assembly roars, "Agreed!" Hands squeeze his shoulders. White feints a punch at him.

*All I have is my life, and you can take that anytime,* Vaun thinks. All his life he had been conscious of being better, and now he is suddenly surrounded by his equals, at least three hundred of them. A hall of mirrors. He thinks of being imprisoned in a faceted crystal.

When he does not reply, Abbot smiles at him sadly, then goes on to other business. "Medical report. Qualified?"

"Medic," says a voice from the back. Vaun cranes his neck to see the speaker, and then realizes that it doesn't matter. "One dead. He died well, and did not suffer."

"We mourn our loss," Abbot says solemnly, and again comes the chorus. "Agreed!"

Vaun stares at his own knees. He should have known that shooting a unit of the Brotherhood would be pointless, and stupid.

"Specialty?" Abbot inquired.

"No identification yet," says the invisible medic. "We'll inform his prior as soon as we can. One ventilation technician wounded, but it's a clean flesh wound. He won't even have a scar." That news brings a cheer.

Abbot turns to Vaun. "We have lost a brother and gained one. Will you be happier using a personal name for a while, Brother?"

"Commodore Vaun, Ultian Command." It is hard to sound formal and disciplined when a four-year-old has just discovered that you unzip down the front . . . This toleration is impossible! How can they not bear a grudge?

"Brother Vaun." Abbot's baby is refusing the nipple. He tucks the bottle in a pocket, and adjusts the youngster on his shoulder. His movements are confident and efficient. "Obviously you are not the one we hoped for."

"Prior, you mean?"

"That was his title, leader of a small group. We have other titles also. You speak Andilian, though."

"They . . . I mean *we*," Vaun says grimly, "*we* mind bled him."

He feels the whole congregation shudder, and a few of the youngsters cry out.

Abbot's expression turns black. "We honor his memory!"

"Agreed!" chorus the brethren again.

"Will you tell us of him, and what he achieved?"

"Why should I? We're all about to die!"

"If you refer to the missiles, then you can set your mind at ease. Qualified?"

"Gravitics," says a Brown, sitting on the far side from Vaun. "They fired four, and one went wide. We absorbed the others. No sweat. They've done some damage to the com equipment with beams, but nothing serious. They won't try anything more for a while, because we're over populated country." He grins across at Vaun, and a lot of the youngsters grin also.

It may be a bluff, of course, but it would be a very odd one. A rush of relief tells Vaun that he believes; his dread had lessened considerably. "Absorbed?" he demands.

"Swallowed them in singularities. It happened over the ocean, so the radiation flash did them no great harm, but it has probably knocked out planetary communications for a while."

"You can't turn a Q ship that fast!"

Q ships can accelerate instantly in a straight line, but to rotate a rock without breaking it up or making it spin is a brute of a job. Yet Vaun's words create a hundred smiles.

Abbot says, "You think like a spacer, Brother Vaun. Let us hope we can teach you better habits! We turn the projectors instead. We shall gladly show you, later. But, please, will you tell us now of our late brother?''

It makes sense. In fact, it is glaringly obvious, and if Ultian Command has never thought of it, that must be because no one has ever bothered to consider a Q ship as a military craft. Again Vaun reflects that he is dealing with an organization of boys as smart and effective as . . . as Prior was.

So now he is a prisoner in an impregnable fortress. But if Ultian Command cannot damage the Q ship, then equally the Brotherhood can hardly conquer a planet. Standoff. Vaun's outlook has suddenly changed dramatically. He scowls around at the sea of expectant Vaun-faces.

''He came very close,'' he admits.

''Louder, please, Brother.''

''Prior almost succeeded. It was only some very bad luck that balked him.'' Reluctantly Vaun begins to tell the story, and every time he hesitates Abbot shoots a penetrating question and drags out more details. An audience so attentive is hard to resist—soon he is telling it all. The brethren listen in solemn silence, except for some of the very young, who drift off to sleep or play quietly with their guardians' hair, or ears, or lips.

All the while some part of him wonders how it would feel to strip off his uniform and just blend into this group. Shed the Patrol, shed his childhood, and just vanish into the Brotherhood, never exactly like a hive-reared unit, perhaps, but close enough, if they will accept him, as Raj and Dice accepted him. Not a black-haired freak, not a mudslug peon . . .

Valhal is an impossible prize now. And Maeve . . . Maeve never said good-bye. Besides, the things he did with the girl! The memory is sickening. Degrading animal behavior!

At last he stops and Abbot asks no more questions. Instead, he turns around slowly, holding out his free hand to invite comments, and no one speaks.

Vaun, too, looks around at all the somber faces. He feels strangely ashamed, and angry at himself for that shame. He feels misery at bringing such obvious misery to a group that . . . that he does not want to make miserable. A once-traitor may tell himself that he acts from conviction, but a twice-traitor cannot.

''Prior raped my mother!'' he says defiantly. ''He tried to conquer the planet.''

''His actions resulted in your existence, Brother,'' Abbot says softly. ''How can you condemn them? And he wanted to rescue the planet, not conquer it. I see we must justify our motives. Qualified?''

A Yellow not far to Vaun's right says, ''History,'' as another voice says, ''Political science,'' and others, ''Philosophy . . . Psychology . . . Defense . . .''

Abbot has Dice's grin. ''Your choice, Brother.''

''History.''

Yellow speaks, then. ''Have you ever heard of *Homo erectus*, Brother Vaun?''

''No.''

''It was one of our predecessor species, back on Earth. It was more than animal, less than human. But when some members of *Homo erectus* evolved into modern humanity by natural selection, their type spread across the planet. Unimproved *erectus* died out everywhere. It is the way of the universe, the secret of life's progress. The better must replace the inferior. It cannot help but do so.''

''Are you saying our ancestors killed this inferior species? I demand proof.''

''I can give you no proof, but I ask what else was capable of destroying *erectus*, who had prevailed for a million years and settled a world? Nor can I produce, here and now, proof of historical events, although we do have records available, if you will believe them. The Brotherhood did not originate on Avalon, Vaun, but our experience there repeats what has happened on other worlds. The randoms see *Homo factus* as a danger to them, and they will not tolerate us. Can you believe that?''

Toleration? Vaun recalls his childhood. He recalls Olmin's attempts to bleach black hair to fair. He resists the interference. ''But if we are superior, should we not be superior in tolerance and compassion? Can we not teach them the value of cooperation?'' He senses anger and disagreement all around him, but only Yellow speaks.

''We have tried, many times. The wild stock never honor their commitments for long. Driven by fear, sooner or later they attack our hives. On Avalon alone, four hives have been wiped out that we know of—Xanacor, Monad, Wilth Hills, Gothin. We do not know what other tragedies may have occurred in the twenty-one years we have been traveling. Randoms lived in peace within at least two of those hives I listed, and they were hunted down and destroyed also, as traitors. Pogroms against minorities are a universal pattern of human history, on every world mankind has ever settled. The only difference with us is that the marauders do not have their usual opportunities to include rape among their customary abominations of mindless slaughter, torture, and child killing.''

Vaun thinks of Roker and Ultian Command, of their hatred and fear and what they did to Prior. He also remembers the crew of the shuttle—his crew, foully murdered. Neither side in this war will recognize the other as human.

Yellow has apparently finished; Abbot takes up the argument from the center of the floor. "Do you regard yourself as inferior to a random, Brother Vaun? You are superior to them in strength and wit and every talent. Do you have less right to life than one of them?"

"No."

"They will not agree. Now answer me this: Had Prior arrived in your home village with a baby brother and asked that it be reared . . . Had he offered to pay for its food and upkeep and education . . . Would that child have been accepted and cherished as a random baby would be under the circumstances?" He pats the infant resting on his shoulder. As he turns to survey the audience, Vaun sees that the baby has been dribbling milk on Abbot's shoulder, and for some reason that tiny detail hurts.

"What had my mother . . . foster mother . . . done to deserve what he did to her?" he shouts angrily.

"Nothing. What had Prior done to deserve what happened to him?"

"He had committed a cowardly, brutal attack on a helpless girl!"

"Was that his crime? Is mind bleeding the usual punishment for rape?"

Vaun does not reply. The Patrol's usual reaction to a charge of rape would be a fast cover-up.

Abbot answers his own question. "No, his crime was that he sought the continuation of his race, which was not the random's race, and that they will never permit. They deny your right to exist and perpetuate your genes, Brother."

Still Vaun is silent.

"If two contest," Abbot says grimly, "and one will never accept the other's existence, then that other's only choices are suicide or struggle. Which will you choose? Which will you have us choose?"

Vaun looks down at Pink on his lap, a cuddly, black-haired toddler. He can never father such a child. He can only work to support a hive that will manufacture more copies of himself, like this one. Seeing his attention, Pink smiles up at him trustfully.

"Or answer this, Brother," Abbot persists. "If we seek peace, if we now contact the Patrol on Ult and request some unused corner of a desert somewhere to establish ourselves—and we are only a few hundred among many billion—what will their answer be?''

''They will accept eagerly, and then strike at you when you are least able to resist.''

Abbot waits a moment, and then says, ''So the only compassion we can offer is to kill ourselves. Is that what you recommend?''

Silence.

He persists, as soft as silk and as sharp as steel. ''Brother, they are not of our species! We do not interbreed.''

''That's the whole point, isn't it?'' Vaun says hoarsely. ''That excuses everything! What was done to the girl and the spacers and everything! They're just animals.''

''More than animals, but less than we.''

''And to them, we are only artifacts and therefore less than they!''

Abbot sighs. ''Nobody picks his team in this game! He is born to it. Tell us now where your loyalty lies?''

Vaun's eyes have filled with tears. Valhal . . . riches and fame . . . carnal pleasure with Maeve . . . Those ambitions seem tawdry and shameful now, when his brothers are in danger.

Pink reaches up in wonder to touch the tears on his cheeks.

''You expect me to believe that you will trust me, after what I have done? You cannot! I came here to kill you!''

''Then go ahead. Start with that babe on your lap.''

''Me!'' White says, baring teeth and hooking his fingers into claws. ''Tear me to shreds!''

''Good idea!'' Black mutters, and cuffs his ear.

Abbot walks closer to Vaun. ''You acted from ignorance, and we can cure ignorance. We already have, I think. No brother will ever knowingly act against his brethren, his hive. Certainly we shall trust you hereafter. Do you want to be trusted?''

So now Vaun knows the answer to Frisde's question. He knows what the brethren tender. She offers fame and power and wealth, and they outbid her easily.

Love!

''Yes! Yes, please!''

His two neighbors smile at him, and the hands on his shoulders squeeze hard.

''We accept you gladly, Brother—but I do not think that is possible.'' Again Abbot rotates slowly to survey his audience. He seems to find no comfort, and again addresses Vaun. ''From what you have told us, we cannot hope to establish a hive on Ult.''

''Then you must go on!'' Vaun says. ''Go on to the frontier

worlds! Or else go back to Avalon!'' And he will go with his brethren . . .

Silence tells him that there is something wrong with his conclusions. The mood has changed. No one will meet his eyes now. One or two of the youngsters are whimpering, and the older boys whisper comfort and courage in their ears.

"Those options are not available to us," Abbot says softly. "We risked everything on Prior and on secrecy. Both have failed us. The ship must be realigned and allowed to cool before it can undertake another voyage. Forgive me!—of course a spacer knows that. No, hear me out. We should find the same problems back at Avalon, anyway."

"Bethyt is nearer—only two and a half elwies."

"Seven transit years . . . still too far, and still the same problems." The baby whimpers; Abbot moves it back to the crook of his arm and carefully offers it the bottle again before continuing.

"Let me tell you a story. The crew of the shuttle was murdered, all except you. Your attempts to pass as Prior were successful, and we accepted you. You watched from the bridge as we negated the Patrol's attempts to destroy us. Believing you to be Prior, we did not guard you closely. Like all interstellar ships, this one carries a destruct device, for that is—"

"No!"

"Hear me out. Since ancient times, the Space Patrol has always insisted on that, in case of infestation by aliens. Unobserved, you were able to start the destruct sequence. You raced back to the pilot boat, disconnected—"

"No! No!"

"There is only one of us who may survive, Brother. Only one of us will be welcome back on Ult."

"Then choose another!" Vaun shouts. He tries to rise, but strong hands hold him in place. "I will stay!"

"No other would be able to pass as you," Abbot insists. "Qualified?"

"Bio," says an identical voice somewhere. "You are correct, Abbot. They will have tagged him somehow. Strontium, for example. Small doses will replace calcium in the bones, and leave an unmistakable signature. There are so many possibilities that we should need days to test for them all, but they will know at once if we attempt a substitution. Mind bleeding takes too long anyway."

"I won't go!" Vaun yells. "I killed one of you, and wounded another! I cooperated in what they did to Prior. I betrayed Raj and Dice. *I will not betray you anymore!*"

Abbot strides forward to confront him like a reflection. "Listen! By going back you will not betray us, you will serve the Brotherhood!"

"What?"

The face so like his own smiles his own smile at him. "You have an opportunity none of the rest of us have. Do exactly what they want, Brother Vaun! Serve their purpose that you may ultimately serve ours . . . which is also yours. You go back, and we perish. We are only a few hundred units—the Brotherhood can replace us easily. But you will be established as loyal to the randoms, and be honored. *The Brotherhood will try again!*"

"What? When? How?"

"I have no idea. But it will never give up. Maybe not for centuries, but maybe in your lifetime. And the next time you will be trusted, and you will have a better chance to aid our cause."

"I won't! I can't!"

Abbot turns to look around the silent, somber company. "Has anyone an alternative to propose?"

No one responds.

"Are we agreed?"

This time the response is a deep, sad rumble. "Agreed!"

"Surely you can save some?" Vaun whimpers. "Some might survive a pogrom. The ship might make it back to Avalon!"

"This way is better," Abbot insists. "I have told you—we do not matter. You are truly on our side now?"

"Yes, yes!"

"Then this is your duty, Brother Vaun. If you feel you committed crimes against your brethren—and no one but you has said so— then this is your chance to redeem them. Perhaps it will be easier for you, but to any of us what I propose would be torture, a life alone, among wild stock. Blue . . . Black . . . take him back to the patrol boat, and then to the bridge, and lead him through the scenario. Go through it all twice or three times, if needs be, until he is sure of the story. Then see him on his way."

A scramble of limbs and bodies, and Vaun finds himself on his feet, with a brother flanking him on either side.

"We shall come back here afterward," Black says. "There will be time."

"Of course," Abbot agrees. "Now go."

Later, as Vaun and his two companions are returning from the bridge where the destruct device now flashes seconds, heading for the patrol boat that will carry him away to exile, they pass by the domed hall, and along the entrance tunnel comes a sound Vaun thinks will haunt him forever—baritone and treble soaring together, the sound of the brethren singing.

T HE ANCIENT SETTLEMENT of Kohab was exactly what it seemed—deserted. Any stray visitor would naturally check the buildings first, and find nothing there but pepods and traces of other visitors years before. The hive was hidden in the old mine tunnels, with only its torches of necessity kept aboveground.

The salty wind gusted and blustered over the stony moor, forcing Vaun to lean into it as young Tan guided him. Trekking westward, they had it right in their faces. The three adult boys were following close behind, escorting Feirn and Blade at the lens of Vaun's handbeam. With the Sheerfire tucked away in the hangar and the countryside rife with pepods, the two randoms weren't going anywhere anyway.

Vaun had put them out of his mind for the time being. He felt almost light-headed, partly from lack of sleep, partly from the exhilaration of finding himself with his brethren, a long lifetime after he had parted from Dice and Raj. His kin. His people. He felt grateful for the wind to explain the watering of his eyes.

Tan was bearing the Giantkiller, but then he slid it off his shoulder and peered at it. Frowning, he hefted it in both hands. "Sure is heavy!" He sighed, then staggered in a stray gust.

"I'll carry it for you," Vaun said, glad of an excuse to remove such a catastrophe-creator from nimble adolescent fingers.

"Oh no, I just meant that the Series Twelve are much lighter. They have two more charges in the magazine than this old relic, and the sighting is calibrated at forty-hertzian increments out to a range of—"

"You're a smart ass, you know that?"

The lad grinned with delight. "Of course! We all are, and you old units are all nervous hens. That bushie over there, the pepod? I could pick it off for you with this, easy."

Vaun thumped his shoulder in boy-to-boy fashion. No one had

ever called him an 'old unit' before, but of course he was, and of course he could not help liking this youngster. The youngster, for his part, was treating Vaun as he would any of his other adult brethren, as if they had shared toothbrushes all their lives. Back in the world of the wild stock, young males usually regarded Admiral Vaun as a demigod. The change was refreshing.

And Vaun had no love for pepods. "Go ahead. Let's see you."

Tan grinned, then sighed regretfully. "No shooting aboveground at Kohab. Too remote—shows up to satellites."

Something in that remark implied that there were other places where such activity was permitted. Other hives?

"Besides," Tan said wisely, "we try to keep on their good side, and shooting them isn't part of our research program."

"Your specialty?"

Tan nodded proudly, and slung the gun on his shoulder again.

"Teach me," Vaun said, mentally contrasting this lithe slip of a lad with the other pepod expert he had met, the late human haystack, Quild. The two had nothing in common except an obvious desire to talk about pepods. There were many of the vermin in sight, scattered around without pattern. He now believed himself to be immune, although he would like to have that supposition confirmed before he tested it.

"Oh, they're our biggest asset!" Tan said. "I mean look at the ground."

"What about the ground?"

"Rocks, see? They keep turning over the slag, so our tracks never show. Keeps the hive hidden. And we don't use screamers now, so any wilds that blunder in assume there's nobody here. And they're great guard dogs! We're getting to know a lot of their communication, just lately."

"And they don't attack the . . . us?"

Tan shook his head. His dark eyes twinkled. "We didn't know that until not very long ago. All the early work here was done behind screamers. Then one day a toddler wandered off and made friends with a pepod! Climbed right inside!"

"Yes?" Vaun said, suspecting what was coming.

"Actually . . ." Tan glanced behind him and then lowered his voice. "It was this unit." He blushed. "Least, I think it was. I think I remember doing it, but I suppose I might have just seen another of my crop doing it, and be remembering that."

"Then your choice of specialty is understandable."

"Oh, that was just the luck of the draw. Lucky for me! I'm glad I'm a pepodist. I enjoy being a pepodist. Some units get stuck with specialties where they have to spend all their time reading books, for years and years, but there's no book to read on the bushies! We're writing it. There are four of us, and we're doing very . . . or we were, until last night.'' He pulled a face. ''Weren't counting on *that*!''

Curious, Vaun just strode along, and in a moment Tan added, ''Thirteen thousand dead? We'd expected a lot more. A *lot* more!''

''It was almost twice that.''

''Really? Great! Of course, it would have been a lot more than that, even, without you!''

''Me? What did I have to do with it?''

''You restored order! I know you had to! Bishop told us what a smart move it was.''

''I don't think I follow.''

''Well, I mean . . .'' Tan sounded surprised. ''The way you put it down! We were watching the pubcom, and there you were! Even the randoms were saying that only Admiral Vaun could have done what you managed, and how lucky everyone was that the Patrol had you on hand to organize the relief. We all had a good laugh!''

After a moment he added, ''Well . . . to be honest, Brother . . . some of us wondered, even after Bishop explained. But you turning up here like this today . . . I mean, you don't mind me saying this, do you? It just seemed so funny, seeing you helping the randoms.''

''No, I don't mind. I understand.''

''Oh, good! It's all right now, of course,'' Tan said hastily. ''Now you've come. No one'll doubt any more. And Bishop did explain how it helped, and why you were doing it, taking their side, I mean, like, next time you won't be there, will you? And without you, the stupid randoms'll make their usual mess of things, and it'll be much worse than they expect. So that's good, but it was a shame it happened accidentally like that. The bushies never reacted that way before. Do you know why?''

''Yes,'' Vaun said, but he wanted to keep Tan's busy tongue at work. ''It's a long story. How well can you control them usually?''

''Not much. I mean, pepods aren't *smart*. You can't explain astronomy or evolution to a pepod, no matter how many you link up. And they've not much memory. You can say, 'This biped good, that biped bad.' That's about as far as it goes. Next day it's almost all gone again. Even the Great Pepod is dumber than a dog. Else it wouldn't have attacked last night.''

The Great Pepod was presumably the same phenomenon as the late Professor Quild's ''holographic continuum.'' Vaun preferred Tan's terminology.

"How about, 'Riot!'? Will that work? You going to be able to repeat last night? Can you rouse the Great Pepod deliberately?"

"Sure!" Tan insisted. "They'll play their part on Die Day." He sighed. "There won't be so many, though, will there?"

"No," Vaun agreed, thinking of the firestorms he had unleashed. "And the surprise won't be so great."

"Pity."

Did the kid realize what he was saying? Had he thought through the consequences?

"Tan, I mean Brother . . . Do you know what happens to people when pepods go berserk? You ever seen it?"

"Yes."

Vaun shot him a startled glance, but the youngster did not seem to notice. He went blithely on, yelling over the gale. "Of course it's unkind, but it has to be done, doesn't it? I mean, we can't let them make the planet totally uninhabitable. We have to get their population down to sustainable limits somehow. If they breed like vermin, then they must expect to be treated like vermin."

So that was what he had been brought up to believe? Prior had said much the same, Vaun remembered—the Brotherhood's objective was to domesticate the wild stock. After seeing today what overpopulation had done to the once-fertile continent of Thisly, Vaun could admit that the argument had some validity.

Not the same species, Abbot had said.

"Hey!" said a voice at their back. "Nipper!"

Tan spun around, scowling. "Meaning me?"

"Yes, you," said Orange. "Let's detour around those." He nodded at a group of pepods scrabbling among the pebbles just ahead.

"It's all right. They're far enough away."

"No, let's not take any risks."

"I'm a pepodist, remember!" Tan announced grandly, raising his chin. "Prior sent me along to keep an eye on you and the bushies."

"I'm one too," Orange said gently. "And he sent *me* along to keep an eye on *you*."

The lad deflated, and turned pink. Looking about three years younger than he had a moment before, he muttered, *"Freckles!"* as if that was an obscenity. Green and Violet were smirking.

Orange laughed, but without malice. "Normally you'd be correct, Brother, but we've got two wild stock with us."

"Still awright," Tan mumbled. "Outside attack radius."

"Normally, yes. But the bushies may still be edgy, after last night, and we don't want them getting used to seeing us associating with randoms, okay? So let's play it safe and go around.''

Tan stalked off angrily at an angle to his previous course. The adults followed, grinning.

The pepods continued their scavenging, paying no attention as the two processions walked by at a safe distance. Straight ahead now, a weed-choked tunnel mouth came into view.

Vaun turned to his new neighbor, Orange. ''That's the hive, I assume?''

''That's it. Welcome home.''

*Home!* Yes, he did feel as if he was coming home, home from a lifetime sojourn in foreign lands. Surely such a feeling must be just imagined? Could it be genetic?

Orange looked chilled. The absence of a jacket might be mere bravado, or the need to let his companions see the color of his shirt—or the hive might be short of resources.

''Er . . . Admiral?''

Vaun gave him a hurt look.

He smiled and said, ''Brother?''

''Yes?''

''If we have to put down these randoms anyway . . . we use randoms in our conditioning program.''

More than the wind caused Vaun to shiver then. He glanced around at the captives. Feirn was still clinging tightly to Blade, and having trouble with her impractical shoes on the stony ground. Blade was steadying her, but his eyes said he had caught the deadly implications of Orange's remark.

''We dope them first, of course,'' Orange added. ''They don't feel anything. Or not much.''

''Well, they might as well die usefully,'' Vaun agreed.

Blade's mauve eyes flickered. The girl had not heard, or not understood.

Very soon now Vaun must choose between the two species, random and brother. In a sense, he had never really had a choice before. He could have refused Raj, maybe, and stayed in the village, but then he had not known the game or the stakes. Roker had never offered Vaun a thinkable alternative. *Cooperate or die* was no choice. He had declared his loyalty to the Brotherhood in the Q ship, but it had brought him no freedom of action, for Abbot had immediately thrown him out, sending him back to Ult and the wild stock.

Ever since then he had served the Patrol, but that was what Abbot had told him to do, to demonstrate his loyalty so the Patrol would trust him and he could betray it eventually—now.

Where did the pendulum stop?

Very soon he must answer that question. From then on there could be no neutrality, no evading the issue. Then he would be a mass murderer also, one way or the other.

And a traitor, one way or the other.

The weeds masking the tunnel mouth, he noted, were artificial. Tan was waiting there with a broad grin, his juvenile sulks forgotten. "Welcome to Kohab Hive, Admiral Vaun."

"Meaning me?"

The youth grinned ever wider. "Brother!"

"Brother!" Vaun agreed.

Tan proudly put a hand on his shoulder, and led him inside.

Home at last.

Love.

A HEAVY BLACK drape blocked the tunnel, then behind that another. Tan pushed it aside and shouted, "Hey, guys, we got a visitor!" Four brethren had been sitting there reading, and they exploded to their feet with yells. Blinking in unfamiliar gloom, Vaun was once more mobbed by brothers.

Even here, in remote Kohab, he could not escape the hero worship, but now it brought tears to his eyes. So long they had trusted him! Barely a week went by without Admiral Vaun appearing in public somewhere on Ult—making speeches, leading appeals, dedicating monuments. He was the most celebrated celebrity Ult had ever known, the lion of the randoms, vanquisher of the Brotherhood. His unsuspected brethren had watched all his worldwide antics on pubcom and never once doubted that he was secretly on their side.

Prior had known. *When the chips are down, you'll side with your kin.* And Abbot. *No brother will ever act against his hive.* Even Raj, who had promised to die for him. *You belong with us.*

And Maeve, the previous night. *They love one another, don't they?*

He had come home at last, to kin and hive.

As the hugs and backslapping died away, he saw the girl's accusing glare, and Blade's mauve eyes staring impassively, and for a moment shadows cooled his joy. But he had not invited either of them along. She was a stowaway. Every spacer officer swore to risk his life . . . So one had risked it and lost! Vaun had not known what was going to happen. He was not responsible for either of those two.

"Brother Vaun?" Green was shouting from a corner, clutching a telephone. He might be the Green who had met Vaun at the hangar, or he might be the Green who had been on guard duty. It didn't matter. A telephone?

Vaun limped over to him. The long hike had made his knee ache.

"Bishop wants to know if it's urgent."

Vaun shook his head wearily.

"He's decanting a baby," Green explained, grinning. "Says we'll have a meeting after dinner, if that's soon enough."

"That'll be fine."

Green spoke to the phone, listened. "He wants to know when you're going back?"

Going back? The shock was a wrench of physical pain. Going back? But of course he would have to go back! They had plans for him. The Q ship was coming. Armageddon. *Die Day,* they had said. He was the king cuckoo, the Trojan horse. His work was not finished. He forced out the right answer. "Whenever he wants me to go back."

Green passed the word.

Primitive, primitive! Telephones? Curtains? Artificial weeds cloaking the entrance? The guardroom was merely a wide place in the tunnel, furnished with rough, homemade chairs. Vaun could see no sign of modern security equipment at all. Young Tan was stacking Vaun's Giantkiller on a rack beside a couple of dozen other assault weapons, and those looked impressive enough, but everything else was shoddy and make-do and antique.

Yet . . . a miracle, really. Dice and Cessine had achieved a miracle. Whatever posthumous assistance they had had from Abbot, they had worked a miracle to build a functioning hive and keep it secret. How on Ult had they ever financed it all? How in hell did they feed their brood? Biotech equipment to make babies would never have come cheap, not to mention the torches he had seen in the hangar. Food and clothing and the bare necessities of life . . .

The wonder was not that the brethren of Kohab lived simply, the wonder was that they lived at all. Randoms could never have done it. Vaun felt pride, and overwhelming admiration.

And shame. Why had they never asked him for help?

Green spoke again. "He wants to know who the two wilds are, and if they're important."

Blade and Feirn were certainly listening, but Vaun did not look at them. "No. They're stowaways. They're dispensable."

He heard a girlish whimper behind him.

"Kid here suggested the storeroom in the air plant," Green told the phone. "Yeh, okay." He hung the antique back on its rest. "Yellow, Blue, Bishop says take the randoms down to the air plant, okay?" He turned to gaze admiringly at Vaun. "Great to have you with us at last, Brother."

"It's great to be here at last."

"Exciting to realize that Die Day is getting so close!"

"Um," Vaun said.

Tan materialized in front of him, eager to please his new friend. "Show you around, Brother?"

Vaun forced a smile. He was incredibly weary, for he had barely slept in three nights, but he knew he was too excited to sleep. "How about a shower and some clean clothes to start with? I feel like I've just come from a masquerade ball in this rig."

"Vaun!" Feirn screamed. Yellow was trying to make her move, jabbing a gun at her. "Vaun, stop playing games!"

Blade tried to hush her; she lurched past him to get at Vaun, but Blue blocked her. "Vaun! Vaun! Do something!"

"I am going to do something. I am going to have a shower. Come along if you want, but don't expect separate facilities here."

She recoiled against Blade, staring unbelievably at her former hero. Blade put an arm around her. He was as pale as she was. Ever since he had been seven years old, he had said, he had wanted to be like Admiral Vaun.

Tough.

Heroes have their off-days too.

Vaun turned back to Tan. "Lead the way, Brother."

T HE TUNNELS WERE mostly narrow and chilly and dim.
They branched and intersected with the complexity of a spider's web, many still cluttered with rusted rails, overhead pipes and ducts. Vaun struggled to recall all the varied uses Kohab had known, but he could remember only germ warfare laboratory. The antique telephone was easier to understand now. Whenever possible, the brethren had adapted the relics they had found already in place. Beside, high tech would be much more likely to reveal itself to the Patrol's constant monitoring of the planet, and the hive's only real defense was secrecy. He understood, but he felt as if he had stumbled into a historical drama, or back through a major time warp. Here and there he saw patches of brilliantly colored mosaic floor and wall paintings, but obviously the brethren of Kohab Hive had rarely had time or money for art.

Again and again he was dazzled by flashes of Prior's childhood memories and his own remembered glimpses of *Unity*. This dingy catacomb was not the rustic comfort of Monad, but the steady stream of brethren was stunningly familiar. They came in all sizes, from chattering toddlers up to exact replicas of himself. Slacks and garish shirt, dark hair and astonished smile . . . The pattern repeated over and over. Proudly Tan introduced him, over and over. Hugs and backslaps and crushing grips by the score, over and over. Eager questions about the pepod attack, and how long he was staying, and what happened to his face—his brothers were surprisingly concerned about his bruises.

Others were heading where he was going; he soon moved within a chattering, joking crowd of brothers. Monad and Prior's childhood . . . *I am Blue. I am Yellow. I am Red. I am all colors.* As he neared the showers he heard familiar sounds of merriment and smelled the soapy steam; the tunnel there was more finished than elsewhere, all tiled in brilliance.

Suddenly he was tearing off his clothes in the middle of a dozen boys tearing off their clothes. He had more to shed; they waited for him and then waved him forward in the place of honor. Joyfully naked and anonymous, leading a laughing band of replicas, he ran through a doorway and straight into a bucketful of icy water. He leapt for the culprit, but lost him in the fog and crowd.

Too late, Prior's memories warned him how uninhibited the brethren became when they shed their color coding. All hive showers were a raucous, steamy, roughhousing mayhem, with more high spirits than a distillery. Even the adults indulged in juvenile horseplay, while the adolescents behaved like lunatics, and the small fry screamed and shrieked and mobbed without mercy.

He had known, too, that small brethren were as resistant to control as cubs of any other species, so that youngsters bore serial numbers stained on their buttocks. Now he discovered that an adult brother with tooth scars in that location was an obvious target for buffoonery. The new brother also had a bruised face, so he could not hide. As soon as he escaped the swarm of small fry, then the grown-ups pointed him out again. In a sense it was like being chased by the ripper pack of the village, but this was fun and very touching. About fifty brethren of all sizes tried to romp with the new brother in the shower room, and twice that many when he took refuge in the pool, which was a flooded mine tunnel and cold as a drill sergeant's heart.

The process was strangely therapeutic. Vaun rollicked in the shrieking tidal wave madhouse until he was turning blue all over, and by the time he staggered ashore he had forgotten wars, interspecies rivalries, deadly Q ships, the lot. Food and sleep, he decided, and the planet could pull down its blinds until he returned. He hung his towel on a rail with all the others, and snatched shoes and clothes from the baskets—perfect fit, of course. From habit he chose a white shirt, but it was a thin rag of a thing. Better than he'd had in his childhood, but not like admirals wore.

The foolery was over; he had come home at last.

He headed for the door, and was accosted by an adolescent waiting there, still wet-haired from the showers. His shirt was gray, his grin familiar. "Show you around now, Brother?" he asked hopefully.

Now Vaun knew why bruises bothered brethren, but he said, "Sure."

So Gray, who had been Tan, led him off to explore Kohab Hive. Apart from a few odd glances at his face, though, Vaun no longer attracted attention from passersby. For the first time in his life, he was one of *them*.

Library. Kitchens. Dormitories. Generating room. Housekeeping. Feeling sleepy. Kindergarten. Schoolrooms. Powerplant.

The most impressive was the nidus. Fifty-five tanks, Gray said proudly, incubation down to two hundred twenty days—more than a baby a week now. Vaun was saved from further exploration by a scratchy public announcement that ptomaine pie was available now if anyone was hungry.

The main hall was much larger than a mere tunnel. It must have been created for some purpose other than mining, but it looked old, predating the Brotherhood's occupation. A couple of hundred brethren were eating there at long tables and benches, and the steamy scent made Vaun's mouth water copiously.

Ptomaine pie was not the gourmet food of Valhal, but he was going to enjoy it more. Collecting a heaped plateful, he headed for an empty space at the end of a table, and sat next to a Green, remembering to huddle tight against him in brotherly fashion. Then young Gray rammed in beside him like a landslide.

Green flashed Vaun a smile of welcome, but obviously did not register that he was anyone unusual, because he immediately turned his attention back to the boy across the table, another Green. "Bishop takes knight."

His reflection pondered a moment, then said uneasily, "Queen takes bishop."

"*Bishop takes queen!*"

"Oh balls!" said the other.

Having missed the start of the game, Vaun could not find it interesting, although he could tell from the way his neighbor promoted pawns that he must be a devious player. And Gray had sniggered knowingly, which was a reminder that there were no dullards among the brethren.

Vaun tried to concentrate on his meal, but he was too tired to be truly hungry. Even the thrill of being with his brothers was fading before the onslaught of fatigue. He would have to go back, of course, back to Valhal and Hiport and the ghastly routine of a public clown. That was a dread thought, but unavoidable. He was more than a pawn in the Brotherhood's game this time.

The Q ship was coming—everybody dead in eleven weeks, who cares? It would be ironic if the Brotherhood destroyed the planet when there was already an established hive on it, and perhaps more than one. But the brethren at the landing strip had talked of "Armageddon." They were training the pepods to attack on command.

However ignorant the rest of the world was, the brethren obviously knew about the Q ship.

His eyelids kept drooping until he thought he would fall asleep at the table. Whenever he opened his mouth to eat, he started yawning. Repeatedly he caught himself nodding and forced his head up. Every time his eyes met anyone else's, that boy would smile at him. It wasn't just him. They smiled at one another, they sat tight together, they touched in passing. At least a third of the adults were occupied in caring for children, although they often passed them around. There was something enormously appealing about this easy friendship, this one gigantic family. No complaints, no arguments, no fights or jealousies.

*All boys are created equal.*

He had come home at last.

A finger touched his ear and he looked up, blinking at a brown shirt and the inevitable smile.

"I bet you almost bled to death from that."

"Dice!" Vaun started to rise and was pushed down. Brown swung around the end of the table and the close-packed occupants of the opposite bench somehow made room for him.

"This unit was Dice once," he admitted. His mouth still smiled, but his eyes were wary.

"You're still the same! You haven't changed. You're exactly the boy I remember on the boat, long ago."

Dice shook his head vigorously. "That's not true! The years leave scars." He cocked a dark eyebrow. "But I expect that's better than what happened to Raj?"

Vaun winced. There was nothing to say to that.

Odd . . . Prior, and Abbot, and the rest . . . Vaun had compared every adult brother he had ever met to his memories of Dice. And now he felt strangely cheated to see that Dice was just like all of them. Vaun would not recognize him the next time they met.

"And so you're Bishop?"

"No. We have some specialists in politics and strategy to handle that."

"On *Unity* Abbot was the senior."

Dice shrugged again. "We do it otherwise. We outgrew amateur leadership, I suppose. I'm just a self-taught genetic engineer, remember? I do hold the galactic record for diaper changing, of course."

"You've done marvelously. A magnificent life's work! And Cessine?"

"He's . . . probably here somewhere."

The hesitation had been slight, but it might imply that there were other places Cessine might be. Other hives, possibly. That problem could wait for *yawn!* . . . tomorrow.

Dice's arrival had interrupted the mental chess game. The Green sitting next to Vaun was openly listening, grinning. Now he said, "This unit is Bishop sometimes. Hadn't realized who you were!" He gave Vaun a hug. The rest of the diners at the table had stopped talking to eavesdrop.

*"Birthmarks!"* said his opponent. "I'm playing *chess* against *Bishop*?"

"You were doing fine!" Vaun's neighbor said.

The other snorted and gathered up his dishes. "I concede! I should have guessed when you dropped me your queen so easy. Maybe we can meet on my turf sometime?"

"You gave me a lesson this morning in the gym. I know those karate hands."

The other rose and smiled ruefully. "Next time tell me who you are."

"Not likely!" Green chuckled as his double stalked away, then turned his grin on Vaun again, and thumped his shoulder. "Welcome, Brother! Welcome!"

"It's great to be here."

"Great to have you! And we have so much to talk about! When are you going back?"

"Huh? Whenever you want. I told you that already!"

Bishop chuckled. "I said I was Bishop sometimes. Others are Bishop other times, okay? What else have you told 'me'?"

"Not a damn thing."

"Good. So, how'd you find us?"

"Pepods."

"Ah. 'Fraid of that. You don't mind talking and eating at the same time?" He glanced around, and Vaun realized that a crowd had gathered already, and packed in like sand. A close-knit family like this one would be very sensitive to unusual events, and today he was one of those. Youngsters were standing on the tables to see, some of them holding their plates and still eating. Others were scaling adults like trees to sit on their heads or shoulders. Inquisitive toddlers came burrowing in through the undergrowth of legs.

Having trouble getting an arm free, Bishop hauled a tiny microphone from his pocket and laid it on the table before him. He raised his voice slightly. "Hey, guys!"

The words echoed, and the babble of talk stopped instantly, leaving the hall silent.

"Most of you have probably heard already. Our lost sheep is here at last. Welcome Brother Vaun!"

The roar was deafening. Bishop grinned sideways at Vaun, who blinked to ease the prickling under his eyelids.

"We need to hear his news, and we need to talk about pepods. Qualified?"

"Qualified," said Gray quickly at Vaun's other elbow.

"Mm," Bishop said doubtfully. "All right. Listen close, Little Expert. Tell us, Brother." He turned the mike slightly.

Vaun gathered his fading wits. "It was Roker's doing. He'd dug up a man who claimed to be able to talk to the beasties."

"Quild?" asked Gray quickly.

"Yes, Quild."

"I've read his stuff. It's crap."

"You may find yourself more familiar with crap if you keep interrupting," Bishop remarked gently. "Shoveling it. Carry on, White."

Not *Vaun*! Not *Admiral*! *White!*

It felt good to be just "White."

"He thought that pepods somewhere might know where Dice and Cessine had been hiding all these years and could tell the network."

Gray snorted disbelievingly, but Bishop's face lit up.

"They don't suspect we have a hive?"

"Not a clue. I'm certain."

The hall rustled excitedly at the good news. All around Vaun, faces were smiling, with one exception—Dice. Vaun caught a glimpse of something odd on that unit's face, something he resented. Perhaps it was only satisfaction at having so deceived a whole planet, and perhaps fatigue was making Vaun testy, but something prompted him to add, "I've always believed, of course, and I knew you'd get in touch with me when the time came."

"Of course," Bishop agreed.

Now why had Vaun said that? He was still playing silly random games. He had picked up the randoms' bad habits, and lied to his brethren. He was groggy from lack of sleep. Why not just admit that Abbot and Dice had totally fooled him as well as everyone else? Nobody cared here about status, or scoring points. The generous thing would be to apologize right away and confess.

Not easy for an admiral, a famous hero, to shed the habits of a lifetime. His audience was waiting.

"So Roker organized a meeting . . ." He related how the pepod seance had gone wrong, and how he had used the records to identify

Kohab as the source of the disturbance. He did not mention Feirn's part in that. "Obviously someone else was messing around with the beasties, and at a very remote location. Having just learned that I was immune to pepods, I could guess who that someone was. The only way I could think of to warn you, was to come in person—and I couldn't resist a chance to visit the hive at last."

That was another lie, or a repeat of the first one. He'd expected to find two brothers, not hundreds.

He caught himself in an enormous yawn, and mumbled an apology. "So," he concluded, "I bring sad news. Sooner or later someone will make the same discovery as I did, even if it's only counsel for the defense."

"Not if you block them!" Bishop said, grinning. "The sooner we get you back in position the better, Brother! Lock up the data, delay the inquiry . . . That's exactly the sort of help you'll be able to give us between now and Armageddon. Invaluable!"

Vaun did not want to be sent back. He wanted to stay, and yet obviously he could be far more valuable to the Brotherhood as a traitor working within the Patrol than he could be changing diapers at Kohab. His personal feelings would carry no weight in the matter. He would shock the whole hive if he even admitted to having any.

Bishop squirmed a hand loose and scratched his head. He smiled at young Gray. "All right, Pepodist? Got all that?"

As the lad nodded, a voice called out, "Prior, pepodists. Got a question for Brother Vaun."

"Go ahead, Prior," said Bishop.

"We've managed to increase the pepods' privacy radius by twenty-four percent in the last five years. Not just here—the effect shows as far away as Ralgrove. Has that been noticed?"

"I haven't any idea," Vaun told the mike. "No one mentioned it." Was Ralgrove another hive? And *how* had the radius been increased? And measured? Quild had used felons for his research. Judged on ruthlessness, there wasn't much to choose between sides in this war.

"Any more questions for our newcomer?" Bishop demanded. The hall stayed silent. "Then back to the trough, all of you. We'll have a formal ruckus in the morning." He slipped the mike back in his pocket.

Eating resumed, and the youngsters on the tables dropped out of sight.

"These two randoms you brought, Brother," Bishop said. "They're a breeding pair?"

"I think they're at the courtship stage, why?"

"Just curious. They've been engaging in coitus."

"They've been what?"

"We have a camera on them, of course. I found a gaggle of small fry gathered around the monitor, having fits at the show they were putting on. I think it's coitus—no clothes on, bouncing around on top of each other?"

"That sounds right," Vaun muttered. He wondered whose idea that had been. Feirn had found her hero at last? Conscious of a hundred questioning eyes on him, he added uneasily, "It's more fun than it looks, actually."

"It made me feel sick, so I didn't watch. Can you explain away their disappearance when you get back?"

"If I go soon. Nobody knows they came with me." Vaun considered the prospect of a return to lonely Valhal. He wondered if he could ask for a few brethren to keep him company . . . but that would be an unthinkable breach of security.

He thought glumly of that shadowy reconciliation he and Maeve had sketched in the night. He would not dare follow up on that now. Maeve was shrewd, and he had never had much success at deceiving her.

"I need some sleep, and then I'd best leave. Tell me about Armageddon."

"Did not Abbot explain, Brother?" Dice asked softly.

Bishop had opened his mouth to speak; he shut it in silence. Of course, Dice was not hive-bred like all the rest. Dice had lived in the randoms' world, the jungle. Now Dice was suspicious. He did not trust the new brother, and that realization seemed to settle over the audience like a cold dew. Fifty identical faces registered identical shock.

Tremors of danger jangled Vaun's antennae. He took a deep breath to clear his head, and pushed away his half-eaten meal.

"Of course he didn't! Would you? I wouldn't have told me the truth! Frisde's goons were as suspicious as . . . as I don't know what. Do you think they greeted me with open arms? Abbot knew I would be put through the grinder when I got back. He told me only enough so I would know what to do. The rest I worked out later. Much later."

*About three hours ago* . . . He wondered if Lieutenant Blade understood that, and why he wondered that.

There was a pause, and Bishop left the questioning to Dice.

"What did you work out, Brother?" The smile and the voice were gentle. The steady, dark stare was not.

"That there was a fifth plan. I . . . Roker . . . the Patrol had worked out four possible strategies the Brotherhood might use. There was a fifth. Eventually I realized that the moment *Unity* had turned off her fireballs, she'd received a tight-beam message. I'd guess that it originated right here, in Kohab, since you'd opened your marine lab or whatever it was in '99, the year after we met. This is where you and Cessine were hiding."

"Full marks so far," Dice said softly.

Vaun began to relax, very slightly. "Roker was determined that the Q ship would launch no shuttles, ferry down no illegal immigrants. But he couldn't monitor a billion meteors, all moving at high velocity. The self-destruct was a blind to cover a homing probe. One small, automated, untraceable probe among all that flying crap."

"They died that we might live," Bishop said, as if that was a familiar liturgy.

"Agreed!" rumbled the surrounding brethren.

"That probe brought you all the know-how and supplies you needed in order to found the hive," Vaun concluded, "a do-it-yourself baby factory. So Abbot won. The Patrol lost." He yawned again. "It must have amused you to see me being hailed as a conquering hero, fêted and honored?"

"I'm not sure that 'amused' is the word." Dice smiled bitterly. "I mostly wished you were here to do your share of the diapers and nose wiping."

That was a capitulation, at least a partial capitulation.

"If you'd ever asked me, I'd have done anything to help," Vaun said.

He would have done so, of course.

"Couldn't risk it," Dice said with another dark, ambiguous stare.

"I suppose not."

Bishop grinned . . . very friendly . . . "So when did you work it out, Brother?" Bishop had specialized in intrigue. Most likely he had been designed for it, in the discretionary five percent of his genes. For the first time in his life, Vaun was up against someone smarter than himself.

"I don't remember exactly."

"Long time ago?" He wanted to know how long Vaun had guarded the great secret.

And the answer was that Vaun never had.

He would have done so, of course.

"Probably. Excuse my yawning like this. I haven't slept in weeks. Why? What matters is that I'm going to have to scamper back to

Valhal before anyone wonders where I got to. And I couldn't fly a paper dart right now . . ." Vaun stretched sleepily, and went on the offensive. "Abbot did something else, too. Right at the end, he must have reported back. He radioed to Scyth. There were no Q ships blocking Scyth at that time, nor Avalon . . . so why Scyth?"

"I suppose he wasn't sure what the Brotherhood's situation was on Avalon." Bishop had been pushed forward hard against the table by the crush; he was supporting one cheek with a hand, twisted around to regard Vaun with an unwinking, dark stare. He looked uncomfortable and totally unaware of the fact. "Do you know—now?"

"Avalonian Command claims to have wiped . . . us . . . out."

"Interpatrol report?"

"Yes."

"Could be crap."

"Yes. So Scyth waited . . . Let's see . . . The message would have taken seven years to get there, so Scyth waited twenty-five years or so, and then dispatched this next Q ship. Tell me about Armageddon."

"It's a blind, is all. It'll make a very close pass, but it'll miss." Bishop was speaking just a little too loudly. "How much do you know about Scyth?"

"I know that the Brotherhood took advantage of the chaos caused by the Great Plague. They infiltrated all the governments after that."

Bishop frowned thoughtfully. "The Patrol here knows that much?"

It hadn't. It did now. Tham had made the discovery, but he hadn't seen the importance of the information until Vaun had told him of the coming Q ship. Then he had understood. Distrusting Vaun, the dying commodore had sent him the Ootharsis of Isquat file in cipher, knowing that nothing would draw Roker's attention to it more surely than that. And, of course, Tham's security had recorded the conversation, and thus the password.

Roker had died also—but then Vaun himself had sent Tham's file to Acting High Admiral Weald . . . Damnation!

"I think the Patrol knows," he muttered, aware of the many sharp eyes watching him.

Bishop nodded. "We'll turn the public panic to our advantage. You'll have a big part to play then. We can talk about it in the morning." He glanced around the audience.

Bishop was lying.

And Scyth gone silent. Was that when the Brotherhood made its move to take absolute control? Better not ask too many questions.

Vaun rubbed his eyes groggily. He could *smell* the suspicion now. Dice had passed the baton and Bishop had accepted it. By telling a known untruth, he'd just sent out a signal to everyone within earshot.

He struggled to his feet, aching in every joint. "It's great to be here," he said. "But I'm bushed. Would some kind brother show me some place I can fall over and not get stepped on for about twelve hours?"

In a clamor of treble voices, about twenty of the youngsters underfoot volunteered. None of the adult boys did; they were going to stay for the resumption of the meeting.

"One last question, Brother White."

"Yes, Your Holiness?"

"Those two randoms you brought?"

Vaun stared down angrily at the so-familiar face. Did his own ever look so dangerous? "I know—you want to feed 'em to pepods. Do what the fuck you like with them."

"It's just that dawn's the best time," Bishop said.

Roker's question . . . Whose side are you on?

Prior with no top to his head. Raj and Prosy tortured to death. Tong poisoned with a virus. Olmin's little peepee experiments. Doggoth. Pepods. Abbot and *Unity*—they died that we might live.

Maeve the traitor.

Vaun said, "Sure. To hell with randoms! I don't care if you fry 'em for breakfast. Now will you excuse me?"

"Of course. If you're sure you don't want to hang around for the singsong?"

Vaun shivers. "Maybe another night." He lets one of his smallest brothers take his hand and lead him off to bed.

T HE DORMITORY TUNNELS were dim and low, a vague labyrinth of mysterious silence. Straw-filled pallets lay along both sides, many already occupied. Some boys were reading, their faces gleaming spectrally in the light of their books, and they did not look up. Others were already asleep, mostly small fry. No sound of snoring echoed along those rocky walls. Snoring would be a design fault.

Krantz! He was tired. Sleep for a week. He came to an empty place that looked no better or worse than any other.

"Thanks," he whispered to his diminutive guide. "I can manage now." He hauled off his shirt. When he looked down, he saw that the lad was grinning gap-toothed at him, and tugging at his own buttons. He pointed a stubby finger at his feet.

"You undo my thoolatheth?"

Admiral Vaun knelt down and undressed his nameless little brother.

"And tuck me in?"

"Certainly. But see that black shirt?"

The lad nodded, shivering because he had nothing on.

"Take this one over there and bring me his, okay?"

His brother twisted a finger inside an ear for a moment while he thought about it. "Why?

"It's a joke. Tell you about it in the morning."

"Okay." Taking Vaun's white shirt, he set off, unwittingly revealing that he was Number 516. In a moment he came back with the black shirt, and put it on Vaun's blanket. Then he scrambled quickly under his own. No one noticed what toddlers did.

"Thanks," Vaun said, smiling conspiratorially. Comfortably tucked in, Number 516 demanded a good-night hug and a kiss, too—he knew his rights. Then Vaun crawled under his own blanket and they smiled sleepily across at each other. The pillows could certainly use a wash.

He thought, *They were engaging in coitus.*

Crazy, crazy randoms!

He was asleep.

T HE SUN SHINES all day, every day. The trees are bowed by the weight of blossom.

Surf rolls into the bay and seabirds wheel under a perfect sky. Warm waves lap the shining sands.

The Dreamer runs over the beach, hand in hand with his lover.

In the great empty ballroom music soars, and they dance naked under the glittering crystal of the chandeliers.

They make love—in bed, on the beach, on a couch under the glittering crystal of the chandeliers. In sunshine and under the stars.

Within the dark mystery of her hair glints red, and he kisses every freckle.

Sometimes they throw great parties, for kings and ministers and presidents. Gladly they send them on their way again, and are alone with each other.

Day follows day. She laughs almost fearfully. "How long can it last? How long can mortals be so happy?"

"Forever!" the Dreamer tells her. "The hero and heroine always live happily ever after. That is mandatory."

Yet sometimes there are sad farewells, when the lovemaking becomes frenzied because the Dreamer must depart to suffer through endless, excruciating ceremonies in far countries: honors and speeches, banquets and empty ritual. Always he rushes back to his lover, and absence has made the loving even sweeter.

The hero's return.

The hero's welcome, in the arms of his love.

She laughs, her face flushed with happiness as she looks up at him from the pillow. "I wasn't ever Roker's mistress. I wasn't hostess here for Roker. I never did this with Roker."

"That's good," says the Dreamer. "I'm glad you're telling me now so there won't be any misunderstandings later."

"And you don't act like a great celebrity, or a spacer stud, or a social snob . . ."

Penetration, and she screams with joy.

261

Climax, and he gibbers in ecstasy.

The Dream changes. They are dancing.

"This is crazy!"

"You made me crazy! I am crazy in love."

"Not that."

"Then what?"

"Dancing with bare feet. I stick to the floor. We ought to wear socks, at least."

"Socks are not romantic," he says, and sweeps her naked body into his arms and carries her to the nearest couch. "I'll show you romantic."

The hero's reward.

U P, UP FROM a bottomless darkness . . . Effort . . . Struggle . . .

It was the hardest thing he had ever done.

His brain was sand, his body a rock. His eyelids were marble tombstones, but he forced them to open.

Above him, the roof of the tunnel was faintly visible in the light of glow lamps spaced well apart. Close on either hand, he heard quiet breathing.

*Maeve's daughter?* Pepods?

*Oh shit!*

He heaved himself up to a sitting position, and thought that his joints creaked like unoiled doors. His skull was full of mud. The tunnel was full of sleeping brethren. Healthy boys, hard workers, sleeping soundly.

He shivered, feeling the cold of the rock sunk deep in his being. The temptation to fall back and sleep again was a promise of Paradise . . . Cruel destiny, to have to leave that humble, worn rag of a blanket.

Arkady was very close to Hiport!

*Hell!* He reached for his clothes.

Security here was as primitive as coal. The brethren trusted one another absolutely, and relied on secrecy to defend them against the outside world. Bishop might have thought to install a camera in the dormitory, but it was not likely. If he had, then the switching of shirts should have put it in the wrong place—inspecting faces for bruises would have been a big operation.

Vaun wondered if his bruises had faded much in the night.

Half a night.

One thing a boy learned in Doggoth was waking to order.

THE CORRIDORS WERE dim and almost deserted. A few sleepy boys wandered the corridors, but whatever business they were on had nothing to do with security or guard duty. They exchanged smiles and nods with their black-shirted brother, and went on without having really noticed him at all.

Finding the air plant was easy. It was hot and stunningly noisy, filled with a mind-numbing throb of archaic machinery, monstrous black shapes vibrating in the shadows of what had probably once been a shaft. Huge ducts and girders led off from it in various directions, vanishing into rock and overhead darkness. The place looked deserted, as if no one had visited it for years.

There was at least one camera somewhere, though.

Vaun could see only one other door. It was a plate steel antiquity, rusty and solid and unrevealing. He stood for a while in a corner to study it, struggling to make his sleep-sodden brain do its duty.

Duty? He was sorely tempted to say *The hell with it!* and just go back to bed. Any bed. There had been several empty pallets with no clothes on them and no dark-haired head on the pillow. Any of them was his for the taking. This was where he belonged. This was what he'd been born for . . . conceived for, designed for.

Shit.

Maeve's daughter.

Pepods.

After a while he felt himself starting to wilt in the heat, and that roused him to move. He was mostly worried by the key hanging on a nail in plain sight by the jamb—it seemed too easy. The key could be a trap, booby-trapped somehow. The hinges were visible, and a ramshackle tool bench nearby was littered with implements and junk. He could hammer the pins out of the hinges—except they were well rusted in and he would make a lot of noise.

The hell with it. He went to the bench and selected a weighty ball-peen hammer . . . to disable the camera, he told himself, while suspecting he needed it more to satisfy some atavistic craving for a weapon. He marched over to the cell door and took down the key.

The lock squeaked. The hinges creaked alarmingly, a shrill scream of alarm rising over the basso background roar of the compressors. He opened the door just wide enough for him to peer inside, gagging at the musty stench that greeted him, the rot of centuries.

The room was very small, the floor filthy and littered. At the far side, a shapeless bundle of blankets was already starting to stir. If he were going to put a camera in here, he would put it right above the door, high up. He squeaked the door a little further and slipped inside.

Near the ceiling, above his head, a black limpet about the size of his thumb clung to the rock. It was unobtrusive, but newer than anything else, unmarked by the pervasive dirt. He swung the hammer up and crushed it, and was showered with dust. Unless the watchers had noticed the sudden brightness of the door opening, they would assume a malfunction—those must be commonplace in the archaic junk market. And it might operate only in the infrared anyway. He stared all around, looking for others.

"Admiral Vaun?" Blade asked softly. He was sitting up, and he did not seem to have any clothes on.

Feirn mumbled sleepily beside him, and groped for the blanket. She said, *"Eek!"* as her hand found Blade instead.

"Get dressed! And hurry!" Of course, Vaun could have gone around by the washroom and stolen some hive garments, but those would not disguise either the girl's red hair nor the boy's height. Somehow they must avoid being seen at all on the way out.

"Is this a rescue, sir?" Blade was not moving.

"Of course it's a rescue! You think I came to kiss you good-night?"

"Is this wise, sir?"

"What the hell do you mean, 'Is this wise?' "

"Won't they be sending you back, sir? I mean, don't they expect you to resume your duties with the Patrol?"

"What of it?"

"Well, sir. If we try to escape and don't succeed, then there will be no way to warn Hiport about this hive. Even if we do get away, they will guess that you helped us."

"Idiot!" snarled the girl. She, at least, was scrabbling into her garments, but Blade was just sitting.

"You have a touching faith in my loyalty, Lieutenant!"

"Your presence here now would seem to vindicate my trust, sir."

"God's tits, boy! Get dressed! Now!"

"I still think the tactic is questionable, sir."

"They're threatening to throw you both to the pepods, you clatterbrain!"

"I am aware of that, sir. But our fate is not important compared to the fate of the planet. I think you should play along with them, sir. I really do!"

The girl was almost dressed. She said, "Blade!" furiously. "You can't mean that! One minute you say you love me, and the next minute you want to feed me to pepods?"

The kid was absolutely, one hundred percent right, though. Vaun should not be here. Even if he believed that the hive no longer trusted him, he would have a much better chance of escaping on his own. He ought to slam the door, lock it again, and walk out by himself. Or go back to bed.

He hefted the hammer, fighting a fierce urge to throw it. "I have given you an order, Lieutenant!"

"Sir!" Blade spasmed into motion, but he still argued. "If they trust you, sir, then you could order a strike in force, and in proper order." He was on his feet already, zipping his pants; speed dressing was a Doggoth specialty. "If you release us and come with us, and do manage to get away, then they will have time to evacuate at least some of—"

"You idiotic numskull! Spare me your woolly idealistic heroics!" Vaun slipped back out of the cell with relief, gasping some welcome fresh air.

The corridor beyond remained deserted; nothing had changed. The captives followed him, Blade still furiously buttoning. The girl had an arm around him.

"This is for real, isn't it?" she demanded, glaring at Vaun as if she suspected he was about to turn into someone else. "Last night I really thought you'd gone over to their side!" She had transferred her hero worship to a new hero, obviously. Fine by him, but Maeve would not be pleased.

"So did I."

"What!?"

*They wouldn't have me.* Still carrying the hammer, he led the way out into the tunnel.

What had the brethren decided after he left the hall? He didn't know. He didn't want to know, not now.

He walked as fast as he could, but this was one of the unimproved parts of the mine, with ancient rails on the floor and many overhead ducts and dangling cables. The lights were matted with webs, everything was deep with the megafilth of centuries. "I don't suppose you noticed any com equipment around, did you?"

"None, sir." The lieutenant was practically dancing as he tried to stay close to Vaun and also negotiate the rough terrain, while adjusting his long stride to that of the girl clinging to him, and not bang his head.

"Then listen," Vaun said, "both of you. We may have to split up. Can you fly a torch, Feirn?"

"Not as well as Blade."

"Few can. The torches may be locked. They may have disabled the Sheerfire. But if we get the chance, we should scatter, understand? They'll follow and try to bring us down."

"I won't leave Blade!"

"You have your orders, Lieutenant." Vaun stopped talking while he negotiated an ominous hole in the floor. "There's at least one more hive somewhere, possibly at a place called Ralgrove. Got that?"

"Yes, sir. Ralgrove." Blade scooped Feirn bodily over the ditch with him, using one arm and not braking stride. "I see why we need a com, sir. Do you think they even have them in their torches?"

"Probably not. Not even for emergencies." The brethren would sooner die than imperil security.

"The nearest strip is at Fondport, sir. Twenty kilometers south."

Vaun wondered if he should have promoted Blade to a higher rank than lieutenant. Of course, if they came out of this alive, the kid would be a commodore tomorrow. Their chances were about three in a billion. He signaled a halt as they reached the first crossing. He knelt and peered around the corner, both ways. There was no one coming. "Right," he said, rising.

"Left, sir," said Blade. "If we're going back to the exit, that is."

"Please yourself." Vaun went left, and the other two followed. Probably either way would do, but the way the captives had been brought might be shorter. This was one of the improved tunnels, paved and clean, and it seemed to go on forever. The night lighting was dim, but anyone who stepped in from a crosstunnel was going to see well enough to notice two very odd brethren, even at a distance.

At the next intersection he stopped his companions and walked boldly ahead, glancing to right and left. Seeing no one, he beckoned for the others to come, and they dashed across to him, hand in hand.

He hurried onward. "Our main message, the one we must get through, is to neuron this place soonest. Ralgrove should be investigated. This one—*fry it!*" What of Number 516? He had kissed the child good-night and now he wanted to melt every cell in his brain before he woke up. But even if he could save the innocents, they wouldn't stay innocent. In fifteen years or so, Number 516 would have all the deadly potential Dice had had when Vaun first met him. Roker's talk of an infection had been realistic. Every spore must die.

Think *Armageddon* instead!

And how to convince the Patrol? "Trouble is, I don't know the codes."

The day code would have changed since he left Valhal. The fences would open for most admirals, for they could be identified by voice or face, but Admiral Vaun was a special case. The systems had special procedures for him, and they would certainly talk back to a lieutenant, especially if this one was already posted AWOL.

"I could get through, sir."

"So could I," said the girl.

"You? How?"

Feirn laughed harshly. "Think any pubcom station would resist a beat like this one? Petly'll wet his pants. Then he'll call the Patrol for comment, right? And Petly can get high up, fast! I know—I've seen him do it."

Messy! But it would suffice if only the girl escaped. And, of course, Blade's mother was quartermaster at Hiport, so he might be able to get through to Weald or Phalo faster even than Vaun could. Infuriating, superhumanly efficient young upstart!

Another intersection . . . He went forward, and still saw no other pedestrians. How long could this luck last? Again he beckoned for his companions to join him. When they caught up with him, he said, "If we can get out, we scatter. If they have coms in their torches, then get through to Hiport as soon as you're airborne!" The Sheerfire would be speedier than a torch; but its electronics were dead. Blade knew all that. Time would tell, maybe.

And there was going to be pepod trouble. The pepods would

react to humans but not brethren. Time to think about pepods when they got out of the hive.

"They're training the pepods to be a weapon, of course. Report that. And the Q ship. It's going to look like a near-miss, but it's not a rock, it's a boat."

"Unmanned, then," Blade said.

"Yes, unmanned."

"Told you that, sweetheart!" the girl said. "Didn't I?"

"Yes, honey."

"I said no one would send a Q ship across interstellar space just to give someone a bad fright twenty-five years in the future! You didn't believe me, darling."

Oh, Krantz! They were into the lovebird stage.

"Yes, I did, dear. Sir, we go right here."

Vaun turned right without questioning. This tunnel sloped steeply upward, and it was pleasantly dim.

"The brethren are talking about *Armageddon*!" he said. "It'll be a tin boat, not a rock. Or maybe a very small rock, able to take the tidals from a course correction at three hundred millies. So it'll *seem* to be going to fly by, and then it'll veer at the last minute and impact. My guess is that it'll take out Hiport."

The girl gasped. "But why, Vaun?"

"To destroy Ultian Command. No more central control. It will devastate the planet—earthquakes, no communications, no solar power, no harvests for years. Billions dying. Chaos and anarchy. I sent Weald a file—it's all in there. Got that?"

"Yes, sir."

"Yes, Vaun."

"*Back!*" He shoved; Blade wheeled and dragged the girl back with him to the sidetunnel they had just passed. Vaun carried on as if nothing had happened, climbing toward the two brethren who had just appeared up ahead. The lighting was dim—would they have noticed?

Apparently not. They were deep in talk, and passed him with vague nods. He turned off into the tunnel they had come from, then stopped and peered back around the corner until they had vanished. His knees were shaking. Time oozed by in drips of sweat as he waited for Blade to conclude that the coast was clear and follow. He was dismayed to realize how easily he had come to trust his self-appointed deputy.

Trust . . . Apocalypse . . . Meteor impact and pepod attack . . . Communication breakdown. Then famine and pestilence and civil war and breakdown of order . . . Petty warlords taking control with their own militias . . .

What leader could ever refuse an efficient, trustworthy subordinate? Or a fearless bodyguard, loyal to the death? Or ruthless mercenaries, genius advisers? Or officials utterly incorruptible, immune to both gold and girls? As deputies, the brethren would be irresistible and very soon make themselves indispensable in all the high places. If your opponent has one, then you must have one . . . Just intelligent cyborgs, of course, but very handy.

And in twenty years or so, the knives would turn in their users' hands—all of them at the same instant. The Master Race would rule. The wild stock would be domesticated, and Ult would go silent. It had worked on Scyth, and perhaps on a thousand other worlds.

The two human fugitives emerged from their sidetunnel and came racing along to meet him. He held out the hammer so they would recognize him—even so, he noted that Blade took a hard look at the bruises that distinguished the one good brother. The traitor.

Without a word, they resumed their march, hurrying now with a shared sense of urgency. Time was running out. They must reach the torches before dawn.

More turns . . . more frantic dashes and pauses to peer around corners . . . Twice more they hid from wandering brethren. They must be close to the entrance now, and the hive seemed to be stirring into life. Blade's memory of the route had been faultless.

And then they were all three jammed into a dead-end crevice, hardly breathing as a troop of four brothers went trudging by, muttering sleepily. Vaun suspected they were the night watch from the gate coming off duty. Pity . . . the replacements would be more alert. But the four had gone by and it was only a matter of minutes before the fugitives could try their break for freedom.

The boys stayed silent.

"Sweetheart?" Feirn whispered.

Blade said, "Dearest?" It was nauseating.

"What *good* are we going to do? If the Q ship is going to hit the world . . . I thought Q ships couldn't be stopped?"

"This one can, I think. They can't hit Hiport from Scyth."

Good boy—he'd seen the one slim chance.

"Huh?"

"It probably can't even hit the planet from seven elwies, and certainly not a bull's-eye on Hiport, if the admiral is right and that's its target. It'll have to make a sighting."

"I don't follow."

His voice was very low and patient, but he was talking to Vaun also. "It will have to shut off its fireballs for course confirmation. Maybe for only a minute or so, but when it does, it's vulnerable. Right, sir?"

"Right. I hope that's right."

It was right in theory, and a tin boat was a lot more vulnerable to hardbeams than a rock, but it was going to call for some very, very nimble work by the Patrol.

It didn't sound like Ultian Command, somehow. It would take everything the Patrol could put in the sky, and then some. Roker might have been able to organize it. Maybe Vaun himself could, if the Patrol would let him. Weald, Phalo . . . not too likely.

A hell of a slim chance, but it was all they had.

"Let's go," Vaun whispered. "Every boy—and girl—for himself. I'll try for the gun rack. You two wait a minute, then sprint for the door, okay?"

"Yes, sir."

"Kiss me, darling."

Vaun left them to it.

He dropped the useless hammer, made sure the tunnel was empty, then stepped out into the passage and ran for the guard room.

T RUST . . . THE WHOLE system was based on trust, the certainty that a boy was who he said he was.

On his arrival the previous day, he had seen no signs of electronic trickery. The hive's only real defense was its enemies' ignorance of its existence.

He strolled into the guardroom. Four boys were sitting there, muffled in blankets, reading books. They were amateurs in security, he assumed, specialists in other disciplines who had drawn an unwelcome tour of sentry duty in addition to their regular labors. That explained why they were all huddled together—unusual to find the Brotherhood being inefficient. They did not even look up at him.

"Prior," he said, and walked over to the gun rack.

His Giantkiller was there, but there were two newer-seeming versions beside it in the rack, and he recalled Tan's remark about those being lighter. He slung one on his shoulder, tucked a handbeam into his belt, and turned to go. "How's the weather out there?"

"Cold," said a grumpy voice. "You'll need a coat."

Perhaps there was a password. Perhaps the light fell on his bruised face. Perhaps he walked like an admiral. One of the books clanked to the floor, one of the guards struggled to unwrap himself. "Hey! Aren't you . . ." Moving in unconscious unison, they threw off their blankets and sprang from their chairs, not even glancing at one another—four of them, each one glaring at Vaun, each as good as he.

They were between him and the exit tunnel. He backed against the wall, holding them at bay with the Giantkiller. His own face repeated four times stared back at him in shock and horror.

"Stay where you are!" he barked, but it didn't work.

At that moment Blade and Feirn sprinted in and dashed for the exit. The guards again moved like one, jumping to block them.

*"Stop!"*

This time everyone froze. Tableau. Standoff.

"Please, Brothers! Don't make me kill you!"

Vaun was against one side wall, Blade and the girl against the other. The four brethren blocked the exit—White, Yellow, Red, Brown.

"Who's Prior?" Vaun demanded. He felt sick. This wasn't going to work.

"I am," White said hoarsely. He stuck out his chin. "You will have to kill us, you know!" He sounded younger than he looked.

"I shall if I must. So why die needlessly? I can gun you down and we'll get away and you'll be dead. You go ahead of us. When we leave, I'll not shoot you, I swear."

If White moved first, it was by only a fraction of a second—all four took a step forward.

"Oh, stop that!" Vaun shouted. Sweat was running into his eyes. "You can't shoot your brothers!"

"I can. I did. I shot two on *Unity*!"

The guards gulped in horror. The whites of their eyes showed all around the irises.

Vaun had never told anyone that before. No one. Not even Maeve. And that time he had been out of his mind with fear. This was in cold blood.

''And I helped mind bleed Prior! I have a design fault, remember? That was what they decided last night, wasn't it?''

He wished instantly that he had not asked that question. He did not *want* to know what had been decided after he left the hall.

Yellow took a deep breath, as if surprised. ''No,'' he said. ''Never. We decided you'd been damaged, though.''

Blade tried a move, and Brown sidestepped to block him. Vaun shouted, *''Stop!''* again.

''Not your fault, Brother,'' Yellow went on. He was the youngest, not quite an adult. Eighteen, maybe, but apparently the only one who'd been at the meeting. ''But we decided we daren't risk sending you back.''

''Kill me, you mean.'' All this talk was crazy. Time was running out. Someone would come. Dawn would come. But he did want to know, really. Just in case.

White shook his head, and eased forward imperceptibly. ''Brother doesn't kill brother! Sending you back is too great a risk, but we want you to stay and help here.''

There was a jagged lump in Vaun's throat. ''Crap! Either you trust me or you don't!''

''Listen!'' White said urgently. His face was shining wet in the dim light of the glow lamps. ''We do trust you, Brother, but we just don't dare send you back. You're welcome to stay with us, always! You're one of us. You've suffered out there alone long enough, and been damaged, and we want you here in the hive. We need you here to advise us. Honored, and loved. I swear this on the Brotherhood.''

Krantz! It was so tempting, Vaun wanted to scream. He dared not look at Blade or the girl. His brothers. Really wanting him? Even *needing* him a little?

''You can't trust me,'' he muttered angrily. ''Not now.''

''Tell me what's wrong, Brother,'' White said gently. ''Is it Die Day? Armageddon?''

''Maybe,'' Vaun admitted. His hands were shaking.

''It'll happen anyway! We can show you the numbers. Projections. The famines have started. Their whole ecology's about to collapse.'' White was pleading—why did he have to seem so infernally sincere? ''I can't lie to you, Brother, you know that! We're certain: twenty years, maybe thirty . . . Total disaster! We can show you!''

''Mortality doesn't excuse murder!''

''Ah!'' Red shouted with relief. ''It's these two randoms! That's it, isn't it, Brother? You didn't say they were your friends! You said to kill them. If that's what's bothering you, we'll not hurt them, I'll promise you that. I'll promise my own life. It's all I've got, but I swear I'll put it ahead of theirs. Trust me, Brother.'' The other three chorused agreement.

Vaun moaned. The gun was drooping in his hands, and trembling.

"You can't put a couple of *them* ahead of the hive!" Brown protested. "One of them's a female."

Maeve's daughter.

Vaun glanced at the two scared faces of the wilds and then hastily back at the brethren, as all four lurched forward a pace. He jerked the gun up and they stopped.

"It's obvious that you've never been laid by an expert, sonny!"

Brown flinched. "No. No desire to . . . But if you need that, we won't mind if you keep her."

*"No!"* Feirn shouted. "Not me! I'm not the one he loves. He's doing this for—"

Blade hushed her. He was clutching her tight with both arms, watching bleakly as their mutual future was decided.

"You can't trust me ever again!" Vaun insisted. *Oh, tell me I'm wrong!* "I wasn't lying about shooting brothers on the Q ship! I'm trying to escape now. How can you ever trust me in the future?"

"We love you, of course," White said, "and expect you to love us. We'll put a mark on you so we'll know—"

*"A mark?"* Vaun yelled. "How could I be one of you if I had a *mark* on me? I'd be the One With the Mark, you idiot!" An outcast still. A stranger again. On, no! "An *X* on the forehead, perhaps? Offer declined! Now turn around and start marching out in good order!"

"We can't!" White shouted. "We just can't. You know that! We don't want to be shot, and we believe you when you say you will, but we must be loyal to the hive. You ought to know that."

He did know that. He'd known it all along. "Crazy defective artifacts!" *Raj, how often must I betray you?*

Yellow, the youngest, sniffed loudly. He wiped his nose on his sleeve, but he wasn't even looking to the others for guidance. He couldn't shift his feet if that move would hurt the hive.

Vaun gestured with the gun. "I'll count to three, and then I burn off your legs. One!" He knew that if it were him, he would jump on "Two."

"Two!"

They jumped. The cave blazed with green light. There was no time for fancy disablement, and a Giantkiller wasn't a scalpel, and it was not designed for use in a confined space. He flashed them totally away. The explosion recoiled, hurling him to the floor, scorching his face, banging his ears like mallet blows, splattered him with falling gravel, chunks of burning meat, and gravy.

H E WANTED TO scream and tear off his skin. He needed to throw up and cough out his lungs and lie down and weep for a year; but he was driven by the frantic urgency of knowing that he must close the tunnel before anyone else came. He *must* not kill any more of his brethren.

Blade was barely conscious, half-stunned by flying rock, with his own blood streaming over the unspeakable soup that had sprayed all three of them. Somehow the other two bore him outside between them, staggering and reeling. The remains of the doorway curtains still smoldered, the floor was covered with debris, and the Brotherhood would be pouring up that tunnel like hornets any second now. Vaun could hold them off forever, but he must not. Somewhere in the bottom of his mind he knew he was being illogical about this, that he was planning to wipe out the whole hive before the day was out, but that was different. Mass murder was much easier than killing people you could see.

The night was cold, the ground glinting with frost in Angel's eerie blue glare. The east was brightening, though.

His face smarted with burns, and he seemed to have twisted his knee again. His ribs ached as if they had been kicked and his ears sang.

Feirn moaned. "Gotta rest, Vaun!"

"No. Too close still."

"Am awright," Blade muttered, although his feet were dragging on the rocks.

Feirn collapsed, and he fell on top of her, and Vaun almost on top of Blade. The tunnel mouth was still too near for safety, but this would have to do, for the Brotherhood would start spurting out of there any minute. Trouble was, all he had was the Giantkiller, and hardbeams were not much good against rock.

As the girl tried to rise, he pushed her down again. "Cover your ears!" he snapped.

Blade made querying noises and she hugged him. Vaun knelt by a sizable boulder. With trembling, sticky fingers, he set up the Giantkiller on its tripod, and flopped on the icy stones to aim it. He set three seconds' delay and maximum flash. He rolled away and put his head behind the boulder, shouting a final warning.

Maximum flash from a Giantkiller was a major disaster. He really thought he'd killed himself that time. Rocks rattled down like hail. He could smell burning hair, and when he fingered his scalp he discovered why. Ears ringing, ribs worse than ever . . . He tried to rise and sank back, groaning.

He had won a small respite. Certainly no one would ever come through that tunnel again. He hoped no one had been trying to. Of course, there must be other exits—he had no doubt of that—but at least now he needn't stand here and hold off the brethren at gunpoint, shooting them down as they marched to destruction like a thousand Abbots. That was what he'd been afraid of.

He hauled himself shakily to his feet, just as Feirn rose also. She'd lost most of her hair, and she had a second-degree burn on her forehead. The rest of her face looked as if it had been punched a few times; her clothes were tattered beyond the limits of decency and even charred in places.

The sky was brightening. He was frozen and shivering uncontrollably.

Blade was on his knees, another nightmare scarecrow of burns and bloodstains, the remains of his uniform hanging on him in rags. From the way he was clutching his right arm, he had a broken collarbone. Could even Blade fly a torch one-handed?

They were a trio of corpses, but apparently all mobile.

Vaun spat to clear dirt from his mouth. "Let's go," he said.

A SINGLE, PIERCING point of blue light, Angel stood high to the north. Dead ahead, dawn flared gold on the hills; the fugitives threw double shadows as they stumbled over the rocky ground. The air was still and bitter cold.

Vaun burned with intolerable anger. It hurt much worse than his physical wounds, for his body was numb, too frozen even to shiver. He could no longer feel the rocks under this thin-soled shoes or the sting of his burns; only his ribs still ached. He raged instead at his brothers' futile deaths.

How could they have been so stupid? The forgotten geniuses who had designed the brethren should have included more pliability. Such implacable stubbornness was a design fault in the whole genotype. Easy to say that a single unit was unimportant and only the Brotherhood itself mattered—he did not feel unimportant! White and Red and Brown and Yellow had not felt unimportant. They had wanted to die no more than he had wanted to kill them, but their chromosomes had insisted that they defend the hive's interest to the death, as a poisonfang defended its young.

And now he must kill them all. Dice. Bishop. Little 516, and Tan—who would still be Gray until he next changed his shirt. Cessine, whom Vaun had never met . . . had probably never met. All of them.

He had made his choice. There was no doubt now which side he supported, or where his loyalties lay.

It was not necessarily the winning team.

The same intransigence that had forced his four brothers to die determined that the Brotherhood as a whole would never give up. There was probably at least one other hive somewhere; simple common sense would have made that a priority. Had he been Bishop, he would certainly have taken other precautions also. He would have set up secret depots of know-how and supplies at a dozen places around the planet. As long as even one unit remained operative, he would seek out one of those depots and set to work establishing another hive. In another forty or fifty years it would start all over. Infestation, Roker had called it.

And even if the Patrol was alerted and could act in time to scotch Kohab Hive before it was evacuated, even if it could find the other hive or hives, even if it could hunt down and kill every single unit on the planet, the war would be far from won.

The Q ship was still coming. Yes, knowing it was only a boat made the odds look less impossible, and it must shut down its fireballs momentarily to make a course correction. But a boat was nimble in a way no rock ever could be, and that brief window of maximum vulnerability was going to be very hard to find. Almost certainly that window was also intended to let the brethren signal what action they wanted the missile to take, what target would best suit their purpose. Losing Hiport was not the worst that could happen to Ult, for a meteor impacting an ocean was vastly more destructive than a land strike. What was the built-in default instruction?

He stumbled as a rock rolled underfoot; the Giantkiller banged painfully against his burns und bruises. The stab of pain cut through his numbness and brought him back to the present. Feirn, now, was in the best shape of the three. Blade was leaning heavily on her, and at times seemed hardly conscious, but Vaun's offers of help had been refused.

He pummeled his wits to work. Something missing?

Two things missing. Pepods, and pursuit. To blunder into either would bring disaster, and yet the fugitives were instinctively staying on low ground, staggering along the gullies between the ancient hummocks of slag. They were still heading toward dawn, a little south of east; that was the right direction, but he should survey the terrain.

Croaking a wordless order, he veered up the nearest slope. Blade and the girl came stumbling after him. Frost-white rocks slithered underfoot. Vaun reeled onto the summit and sank down wearily to sit on a small cairn of rocks stacked there by some ancient unknown hand. He stared out blearily at the barren landscape.

The main saddle lay to the south. Northward was the closer hill, and the mine lay under that. If there were other exits—and there must be other exits—they lay in that direction. Far off to the east, the dawn's glow shone on the frosty tarmac of the strip, making it shine like a promised jewel. That was the prize. The brethren knew that, too. First to the strip wins.

Blade had sunk to the ground and laid his head on his knees. He seemed to be concussed, and that was worrisome. Vaun needed Blade to take care of the girl if they had to split up. He needed

Blade to escape if he got killed. He needed Blade to reduce the odds of that happening.

"Pepods!" Feirn said, pointing. She was upright, but swaying on her feet.

Pepods.

A sizable thicket lay dead ahead—in fact, there were pepods near the base of the slope, too close to the two humans for comfort. That could not be all of the vermin, though. Shielding his eyes from the dawn glare, Vaun peered at the distant strip itself. He decided there was at least one more thicket barring the way, but the range was too great for him to tell whether there were pepods near the hangar itself. If there were, then the two humans would not be leaving. It seemed unfair that the Brotherhood should have such an advantage in this deadly game—that insensate vegetables might thus determine the fate of a planet.

South? "Can't see any to the south," he croaked. He could use a drink. And food. And sleep. And his battered carcass ached and throbbed in a dozen places. No time for self-pity . . . "We'll have to detour that way."

"They'll come from over there, won't they, Vaun?" Feirn was gazing northward.

Vaun grunted agreement. Pursuit would come from the north; common sense said not to detour north. There were more pepods to the northeast, anyway. That looked like the largest thicket of all, or perhaps they just happened to be displayed there by some trick of topography. The slaggy mounds were alive with them, but of course the brethren could run right through. Pepods were no obstacle to the brethren. Unfair, unfair!

"We'll have to cut south to get round the pepods."

Blade had apparently been listening. He looked up grimly, his face a mask of blood with two shocked eyes in it. "Feirn and I do, sir. You go straight."

Vaun took a dead breath to fuel an admiral's bellow, and then let it out slowly.

"Pepods won't notice you, will they?" Blade mumbled.

"No," Vaun admitted. As much as he hated the thought of separating, there was no possible argument against it. With a world at stake, it was every boy for himself now. "Yes. Devil take the hindmost, I'm afraid. You two cut around that way, and I'll risk the pepods. Good luck, both of you."

They were a pathetic-looking pair. If they were his reason for ratting on his brothers, then he had a strange set of values.

The girl had never had eyelashes. Now she had only one eyebrow and half her hair was frizzed away. She must be in considerable pain, but she was bearing up well—for a civilian. Two days ago her body had excited him almost to madness; she was a disgusting sight now.

Blade's torpor was ominous, especially in a boy who had previously demonstrated such rigorous self-control. Courage could only push physical limits so far. He stayed hunched over to favor his useless arm; his face seemed thinner and longer under its mask of blood. Of the three of them, Blade was probably nearest the edge.

Vaun made a final scan of the landscape, trying to memorize the extent of the nearest pepod thicket, and the locations of the other two. He did not expect to see any of his brethren. They would stay out of sight and run like hell for the strip. First boy there wins. They were fresh and unwounded. They might have farther to come, but brethren were built for speed, as Tham had said long ago. -

*They would stay out of sight . . .*

Too late that thought registered. He started to rise as Feirn yelled and hurled herself at him. They toppled over together, a sharp explosion snapped the silence of the morning. The cairn he had just left erupted and shattered in green light. He curled up tight as fragments thumped and clattered all around him; he yelped at a couple of sharp impacts.

It must have been a long shot to have missed, though. Vaun had won the Doggoth marksmanship medal five years in a row.

No more firing. Only the ringing in his ears spoiled the silence. He opened his eyes. "Thanks!" he said. "What did you see?"

There was no answer. He twisted around, and Feirn had gone. He pushed himself up on his hands and knees.

Blade was still there, lying with arms and legs spread at odd angles, facedown in a patch of red weeds. Where the back of his head should have been was a bloody rock. Blood and brains had splashed out all around, on the vegetation and the stones.

Strange that the one thing that was absolutely inevitable for everyone always seemed so unthinkable, and always came so unexpectedly.

The misfortunes of war! What good are all your medals now, Lieutenant? You worked like hell for them, you said, to be like Admiral Vaun, you said. But you forgot *luck*, Lieutenant. You didn't put *luck* in your recipe, and Admiral Vaun was always a lucky shit— didn't you know that? And you were an unlucky son of a bitch. Admiral Vaun went from mud hovel to the top of the dungpile in one big bound, but he didn't do it with medals, he did it with *luck*. You won no medal for luck, did you?

You won't ever see that strealer mounted, Lieutenant.

Suddenly Vaun retched. Heedless of aches and biting pains, he scrambled away from the corpse, moving on all fours, dragging the Giantkiller. He wriggled down below the skyline, until he felt safe.

Feirn was halfway up the opposite slope, trudging gamely southeast, hair on one side of her head blowing like copper flame in the wind. The other side of her scalp was bald. He hurried after her.

Poor Blade! Freak accident. That sort of thing was supposed to happen to the other guys, the bad guys, not to the good guys. But Red and Brown and White and Yellow hadn't thought of themselves as bad guys. They hadn't thought of Vaun as a bad guy, either. They'd wanted to help their unfortunate damaged brother. The crew of *Unity* hadn't been bad guys. They'd been unlucky, because Prior had been unlucky.

Feirn paid no attention when he reached her side.

"Feirn . . ."

"I know. I saw." She continued to hurry straight ahead.

"This is war, and . . ." He stopped, feeling that silence might be a better tribute, knowing that the words must be said. He put an arm around her. "I am very sorry," he muttered. "He was a fine boy. I liked him."

For a moment she leaned against him as they walked. "Vaun, I was wrong."

"Wrong about what?"

"About Blade. He made love very well."

*Krantz!*

She shook off his arm. "Now get the hell out of here!" she said shrilly.

"Feirn—"

She stopped and pointed east. "You go that way! I cut around to the south. That was what we agreed." She glared up at him with a face like a death mask, pallid skin scorched in places and swollen, grotesquely smeared with filth and blood. Her blue eyes were unnaturally, crazily bright.

"Nonsense." He tried to put an arm around her again, and she backed away. "We go together."

"Vaun! Did you do all this just to rescue *Blade*?" There was a squeak of hysteria in her voice, but there was more anger.

"Of course not."

"To rescue *me*, then? Is that all?"

He hesitated, staring at her, astonished by her fury. He had never observed the resemblance to Maeve so strong—it made him want to lash out with angry, hurting words. Maeve had always been the only person who could hurt him, and he supposed he'd always resented that ability. Even after he'd thrown her out, he'd known that she could still hurt him . . . What was the question? . . . Doing this to rescue Maeve's daughter?

"Not entirely. Partly."

"Don't be a fool!" she yelled. "This is a world we're talking about! This is a war! Blade was right—we don't matter! You and I don't matter! The world does! You go straight! I'll cut around. Devil take the hindmost, you said."

"I can't leave you!" Go back to face Maeve . . .

"Yes, you can! You must! If that was me up there, and Blade down here, you'd split up, wouldn't you?"

"I suppose so."

"Then go!" she screamed, pointing. "Hurry!"

Still he hesitated.

Feirn stamped her foot furiously, and staggered as her ankle twisted. "Ouch!" He reached out to steady her, their eyes met— and suddenly they both laughed.

"Dumb!" he said. "Come on, let's go together."

"Please, Vaun! I can walk and I can fly a torch! Two have twice the chance of getting word through! Stop being a fucking romantic idiot!"

Who was she to call him a romantic idiot?

"For Blade's sake!" she begged. "Don't let him have died in vain."

She was right, of course. He could go straight, and probably faster. Two had twice the chance.

"All right. If you see me get away, then you climb that south hill." He pointed. "I'll send a torch there to pick you up."

She might have tried to smile, but either contempt or pain turned it into a grimace. "Thanks worlds! Scat!"

"You're your mother's daughter, Feirn! You've got courage!"

She screamed wordlessly at him, and turned, staggering away over the shingly ground.

She was absolutely right, of course.

Vaun faced to the east. He forced himself up to a jog, and deliberately headed for the nearest pair of pepods that chittered and scrabbled at the base of the next hill. He ran right between them, but they ignored him, although his scalp pricked and his gut knotted. *Nivel! Quild! Roker!* He passed by safely, and after that it was easier. There were hundreds of them, yet soon he was paying them no more heed than thorn bushes.

After a while, he realized that the Giantkiller still dangled on his shoulder. He should have given it to Feirn, although even a wide-spectrum weapon like that would probably not prevail against a whole thicket of pepods; they were just too damned fast.

He did not try to run full out. Even a slow jog was hard to maintain on such rocky ground; a twisted ankle would finish him. That was another worry the pursuit did not have, for there were many more of them. They were certainly armed, so if even one of them won the race, that would count as a victory. Again Vaun thought how unfair this contest was, and anger fueled his aching muscles.

Soon he had to slow down even more. His ribs felt like red-hot bars in his chest, and one knee kept threatening to give way under him.

Damn them! He was going to win this race if it killed him!

It would certainly kill them.

He preferred not to think about that. He had made his decision; he must live with it. Or die with it. If they took him alive, he supposed they would kill him this time. He could not live in the hive now. Mark or no mark, he would die of shame.

He wondered how Feirn was doing. She had farther to go, and she was only human. She was in at least as bad a shape as he was, but she had turned out to be much tougher than he had expected. He had never understood her at all. Her motives might be muddled, but she did not lack purpose and drive. She knew what she wanted and went for it—as gate-crasher and stowaway she'd done splendidly. As seductress she'd been balked, but only by events beyond her control. Had Roker not intervened, she'd have gained what she wanted of Vaun very easily. When Vaun slipped out of reach, she'd had her spare hero ready to hand. Now Fate and the Brotherhood had snatched him away.

War! Waste! Good boy, Blade, wasted.

And poor little redhead. If the brethren didn't get her, then the pepods would.

How would he ever face Maeve if Feirn died in this mess? Of course, that was a very hypothetical situation at the moment; he was not very likely to see Maeve again.

The sun was dazzling, right in his eyes. He was staggering a lot now. He suspected he had lost blood somewhere, or else it was mere pain that was sapping his strength. He wondered what was fueling him now—rage? Pride? Probably shame—it was easy to shine in a collection of randoms, but when he tried to compete against his own kind he balled-up utterly.

He'd long since passed through the first group of pepods, and now he could see another of the brutes ahead, so he was almost into the second thicket. That meant he was coming close to the strip. He was going to win this if it killed him . . .

He reeled up the side of a steep hillock with a rocky top, dropping to his knees and scrambling the last bit with his head down. And finally he lay flat and crawled, gasping for breath and nauseated by the pain in his ribs. That was so bad that it let him ignore all the other sore places. He mustn't lie here too long or he'd never get himself on his feet again.

He had trouble focusing his eyes against the sun.

There were pepods almost all the way to the strip. And . . . damnation! . . . there were pepods all around the hangar itself. At least a dozen that he could see from where he was. So Feirn had lost anyway. He felt a shameful release of guilt when he saw that. There was no way he could have gotten Feirn, or Blade, past the vermin without a radio screamer.

So it was up to him, and all his efforts to rescue the two humans had been wasted. He could very likely have walked out of the hive in the night and just left. He could have spared himself all this punishment! Somehow his wounds seemed to hurt much more when he thought of that. Brethren were supposed to be rational, not romantic, girl-rescuing idiots.

He glanced to the north. Pepods thick as flies, everywhere.

And brethren, among them.

At least a dozen specks were moving much too fast to be grazing pepods. Brethren, crossing a wide, flat meadow. Running strongly. They still had farther to go that he did, but they were going much faster. In a few minutes they would . . . Joshual flagging Krantz!

*Beaten!* Defeated!

Right ahead of those runners was a final ridge, and from there they would have a clear view of the hangar and the strip. They could pick him off from there when he arrived, easy. Or they could just blow up the torches with a hardbeam. They could win the race without even completing the course!

When the Brotherhood took the high ground, the game would be lost. There was no wild stock settlement within walking distance, or none that he could reach before he was hunted down from the air.

Beaten!

# H E WANTED TO weep.

It was the sense of failure. He despised himself for betraying the hive, yes, but he hated even more the thought that he had failed the other side through sheer incompetence. Being a fool felt much worse than being a traitor. The cold seeped into his bones, and despair into his soul. Pain and exhaustion nibbled away at his mind, and he felt himself fading, stiffening on the icy rocks of Kohab.

The randoms didn't have a hope now. The Q ship was coming, and when it struck, the brethren would unleash the pepods as well and compound the chaos. Disaster.

Arkady was very close to Hiport.

And there were pepods at Arkady—double jeopardy.

*Chitter!*

Vaun raised his head from the cold stones and peered down the slope. Pepods. Lots of pepods.

He remembered Nivel. A worthless, crippled peasant . . .

If Vaun could somehow draw the pepods away from the hangar, then Feirn might still have a chance of getting through.

He shivered: Now there was a *really* crazy idea.

A suicidal idea. If he provoked one pepod, all the rest would attack him, and there must be a hundred of them in the vicinity. Furthermore, they would turn on Feirn, also, wherever they were. And the disturbance would inform the brethren of his location. Insane.

On the other hand . . .

Pepods apparently distinguished random from brother with no trouble at all. The one that killed Nivel had gone right past Vaun in his ditch, and that had been years before anyone started trying to train them. If a *brother* suddenly turned dangerous . . . what then? Would they attack the solitary random in the area and continue to ignore the brethren? Not likely, surely. And if one brother is bad, aren't all brothers bad? How smart were they?

That depended on how many you linked up, or so Tan had hinted. Well, there were more in view around this hummock than Vaun had seen in his life before. Paging the Great Pepod . . .

And if brother and random were so obviously different, then just maybe the brutes wouldn't react to a random at all on this occasion.

It was a wild card, but it was all he had left in his hand.

"Feirn!" he whispered. "Oh, Feirn! I hope this doesn't undo all my good work, child. If it does, well I'm truly sorry. If it doesn't, then you may yet have a chance." She had nothing to lose now.

He struggled painfully to his knees, and eyed the nearest pepods. His flesh crawled as he remembered Nivel's screams. He made a mental note to keep some reserve in the gun for himself at the end.

The brethren to the north were almost across the meadow. No use waiting until they started up the slope.

If Nivel had found the courage, then he could.

Vaun set the Giantkiller on riotbeam, which could blind humans on an eye shot, but otherwise merely scorched them, with no serious injury. He doubted it would hurt pepods, either, but it might annoy them.

He experimented on the nearest couple, and yes, it annoyed them very much. They spasmed as if he'd given them an electric shock, and their claws and mandibles and pseudolimbs rattled and clattered furiously. From leisurely rock pickers, they became whirling dervishes of fury, going nowhere—flailing around on the spot, unable to locate their assailant.

That was not good enough. He sprayed the thicket at random. *Chitter!!!*

They found him. They came for him, and riotbeam was not an adequate deterrence. He barely had time to toggle higher power before a dozen were almost up the hillock. He burned them with green light. They exploded into orange flames. A few rolled back down the slope; most just stayed where they were, burning and crackling. And the rest kept coming from all directions. He rose to his knees, and then to his feet, firing almost continuously, twisting and turning to keep track. They were so fast! In minutes he had a flaming hedge in front of him, and that was some defense, but they were smart enough, or numerous enough, to come around the ends.

Soon he was gasping and coughing and weeping in the acrid white smoke. The heat of burning pepod licked cruelly at the burns he already had. He had started a war and he was in the thick of it. He was going to suffocate.

Then, in a momentary breather, he heard a distant fusillade.

Between the billows of smoke, he saw green flashes to the north, and white clouds floating up into the china-blue sky.

He laughed aloud. He'd done it! He'd wakened the Great Pepod and set it on the Brotherhood like an attack dog!

Except that he was near the teeth himself. He whirled again and fired, and jumped, and still they kept coming, rushing out of the smoke at him. He built an almost complete ring of fire around his eyrie, and although the horde still thrashed the ground in fury, they were staying beyond it. The first few had already collapsed into burning sticks and disconnected embers. Yet even that seemed to be enough to discourage the others. Now he could rest a moment— at least until he choked to death or the fire burned down or the Giantkiller ran out of charge. With streaming eyes, he sneaked a look at the vid, and it showed twenty percent remaining.

Oh!

How much had he used just to seal the tunnel? Had it been on full charge in the rack?

He must remember to save enough to burn his brains out before the pepods got him. Realizing that he was on his feet, and that scopes could see through smoke better than he could, he sank down to his knees and leaned against a boulder.

*Chitter!!!* said the pepods, gibbering beyond the barricade.

Between his coughing spells Vaun cursed them with every vile oath he could think of. Murderous weeds! Curse of the planet. Couldn't be stamped out without a worldwide simultaneous campaign—which had never proved practical and would have had to find every seed anyway.

Rather like the Brotherhood, in fact.

There was a lot more smoke to the north, and the firing was still continuous. So the brethren were not safely barricaded inside a laager, as he was, and could have no spare time to worry about the airstrip, even if any of them were within sight of it.

The fire was burning low at a couple of spots. He jumped up and flashed a few of the pepods beyond it, widening his barricade.

Sixteen percent charge remaining.

The smoke billowed. He caught glimpses of hundreds of furiously writhing pepods around his fortress. He could hear their clickings as a steady roar. They weren't going to give up.

He peered east. Feirn? The strip looked clear of pepods, as far as he could tell through his tears. There was a thin spot developing on the west of his laager. Feirn, where are you?

*There!* Yes! There she was, one tiny figure running for the strip, and not a pepod in sight! But oh, so far from the hangar still! Hurry!

Then he heard the snap of a firearm and saw a thin line of green light that stretched from the northern horizon to end in his own chest.

As he went down he thought, *Damn! Now I'm not going to know how this ends.*

T HERE IS NO pain, just a great pressure as if a huge lump of ice is growing in his lungs, a strange floating feeling. He cannot even feel the rock beneath him. His eyes blur, but the smoke seems to be thinning.

The question now is whether he can die before the pepods get him. His ears don't seem able to distinguish fire noise from pepod. He tries to find the Giantkiller, but he can't even find his hands.

Hurry, Feirn, hurry! You can do it now, Feirn! Get your ass out of here. Call home. Call your mommy. Call anyone. You'll be a heroine, Feirn. Save the world, Feirn!

Hurry! I want to know what happens.

She should be there by now. What *is* the girl doing? Running a preflight check? Counting the airsickness bags? Hurry, Feirn, hurry! I want to know.

No pain, but the pressure in his chest is growing. He thinks he is about to split apart. Cold, cold . . .

She should be able to make it. No brethren in the way now, no pepods.

Except this is only one hive. There must be others. The Q ship is coming.

The smoke swirls, white and acrid, nipping his eyes. He blinks, trying to see. A brother is kneeling over him. Dice? Bishop? Maybe just an illusion. Vaun can't make out the color of his shirt.

He can't be here. Couldn't have gotten past the pepods.

Vaun says, "Hello?" in a whisper so faint he can't hear himself. He has no air in his lungs. Only blood.

But the brother has heard. He smiles Raj's smile. "There's help coming, Brother! Hang on!"

Illusion.

"We'll save you, Brother." It is Abbot's voice, or is it Prior's?

"I'm sorry," Vaun says. "Really sorry. I was damaged, you see. I wasn't hive-bred, and by the time I really knew who I was, I was imprinted with loyalty to the wrong hive. I didn't want to kill you, Brother."

The other takes his hand, and rubs it. Vaun sees that, does not feel it.

"It's all right!" Sounds like Bishop. Fades into smoke; fades back again. "We understand, Brother Vaun. And it doesn't really matter. Perhaps this hive will be destroyed, but that will not end the struggle. The randoms will fail in the end. Unsuccessful species die out. Successful species produce even better, and *then* die out. We are the Master Race, and eventually we must prevail."

What does a Master Race do with the wild stock when it attains control? Put them in reserves, or zoos? In concentration camps? Gas a billion or two now and then? How big a grave for a billion people? Ten billion?

Scyth went silent. Thousands of worlds have gone silent, so that the others will not find out and be prepared.

Vaun says, "Yes, we are the Master Race. But when we have achieved perfection, what do we do then?"

Raj just smiles, and does not answer.

Life is struggle.

Then a great roar—he hears that. Something booms overhead, dark and bright against the baby-blue sky, and is gone.

"A torch!" he says. "She made it! I'm not dreaming, am I?"

Abbot shakes his head. "Not dreaming that. She made it. And listen!"

Vaun hears nothing, but he feels the ground tremble.

"Fuel tanks exploding," his brother explains, smiling sadly. "The random turned the jets on the hangar. She torched the hangar with the torch! There will be no pursuit, and no evacuation."

*Bravely done! Safe journey, friend Feirn. Send marines soonest! Tell your mother I maybe did love her a little, perhaps.*

*Hell, tell her I do love her and always did.*

Flash. The ground heaves, the hard rocks under his back.

"That was the Sheerfire," he says silently, and closes his eyes. He wants to die before the pepods come for him, but when he looks again, the vague shape is still kneeling over him in the drifting smoke.

"I wish I understood," Bishop says. "Even if you weren't hive-bred . . . We are supposed to be rational. I wish I knew why you chose the losing side.''

"They called me a hero, but I never was a hero. I was always just a traitor."

"Yet I think the Patrol may soon put up a monument here—to a hero."

"To Feirn, you mean? A heroine?"

"No," Raj says, smiling. "Nor to Blade. There are wins and there are losses. The details vary, but the end is inevitable. You must know that. A hero might choose the losing side, but why should a traitor?"

If Vaun could breathe he might say something like, *Life is struggle and becoming. Perfection is failure. If God loves us, it is not in spite of our faults, it is because of them.* Who said that? Sounds like some of Tham's sentimental crap.

And his brother would never understand.

"Because I think of them as people."

His brother frowns. "Ah. That is a serious error. They do not think of us as people!"

"I do."

"Of course. But you can never play on two teams. If you try to stay in the middle, you get hit from both sides."

"It was ever thus," Vaun agrees—or would agree, if he could breathe.

The Brotherhood is humanity's greatest success, and its greatest folly. It is fitting, maybe, that *Homo sapiens* will fall to its own creation.

"Here come the others," Bishop says. "It is time to go."

Then blood rushes from Vaun's mouth. A clamor of trumpet roars in his head and the sky darkens as his brothers crowd in. He is glad the pepods aren't going to get him. This way's better. He smiles a farewell to his brothers, and the brothers all smile back with Raj's smile.

He isn't going to know how it ends. But he wouldn't have found out anyway. It won't end. On world after world, the Brotherhood will keep trying, either winning or losing and trying again. Life is struggle. And this one will go on forever, and to the farthest stars.

# APPENDIX A: Timing

RELATIVISTIC EFFECTS ARE negligible at one-third light speed, but there is considerable time lag. A Q ship takes 12 years to travel between Avalon and Ult from the point of view of the passengers—neglecting time for acceleration and deceleration, which adds a few months. An observer on Ult, though, sees the ship taking only 8 years, and an observer on Avalon 16 years.

*A Boy's Book of Space*
(59th Edition, Cashalix, 29302)

# APPENDIX B: Q Ships

T HE MOST REMARKABLE feature of the Q drive is that its performance is almost independent of the size of the payload. In theory, a standard Q drive could move a planet. In practice, radiation and tidal stress set limits, which may best be illustrated by comparing the two types of Q ship, rocks and boats.

Despite the universal designation "rocks," interstellar vessels are never fashioned from stony meteorite material, only from the nickel-iron variety. Asteroids of that type represent fragments of the cooled cores of differentiated planetesimals. Although originally homogeneous, they have been spalled from larger bodies by violent collisions; all of them now contain flaws and hidden fractures. The larger the rock, the greater the stress and the more numerous the flaws.

Because the Q drive works by pulling, not pushing, starships are in constant danger of falling apart. Ships as large as ten kilometers in diameter have been reported, hollowed out by generations of inhabitants into vast metallic cheeses. In the past, foolhardy souls attempted to convert even larger bodies, only to have their masterpieces fall apart along preexisting planes of weakness and swallow themselves. As tensional stress is greatest during acceleration and deceleration, Patrol regulations limit rocks to a velocity increment of one-half gee.

The Patrol also sets an absolute speed limit for rocks of 333 millicees, or one-third light speed, and less than that in certain areas of high dust content. The danger is radiation, for nowhere is space ever a perfect vacuum. Even at rest, a Q drive singularity will devour stray molecules, and when traveling at interstellar velocities, it sweeps up the galactic medium—gas and dust and stray cometary debris. Matter ripped apart by an infinite gravity gradient is converted to radiation, some of which escapes absorption. Depending on the speed of transit and the nature of the medium, frequencies from radio waves to hard gamma may be found in the resulting fireball. Gravitational redshift lengthens the wavelength of the radiation, which is why the first Q ships detected were for many years mistaken for quasars.

Thus the forward quasi mass not only provides the impetus to drive the ship, but also protects it from potentially disastrous impact. Several hundred meters of nickel-iron will suffice to shield the crew, but the rock itself corrodes at the molecular level, and in extreme cases may even melt. The main reason Q ships star-hop and shun very long runs is that years of stress at high temperatures tend to stretch the rock itself. During world stops, part of the Patrol's standard refurbishment procedure is to rotate the drive 90 degrees, distributing the stress along another axis.

Boats, in contrast, are metal-skin vessels. No matter how large, they mass less than a millionth as much as their big brothers. With their small dimensions and superior tensile strength, they are little affected by tidal stress, and can safely accelerate at dozens of gees. Ironically, such extreme acceleration is unnecessary, as boats can never approach interstellar velocities without frying their occupants. They are restricted to interplanetary work, except for a small role in interstellar exploration as unmanned probes . . .

Rigorous explanation of the Q drive requires an analysis based on Morganian gravity waves. In lay terms the projectors may be described as creating virtual masses having location, infinitesimal duration, and no dimensions. The Q ship is impelled by its efforts to fall into a hole that is constantly appearing in front of it and vanishing before the ship arrives. The Patrol decries the popular terms "bootstrap machine" and "celestial carrot" . . .

If a Q drive projector merely created a single transitory quasi mass, it would violate the laws of conservation, but a single quasi mass is no more possible than a single magnetic monopole. The two virtual masses have opposite signs, and may be thought of as quasi matter and quasi antimatter, with a net pseudomass of zero. As both matter and antimatter have the same gravitational results, both act to draw the ship toward them.

Caught within two steep gravity gradients, each of which defines a different apparent center of mass (ACM), a rock must still move as a unit, and therefore a single effective center of mass (ECM) may be defined. The ship is accelerated or decelerated by moving the Moganian projector forward or aft of the ECM—which may not correspond exactly with the rest center of mass (RCM) even when the ship is traveling at constant velocity. At such times, bodies—

including human bodies—situated forward of the ECM are accelerated faster than the ship, and hence sense "down" as being toward the bow. Aft of the ECM, the apparent gravity field is reversed, in an interesting Einsteinian comparison of gravity and inertia. Apparent gravitational effects during acceleration are more complex. . . .

The quasi masses created are not as large as commonly believed. Typically, they are located about fifteen kilometers away from the ship. Assuming a ship diameter of five kilometers, an Earthlike mass would generate a gravitational field of almost 200,000 gee at the bow—somewhat excessive—and little more than half that at the rear. Add in the opposing effects of the rear quasi mass, and the result is a gravity gradient enough to disrupt any matter ever envisioned. A quasi mass equivalent to a small asteroid is adequate, and a Q ship may approach a planet without causing disaster, or even any appreciable tidal disturbance in the oceans. Remember though, that the quasi masses have no dimensions and thus constitute singularities. At close quarters the gravitational *gradient* becomes effectively infinite.

The aft quasi mass does more than maintain the laws of physics. Because space is never empty, a Q ship cannot just coast after reaching cruising velocity. The forward singularity must be maintained to defend the ship from impact with the galactic medium, and thus without the braking action of the rear quasi mass, Q ships would accelerate indefinitely to relativistic speeds. Once the desired velocity has been obtained, therefore, the projector is moved forward until the attractions balance, and net acceleration becomes zero. For deceleration, of course, the projector is merely moved farther forward yet.

Rocks are not designed to be nimble; space is so huge that they can normally just line up on their targets and go. Any significant change of course at high velocity would require displacing the forward singularity with respect to the line of flight, thus exposing the rock itself to the impact of the interstellar medium . . .

The Q drive itself should not be confused with pseudogravity, which is a short-range, low-intensity field used mainly to make shipboard life more comfortable for crew and passengers when the Q drive in not in use . . .

                                                                    Ibid.

# About the Author

After thirty years as a petroleum geologist, Dave Duncan discovered that inventing his own worlds was much easier (and more fun) than trying to make sense of the real one. Since then he has been making up for his wasted youth, having turned out a dozen novels within five years. He alternates between fantasy and science fiction and shows no signs of going back to earning an honest living.

# FANTASY
# NOVELS
# THAT COME TO LIFE
## by
# DAVE DUNCAN